"Before... ...re is one other thing I would like to ask: what is your people's belief concerning the great catastrophe that befell the world long ago?"

Hael paused, remembering old tales heard as a child. "We have a tradition that once spirits were far more powerful than they are now. They took control of men, and made them mad. Men had great fire magic in those days and killed one another with it. At last, they even hurled fiery spears at the Moon and wounded her so that the scars are still visible. When most of the people were dead, the spirits lost their great power, and men have been living sensibly ever since."

Malk nodded. "I have heard many, many tales of the catastrophe. Yours is not the only one to mention fiery spears. Some legends speak of the Great Plagues, and some of the Years of Heat, and some of the great mountains from the sky that fell into the sea. Some wise ones speak of a great time of evil, when catastrophes struck one after the other, and I think this may be the truth."

Hael's head buzzed with all this new knowledge. Also with wine. "We thank you for your hospitality," he said, "but now we must go. Perhaps you will come by our camp tonight and we can continue this talk. We will make you welcome."

"We promise not to make you drink milk and blood," Danats said.

Tor Books by John Maddox Roberts

Cestus Dei
King of the Wood

THE CINGULUM

The Cingulum
Cloak of Illusion
The Sword, The Jewel, and The Mirror

THE ADVENTURES OF CONAN

Conan the Bold
Conan the Champion
Conan the Marauder
Conan the Valorous

JOHN MADDOX ROBERTS
THE
ISLANDER

BOOK ONE OF STORMLANDS

TOR
fantasy

A TOM DOHERTY ASSOCIATES BOOK
NEW YORK

**For the Fantastic Four
with affection and expectations:**

**Loston Wallace
Ann Meade
Scott Mullins
Jason Adams**

THE ISLANDER

A Tor Book
Published by Tom Doherty Associates, Inc.
49 West 24th St.
New York, NY 10010

Cover art by Ken Kelly

ISBN: 0-812-50627-8

First edition: December 1990

Printed in the United States of America

0 9 8 7 6 5 4 3 2 1

ONE

The boy's name was Hael. He did not think of himself as a boy any longer, though. He had undergone his initiation into the fraternity of junior warriors, entitled to bear arms and to move from the enclosure of his family to the camp of his fraternity. This status was the dream of every boy of the Shasinn people, although the initiation itself was arduous and frightening. Not every boy who began the ordeal survived to receive his spear.

Hael leaned on the spear he had taken so proudly from the hand of a retiring senior warrior. It was a foot taller than himself as he held it braced with his outstretched right arm, the sole of one bare foot resting against the knee of his other leg.

Silent and unmoving as a statue, he stood at the lip of a granite crag, watching over the herd of kagga assigned to the Night-Cat fraternity. There were hundreds of the beasts within his view, but if a single animal had been missing, he would have known. The animals were the whole tribe's wealth, pampered and petted. The older herdsman could name each one, and recite its lineage. They were kept for their milk and hair, and were killed for meat only at certain important rituals. Otherwise the meat was eaten only when one died or had to be killed through misfortune. A few were solid colors; black, brown, red or white, but most were dapples. Each had four horns, those of the males long and curling, those of the females short and straight. They stood near five feet at the shoulder, with heads balanced on long, graceful necks.

Hael was a handsome youth, with long arms and legs, and a narrow waist. His wide shoulders had not yet attained the full bulk of maturity, although he had already developed great strength by the incessant wrestling which was his people's favorite sport. His skin was almost the color of polished bronze, the color of his spear. His hair was a darker shade of bronze, cut for the first time at his initiation, and not yet grown long enough to plait into the innumerable tiny braids worn by all junior warriors. It would not be cut again until he was made a senior warrior, in seven to ten years' time. At that time he would be allowed to move back into the family enclosure, to marry and to own livestock.

A leather thong supported his only garment, a loincloth made from the beautifully mottled skin of a forest night-cat. Above his elbows and knees he wore bands made from the long neck-fur of the same animal, the totem of his fraternity; another band of its skin circled his brow. As a part of his initiation, he had had to go alone into the mountain forest to hunt the animal. It was this part of the ritual that killed more of that fraternity than any other. The Shasinn were chiefly herdsmen, forbidden to hunt except for certain ritual purposes, or to kill marauding predators. They thought little of all other peoples, who lived by hunting, or scratching the soil, or dragging nets across the waters for fish.

Hael's eyes were blue above prominent cheekbones, as was true of all his tribe. His neck was encircled by a necklace of night-cat teeth alternating with the beast's claws. From a strap around his shoulder hung a small pouch and a waterskin.

The garments and ornaments he wore and the spear he carried were his only possessions, nor did he feel need for any others. Of all things, he prized the spear most highly. He could contemplate its beauty for hours, and sometimes did. A third of its length was the bronze head, a narrow, swordlike blade of a graceful leaf shape, the keen edges made of precious steel, cunningly mated to the softer, lustrous red-gold metal. Another third was spirally fluted bronze butt-spike, its terminal three inches a diamond-shaped point to hold the weapon upright when stuck in the ground or used as a secondary weapon at need. The middle third was finely checked flamewood, once streaked scarlet and yellow but now a dark gold from the continuous handling of previous owners.

Below him he could also see a dozen of his brothers of the fraternity, the younger ones standing as still as himself around the herd, the older ones walking among the kagga in a ceaseless search for sickness, injury or distress, patting and

speaking soothing words, crooning ancient herding songs, checking the females for progress in
calving, pulling off the bloated ticks that plagued
all animal life.

To either side of the crag upon which he stood
was forest, which stretched up the slope behind
him, into the hills beyond. He felt the presence of
its myriad animals, its birds and insects, its tiny
man-of-the-trees, even the despised hunters with
their bows and poisoned arrows. The shore far
away was rimmed with villages of fishermen
whose long, sleek boats impressed the Shasinn,
though they would never have admitted it. In the
lowlands were people who could tear the land
with curved sticks and plant seeds or cuttings and
coax living, edible things to grow. Hael knew that
this was no fit life for a warrior.

Far away, near the eastern horizon, lay a gray
arc of water, the sea that separated the Cloud Islands from the great mainland. He knew that his
tribe dwelled on one of the largest and northernmost of the islands, called Gale, but the island was
very large, home to many peoples, and it seemed
like the whole world to him. He thought of the
mainland as a narrow strip of land, like a very
long island, somewhere across the water, just beyond sight.

Beyond the water was the greatest mystery; the
Men with Hairy Faces in their huge boats, ten or
twenty times the size of the fisherfolk's boats.
These came a few times each year to trade metal
and cloth and other wonderful things for the
meat and cheeses, the hides, dried fish, bird feathers and pearls of the island people. Sometimes
they also came to raid for children and fair young

women to take as slaves. The men they never took alive, or regretted it if they did. The farmers and fishers were not glorious warriors like the herdsmen with their warrior fraternities, but they were tough, cunning fighters. The Men with Hairy Faces never went far enough inland to bother the hunters.

All these things swarmed through Hael's mind as he watched over the fraternity's herd, and never did any of it make his attention swerve in the slightest degree. Behind him, above the western peaks, tremendous clouds piled as they did every evening. At another time, sharing this vantage point with a brother, he might turn to contemplate their majesty, but since he was alone on this evening, he did not do so, although watching the great clouds was among his chiefest pleasures.

As the light of the sky dimmed, a pale form thrust above the water to the east. It worked its way above the horizon slowly as if wounded, and wounded it was. The Moon shone pale in the turquoise that was quickly deepening toward purple, but its surface showed ghastly streaks and splotches of black amid the virgin white.

As it cleared the horizon, Hael raised a hand to his brow, palm outward, and bowed his head, the first true movement he had made in an hour. "Forgive us, O Moon," he intoned. "In our folly, we, foolish men, have hurt you. Do not withhold from us the rain, nor the tides that bring the fish, nor the seasons that quicken the female of all kinds."

Finished, he resumed his stance. The prayer was ancient, and he could see his brothers below repeating it as the Moon became visible to them. Like all his people, he felt strange praying to the

Moon for fish, because fish as food were an abomination to the herdsmen. But he knew that people must live together, if not necessarily like or understand each other, and he assumed that the fishers must include the Shasinn's kagga in their morning devotions to the Sun.

Young and tireless as he was, he felt gratitude when the night watch came to relieve him. He smiled when the other arrived, scrambling up the rocky surface to the lip of the crag.

"Go below and seek the comfort of the fires, fortunate fellow, while I keep watch by night!" It was, of course, Danats, who had brought a blanket of woven kagga hair against the chill, and a wrapped bundle of snacks to stay the pangs of hunger lest he starve before breakfast. Danats loved food as others loved their women or the spirits.

"My heart shall mourn," said Hael, "knowing that you stand here beneath the stars until the next turning of the Moon, when it shall become my duty."

Danats picked up the blanket and wrapped it about his shoulders, although the chill had not yet come. "I'll see few stars this night, unless those clouds lie. Hard rain tonight, brother."

"Without rain there is no grass, and then what would the kagga eat?" He was not worried about Danats. A blanket of kagga hair would shed water like the feathers of the diving birds, and the Shasinn enjoyed rain, save when an over-hard wind blew it.

Still he lingered to keep the other company. He and Danats shared a special relationship. While all the fraternity were brothers, *Fastan*, he and

Danats also had the closest bond. They were *Chabas-Fastan*. On the last night of the initiation ceremony, they had circumcised each other, inexpertly and with a dull flint knife. The term meant "foreskin-brothers" and it was a bond for life, obliging them to reciprocal duties. One would have night watch while the other watched by day. One would nurse the other while sick or wounded. In battle, they would always fight side by side. When one was detailed for duty elsewhere, the other would stay with the herd. The relationship lasted through life. In senior warrior or elder status, they would be the protectors of each other's children, one taking the place of parent if the other should die. It was a terrible fate among the Shasinn if one of a pair died while they were still young men, for the bond could not be replaced. It was even worse than being an orphan. Since Hael was already an orphan, the loss of his *Chabas-Fastan* Danats was something that did not bear thinking about.

"Have you enough food?" Hael asked, prodding a fat bundle with his toe. "I would not wish to come here tomorrow and find only a miserable skeleton, picked over by the less fastidious scavengers."

"Go below, slothful one. Leave it to the real men to stand watch at night. Eat dinner like the idler that you are, then seek out the women to court, while I remain a slave to duty."

"I thank you for the suggestion," Hael said, drily. "After all, soon the women go into four long nights of seclusion, prior to their Calving Festival, and then we will all be too busy to court."

Danats sighed. "All too true. Ah, well, a man

may always polish his own spear, as they say. Go, child, while you have light to see your way. It would be my duty to pass the spear through your neck like a crippled kagga, should you break a leg."

Hael chuckled as he went down the craggy slope, although Danats's joke was not all that great an exaggeration. A few minutes later, he was at the fires of the encampment.

Small fires burned within the circle of huts, and he could smell meat grilling. Since it was not the time for a festival, he knew that an animal must have come to an untimely end. The fires were fueled by thornwood and kagga dung, dried and pressed. Fuel was gathered by the women and delivered to the encampments on most days. In return, the young men helped them carry the heavy water jugs from the stream to the village. This was a duty they always complained of, yet looked forward to eagerly, for it was a chance to preen before the women, to flirt while still young and pay serious court as senior warrior status drew near.

He strode to the fire nearest the hut he and Danats shared and drove the butt-spike of his spear into the earth next to a low stool of polished wood. These simple seats were owned by the fraternity, to spare their hard-earned cat pelts. There were three other men at the fire, and as he sat one of them passed him a wide bowl of kagga milk. He drank and passed it to the man on his right. The milk was still warm from the kagga cow, and had this not been a night when they had meat, the milk would have been mixed with blood drawn from the neck-vein of a calf.

"Who do we thank?" he asked, gesturing toward the chunks of meat skewered on two-foot thorns, slanted over the low coals at the edge of the fire.

"The Fur Snakes," said Raba, polishing the bronze knife in which he took inordinate pride. "Lightning killed two yearlings in yesterday's storm." He grinned, showing a gap between his front teeth. "Their misfortune is our good luck." The meat from such a kill was parceled out among the tribe, with the best pieces going to the senior warriors and elders, and none at all to the fraternity whose herd suffered the loss. The Fur Snake fraternity would have to dust their hair with ashes and mourn for three days, fasting and drinking only water.

Hael took a thorn from the fire and sniffed the meat, then replaced it to grill a while longer. Although the herdsmen drank the blood of living animals, they feared undercooked meat, which might still contain a small part of the dead animal's spirit. These spirits could be spiteful and resent being eaten. Their revenge could range from mere embarrassment to agonizing death.

The darkness was almost complete, but the clouds piled high to the west were fitfully illuminated by lightning flashes. Thunder rolled faintly in the distance, gradually growing stronger as the lightning increased. In a great storm, the sound would be continuous, like the beating of drums at a festival. The rains came from the west almost nightly for six months of the year, sometimes with winds of terrible force. It was for these disturbances that the islands and the nearby mainland were known as the Stormlands.

He raised his head and smelled the rain-laden

breeze. "West winds for two more moons. No ships of the Hairy Ones until then."

Luo laughed and cast a handful of grass at him. "Hael wishes to be a spirit-speaker. See, already he prophesies! He tells us when the east winds will come, as if we could not have predicted that from our mothers' wombs. Have the spirits informed you of any other important matters, brother?"

Hael laughed with the others, but without their carelessness. This was one of the things that set him apart from the others. It was well known among his age group that Hael took things too seriously, that he saw importance in things that most youths ignored. Sometimes he felt that he truly should have become a spirit-speaker, but that was not to be his fate. No boy whose parents were dead could become apprentice to a spirit-speaker.

"Who else would care about the Men with Hairy Faces?" Raba asked. "Or any other people who own no livestock? Only Hael. You may not believe this, but I have seen him speaking with a farmer, as if to an actual person."

The others let their eyes go wide in mock amazement. "No!" said the third youth, whose name was Pendu. "Even Hael is not so undignified. Perhaps the soil-ripper had a pretty daughter."

"I have to know about the doings of our neighbors and visitors," Hael told them, "because someday I shall be a great elder, and have to manage you all as you become fat and lazy, having passed your spears on to just such young fools as you are now. With the tribe in the hands of such worthless elders, I may have to beg charity of our neighbors."

The others hooted. "Sharp spear, sharp tongue!" quoted Luo, who always seemed to have the greatest stock of the tribe's proverbs. He snatched up a thorn and sniffed the meat, sighed loudly and bit into it. Seeing this, the others began to eat, taking small bites while passing the milk bowl around.

The Shasinn were abstemious eaters, prizing their lean physiques and their ability to endure long privation. On raids, they could go on for days, drinking only from streams and eating only a few lumps of hard cheese or some strings of tough, dried meat. A man who ate too much or too quickly was thought to show poor character. Danats was mocked unmercifully for his love of eating.

When the eating was done, Hael went a little way from the fire and gazed upward at the stars. There were still many visible despite the swiftly gathering clouds. He could name many of them, and any herdsman could trace the patterns they formed in the night sky. The words for these were very ancient, some of them beasts such as no living man had seen. The Fish, the Crab and the Scorpion were common creatures, but what was the Goat-Fish, or the Ram, the Lion, the Bull? It was said that a bull had been a thing like a male kagga, but with only two horns, and that a ram was like a mountain curl-horn, but without the large, wood-gnawing front teeth. The lion was known to have been a cat, even larger than the night-cat, perhaps as large as the clouded terror-cat of the lowland jungles to the south, but maned like the great sleens that came up from the sea to sun themselves on the tidal rocks. These mysterious animals had not existed since the Days of Evil, when men had used sorcery to attack one another, men whose pride had been so great that they had even attacked the Moon. Of all such past things, or anything so long ago as to be nearly forgotten, it was said, "not since the Moon was white."

Before the doorway to his hut he again spiked his spear upright, where he could grasp it with his right hand as he came out. Before first entering the hut they had built together, he and Danats had cast the bones for this favored position, and Hael had won. Danats would always have to reach across to his left to retrieve his spear. From his pouch Hael took a long sheath of dried gut taken from a grass-cat. He slipped it down over the head and shaft of the spear. The bronze would not be harmed by water, but the rare steel of the edges could rust and a soaking could damage the fine wood.

Satisfied that his weapon was cared for he was about to crawl inside when the rain began. He removed belt, loincloth and pouch and tossed them inside, then stood for a few minutes in the warm downpour, letting it wash the day's dust from his body. All around him fires hissed in the wet as laughing youths shoveled coals and ashes into clay pots to store in the fire-hut, so that they would have fire in the morning without the arduous task of twirling a fire-stick with a bow. Few of them had enough fire magic to perform this task well, although Hael had seen mountain hunters raise a fire in the time it would take him to walk across the encampment and back to his hut. They had sung a low-voiced chant as they did it, and he had never been able to hear it clearly enough to imitate it. He was certain that the chant contained their fire magic.

On hands and knees he crawled through the low opening and into the smoke-scented interior of his hut. A tiny pot of kreeswood charcoal smoldered by the door. Its smoke had a pleasantly astringent sting, and would ward off the worst of the night's biting insects. Hael took a few more tiny black lumps from a bag that hung on a wall peg and tossed them onto the glowing ones in the bowl. He settled onto his bed of hide thrown over a mat of fragrant grasses and lay on his back, head resting on laced fingers as he listened to the rain drumming above him. The hut was dome-shaped, made of a frame of bent saplings overlaid with a skin of close-sewn bark. It was a comfortable dwelling, but the Shasinn lived their lives outdoors and rarely went inside save to sleep, make love or take refuge from inclement weather.

Outside and far away, he could hear the roar of one of the great predators, perhaps angry at the rain for spoiling its hunting. Night birds called to one another. Slowly, his eyes closed and the night sounds merged into his dreams, which were filled with vague, disturbing shapes. Sometimes he dreamed of things he knew, other times of things nobody he knew had seen. Many people claimed to dream of things that came to pass, but Hael did not like to think that some of the things he dreamed of would really happen.

He woke to the song of the fishbats returning to their caves where they would sleep the day away. Not bothering to don his pelt, he crawled out of the hut and walked to the great water jar that stood in the center of the camp. He splashed water in his face and rinsed out his mouth as the pearly gray light began to spread from the east. The jar stood next to the camp shed, a thatch roof supported by poles and protecting the warriors' hide shields, their drums and the few odd bits of furniture they required. There were some practice spears and targets, sticks for stick-fighting, pots of paint and oil.

"Hael!"

He turned to see who had called. Gasam walked toward him. Although all the fraternity were nominally equals, Gasam was the oldest and therefore the acknowledged leader. He was also Hael's foster brother, and the two had detested one another all their lives, but the customs of the fraternity forced them to behave with civility. The older youth was fully grown, with a broad chest and long, swelling muscles. He was fond of face-paint and wore numerous adornments of copper and beadwork. He even owned a fine shortsword, one of only three in the fraternity.

"You have water duty this morning," Gasam said. "You are excused herd watch until afternoon." He said this politely enough, but the tilt of his head and the tone of his voice were sufficient to express his disdain.

"Why always me?" Hael made the ritual complaint to hide both his irritation with Gasam and his elation at having the duty. It had been five days since he had been to the river to help the women. He hoped that Larissa would be there. "Warriors should fight and guard cattle, not bear burdens."

"Real warriors do not have to," Gasam said. In

truth, he was as inexperienced at raiding as any other new-made member of the fraternity, but he liked to pretend otherwise. As compensation for having had to remain boys for so long, the older members of the fraternity got to lord it over the young ones, and did not have to perform labor on such details, but only supervised. "Kampo will meet you and the others at the spirit-pole when the sun is up."

Hael hurried to the hut shared by Luo and Raba. The two stood outside, stretching, yawning and scratching. Luo saw him first and said, "Don't tell us. You carry water this morning. So do we. Gasam, that glorious champion among men, has just told us."

"And now," Raba said, "you wish me to work my magic, to make you shine and sparkle so that the women will think you comely. Well, you are ugly beyond belief, but I will see what may be done." He reached into the hut and brought out a flat wooden case. Inside it were several tiny pots of pigment and a number of small brushes. Deftly, he outlined Hael's eyes with black, then drew a series of blue lines down his wide cheekbones. With the tip of one finger, he made a series of red dots along Hael's jawline. With a final vertical yellow stripe on the chin, he stood back and admired his handiwork. "There. Perhaps now you will not frighten them."

"Thank you, Raba. In return, I will not tell them about you and the she-kagga." He trotted off to his own hut and put on his loincloth and fur ornaments. Tying his headband, he felt impatient for the time when his hair would be long enough to dress properly. He stripped the sheath from his spear, rolled and stored it in his pouch, then took the weapon to the shed, where many of the young warriors now stood washing themselves and splashing each other amid much laughter.

At a corner of the shed's wooden platform, next to a rack of javelins and a pile of bronzewood throwing-sticks, stood a pot of fistnut oil. The fistnut tree grew in profusion along the coast. Its nut, which was shaped remarkably like a human fist, was inedible, but it yielded an abundance of fragrant oil useful for protecting metal, making leather supple, waterproofing cloth and bark, and many other purposes. Hael applied a thin coat to the metal parts of his spear, then rubbed a little onto his arms, shoulders and chest, giving his skin a high, golden gloss. What remained on his palms he rubbed into the shaft of his spear.

Walking easily, his spear slanted across one shoulder, he crossed the compound to the spirit-pole. This was the camp's protective totem symbol, a bronzewood shaft as thick as a man's leg and half again man height, carved with spirit symbols and surmounted by a night-cat skull. Moving the pole when they broke camp to change pastures was a grueling task. Bronzewood was not named for its color, which was almost black, but for the density, weight and hardness of the wood.

Before the sun was a finger's breadth above the horizon, the water-carriers had gathered: nine young warriors and Kampo, an older youth with a lazy, easy-going manner. He was exceptionally handsome, even among the Shasinn, a comely people, and he wore many strings of colorful trade-beads. He was also the proud possessor of a necklet of hammered silver. When all the young men were assembled he raised his spear and the group trotted away. This was their usual gait when there were more than a few steps to be covered, and they could maintain it for hours, even encumbered with their heavy shields.

Two miles from the encampment lay the village, situated in a bend of the shallow Bunda River. It was an untidy sprawl of perhaps fifty huts and a few long gathering-halls, with livestock pens around its periphery, the whole surrounded by a palisade which was topped by a tangle of thorn bushes. The palisade was to protect people and livestock from predators that hunted by night, for the Shasinn always fought in the open field, never from behind walls.

They did not go into the village, but turned aside toward the watering place. This was a basin excavated into the side of the riverbank and lined with flat stones, where silt and mud could settle out of the water to be used by the village. They could see a group of women leaving the village as they reached the pool.

The women arrived a few minutes later, escorted by a few senior warriors. The women wore simple garments of trade cloth in bright colors; some were vividly patterned. The married women wore theirs wrapped carefully closed from armpits to knees. The unmarried ones wore the long lengths of cloth loosely, knotted over one shoulder, the bolder ones leaving theirs open down one side. There was an art to wearing the cloth thus and not allowing it to gape open, letting the men think they were seeing more than was actually the case.

With the women safely delivered, the senior

warriors walked back to the village. Hael and the rest did not doubt that they sighed inwardly for their days as junior warriors, with no cares or responsibilities beyond fighting and caring for the herds. It did not occur to the young warriors that someday they, too, would want wives and children, property and status.

Amid laughter and bawdy jokes, the women waded into the water and began filling the tall jars. Standing on the bank, the men set the jars upright on level ground. The youths made a great show of handling the ponderous, sloshing jars as if they weighed nothing while the women made fun of the obvious strain they nonetheless showed.

Hael admired the women, who were as beautiful as the men were handsome. He did not know that travelers who had been to the islands considered the Shasinn to be the comeliest people in existence, but it would not have surprised him. The women took greater care than the men to protect their skin from the sun, using hats and veils and lotions, so that they were mostly of a pale gold complexion. Their hair ranged from deep copper to almost white, and their eyes were every shade of blue. They were slender but strong, and moved with exceptional grace.

Downstream, a crowd of children drove a small herd of quil into the water for their daily bath. The fat, placid animals were as large as kagga, but needed to spend an hour or more every day soaking in running water. They were very stupid and easy prey for predators, and so had to be guarded at all times, but twice each year, at mating time, they grew incredibly long, fine hair that seemed to weigh nothing. When it was shed, the Shasinn traded it by the bale to the Men with Hairy Faces, who took it to the mainland, where it was woven into a beautiful and very costly fabric. Bare as fish, the children screamed and splashed in the water, scrubbing themselves and the quil, watched over by a detail from the Grass-Cat fraternity.

Thinking of the Men with Hairy Faces, Hael ran his fingers over his own face, careful not to disturb his paint. His skin was smooth, as it had been for weeks. None of the island people had facial hair as abundant as that of the men who came from the mainland, but as they neared manhood the boys would acquire a few scraggly, wiry hairs on chin and upper lip. These were easily plucked, and after a year or two, no more would grow.

He was especially concerned now to look his best, because Larissa was indeed among the women. Even in the midst of such beautiful women she shone. Among a race distinguished by wide brows and cheekbones, her narrower features gave her a touch of the exotic. Her eyes were deep violet, a rare shade, with dark rims around the irises. Most startling of all were her eyebrows. Despite hair that was nearly white, her eyebrows were so dark they appeared almost black. These features had made her a rather plain child, sometimes mocked by the others, but never cruelly, because of her father's high rank as an elder and her mother's status as head midwife. As she became a woman, these had in some magical fashion become the marks of a great beauty.

Hael had known her all his life. As children they had played together, bathed the quil together and done all the things tribal children were accustomed to do. In those days they had been close, the oddities of appearance that had set her apart from the other children had been matched by the deficiencies of family which had plagued him. He had lost his mother in the birth of her second child, who had also perished, and his father mere months later in a raid by a hereditary enemy tribe of the Shasinn. He had become a fosterling of an aunt and her husband, but they had taken him only as an obligation. The couple were of good status, but as a fosterling he could not share it: not like their natural child, Gasam, who was nearly seven years older. He had been as close to an outcast as the close-knit Shasinn could produce.

Lately, it had been different. Simply by living long enough, he had been inducted into a warrior fraternity. He now had a respectable status, a start in life, in spite of his familial handicaps. He had hoped that this would make him desirable to Larissa. Now, though, she was one of the tribe's great beauties, and half of the young men were trying out their mostly dismal skills at composing poems and songs to her beauty, her grace, her eventual position as one of the tribe's leading women.

She wore a mantle of red-and-white checked cloth, and her arms flashed with ornaments of bronze and silver; she wore hoops of gold in her ears. This jewelry represented the price of a small herd of kagga, wealth she would bring to her husband when she married. He elbowed others aside to be the one who took the filled water jars from her hands. Her teeth flashed bright as she smiled at him and his heart swelled at her nearness.

When the jars were filled the warriors took the

larger ones by the looping handles and balanced them on their heads and began to walk to the village, their spears held casually at their sides. The women made critical comments on the young men's dress and grooming, and the poise with which they carried their burdens.

"Luo is spilling water," said one. "I think there must be something wrong with the way his head is shaped."

"He took too many falls on it when we were wrestling," Pendu said. "I thought it was the safest place to drop him."

"Kampo's backside sways nicely when he carries water," said Binalla, who was known to favor the older youths. The men laughed and hooted and complimented Kampo on his comely bottom.

"Enjoy these while you can," said Tinatta, a woman old enough to have lines in her face, but not old enough for retired matron status. "When they become senior warriors, they are useless. They want to do nothing but count their livestock and drink ghul and seduce each other's wives." The other married women moaned agreement.

Larissa walked beside Hael and his mind sped, preparing clever banter to trade with her. If he became tongue-tied, he would not be able to bear the humiliation. She smelled sweetly of fistnut oil in which flower petals had been steeped.

"Your face paint is very well done, Hael," she said. She sighed dramatically. "I wish women were allowed to wear paint in the mornings."

Understanding immediately what was called for he said, "You need no paint to enhance your beauty, morning or evening, Larissa."

She smiled, an expression that made dimples

appear beneath her eyes. "You are a flatterer. I have been warned." She made a show of scanning the line of young warriors. "But where is Gasam this morning?"

Hael flushed with mortified anger. He knew that she was practicing one of her wiles against him. He also knew that she had picked the most effective one.

"He is at the camp, pretending to be a great warrior, too good for mere work such as this. Why, have you become like Binalla, to favor elders?"

She beamed with satisfaction, knowing that her barb had sunk deep. "Why not? He is handsome, and he is the leader of the Night-Cats, and one day he will be an important senior warrior."

"We have no leader," Hael insisted. "He is just older. It was his bad luck to be just too young for initiation the last time warriors were made."

She laughed and passed on to talk with the other women. He did not doubt that she would boast of how she had put him in his place.

"If men and women were allowed to wrestle, brother," Raba said, "I think you just lost three falls out of three."

"The ways of women are strange," Luo added. "The mighty Gasam, warrior of great repute, wins this contest merely by not being here."

Hael said nothing. They neared the entrance to the palisade. Just without the gate stood the village's spirit-pole. It was very old, intricately carved and decorated each year with the tails of sacrificial kagga. Beside it on a carved stool sat the spirit-speaker, Tata Mal. He nodded to the young men and the women as they passed, his lined face shaded by his hat of woven reeds.

Tata Mal's eyes lingered on Hael as the youth passed, waving courteously with the back of his hand. It had been a terrible stroke of bad fortune that the boy had been orphaned young, for no other youth in the village had shown such promise to be a spirit-speaker. Once, when the college of spirit-speakers had held their yearly meeting, Tata Mal had dared to ask that an exception be made, so that he could take Hael as apprentice. After much debate and argument, it was voted that the ancient rule should stand. After all, if an orphan were allowed to learn their arts, who knew where it might end?

It pained him that he had never found a suitable apprentice. The boy he had finally been forced to accept had little aptitude. He was certain that the spirits took a singular interest in Hael, and that might be why the youth was so afflicted with misfortunes. First the loss of his parents, then his adoption by an uncaring family, and his torment by his foster-brother Gasam; then the crowning misfortune: to end up in the same fraternity as Gasam.

Tata Mal did not like to think about Gasam. He sensed a potential for great evil in the young man, although so far it had been manifested only in bullying behavior. Since warrior initiations came so many years apart, there were always a few who missed the chance to be initiated because they were not quite old enough, by a year or even less. These had to wait until they were grown men of twenty or more years before they could even achieve the status of junior warrior.

Most took this in good part, like Kampo. They were still officially boys when others were almost ready to marry, but that was simply by custom, and in any case no male had much authority until well into his senior years. When they were at last initiated, there were compensations for the long wait. They were the natural leaders of the others, many of whom were no more than fifteen years of age. They did not stand night watch, and they could pass their days practicing for war and wandering among the herds, enjoying the care of this living wealth. When they graduated to senior warrior status, they would be the most experienced men, the leaders in the raids and battles, the most desirable husbands.

But some were twisted by the long wait, and Gasam was one such. He was a loose-haired boy during years when he longed to wear warrior braids. He carried a quil-herding stick when he felt it was his right to carry the spear. He burned with envy, listening to youths no more than a year his elder boasting of battles, of bloodied spears and herds of kagga taken from their enemies.

And yet, there was something more about the boy than these rather common unpleasantnesses. There was a scope for mischief that the old man could only sense. He pondered this as he scratched his knee and watched a stubby clay chimney a few feet away. Presently the small, furry head of a horndigger poked out the top of the chimney and surveyed the surroundings. Its sleek head was earless, with tiny eyes, and a short, forked horn thrust upward from its nose. Its powerful digging claws appeared next, then the rest of the animal, followed by its family. They began to forage for seeds and nuts, a diminutive brood the same color as the earth they tunneled in.

"What of it, eh, horndiggers?" Tata Mal asked them. "Why is it that I sense this evil? Surely you must hold converse with the spirits beneath the earth." The horndiggers said nothing, as he had known they would not. They were animals without spiritual qualities. They paid him no heed, because they were not interested in men. The predatory birds and daybats kept them scanning the skies. Serpents and lizards and furry things with sharp teeth made them pay attention to the surrounding grass, but man was just a towering, clumsy creature of no possible interest.

Idly, Tata Mal rattled the strings of bones that draped his withered chest. He was old, and he knew he was being selfish in hoping that he would not live to see this coming evil he sensed. His hair was white, he could no longer see faraway things as clearly as he used to, and now he felt no special regrets about leaving this world.

Hael set his jar in the village's central shed, a long, low-roofed, wall-less structure. When the jars were stored a woman of middle years came and clapped her hands for attention. It was Umarra, Larissa's mother and the head midwife of the village.

"When the Sun passes noon," she called, "we women retire to the women's lodge for three days of isolation prior to the Calving Festival. You young men are to stay away until the festival is over. While we are in isolation, the senior warriors and the elders may feed themselves or starve as they wish." She added, as ritual demanded, "For anyone who violates the tabus, the punishment is too terrible to mention. Now go and prepare yourselves for many sleepless nights. The calves will begin arriving before the Moon reaches her half phase."

"This is not a duty I look forward to," said Raba as they began to walk toward the village gate. The women's festival purified them so that they would be able to assist the she-kaggas at calving, a thing forbidden to men. It would go on day and night for twenty days or more, with the women amid the herd and the men standing guard, for the sounds and smells of birthing would draw predators from many miles around. The nights would be hideous with the cries of the lurking scavengers.

"But there are chances for glory at such times," Luo pointed out. "You might kill one of the great cats, or even a longneck, without violating tabu, and with the whole village watching. You could then wear its skin for the rest of your days."

Hael slapped him on the shoulder. "How often does it happen thus? Last year, the Spearfang fraternity killed a terror-cat that came up from the jungles at calving time. So many threw their spears at once that each man of the fraternity now wears a strip of pelt large enough to make an armband."

"Hael speaks gloom again," said Raba, arms raised and imploring the sky to witness. "He cannot allow a man to dream without pissing on the fires of glory."

"You do not rate fire yet," Hael told him, "only smouldering coals."

As they left the village, Tata Mal called to him. "Hael, tarry here with me a while." Hael turned aside, and the others set off at a trot. Kampo, in the lead, began a warrior chant and the others took it up in a low voice. As they drew away, Hael squatted by the old man, his spear held before him with both hands. Respectfully, he waited for the elder to speak.

"You enjoy the warrior's life, do you not, Hael?"

"Of course. Who would not?" Hael answered.

"Since you were not fated to be a spirit-speaker, it is well that you find the life agreeable. You seem to get on well with your brothers of the fraternity."

"With most of them, yes," Hael said, judiciously.

"But not with Gasam?"

"There is nothing new about that. In fact, he has never behaved better toward me, since custom now constrains him." He was uncomfortable with the subject, as if speaking of it raised a reality he would rather forget.

"Gasam is new to his warrior status, as are you. Soon he will become more comfortable with it, more confident. Then you must watch out for him. The idea that all junior warriors are equal is untrue. He is in a position to do you much harm, and he will."

"I can protect myself," Hael insisted.

"This is not like an open fight," Tata Mal cautioned. "He will not attack you from in front. Gasam has had more years than you to observe the ways of men. He may set others against you, perhaps without their knowing. He can make trouble for you here, at the village, while you live in the camp."

Hael looked up at the older man. "But why?" he asked earnestly. "We have never liked each other, but I have never threatened him. If he survives his warrior years, he will be a respected elder, with many wives and a great herd. I will do well to have a single wife and a few kagga of my own. Why does he feel he must humble me?"

"He sees something in you, as do I, only he does not like it. You have qualities that make you stand out from the others. You have the seriousness, the gravity of an elder, even though you are younger than the greater part of your brothers. They mock you for it now, but soon they will come to respect it and they will turn to you for advice and, yes, leadership. Gasam will find this intolerable."

Hael watched the clouds drift across the landscape. A herd of branch-horns grazed, seemingly placid but nervous and alert. At first sign of a predator, their slender legs would carry them away in tremendous bounds. "I cannot fight him. It is forbidden within the fraternity. When we are senior warriors I can challenge him to the thorn circle, but that is many years away."

"True. You must watch. Be ever vigilant, and do not hesitate to come to me for advice."

"I thank you, spirit-speaker."

"It is my duty. And now I will give you some advice that is even more unwelcome. It is good for the young men to flirt and court with the young women. They must learn each other's ways and few things in life are more pleasant. But do not set your heart on one woman, especially on one as near your own age as Larissa."

Hael felt the flush rising in his face. "And why not? We have known each other since childhood. Of all the women of the village, she is the one who never held my lack of family against me."

"She was a lonely child. Now she is a beautiful and desirable young woman. Let me see"—the old man rubbed his chin in thought,—"the next full moon will mark your sixteenth year, is that not so?"

"It will."

"She is about the same age, and is marriageable. You will not be able to marry until the next initiation, in about seven years' time, perhaps not for as many as ten years, if it takes that long to accumulate enough uninitiated boys. Do you think she will wait so long to marry?"

"No," Hael said, miserable and heartsick. This was something he had successfully avoided thinking about until now.

"Hael, I will tell you some things that all men must learn eventually, although most do not consider them in the carefree days of youth. Why do we have these customs? Why do we separate the young men from the rest of us, and send them to live in camps, and not allow them to return to the village and own property and marry until they are of mature years?"

"Well," Hael said, thinking, "the kagga must be guarded, and the village protected against attack. Someone must go out on raids."

"Other peoples do all these things without warrior fraternities. Within the next year or two Larissa will marry a senior warrior or an elder, for the excellent reason that there is no one else for a girl to marry. *All* young women are married to older men. The oldest, the elders, have more kagga and other livestock, and can make larger bride-presents. What happens when you young warriors bring back kagga from a raid?"

"We hold a feast," Hael answered, already beginning to see where the old man's words were
leading. This was not something easy to think
about, because customs just were; ordinarily they
required no thought.

"Exactly. You kill a few head and throw a feast
for the whole village, pouring out the blood as
thanks to the spirits. Then your fathers get a few
head, and the rest are divided among the elders.
You see? There are far fewer senior warriors than
junior warriors, and fewer still live to be elders.
Most of our customs, especially those involving
warrior duties, have the purpose of keeping you
young troublemakers away from the village, out
of mischief, and poor. The great bulk of the wealth
and all the desirable women go to the senior warriors and the elders. Of those things, the elders
enjoy an even greater disproportion, along with
all real power."

"I had not thought of it that way," Hael admitted. "I had always thought we did as we did because—well, because it was *right*. Because we are
Shasinn, and these things are right for Shasinn."

Tata Mal took his divining-bones from his pouch
and tossed them at his feet, gathered them up,
tossed them again. Apparently satisfied with what
he saw, he gathered them up and replaced them
in his pouch. "They are not bad customs," he continued. "People must have customs and tabus to
guide them, or all life slides into chaos. Our customs suit us well, although they would not be good
for the farmers or hunters or fishers, and none of
us knows what customs rule the people from
across the water. Ours have kept us independent
and powerful and even rich as we judge such

things, which is to say, rich in livestock. And there is much to be said for taking young men at their most troublesome age and making them useful to the whole community."

Hael said nothing, knowing that the spirit-speaker was not finished. He watched the branch-horns, who were now finished with their morning's feeding and walking westward. In the distance, he could see a small group of killer birds chasing something. Their wings were mere stumps, but their great, clawed feet covered ground almost as swiftly as a bounding branch-horn, and their long, hooked beaks ripped flesh as efficiently as the teeth of any of the cats.

"What you must remember," Tata Mal went on, "is that men are motivated by many things other than warrior glory and the esteem of companions. They want wealth, and women and status and power, and they will scheme and conspire to get these things. One who is older, such as Gasam, is more likely to value these things than a youth like you. Remember, he is already preparing for the day when he will be a senior warrior. He will find ways to curry favor with the elders, even from the camp. He may set them against you. Take care, and remember that the mightiest warrior's back is as vulnerable as any other man's."

"Do the spirits tell you all these things?" Hael asked.

"No, the spirits concern themselves with the things of nature. They may be approached concerning the fertility of animals and plants, the hunting of wild predators, the coming of rain and storm, even of fire. But they do not care about the doings of men. I am old and have watched people for a lifetime, and that is how I know their hearts, even when they themselves do not. Also, as a spirit-speaker, I can watch from the outside. I cannot be a warrior, or own property beyond the implements of my trade. A spirit-speaker may marry only once, and may not accumulate wives for status or to form alliances, and my wife died long ago. I may not be a chief or hold a seat in council, only advise. Therefore I cannot long for these things. This bestows a certain clarity upon a spirit-speaker's observation of his fellow men."

Hael got to his feet, sensing that the old man had said what he intended. "I thank you for your advice. You have given me a great deal to occupy my thoughts in the future."

Tata Mal grinned. "There. I have taken the shine from a perfectly good day. Do not let this sadden your heart, Hael. These are years to be enjoyed. But do not forget that the world is a dangerous place, and that wild beasts and tribal enemies may be the least of the dangers."

"I will remember that," Hael said. "Again, I thank you." He turned and set off at a steady lope.

Tata Mal watched him go, relieved that he had done his best to warn the boy, but still uncomfortable. He had not been speaking the exact truth when he said that the spirits cared nothing for man, although most of the time that was true. He was certain that the spirits had an interest in Hael, but this was not something he was allowed to speak of to one who was not an initiate of the college of spirit-speakers. It was all very complicated. He took the divining-bones from his pouch and began to toss them again.

Hael loped over the grass, glorying in the day,

but troubled in his mind by the spirit-speaker's words. The life of a junior warrior was turning out to be more treacherous than he had thought. Still, the day was beautiful, the grass was high, and he had spoken with Larissa, although not satisfactorily. He slowed when he saw a faint ripple in the grass and readied his spear. It might be anything, but among the possibilities was a grass-cat. The beast was not large, but it could easily kill a man taken unawares. The grass-cat was almost magical in its ability to remain undetected until it sprang. At this time of year its pelt was green, the same color as the new grass. Later in the year, in the dry season, it would become yellow-tan.

He relaxed slightly as a large, ungainly beast blundered into view. It was a toonoo, a wild cousin of the quil, bulky with muscle where the quil was fat, and a bit more intelligent. It also had two forward-slanting tusks as long as a man's forearm protruding from its grotesque head. It could be a dangerous creature if provoked, but it rarely attacked if unmolested. Hael remained cautious for it was always possible to offend a beast without intending to. He might be standing too close to its young, which often crouched unmoving in the grass while their mother was foraging nearby. This one looked at him for a moment with its tiny, bone-rimmed eyes, shook its head and trotted into the grass with a loud snort. Hael continued on his way.

TWO

The time of the Calving Festival came, and for a day and a night the men of the village were exiled from the enclosure while the women were purified. Grousing to hide their holiday elation, most of them made their way to the encampments of the warrior fraternities, carrying skins of ghul and bags of provisions. Behind them, the sounds of drum and flute announced the beginning of the women's ceremonies.

In the camps, the young men rested against the arduous weeks ahead, passing the time in wrestling and spear-throwing, stick-fighting and dancing, as they listened to the senior warriors and elders complain of how dull or hard or henpecked their lives were. The skins of ghul were passed around, and although junior warriors were not supposed to drink it, the custom did not carry the force of tabu, and its violation was winked at as long as a young man did not become disgracefully drunk. The drink was made from a crushed fruit pulp mixed with honey and water and stored in jars to ferment for several months. After that the pulp was strained out and the liquid stored in smaller jars or in skins, where it would sometimes keep for a year or more. It was made by women who were specialists, as the craft called for its own peculiar spells and chants. The spirits loved ghul, but when they got into it they turned it sour and undrinkable.

The senior warriors were swaggering, arrogant men for the most part, survivors of the dangerous years of youth. Although they no longer went on the kagga raids, they were the backbone of the tribe's defense in battle. At such times, the formation of junior warriors, the attackers and skirmishers, were called "the spear," while the defensive line of senior warriors who always stood between the enemy and the village were called "the shield." In the great battles, which involved many villages and happened only once or twice in a generation, the seniors of all the villages formed the center of the battleline, while the juniors formed the horn-curved flanks, with the task of encircling the enemy and crushing them against the immovable center.

Senior warriors continued to wear their hair long, but they could wear it clubbed at back, or in a single braid, or sometimes in two thick plaits in front of their ears. They wore kilts or loincloths or brief cloaks of trade cloth in bright colors and vivid patterns. The prouder ones outlined their many scars with red paint.

Elders wrapped themselves in long cloaks and carried no weapons, only walking staffs. Their

graying hair was cropped short and they seldom
wore ornaments. They needed none, for they were
wrapped all about in their status, and each was
wealthy in kagga, wives and children. Most lived
in small family compounds outside the village,
where they maintained huts for each wife and
pens for their personal herds. It was easy to judge
an elder's wealth merely by walking by his compound and counting the number of huts inside.
They needed many children to help guard their
animals, although a few kept prisoner-slaves, a
new custom of no more than three or four generations' practice, and still hotly debated by elders
and spirit-speakers. No more than one man in ten
survived to elder status. Battle, injury, wild beasts
and sickness carried off the rest. Elder women
survived in about the same numbers. Childbirth
and capture by enemies or slavers took the same
toll on them as battle did for the men.

While the older men lounged about in the shade,
the younger ones practiced the arts of war. Some
wrestled violently, raising clouds of dust as they
grunted and struggled, their bodies slippery with
fistnut oil. Others practiced with the throwing-
sticks. These were made of bronzewood, in length
the distance from a man's elbow to his fingertips.
The haft was as thick as a man's thumb, with a
knob at one end, half the size of his fist. They went
into battle with five or six clutched in the hand
behind the shield. They could be thrown with
great accuracy and bone-smashing force. The
young men at practice threw them at each other
in turn, and the one on the receiving end had to
dodge or duck, or he might block it with a small
dancing shield. The crack of a stick meeting one

of the tough little rawhide shields could be heard for hundreds of paces. A few of the most agile would catch the flying sticks and throw them back, but this took the most precise judgment, for a stick could smash a hand to useless splinters of bone and shreds of flesh.

The spear-throwing targets were man-sized cylinders of woven basketry, stuffed with grass. Hael and several others cast at these while a few seniors idled near them, making critical comment. The javelins were about five feet long, no more than a third the weight of the warrior spear. They were of tough wood with six-inch heads of cast bronze. These cheap points were traded by the thousands from the holds of the mainlanders' ships. They were easily retrieved after a battle and would last indefinitely. The valuable, intricately made spears were thrown in battle only if the warrior had a sword or axe as backup weapon, or in a moment of great desperation.

A young man named Sounn picked up a javelin from a pile leaning against a crude rack and hefted it, then strode to the throwing-line. His arm rocked back, then shot forward, and the javelin sped toward one of the nearer targets. It was a fair cast, but he had misjudged the breeze and the point gouged the left side of the target, glanced away and struck into the ground beyond. The senior warriors, a little the worse for the ghul they had drunk, hooted in derision.

"That cast would not have done the day we faced the Asasa!" shouted one, whose many scars proclaimed him a veteran of numerous fights. The Asasa were another herding people, dwelling in the south of the island. Their customs differed from those of the Shasinn, although all the island peoples spoke variations of the same tongue. The young warrior walked away, shamefaced. Enduring such taunts was a part of the burden of the new-made warriors until they proved themselves in battle—or died.

"Hael will show us how to cast the spear."

Hael looked up to see who had spoken, knowing all the time that it was Gasam. The older youth was standing at his ease amid the group of veterans, as if he were their equal. Now that he knew what to expect, it was of some interest to Hael to see how Gasam went about it.

"Show these brave men, Hael," Gasam urged, "lest they think the Night-Cats useless in battle." He turned to the older men, smiling. "You shall see. Not just that nearer target, either. Hael shall cast for the farthest."

"Yes, show us, Hael," said a man whose temple-braids dangled to his chest, his voice uneven from the ghul he had drunk.

Wordlessly, Hael stepped over to the rack of javelins. Gasam had chosen carefully. He would not have challenged Hael to wrestle, or to a mock fight with shields and practice spears, because Hael excelled in those exercises, even though he had not yet reached his full growth. If he had a single weakness as a warrior, it was the long cast with the javelin. Still growing, the ratio of arm length and hand-to-eye distance changed fractionally each month, making it difficult to achieve more than adequate skill where such minute, if unconscious, calculations were called for.

He jammed his spear-butt into the dirt and selected a javelin. Placing its rounded butt on a flat stone, he spun it between his palms, checking the shaft for straightness. It wobbled slightly and he chose another. This one was straight, but when he grasped the point and twisted, he could feel that the head was slightly loose. He rejected another because the bronze point was bent. At last he found one that seemed satisfactory, and he stepped to the throwing-line. The usual banter ceased, because everyone could sense that a challenge had been issued, although Gasam had been careful to sound otherwise.

The farthest target was fifty paces away, an easy shot for a hunter's arrow, but difficult for an accurate javelin-cast. There were tribes who threw the javelin for mere distance, but the Shasinn were not among them, holding that a weapon that does not strike an enemy is not a weapon, but a toy. In consequence, they did not bother to cast beyond distances at which they could count on a fatal hit.

He picked up a handful of dust and cast it up, watching its fall for wind speed and direction. He also watched the gentle waving of the grass near the target, as the wind was capricious and did not always blow the same even over short distances. He turned and went back twenty paces at a lanky, loose-jointed trot. He stopped, turned and raised the javelin to shoulder level.

His first step was almost a leap, although made slowly. The next was shorter and swifter, as was each subsequent stride. His spear hand swept back to its farthest reach and he made a short hop. As his left foot struck the ground his arm, nearly straight, swung forward, the muscles of shoulder, chest and waist working in perfect coordination. As his hand reached the apogee of its arc, the haft slid across his palm and fingers and he gave a final flick of his wrist, giving the javelin the necessary rapid, stabilizing spin. After it had left his hand, he continued to go forward, twisting to his left in follow-through, stopping with a couple of short bounces on his right foot.

The missile arched upward, the sunlight flashing from its twirling bronze point. Midway it leveled and slowed, then its point dipped and it began to descend, picking up speed as the pull of gravity took inexorable hold. Nobody breathed as it sped the last thirty paces. The point struck the target precisely in the center, at the height of a man's chest, the angle such that only by seeing the weapon in time and raising his shield could a warrior save himself. The bronze lodged in the slender pole that was anchored in the ground to hold the target upright, causing the whole construction to sway dramatically.

The watching warriors whistled and tapped their spear-butts on the ground in appreciation. The other Night-Cats cheered. "There!" said Gasam with a false laugh and a forced smile. "You see?"

The veterans went to find more ghul. As they filed past Hael, one said, "A fine cast, young Hael. When you can make it with a shield on your arm, you will be ready for real battle."

The last of them grinned and clapped Hael on the shoulder. "Don't listen to fools like him. Drunk or sober, with or without a shield, he could never have made that cast."

As Gasam walked by, he said nothing, but he did not bother to hide an expression compounded of disdain and hostility. Luo came over with Raba and Pendu. Luo wagged his right hand in wonder.

"When did you become a champion with the javelin? Have you been practicing at some other camp? You were not that good last month."

"He spoke with the old spirit-speaker a few days ago," Pendu said. "Tata Mal must have given him a spell to make the spear fly true."

"You are superstitious," Raba sneered. "Don't you know there are no spells to assist warrior skills? If there were, we would all be defeated by little armies of spirit-speakers."

"I used no spells," Hael said quietly, in the serious way he had that always seemed strange to them. "I did not have to. I simply dared not miss."

The women's festival was a success, for the last note of the drum had barely faded in the gray light of early morning when the she-kaggas began groaning in birth-pains. Red-eyed from lack of sleep, the women began to trudge out to the herds. Nearly everyone in the village took part, except for a few elders and their children who had to tend to personal herds.

The herds had been gathered in a single pasture so that there should be safe, centralized forage for all the beasts during the vulnerable calving time. All the warrior fraternities gathered and the chiefs assigned them sectors to guard, with the senior warriors in a continuous circle nearest the herd. The greatest danger was from wild beasts. Rival Shasinn and the other herding peoples would not raid at calving time, both because of custom and because they were similarly occupied at this season. Not all peoples observed herdsmen's customs, however, and for this reason the senior warriors carried shields as well as their spears.

It was a time of hard work and little sleep, but there was a feeling of holiday as well. Children under the watchful eyes of the warriors spent the days gathering fuel for each night's fires, and these burned around the periphery to provide the women with light and to keep the beasts at bay. The smells of blood and afterbirth, and the bleating of newborn kagga made cowardly scavengers bold. The roars of the great cats could be heard, and the hissings of the spearteeth. Killer birds patrolled the grasslands but they were no danger, since smells and sounds meant nothing to them. They only pursued movement. The predatory reptiles never strayed far from the streams.

Runners went from village to village, spreading word of wild beast sightings or fetching women who were notably skilled in particular birthing problems. The spirit-speakers wandered from one herd to another, performing required rituals, or persuading the spirits to aid the she-kaggas in delivery, driving away the spirits of sickness. Day and night, the songs of the women and the warriors could be heard above the noises of the massed animals.

"I cannot decide," said Luo, swishing the air about him with a kagga tail, "which is worse: these skulking stripers, or the flies." The animals he referred to lurked in the grass. They were not large, weighing around thirty pounds full grown, but their oversized jaws were extremely powerful and lined with stout, sharp teeth. They ran in packs and usually ate carrion, but they were always eager to attack the young or crippled. The flies were everywhere. By the fifth day they clustered thick on everything and everyone near the herd.

"I prefer the stripers," Hael said. "Flies are like ticks; they are a part of life when you raise livestock, but this is intolerable. I will be happy when we can split up the herds and move them to fresh pasture. It's getting difficult to breathe."

There were a dozen of the young men patrolling the southern periphery of the herd. Heavy brush grew close in this area, making good cover for predators both four- and two-legged. They were making for the nearest fire, a tall blaze tended by children who were building it up in the gathering dusk. Covered jars of milk and blood, pots of honey and piles of fruit and cooked grain stood near the flames.

The plant foods were forbidden for the young warriors, but when they reached the fire they passed around the milk and blood, which they swallowed thirstily, mixed with honey. As the darkness deepened the biting insects began to replace the flies. The kagga-tail whisks flickered in the firelight, making the men look like strange hybrid animals.

A small group of warriors wearing the dark pelt of the fur snake arrived at the fire. "Any cats?" they asked.

"None," Hael said. "You?"

"We smelled grass-cat piss over to the east. We think there's a big one working its way close."

"The cats are not dangerous if you're alert," said another of the newcomers. "Two or three men with spears who know what they're doing can handle any cat. It's a good thing the fur snakes are dormant this time of year." The Fur Snakes were always reminding people of how dangerous their totem animal could be, since they were so seldom seen. They were not true snakes, having tiny, useless legs. They were as thick as a man's thigh, and three times man length, with narrow jaws and hooked teeth. Dwelling in the tunnels dug by the larger burrowing animals, they lay quietly, with only their sensitive noses above ground. They could shoot out with blinding speed to seize passing animals or humans.

"If you killed one," Raba observed, "they cannot be all that dangerous. The night-cat, on the other hand—"

His words were interrupted when a runner arrived. He halted by the fire, leaning over with hands braced on knees, breathing heavily. He had clearly been running long and hard, and all stayed silent until he could catch his breath. When he straightened, a Fur Snake handed him a skin of water. The runner rinsed out his mouth and spat, then swallowed two or three tiny mouthfuls. He panted out his message between gasps.

"I am Tusa. From Lingasa. Killer Bird Fraternity." The bird's black backfeathers were worked into the youth's hair. "We have found sign. A longneck. Maybe headed this way."

"I'll get the chiefs," Luo said, darting from the firelight.

All gripped their spears and looked outward from the brightness of the fire; the surrounding darkness was nearly complete. They concentrated on looking manly, but succeeded principally in looking frightened. The longneck was the deadliest of all the predators. Its bulk was five or six times that of a man, but its short, powerful legs kept it low in the grass, difficult to see until it was too late. Its long, flexible neck gave it a swift, serpentlike strike and its triangular head was armed with terrible teeth. Even its tail was deadly, a muscular whip that could snap a man's spine. They were rare creatures, but one showed up every ten years or so to plague the herds and villages. Worse, the animal was of great magical significance, and tabu to kill except under special conditions. Since no single man had ever been known to kill one, there was no Longneck warrior fraternity.

A few minutes later several elders arrived, accompanied by a small group of the more important senior warriors bearing shields. Tata Mal was with them.

Minda, Speaker of the Chief's Council, took Tusa by the shoulder. "Tell us what you've seen."

The youth was better recovered now. "This afternoon, when the Sun was halfway past zenith, some of our guards saw a commotion in the grass. Something big was moving through but keeping low. It did not look up over the grass every few paces, as a cat will, and there was only one, not a pack like the scavengers, the stripers and the spotted ones. The guards quartered behind it and cut its trail. Soon they found droppings such as they had never seen before, and smelled extremely rank urine. The pawmarks were big," he held his hands eight inches apart to demonstrate, "with deep clawmarks, so it cannot sheathe its claws as the cats can. They were almost certain what it was, but they called in an old hunter who lives in our village, who sharpens spears and makes fire magic for his food. He said it is certainly a longneck. Our best runners were detailed to warn the nearby villages. I am the swiftest and was sent here, because it was moving this way." He took a few deep breaths. He still streamed with sweat. "My totem gave me extra fleetness of foot. I feared to meet the thing at every step."

"You are a brave lad," Minda said. Then, "Who is swiftest here? Luo? Go north and warn the people of Motuta. Their calving meadow this year is to the south of the village. You should see their fires before you are out of sight of ours. Go like the wind." Luo set off without a word.

The chief looked most serious. "Tata Mal, how do we stand here? A longneck in the midst of blood can go mad, killing until there is nothing left to kill."

"This is calving time, Minda. The women's rites have been completed, the birthing proceeds. At such times, no animal is sacred, none lies under tabu if it attacks the people or the stock, not even a longneck." At any other time it was a terrible offence to kill a longneck, even in self-defense. The ritual purification could require years, when the circumstances were not such that the malefactor must be killed outright. "This night, and until the birthing is done, a longneck may be killed if it attacks, and nothing but honor to the slayers."

"Good. I was sure that was the case, but I wanted those here to hear it from your own lips. Warriors!" The seniors smacked the inner sides of their shields with their spear-laden fists. "Go and warn the people, see that all the outlying guards are on the alert. If the creature attacks, everyone must come at once to repel it. But I want no false alarms. Tonight, every boy will see a long-neck in each shifting shadow. And no glory-hunting either. One man with one spear is no match for this creature. When I was a junior warrior the Grass-Cats killed one that attacked the women at a watering place. Five of them put their spears through it, and it killed two before it died. The three survivors had to stay isolated in mourning for the next year."

"They were lucky at that," Tata Mal said. "The spirit-speakers decided that most of the guilt could be put on the two dead men. There are far worse things than a year spent in mourning."

The senior warriors dashed off and the elders conversed among themselves in low voices. The runner sat on the ground and a wide-eyed child brought him a bowl of blood-laced milk. Exhausted as he was, he had a smile for the child's worshipful expression. Hael caught his brothers' eyes and jerked his head to one side. They followed him out of the circle of firelight. Away from the fire, they began to trot toward their assigned sector.

"A longneck!" said Pendu. "Even if it takes five of us, that is enough pelt for each man to have a whole cloak!"

"This beast will wear your pelt in his teeth, fool," Raba said, in no spirit of banter but in earnest. "Minda spoke good sense. Against a longneck, twenty to one is not bad odds, and if I cast my spear at it, I will run until someone comes and tells me it is dead. Is that not wise, Hael?"

"It is best to be cautious with such a creature," he agreed. "Each of us has killed a night-cat, and that is an animal with a well-earned reputation for manslaying. But a longneck to a night-cat is what the night-cat is to the little tree-cat that raids bird nests. I for one will seek honor in less foolhardy ways. Any man who fails to raise an alarm because he wants the glory of killing a longneck single-handed deserves what will happen to him."

"At least the tabu is lifted for now," Raba said. "It would be a bad thing, to be punished for protecting the tribe." The thought of such misfortune depressed them. It did not occur to them that it might be an injustice. Ritual law had nothing to do with justice. Justice was for men, tabu and its surrounding laws involved the spirit world. The laws were ancient and unchanging, and the penalties were always harsh.

"We have to keep moving, to patrol our sector," Hael said when they reached one of their boundary marks. "But everyone stay close. We have to spread out some, or it might pass between us, but let no one be out of sight of the two flanking men."

No one disputed his assumption of leadership. This was no time for youthful rivalry. The prospect of encountering a big cat or other predator had been exciting. This was deadly and frightening.

Spread out, they trod their perimeter slowly, on silent feet. They were too far from the fires for the ruddy light to reach, but the scarred moon silvered the grass. From time to time the wind brought to them faintly the sound of chanting and the bawling of kagga. They reached another boundary marker, turned and started back the way they had just come. They had been walking for only a few minutes when their heads all jerked around at once.

"I cannot trust my eyes in this light," said one, "but my nose cannot be fooled. What is that smell?" A shift in the breeze had momentarily carried away the smell of smoke and kagga, and had brought something rank and unfamiliar.

"Since it's something we've never smelled before," Hael said, loud enough for them all to hear, "we can guess what it is. Keep facing to windward and shout when you see movement."

Nervously, spears gripped in both hands, they waited, straining eyes and ears, seeking some warning of the legendary creature's swift attack. The smell grew stronger, then weaker, as if the creature were moving out there, seeking an open spot in their line. But that might be a shift in the wind.

Hael forced himself to relax, as he often did when on guard duty, to empty his mind of vain guesses and deceptive expectations. He let himself become part of the grassland, feeling the movements of its creatures as they went about their small, thoughtless lives. He knew immediately that there were few animals out there tonight. They had sensed the greater predator and had fled.

Then he felt it. Fifty paces ahead of him, and to his left. No movement was visible, there was no sound, but something very large was creeping toward their line. Pendu was the next man to his left, and the creature would pass nearest him. Hael gave a low whistle. It was a signal used in warfare and raiding, to help warriors stay together during the dark hours without using their voices.

Stealthily, he began to move toward the spot

where he sensed the killer. With his spear, he signaled Pendu to stay where he was. With whistles and spear-signals he brought the men to his right around in a wide arc. He heard other whistles as his instructions were relayed, and the men to Pendu's left swung inward as well. When he whistled for them to stop, they formed a broad V, with Pendu at its point and the longneck somewhere within its arms.

It lay quiet, sensing their awareness of it. No wonder the beast was famed for its magic, Hael thought, gripping his spear in sweaty palms. It could see into men's minds. He could feel its presence, but he did not know exactly where it was, or whether it would attack, or try to escape through the open end of the V. A sudden, sharp stench assailed them. The creature was voiding, preparing to attack.

"Be ready!" Hael shouted, "It comes!" The words had barely left his tongue when the grass in front of him exploded and something huge lunged toward him. It was incredible, he thought in the split instant as the nightmare head shot toward him; surely nothing so large could move through the grass, get so close, without making a sound or causing the grass to sway to its movement.

Without thought, he dodged to his right and simultaneously thrust with his spear. He was trying for the throat, but his point grated on jawbone and the weapon was almost jerked from his hand. Desperately, he kept the spear between himself and the beast, knowing that to lose it or to fall would mean his death.

With a shrill, ululating battle-cry, the others

darted in, each man thrusting at the monster, then leaping back to avoid its flashing teeth and slashing claws. Even in the extremity of his terror and exertion, Hael found a place in his heart to feel pride that not one of them dropped his spear and ran or even held back from the desperate battle. The terrible head flailed back toward him. There was no good opportunity for a thrust so he snapped his spear-butt across like a staff, trying to smash the eye; but the bronze glanced from the bony shield that protected it. Still using his spear as a staff, he slashed with the swordlike blade, opening a deep cut the length of the animal's snout. He could hear shouting in the near distance, as other warriors hurried to the scene of the fight.

A youth named Gota lunged at the beast's hindquarters, trying to hamstring it, but in doing so he forgot about the thing's dangerous tail. It lashed out like a great whip, and above the shouting and the sound of the tail meeting flesh Hael could hear the snap of Gota's thighbone. The longneck whirled and drew its head back for a strike at the fallen youth and Hael rushed in, lunging up beneath the jaw. Once again the thing twisted its head too swiftly for a clean thrust to get home and his point jammed against the underside of the heavy jawbone.

A foreleg flashed out, seemingly with no great force, but it caught Hael's thigh and sent him spinning through a full somersault. He landed hard on his back, half stunned, his wind gone, but he saw the longneck looming above him and knew that it was his death. Then he saw spears take it in each flank and it drew back, baffled and roaring.

The rest of the Night-Cats had arrived, and a

few swift runners from other fraternities. In the odd, stretched-out aspect that time assumed during moments of great fear and violence, the battle seemed to have gone on for a long time, but he knew it had only been a very few minutes since the thing had erupted before him. Somebody stood above him. It was Gasam, looking down with a grin he could only interpret as evil. Then he was gone, to join the other warriors.

He hopes I will die, Hael thought, with the great clarity that comes of a serious wound. That was when he knew that he had to live at whatever cost. Gasam could not be allowed to win. He forced himself to one elbow so that he could follow the progress of the fight. At least forty young warriors now surrounded the beast, eager to kill but forced to keep their distance by the thing's multiplicity of weapons and ability to strike in all directions. He saw that Gasam was shouting loudly, giving orders to everyone, but when he darted in it was never close enough to be struck himself.

There was the sound of thunder approaching, yet he remembered that the night had been clear. Then he knew that it was the senior warriors running toward the fight, their spear-butts beating the insides of their shields, the terrifying sound of the Shasinn speeding to battle.

His vision began to shimmer, and he shook his head to clear it. The view steadied and he saw the bright shields loom from the darkness, the lurid glare as men brought torches to illuminate the battle. Now the longneck was whirling, lashing in all directions, squalling horribly. It streamed blood from wounds in head, neck, flank and haunches. The fire dazzled it, the spears and broad shields confused it. Angry and frustrated, it now wanted only to escape. The men were thinnest on the side away from the herd. The animal broke off the fight abruptly, whirled and lunged in that direction. The more nimble junior warriors dived out of its way as if they had grown wings. Three seniors, encumbered by their heavy shields, were not so swift and were knocked flat. By habit of long training they pulled head and legs beneath the protection of their shields, as they did when a picked man lured a big cat to attack his shield while his companions speared it from the sides. Suddenly, as magically as it had come, the longneck was gone.

There was silence. A few men rushed out and cast their spears toward where they thought the thing might be. Minda's voice rang out above the milling crowd. "No pursuit! Do not try to chase it in the dark! We will search for it in the daylight. Bring the wounded to a fire."

The night shook with cheers and a loud warrior chant of victory began. Spears and shields shook rhythmically, and the junior warriors started a leaping dance. It continued for several minutes, then a woman's shrill voice cut through the celebration.

"We are still at work, and the cats and stripers may eat us all while you fools congratulate yourselves! Even if you do not care about us women, come back and protect your livestock!"

Laughing, the men returned to their guard stations. Raba and a senior warrior each grabbed Hael beneath an arm and hauled him to his feet. Until this moment shock and excitement had held the pain in abeyance, but now a wave of sickening agony washed over him and he strove not to cry out. His right thigh was on fire from hip to knee, but that was only the most localized of his pains. He was a mass of suffering from toes to scalp and came near to fainting several times before they reached the fire. He was grateful for the warmth of the flames when they set him down, because he was beginning to shiver with chills in spite of the warm night.

The boys tending the fire made backrests for the wounded, stuffing hide bags with grass. Pendu stuck his spear in the ground next to him. "This will help to identify your corpse in the morning. Your face is altogether unpleasant to look upon just now. Recognizing it in a death-rictus would be far too much to ask of your brothers."

"I will lie with your widows on your grave," Hael responded tiredly.

Pendu laughed and walked away. "He'll be all right," he said to someone. "Insolent and insulting as ever."

Hael was not so sure. In the firelight, he could see that his thigh was striped with four parallel gouges, deep and ragged. They were not bleeding heavily, which might or might not be a bad sign. He would certainly not bleed to death, but infection might kill him. A permanently crippled leg was a prospect no better than death.

After about an hour, Tata Mal arrived with his apprentice. They had gone to the village, returning with a bundle of supplies for treating the injured. He looked at Hael's thigh, probed a bit and said, "This can wait a while. I will see to these others first."

Most were smaller slashes and gouges, and these were treated quickly and the men sent back to their posts. The other serious injury was Gota's broken thigh. Two strong warriors held the youth while Tata Mal tugged on the limb until the broken ends of the bone snapped into place. The youth grimaced terribly, but he made no outcry.

While this was going on, two women came to the fire. They spoke a few words of encouragement to the other wounded, and he recognized their voices as those of Larissa and her mother. They came to stand by him and he looked up, then down again quickly. Both were perfectly naked, because nobody saw any sense in ruining good clothing in a process as messy as calving, and they were both liberally spattered with blood, mucus and other fluids. At such times, it was customary not to look directly at women, and to act otherwise as if they were dressed.

"We hear you were the hero of the evening," Larissa said.

"All were heroes tonight," Hael said, making a mental exception for Gasam. "It was a great fight, and hard to believe no one was killed." He added, hastily, "That is, nobody has died yet." You never knew when a spiteful spirit might be listening.

"That is true," Umarra said, "but you were the one who knew where the beast was when no one else could detect it. It was your spear that saved Gota when the thing would have finished him." As always, he was amazed at the speed with which women learned of these things.

"Tell us about it," Larissa urged, "unless your wounds pain you too much."

With that, there was no way he could escape it. Warrior pride would not allow him to admit that an agonizing, perhaps near-fatal wound might make it difficult to speak, or even cause his voice to shake. Using as few words as possible, he described the night's events. He made light of the way he had known approximately where the beast had been, because he did not understand that himself. There was no need to boast of his own actions. Indeed, once the fight was joined, they were all in equal danger and none of his band had sought to save himself at cost to the others. He ceased his recitation with the receiving of his own wound, saying that he could not see much after that. Thus he was not forced to speak of what he thought to be Gasam's cowardice.

The women seemed satisfied with this, and returned to the kagga, to inform the other tired, laboring women of his account of the night's happenings. He was growing feverish and gray light stained the eastern sky when Tata Mal came to tend his wound. First the old man gave him a potion to swallow, then he set to work on his thigh.

"This could have been much worse. See, the wounds run along the length of the muscles, rather than across them. You would be a cripple for life, had that been the case." He sprinkled powders into the wounds, causing another surge of agony, but by now Hael was too weak even to think of struggling or crying out. Two senior warriors wandered over to observe and make comments.

"Fine wounds," said one. "You will have splendid scars, if you live. You can paint them red for emphasis. These are as good as battle scars."

"I think blue looks better on leg wounds," said the other, for no reason Hael could imagine.

"You two may have some scars of your own to

show," Tata Mal said, "if you catch up to that longneck today."

"It's probably dead by now," said one. "Anyway, it will be far from the herd. We might violate tabu if we kill it thus."

Tata Mal looked up impatiently. "I thought I explained that. It still endangers the herd and the people and this is still calving time." The two looked doubtful as they walked away. "Every fool thinks he is an expert on tabu and ritual law," the old man groused. "They should leave these things to me."

He finished by packing the wounds with old spiderwebs and tying on a loose bandage of trade cloth topped by thin leather. "This should not be too tight. Loosen it if your leg swells, but never let it be loose enough for flies to crawl under it. It is of utmost importance to keep an open wound free of flies. The spirits of infection ride on flies."

With morning light, the men gathered to hunt down the longneck. The old hunter from the village to the south came to assist. He examined the site of the battle while the warriors talked among themselves. Luo, downcast at missing all the excitement, came to see Hael.

"Glory for everyone but me! It isn't fair! And you got out of it with such splendid wounds!"

"You may have them," Hael said, "if you can find a way to take them from me."

Danats joined them. "I should have known you would find a way to get out of guard duty for the rest of the calving season. Now I shall have to stand all your watches."

"You also get to wash me and change my dressings," Hael pointed out. He looked at Raba. "I saw you spear the beast in the flank. Do you think it was fatal?"

Raba shook his head. "The thing has ribs like bronze. Look." He held out his spear and Hael could see how even its stout tip had been blunted. "The others who thrust it in the body say the same. None felt his blade sink in."

"They have strong magic," Tata Mal said, packing up his supplies.

Minda called and half the warriors trotted off to join the hunting party. All the rest had to stay and guard the herd. Hael rested, slipping in and out of delirium. He was clear-headed when the men returned in the afternoon. He could tell by the way they dragged their spears that they had not been successful.

"Still alive?" said Raba as his friends arrived.

"Well, you missed little."

"You didn't find it?" Hael asked.

"We found it," Luo said. "But the senior warriors were in front. They could have finished it."

"It was weakened," Pendu agreed. "Nothing like last night. But they would not get close enough. I think they were still afraid of tabu, no matter what the spirit-speaker says."

"The fools," Tata Mal said. "And what happened to the longneck?"

"We chased it for an hour," Luo said, "Until it got to the swamp down near the farmer's land. We could hear it splashing in there for a while, then it was quiet. The hunter said it was no use trying to catch it after that, so we came back."

"There will be suffering for this," Tata Mal said, darkness in his voice.

The hunter stayed at the encampment that afternoon, to sharpen the spears dulled in the struggle. When he came to sharpen Hael's spear the young man studied him. He was a small man, like all hunters, and wizened like a dried fruit. His skin and hair were very dark, and even his eyes were brown. He wore bone ornaments and dressed in skins.

"What will the longneck do now?" Hael asked.

The hunter stroked the edges of the spear with a flat, palm-sized stone. "He heal." His dialect was guttural, barely intelligible to the Shasinn, but he had lived among them long enough to make himself understood. "Bad wounds. Take many turn of Moon, but he not die."

"Won't he starve?"

The hunter shook his head. "When better, he come out at night, eat carrion. No animal stay with its kill if he want. In time, he come out to hunt."

"Will he stay, or go back to his old hunting grounds?"

The old man shrugged. "Cannot know. Longneck have no home ground. Hunt one place a while, then go to another, not come back for years." He squatted silently for a while, the grating of his stone on the steel edges like the singing of insects. "It will be very bad," he said at last, but Hael was no longer conscious.

THREE

Hael and Danats laughed as they drove the little herd of kagga toward the coast. They had been detailed along with twenty others to take these kagga to the shore for trade. Three elders and a half-dozen senior warriors made up the rest of the party. The kagga were all males that had been culled from the herd for various deficiencies, and gelded to prevent their breeding and to allow them to fatten up for trading purposes.

Hael's hair was now long enough to braid, and the numerous tiny plaits were clubbed behind his neck. The long scars on his thigh were now pink depressions and he no longer limped. To be chosen for this duty was a sign of the rising esteem in which he was held. From the ignominy of his early life he had become one of the tribe's more promising young warriors. The fact galled Gasam, but there was little he had found to do about it.

It was a three-day journey to the coast, constrained as they were by the slow-moving kagga. The ground descended from the grasslands into hilly farmland and thence to the sandy lowland near the sea. Farm children watched them round-eyed as they passed. The fierce warriors of the grasslands were legendary among the settled peoples.

As they neared the water the hardwood trees thinned, replaced by many-branched palms and spiny plants with shapes strange to the herdsmen. There were no grain or vegetable fields here, but fruit orchards stood everywhere along the numerous springs. Water percolated through the island's mountainous interior and emerged here in a hundred places. Some orchards grew spice bushes, and these were very fragrant.

On a broad bay stood Shevna, the island's main trading port. It was no more than a large fisher village with a quay built out into the anchorage and a line of warehouse sheds at the land end of the quay. Circular, palm-thatched huts stood on low stilts along the shore in no particular order. The village was not as fragrant as the spice orchards, and the Shasinn wrinkled their noses at the smell of fish drying on racks everywhere. Only a few boats were visible, those in need of repair. In the evening, there would be dozens of them drawn up on the shore.

Although the village did not smell good, it was clean and the sides of the huts were whitewashed over the plastering of mud. The sound of the surf was pleasant, and the singing of the women melodious as they mended nets. The herdsmen drove their kagga to the pens near the warehouse sheds.

With the stock penned, there was nothing for Hael and Danats to do until the elders were finished with the trading, which might take days. So they made their way to the quay to see what vessels might be anchored in the harbor. They had only been here before as boys, helping to bring in large herds of kagga when the animals were abundant and there was an especially heavy demand for them. At those times, they had been kept under close supervision.

As they passed, women's heads turned, and there was considerable feminine giggling. Many of these women were comely, with brown or black hair predominating. They were plump by Shasinn standards, but this was not necessarily to their detriment. Less attractive were the hands crusted with fish scales, and the frequently bad teeth.

"These women are pretty," said Danats. "The younger ones, at any rate. It would be interesting to try them out, but I don't think I could stomach the smell of fish."

"I've noticed," Hael said, "that they also wrinkle their noses when we get too close."

Danats snorted. "What's wrong with the honest smell of sweat and kagga? It's the way men should smell. Women, too. Not like fish. Their spirits must be very poor, to allow them to eat fish, and to pursue them all day, instead of raising livestock."

Hael pointed at some pens, using his spear to gesture. "They keep some quil and mud-rollers."

"Creatures that eat offal and require no pasture," Danats said, contemptuously. "They need them or they would choke on their own garbage, living in one place all the time as they do."

The two came to the line of warehouse sheds near the land end of the little pier. One of them had been converted for use as a crude tavern, but it was almost deserted, only three or four men seated at the benches of its long tables.

In the harbor were two mainland boats, one anchored in the deep water, the other tied up to the pier, with a line of men carrying bales from its hold to one of the warehouses. The young men strove to maintain the aloof manner proper to Shasinn warriors. The doings of inferior people should be of no interest to them. Still, the boats exerted a powerful fascination. Each was at least twenty paces long and seven or eight wide. Tall posts at stem and stern were carved with the heads of birds and animals, and eyes were painted at their prows near the waterline. It was difficult to believe that objects so large could be built by men's hands and then made to move; to carry men on their backs from island to island, from there to the mainland.

"Do you want to try that place?" Danats said, indicating the tavern.

"We are not supposed to drink their ghul," Hael answered. "Besides, we have no money." Among the Shasinn, only elders were allowed to handle money, which was used solely for dealing with off-islanders. All else was barter. "Let's go out on the pier."

The two walked onto the structure, which was apparently strong but swayed alarmingly, creaking and groaning with the activity of the many men who worked upon it. The warriors strode along the planks, their steps carrying them straight, causing any who encountered them to

stand aside. This earned them dark looks but no
defiance. The reputation of the Shasinn went before them.

Most of the men working on the pier were villagers, but there were off-islanders from the ships
as well, and these watched the two youths with
great curiosity. They stared openly, unlike the is-
landers who politely averted their gaze. Behaving
as if only the vessels and their rigging interested
them, the young warriors studied the outlanders
in turn.

The men from the boats were not all of a type.
Some were tall and slender, like the Shasinn, others short and burly. Many had deep brown skins,
while others were naturally pale, the exposed
parts of them bronzed by sun and wind. Most had
the hairy faces that gave the off-islanders the name
by which they were known to the Shasinn. Some
shaved their face hair and a few seemed to be naturally clean-faced. There were a great variety of
tattoos, paints and decorative scars. They were ornamented and clothed in a multitude of styles, although they wore little because of the heat.

The ships were marvels, built of broad planks
pegged to a framework of wooden ribs. The one
tied up to the pier was decked fore and aft, with
a hold open to the keel in the center. Hael wondered at the big, squarish rocks he could see at
the bottom of the hold. Was it possible that the
boatmen were taking these to some place that suffered from a shortage of rocks?

In the center, the keel thickened to double its
width and at this spot was pierced to step the single mast. The long yard had been dismounted and
lay against a gunwale, its triangular sail bunched

beneath it. Along the top of each gunwale were tholes for six long oars.

The boatmen were unarmed except for a few knives, but Hael saw racks at the stern holding short spears, clubs, a few short, curved swords and even a bin of fist-sized stones. Beside the rack was a stack of small, round shields of hide-covered wicker.

The boat anchored in the harbor appeared to be identical, save that the planks of its sides were painted alternately red and blue, while those of the one tied at the pier were yellow and black. The sails were brown, apparently the rough cloth's natural color. Ropes lay everywhere, some of sleen hide, others of some kind of woven grass.

"You are Shasinn?" The speaker was a short man, heavily muscled. He wore a green kilt with gold-colored fringe. He looked strange to their eyes, but the smile in his beard was friendly.

"We are," Hael said. "You have seen Shasinn before?"

"Yes, here and on other islands. Never many, mostly old men come to the harbor to trade for their kagga. I am Malk, master of the *Wave-Eater*." He slapped the gunwale to show that he meant the boat. His accent was strange, but it was easy to understand; easier even than the speech of the hunters, who lived much nearer.

"Do all boats have names?" Hael asked. He was so fascinated that it was difficult to maintain a properly arrogant, contemptuous attitude.

"Boat?" Malk exclaimed and laughed. "*Wave-Eater* is a ship!"

It was the first time the Shasinn warriors had

ever heard the word. "What is the difference?" Danats asked.

The man hopped nimbly onto the pier. "Boats are what you see these fishermen using. They are much smaller, and they have no keel. The keel is the backbone of the ship."

"Is a ship like an animal?" Hael wanted to know. "You say it has a backbone. I can see that it has ribs and even eyes."

"Yes," said Malk, happy with the conceit, "and it has sails which are wings and oars that are its legs. Attack her, and she can show teeth and claws as well."

"I do not understand," Danats said, "how men can live on a great wooden animal on the water. It does not seem natural. We Shasinn have never liked water we can't wade across."

"You must have been sailors once," Malk insisted. "There are Shasinn on all the larger islands of the Stormlands."

Hael leaned on his spear and thought. "We have old stories that these islands were once all one land. They tell that, very slowly, the land sank, and the sea came in to flood the low places, until the higher lands were separate islands."

Malk, who had been talking to pass the time, took a serious interest. "Say you so? I've heard other stories like that, in many different places in the islands and on the mainland as well. It's my belief that, when a story is consistent, or at least similar, over a great area, there is truth in it." He looked up at the high sun. "I am tired of watching these louts unload my ship. I can do it as well from that wretched tavern. Come join me there, and we can talk in comfort."

"We are not supposed to drink the ghul here," Danats muttered, embarrassed.

"I've seen your elders put it away in this port as efficiently as any sailor." He cocked a shaggy eyebrow at them. "No money, eh? I'd forgotten that you warriors never use it. How does this sound: I invite you to sit and drink with me, that you may satisfy my curiosity about your legends, stories and customs? Among my people, it is considered discourteous to refuse such an invitation. I have always heard that you people pride yourselves on your excellent manners."

"That is true," Hael said, liking the idea. "We are a polite people, and it is especially important to demonstrate our courtesy before visitors. Danats, it seems to me that we would do the tribe a disservice if we were to refuse this stranger's hospitable offer."

Danats pretended a few moments of deep thought, looking down and twirling his spear between his palms. "I am an obedient junior warrior, adhering to all the customs of our tribe, and I realize that, under ordinary circumstances, it would be a great wrong for us to indulge in ghul, especially here at a strange village. But I think you are right. The importance of upholding our people's reputation for good manners outweighs the trifling offences we as junior warriors may commit."

Malk looked quizzically back and forth between them. "Do you go through this every time you feel like breaking the rules?"

Danats laughed as they walked back down the pier. "Don't you find it more fun this way?"

They took seats in the tavern, which was little

more than a shed with a raised wooden floor, a few tables and benches, and a thatched roof. Three sides were enclosed by walls of woven palm-fiber, the fourth was open to the harbor. A covered yard to the rear served as kitchen and storage area.

Hael found the experience enthralling. The benches were not too different from the stools he was used to, although they were higher, but the table was something new. It seemed odd to have things set on this surface near to hand. It was extremely convenient, although he felt a bit hemmed in.

Malk called to the tavern-keeper, a woman of formidable heft whose good humor seemed unaffected by the slackness of business on a hot day. She brought a pitcher and cups of poohranut shell. "You'd better not corrupt these lads, Malk," she said as she set the vessels on the table. "Their elders will take your head back home with them as a souvenir of their visit to town."

"You need not worry," said Hael, seriously. "No one but ourselves would be punished for violating custom."

She beamed at them. "Aren't these the politest lads you've ever met? I'll bet they'd make far better husbands than the louts we're compelled to marry."

Hael and Danats flushed as Malk thanked the woman and ordered some food brought to their table. "Drink in the afternoon, taken without food, is a great folly," he pronounced.

"You shame us with your generosity," Hael said. "We have no way to return it."

"But you have. All sea traders have curiosity about other people, because our livelihood depends on our knowing what others want, need and will pay for. But I am different from most; I like to learn about others' beliefs, their legends and religions." He picked up the pitcher and poured. An amber liquid filled their cups and they drank. It was far finer than any ghul.

"This is good!" Danats proclaimed. "What is it?"

"Wine," Malk said. "There are many kinds, most made from fruit or berries or other plant products rich in sugar." He caught their quizzical looks. "I see I am talking like a sea trader again. It is something that must be made in settled communities, where there are large jars and vats for the settling and aging processes. Your ghul is probably made in skin bags, not so?" The two nodded. "That explains it. Over on the mainland, where there are broad grain fields, men make ale. Once again, a different process. But, I was saying; I like to learn about other people's religions. Who are your gods?"

This word was new to the warriors. "Gods?" Danats asked.

"God?" Malk said, eyebrows going up in perplexity. "There are some who have only one, are you like that?"

"But what is a god?" Hael asked.

"Then it is true, you have none! I have heard that before, but it seems hard to believe." He looked like a man who has just discovered the treasure others said could not exist. "But what supernatural beings do you believe in?"

"Supernatural?" Danats said. It was another new word.

"Well," Malk gestured, trying to get his meaning across, "the unseen things. The invisible world."

"Oh," Hael said, "you mean the spirits? That word you used puzzled us. 'Supernatural,' was it? Yes, the spirits are invisible, but they are as natural as anything else. The wind is invisible, but does that make it less than real?"

"Speaking as a sailor," Malk agreed, "I can attest that it is not. Yet you have no gods. This intrigues me."

Danats refilled his own cup. "You have come to the right man. My *Chabas-Fastan* is almost a spirit-speaker, while I find the spirit world boring. If you need to know about spears or fighting, or kagga or women, ask me. Things of the spirit world are his passion."

"Perhaps you should explain that term," Malk requested. Briefly, Hael explained the relationship between *Chabas-Fastan*. Unlike some aspects of the initiation, this one was common knowledge and not surrounded by tabus. "Truly?" Malk said, smiling and wincing at the same time. "You chopped each other's foreskins off with a piece of flint? No wonder this makes a memorable bond! Circumcision is common among many peoples, but it is usually performed by a priest or surgeon with a sharp knife, while one is an infant." He shook his head in wonder. "Well, to answer your question, a god is like a spirit, only far larger and more powerful. It is like the difference between a man and an inconsequential animal like a mouse. Gods are like men and women, with minds of their own, and whims. They concern themselves with the affairs of men. Most peoples have many gods, or a few, or in some cases a single one. They pray to them for favors or forgiveness. You do none of these things?" Malk leaned across the table, intent on Hael's answer. Clearly, these things meant much to him.

In respect for the other's seriousness, Hael thought well before answering. "What you call a god we do not have at all, unless our spirit-speakers know about them. They do not always tell the rest of us their secrets. We have spirits, and these inhabit everything, for good or bad. Individually, they are not very powerful. But individually a hornet is not powerful, and its sting is a mere annoyance. Hundreds of them together can kill. Spirits influence everything and they have their own requirements. These do not necessarily make sense to us, but the spirits don't care. We must abide by them. We please them, or at least placate them, through proper behavior. This word you used—'pray?'—this we do not do, unless you count our nightly incantation to the Moon. We must forever beg her pardon for having wounded her, although she has never shown signs of resentment that I know of. She is supposed to control rain, tides and fertility, but those things seem to vary whether we speak to her or not."

"You are a most remarkable young man," Malk said. "It is a pleasure to speak to one of serious mind."

The stout woman brought a broad platter of food and set it on the table. There were fruits and flat loaves, preserved vegetables, boiled and baked eggs, and meats. One bowl was covered with a white cloth. With some ceremony, the woman lifted the cloth just enough so Malk could see. "There are salted fish. If you want to keep the company of these boys, don't let them see you eating them. It makes them sick."

Both youths chuckled, made expansive by the wine. "We promise not to get sick," Danats said. "Fish are tabu for us, and we don't like the smell, but everyone else thinks our blood and milk is disgusting, though I cannot imagine why. Surely, the fluids of life, fresh from living animals, should be more agreeable than this carrion." He picked up a skewer of meat and bit into it.

"You will notice," Hael said, "that he does not scorn such 'carrion' as this."

"Of all things," Malk said, picking up a flat loaf and wrapping bits of meat and fish in it, "people make the greatest bother about what they may or may not eat. Everyone has foods that are clean, and others that are unclean. A sailor learns not to be so picky."

"Look!" Danats said, pointing, "A sleen!" Out in the harbor stood a craggy rock. A creature like a great slug was hauling itself laboriously onto the rock. It was a near-shapeless gray mass, hitching itself along on flipperlike front feet, each a broad, webbed paw with bony, imbedded fingers tipped with hooked claws. The fat neck merged into a conical, near-featureless head distinguished only by bulbous eyes. Within minutes, a dozen others joined it.

"They may be wonderful to you inlanders," the big woman said, "but to us they're vermin. They are gluttons—first they take many fish before our men can net them, then they go into the nets to get the ones they missed the first time. Tangle and tear the nets, and many a man has been hauling on a net when the sleen hit it. The jerking of the net can tear fingers off, and that can be lucky. Many have been hauled over the side with their nets and drowned."

"Well, there are nearly a score," said Malk, pointing to the group on the rock. "If they're such a nuisance, why don't your men go out and spear them? You can use every part of a sleen, and get a good price for all of it."

The woman snorted and rattled her necklace of polished bones. "Don't be stupid. It's terrible luck to kill a sleen on Sleen Rock. Do that and we'd never catch another fish for the rest of our lives. Watch, the big bull is coming."

This was the only time Hael had heard the word except in reference to the formation of stars, so he was prepared to see something with two horns on its head. Instead, what he saw was a sleen totally unlike the others. Its hinder parts looked similar, but the shoulders and neck, as they heaved from the water, were covered with a great, golden mane of long hair. Upward from its lower jaw sprang two tusks the size of a man's forearm, white and gleaming in the sun. On clawed feet it squirmed and waddled its way to the crest of the rock. Once there, it bellowed its challenge to the world in an ear-splitting roar.

"Now *that*," Danats said, "is a fine beast. I have always wanted to see one. If it troubles these fisherfolk, then that is only the natural order of things."

The woman swatted him on the back of the head, but not without a slight caress to his neck. "Shame on you! To praise a beast that plagues those under whose roof you shelter. Next you will find a love for the pirates who descend here every few years in their lean ships, to carry off treasure and women."

Danats diplomatically forebore to enquire about the capacity of the ship that might carry off such a woman. Instead he regarded her with great appreciation. "It is our custom to admire all creatures that are splendid of their kind, that show above others the features that make their sort outstanding, whether it be the claws of a predator, the wool of a quil, the backfeathers of a killer bird, or, on a woman, the—"

He was taken under the arm and hauled to his feet. "You two continue your conversation," the woman said. "This one and I shall continue ours out back. You two have food and wine enough to occupy yourselves with in the meantime."

With a silly grin, Danats waved at them as he was hauled off. "Come rescue me if I am gone too long," he called as he was towed out back.

Hael bit into a fruit, wincing at the acid taste. "My brother loves the basic things; food and women and drink. He has little appreciation of spiritual matters."

"Few men have," Malk said. "Most sailors are like your brother, although they may not be such agreeable company. In my travels I have found that men for the most part are slaves to their bellies and loins, and have little use for their heads. But sailors always have gods and spirits to believe in, those they were born with and others they acquire in their travels. In fact, we are famed for the number and variety of our beliefs, some of them held solely by seamen."

"Is it to these gods or to the spirits that you devote your attention?" Hael asked, enthralled.

"For the great things, we pray to the gods of sea and wind; for good weather and favorable winds, for protection from the monsters of the deep. There are lesser gods for smaller matters such as success in trading and protection from pirates. For small matters we seek protection from malicious spirits with spells, chants, amulets and small sacrifices. Spirits aboard a vessel can inflict sickness and small injuries, or they can cause leaks in the sides, or ropes to break, they sour stored wine and spoil preserved food."

Hael was still intrigued by the idea of the ship as a great animal. "Does the ship have a spirit of its own, to see through the eyes on the prow?"

"Oh, yes, each vessel has its own spirit. It is embodied in the figurehead, but that is only symbolic. It actually resides in the keel. You saw that thickened part, where the mast is stepped . . . that is, buried in the wood beneath?" Hael acknowledged that he had. "Well, that is where the ship's spirit lives. The spirits of ships are always female."

"What sort of magic do you use?" Hael wanted to know.

Malk frowned slightly. "In civilized lands magic is mostly practiced by professionals; wizards and priests and such. Are you herdsmen practitioners of magic?"

Hael admired the waves in the green-watered bay. "I would think that sailors would practice the magic of water and wind. We Shasinn have little magic, and most of that involves our herds. The hunters of the mountain country have hunting magic and fire magic, and the farming people have earth magic."

"Surely some of those things are just specialized skills," Malk said. "But one man's skill looks like magic to another who lacks it."

"You used a word a moment ago, 'civilized.' What does that mean?"

Malk refilled their cups. The pitcher had become noticeably lighter. "This is difficult to explain. Over on the mainland, there are people who live in cities. These are like great villages, but a small city will be like all the villages you have ever seen put together. They are built of wood or stone or brick, and few of the people have anything to do with producing food; they do not farm, or herd, or fish." He gestured with his hands, seeking words to describe this difficult concept. "There are people who do nothing but paint pictures, or play music, or buy and sell things. Some are builders or craftsmen, like the smiths who made your spear. There are men who bear arms and do nothing else, and some who make magic, and some who rule others. They put knowledge into symbols called writing and store it like grain. This is what civilization is."

Hael tried to picture such a thing, but he found it difficult. There was nothing in his experience to use as a model. "I would like to see such a place, but we Shasinn do not travel, except to change pasture."

"Perhaps one day you shall travel nonetheless. Stranger things have happened. One of my sailors was a mountaineer. His village was wiped out by an avalanche—that is a great slide of snow down a mountain, which is something else not easy to describe. Suffice it that it is dangerous, and that only he survived. He left the mountains in grief, and had never seen a body of water larger than a small lake until he was a grown man. Now he is a sailor as accomplished as any who was born to the sea."

Danats returned from the back, still wearing his foolish smile. "I have upheld the reputation of the Shasinn," he reported, proceeding to attack the food left on the platter.

"We had better go back," Hael said, "or the elders will come looking for us."

"Before you go," Malk said, "there is one other thing I would like to ask: What is your people's belief concerning the great catastrophe that befell the world long ago?"

Hael paused, remembering old tales heard as a child. "We have a tradition that once spirits were far more powerful than they are now. Perhaps they were like your gods. They took control of men, and made them mad. Men had great fire magic in those days and killed one another with it. At last, they even hurled fiery spears at the Moon and wounded her so that the scars are still visible. When most of the people were dead, the spirits lost their great power, and men have been living sensibly ever since."

Malk nodded. "I have heard many, many tales of the catastrophe. Yours is not the only one to mention the fiery spears. Some legends speak of the Great Plagues, and some of the Years of Heat, and some of great mountains from the sky that fell into the sea. There are so many that they cannot all be true, yet I believe that none of them is really false. Some wise ones speak of a long time of evil, when catastrophes struck one after the other, and I think this may be the truth. It is in the south, for instance, that you hear the plague stories, and tales of the great heat and drought are told among the Kla-homs. Those people migrated into the kingdom of Neva, many generations ago from far inland. And there are many stories of the Sunken Land, always said to be rich and wicked. And many of those sto-ries say that these islands are the highest peaks of that land, which agrees with what you believe about how the Shasinn came to be on different islands without sea travel."

Hael's head buzzed with all this new knowledge. Also with wine. "We thank you for your hospital-ity," he said, "but now we must go. Perhaps you will come by our camp tonight and we can con-tinue this talk. We will make you welcome."

"We promise not to make you drink milk and blood," Danats said. He stood, swaying slightly.

"Perhaps I will do that. However, if loading goes smoothly I will probably sail on the evening tide. It may be that we shall meet again, if not tonight. The *Wave-Eater* calls at this port two or three times every season, when weather permits. For now, I think you two should take a long walk on the beach, and then wash your mouths with sea water, before you report to your elders."

They thanked him again and walked outside. The sun was still high, and they followed Malk's advice, walking along the seashore until they could per-form the act without unnecessary swaying. There was much to admire on the shore. Besides getting a closer look at the sleen on the rock, they saw bizarre starfish, and animals that looked like plants, sway-ing in the tidal pools. There were messy, ill-smelling piles of seaweed swarming with flies and a sea tor-toise sunning itself on the sand, twice the size of a male kagga, the top of its shell as high as their heads.

It watched them with profound disinterest as they walked around it. Best of all was the skeleton of a great sea snake, bleaching in the sunlight at the south end of the little harbor. Alive, its body had been half as thick as a man's, but they measured the skeleton at a full sixty paces. The head was two paces long and a pace across, with six short horns protruding from its crest. The teeth were long and thin, curving back into the mouth, apparently for catching and holding fish.

They asked a woman who sat mending nets about the creature, and learned that sea snakes were exceptionally rare. Few had ever seen a live one, although dead ones washed up on the shores after storms at intervals. It was deemed bad luck to molest the carcasses, so the bones remained for the most part intact until they crumbled. The one they had seen had lain there for a year or more.

As the sky reddened and the fishing boats returned, their triangular sails filled with the evening onshore breeze, Hael and Danats made their way back to the camp by the stock pens. The others were there, waiting impatiently. The elder had already sold the surplus kagga, and they were ready to return to the village. They would get some miles behind them before stopping for the night.

Hael was saddened, because it meant that he would not be able to converse more with Malk. There was always the chance of encountering him again, but Hael thought little of his chances. He would have to accompany another herd to this port, and it would have to be on a day when the *Wave-Eater* was in port, and there might be no more than three such days a season.

When they returned to the Shasinn village, Hael

sought out Tata Mal to discuss what he and the shipmaster had spoken of.

"Gods?" said the spirit-speaker. "I have heard of these. The mainlanders set great store by them."

"But are they real?" Hael asked. He sat in the old man's hut, which was like any other except for the bundles of supplies peculiar to the spirit-speaker's calling.

"Real?" Tata Mal shrugged. "What is real, or not real? If gods want to be, then they may be. It is not for us to determine the realities of the spirit world. What is certain is that men once trafficked with great spirits. It must be so, for how else could they have received fiery spears with which to attack even the Moon?"

"But where did they go? How did the spirits lose their power?"

"They may still be in existence. Perhaps the old, powerful spirits became the gods of the mainlanders. This is nothing to us. Each people have the spirits proper to them. We Shasinn have learned to live with our spirits over many, many generations. It does us no good to meddle with the spirits of others."

This annoyed Hael. "But I am curious about such things. I am like that foreign shipmaster. I want to know what people hold in their hearts concerning the spirit world."

Tata Mal sighed. "I wish you could have been a spirit-speaker. You have the soul of one. But that may not be, and you store up bitterness for yourself by playing at a vocation you may not have."

The old man stretched an aching leg and massaged its stiffening knee. "You are not the only one to be making foolish talk with foreigners, and your case is not the worst."

"What do you mean?" Hael switched at his face with a kagga-tail whisk. They had been at this camp too long, and the flies were very bad. Even the smoke in the hut would not keep them out.

"You remember that a few days before you left, another herd of gelded kagga were taken to the big river port to the south?"

"I remember. I wanted to go, but I think Gasam persuaded Minda not to let me, and to wait for the smaller herd."

"It is of Gasam that I speak. Like you, he spoke with some mainland merchants. Be assured that it was not of the spirit world that he spoke. He wanted to know about their armies and wars, and they told him of the kings who rule on the mainland."

"I think Malk said something of this when he spoke of civilization. He said there were people who did nothing but govern, and those who bore arms and that only. He used the word 'kingdom,' but I didn't get a chance to ask him what it meant."

"It seems these foreigners have what they call kings to rule them. These are not elders, who attain position because of longevity, and the wisdom which we like to believe a long life confers. A man is born to be king, and takes the office when his father dies. And there is only one at any time."

"Just one?" Hael said. "Not a council?"

"Apparently not. A king may have advisers, but his word is final. And he has under him an army of warriors which he can direct against other kings, or against weaker people who like us have no kings. They do not raid sensibly to take kagga, or even women and children for slaves, but to impose their will on others."

"That makes little sense to me," Hael said. "There must be more to it. Foreigners are odd, but the shipmaster Malk seemed to be a sensible person."

"It made good sense to Gasam. He got back two days ago and has been going around saying that we Shasinn should have a king. He says that we are the greatest warriors in the world, and so we should organize an army that would be the most powerful in the world."

Hael laughed in disbelief. "And he thinks that the Shasinn would put up with such a thing? Who would care for the kagga and guard them from raiders if all the warriors were taken away and put in this king's army?"

"Did I say that he spoke intelligibly?" The old man tossed some lumps of kreeswood charcoal on the fire in vain hopes of keeping the flies out. "In fact, he did say something about that. He says that we should make slaves of other people, to care for our livestock and till the soil and do all hand work. We Shasinn should have no duties save to fight and to rule."

"He has gone mad," Hael said. "The Shasinn could never endure a single ruler, and we love our herds too much to allow others to keep them."

"Being mad," Tata Mal said, "does not make him any less dangerous."

FOUR

It was good to be moving again. The grasses had finally given out and the Shasinn councils had met and decided to move to pastures toward the southern tip of the island. After long grazing, pastures required four or five years to recover fully.

Hael climbed to the crest of a hill to watch the scene below. It was a fair sight to the Shasinn: twenty villages and all their livestock on the move at once. The herds stretched as far as he could see, broken up into smaller herds for ease of handling, each surrounded by warriors, women and children. The people carried most of their few inanimate possessions on their backs; the rest were loaded onto the bulky pack beasts called nusks. The Shasinn had little use for these hairy, stupid but strong beasts most of the time, so they kept few. Upon arrival at new pastureland, most of the nusks were traded with neighboring farmers;

when the Shasinn moved on, they traded back. At
their next destination, they would again trade the
big animals off to local people who had need of
them.

A powerful force of warriors strode several
hours' march in front, and there were flanking and
rear forces as well. Hael was part of one of the
flanking forces. It was the third day of the march,
which might require another thirty to complete.
Marching at the speed of the slowest livestock, and
youngest children, on most days only four or five
miles were covered. The island was cut by numerous streams and small rivers, each of which
slowed progress not only as an obstacle to ford,
but because the animals had to be persuaded to
leave the cool water they loved.

When they reached their new land, there would
be pastures to assign, villages to build, warrior
encampments to establish. Their huts they had left
behind them. They would find materials to build
more on their new site. Getting established would
be a long and strenuous period, but exhilarating
as well. They would have to reestablish relations
with neighbors who had not seen them for a number of years. It might be that other herdsmen
would be there grazing their animals on grounds
traditionally Shasinn. If that were the case, there
could be fighting.

The young warriors speculated about this possibility most of all. It would be a chance for them
to prove themselves, something that had been con-
spicuously lacking recently. They had petitioned
Minda to allow them to go on a kagga raid, but
the old man had been unwilling to permit it.

"A raid?" he had said, scornfully. "The last

three years have been the most fruitful in my memory. Why do you think we have traded so many animals this year? Another hundred head would only further overgraze the pasture, which we must leave soon anyway. And you want to raid, just to cover yourselves with glory?" He had chuckled his maddening, superior, wise-elder chuckle. "Come back when pestilence or enemies or drought have reduced the herds and the women and children are thin for lack of milk, and then we shall talk of kagga raiding." They had gone away disappointed, but news of the migration had quickly restored their spirits.

Everyone was relieved to be away from the dust and flies of the older villages. Even after a relatively short distance had been travelled, the grasses were sweeter, the waters were cleaner, and they were away from the vermin that always bred in huge numbers wherever people settled; not only the insects but the mice and their larger cousins, including the blind, hairless rodents that came foraging by night.

Another bonus of the drive was the change of diet. The she-kaggas had little milk to spare from their calves, and it would be unwise to weaken animals by bleeding, but every day an animal would step into a horndigger hole and break a leg, or one would be adjudged too lame to travel or by some other such misfortune have to be killed, so there was plenty of fresh meat. Of necessity, the dietary rules for the junior warriors were suspended.

The big cats avoided this enormous moving mass of humans for the most part, although a few injured cats, unable to catch wild game, were desperate enough to try for a straggling kagga. These were easily killed or driven off. More of a nuisance were packs of stripers and the solitary spotted scavengers. These, unable to believe that such large numbers of animals were leaving, had come along for the march. They made their customary yapping, yowling sounds, sometimes running in demented circles from sheer, baffled frustration. Yet smaller scavengers walked outside of these, and overhead cruised circling flocks of hopeful carrion birds. At night, the great, flapping carrion bats took up the vigil.

All around the little migrating nation, herds of grazing beasts moved aside, upset but philosophical at this strange phenomenon. From his high vantage point, Hael could easily count more than a score of animal types in small or large herds, many with ornate horns, variously colored and wearing every imaginable pattern of stripes, spots and splotches. Near one such group he saw a grass-cat stalking, a green stripe moving through green grass.

Two other warriors came trotting up his hill. From their shields, he recognized Luo and Raba. Since attack could come at any time, all warriors carried their shields as well as their spears on the march. Elliptical and almost as tall as the bearer, the shields were made of stout hide and painted in bright colors. Each man could paint his shield in any pattern he fancied. Some used designs that came to them in dreams, or imitated the patterning of animals they admired, but most simply made random, abstract designs that struck them as attractive. Hael's own shield was vertically striped in yellow and green. Raba's was white and dotted all over with flowerlike splotches in any color he could find. Luo had given his slanting white-and-black stripes in imitation of the hide of the threehorn, for reasons known only to himself.

"What a sight!" Raba exclaimed as the two joined Hael. "Could anything else be so fair?" They set their shields down and leaned on them, each with a foot braced against his other knee in the stork stance.

"No," Hael said. "I am going to be disappointed when we reach the southern pastures. Then it will be years before we see such a sight once again."

They were silent for a while, watching their nation in motion; then Luo spoke. "We are worried about Gasam. He acts more and more strangely each day."

"He volunteered for rear guard," Raba said. "*Volunteered*, when he could have had vanguard or flank. He still has enough favor with the elders to get his pick of assignments, and he chose dust and dung!"

"Have you spoken to Torba?" Hael asked. Torba was Gasam's *Chabas-Fastan*, and would understand Gasam's odd behavior if anyone could.

"He says that Gasam has become a stranger to him. Do you know what is even more unbelievable?" Luo gestured extravagantly to show his puzzlement. "He claims to speak with spirits!"

"Not just any spirit, either," Raba added, "but a special spirit, one with a name he won't divulge. He says it is far more powerful than any ordinary spirit."

This was beginning to sound very bad. "Has he said anything of what this spirit tells him?"

"No," Luo said. "He says the time is not right

yet. I spoke with some of the rear guard this morning at the fire. They say he keeps leaving the guard, running back along our path. He goes poking into the swamps to the east. Possibly that's where his spirit lives."

"He was spending a lot of time down in the swamps before we left," Hael said. This was bizarre behavior for any Shasinn, a people who loved grasslands above all. They could tolerate the mountains and the shores, where their travels sometimes took them, but all Shasinn loathed swamplands, which were full of poisonous creatures and biting insects, deathtraps for men and livestock alike. Surely only evil spirits could live in the swamps.

"The spirit-speakers are growing upset by all this," said Luo. "But Gasam says they are merely jealous, that they try to cling to their influence by denying that any other could possibly hold converse with a spirit."

"We want you to consult with Tata Mal about this," Raba said. "It is complicated to do it this way, but you have not been able to speak with Gasam for months, and none of us have your feeling for the spirits. We can't speak freely with a spirit-speaker as you can."

"I did talk to him about Gasam, a little. That was before he decided to talk with spirits. Does he still babble on about kings and armies of Shasinn?"

"Yes," Raba said, twisting his spear-butt into the ground in perplexity. "And there are some, not many, but some, who like what he says. He is attracting a little group of toadies, mainly from other fraternities, and they are the ones like him, who think they are not appreciated and lack the status they deserve. He even has a few senior warriors listening to him, and he cultivates some elders. He has been seen walking with Borlin a great deal." Borlin was a moderately prosperous elder who possessed a single talent. He was a splendid orator, with a sonorous voice and a wonderful sense of timing and grace of gesture. When it was necessary to send representatives to other tribes, Borlin was always the prime speaker, although others had to plan for him what he was to say, since his powers of thought were not the greatest.

"Say you so?" Hael mused. "He may be demented, but he is evidently not unable to plan his actions. Borlin might be a valuable ally to one such as he. And if he is able to influence people thus . . ."

"Perhaps," Luo said, then added, mysteriously, "but wait until you see him."

Later that day, as Hael waked along beside the herd, he wondered about the nature of madness and of a man who could do things that seemed utterly insane to his people, yet have the esteem of some of them. Could a man feign madness? If so, why? Was it possible that Gasam was not mad at all, but was pursuing some devious purpose of his own, which called for him to make a spectacle of himself? He knew from experience that it was difficult for a junior warrior to attract notice. Separated from the community most of the time, the junior warriors were all but invisible to the people who had influence, spending their days tending kagga and trying to impress each other and the young women.

For the first time, he began to understand that

Gasam might be far more than just a warped young warrior, that he might be something extraordinary, and extraordinarily dangerous. He wanted to attract and impress people. Why else would he cultivate a dull old man like Borlin, save to learn the arts of persuasive speaking? Such foresight was not characteristic of madmen. But what explanation could there be for this pretense of spirit-speaking? Or wandering in the swamps? One thing was certain: He would have to be even more careful of Gasam.

These were thorny, perplexing questions, and it was hard to brood on such a glorious day. Above them towered the majestic clouds, splendidly adorning the blue vault of the sky. Far above the wheeling carrion-eaters flapped a solemn line of hammerheads, each with a body the size of a man's and a wingspan twice its length, slender legs trailing behind their fan-shaped tails. Above a line of trees to his left, the heads of a family of leafers showed. Named for their diet of tree leaves, the leafers had narrow heads atop towering, slender necks. The heads were crowned with broad, palmate horns and their upper lips were drawn out to a long, muscular point which would wrap around a branch and efficiently strip its leaves. Tallest of all animals, they were gentle and inoffensive, but their clawed front feet were adequate defence against all but the most desperate predators.

The flanking force consisted of about sixty warriors, mostly juniors but not assigned by fraternities. Among them walked a few seniors, who would take command in case of attack. The bulk of the senior warriors were with the advance guard and a very few had drawn the unenviable assignment of rear guard. There was no formation, and the guard walked along loosely, spread over a wide area, some solitary like Hael, others conversing in pairs or small groups.

Someone came toward him from the herd, and he saw with lifting heart that it was Larissa. She carried a herding staff and slung across her back was a mesh bag of household goods. "Why look so downcast, Hael? Aren't you enjoying the journey?"

"Very much. I didn't think that I looked gloomy."

"It's how you always look lately. Why have you not come to see me in so long?"

He didn't wish to tell her about Tata Mal's prediction that she would soon be wed to an elder, and nothing either of them could do about it.

"I am a mere junior warrior, with my duties assigned. I can't just leave the camp and visit the village."

She looked at him scornfully. "Gasam doesn't let that bother him. He comes to see me frequently. He comes and goes as he pleases."

"Gasam does a great many unusual things these days," Hael fumed. It was one thing to know a woman was hectoring him, trying to elicit a jealous response. It was another to keep calm under such provocation. "You are not the only one to remark on his eccentricity."

She smiled, knowing that, as usual, her verbal missiles were having effect. "That is true. I've heard seniors and even elders say that he is no ordinary youth. Some have said that he has the makings of a great chieftain."

"They say that?" He was sure that she exaggerated. Or was it that certain? Old stories were full of men who had been ridiculed in youth, then went on to become great heroes, monster-slayers, sages and the like. Should Gasam succeed in making something of himself, this period of peculiarity when he was held by some to scorn would be remembered to his credit.

"Oh, yes. Naturally, being elders, they distrust anyone with new ideas, but he speaks with such authority that people have to give his words serious consideration."

"Did you walk out here to praise Gasam to me? I hear his praises enough from his own lips. And I have yet to hear him speak of you."

He had the bitter satisfaction of seeing her stamp away in stiff-backed anger. Other guards hooted at him, calling out that, once again, Hael had proven to be an inept lover. He answered their jeers with stinging verbal assaults of his own, reflecting that one's fellow warriors were always far easier to deal with than women.

That night, when he came in to eat, he sought out Tata Mal and voiced his unsettled feelings about Gasam.

"Gossip spreads like a grass fire," the old man said. "But, yes, it is true that Gasam claims some sort of spirit power. I can swear with all the authority of my years as a spirit-speaker that Gasam has no more spiritual nature than a stone, and my colleagues agree. But fools believe him." He stared brooding into the fire. "A migration like this is an uneasy time. The rhythms of everyday life are broken, and people become more impressionable, open to outlandish ideas they would scorn in more

settled days. Gasam takes advantage of that. I will
say that for him; he has a great sensitivity to the
weaknesses and credulities of men. He knows how
to say the things that address their fears and their
ambitions. He can seek out the secret weaknesses,
the inner evil of a man and turn it to his use."

Hael nodded. "It is as I was thinking. He is more
than merely mad. He has a purpose. But what can
it be? If he wants men to trust and esteem him,
why does he run to the swamps?"

"I fear that we will all find out sooner than we
like," Tata Mal said, "and that the answer will be
unpleasant."

The rest of the march was enjoyable, and none
of the young men wanted it to end. Each day was
eventful and exciting, and they were seeing land
and people unfamiliar to them. Many of them had
not been through this land since they were small
children. In the evenings they camped by the rivers and watched fishbats come out with the dusk
to hover above the water on leathery wings before
diving to snap up wriggling prey in long, toothy
jaws.

The women, on the other hand, were anxious to
get to their destination, establish villages and set
up housekeeping. Burdened with the care of children and the elderly, they could not share the
young men's unalloyed delight in the migration.
They let their displeasure be known, loudly and
sharply, whenever the young warriors grew too
gleeful.

It had to end, and it did on the thirty-second day
of the march. The older people sang out that the
southern pastures were now all around them. The
kagga were assembled, and all the people called

together while the lands were apportioned by villages.

While preparations were made, Hael wandered about the broad meadow where the kagga had been halted. The grasses were waist-high, and small insects hopped before him at every step. The mountainous country was to the north of them now, ascending from low hills to high peaks in the far distance. The land was well watered, with a few low, swampy areas. He knew that the plain spread for several days' travel to east and west, ending at an abrupt drop-off which descended to a narrow strip of coastal plain. To the south, the coasts joined at a place called by mariners the Cape of Despair. The Shasinn called it nothing at all, since they had no interest in the sea. It was in the midst of these pleasant musings that Hael saw Gasam for the first time since they had abandoned the old warrior camp.

He saw immediately who Luo had meant by his enigmatic words. Gasam had painted his shield black. To one accustomed to the bright colors and patterns of Shasinn shields, the solid black was nothing less than shocking. What, he wondered, could it mean? Or did it mean anything at all? Was it just another affectation intended to distinguish Gasam from ordinary Shasinn warriors? If so it succeeded.

Gasam had grown into a very imposing young man. He was half a head taller than most warriors, a bit taller than Hael himself. His bronze-colored skin was almost brown from exposure, making his pale blue eyes all the more startling. He had gotten rid of the ornaments he used to wear, and he no longer bothered with face paint.

He was now an austere figure, all the more impressive for his undecorated, bulky presence. His stance was assured and his face stern and impassive.

"A good day to you, Hael," he said. That was different, too. His voice had been deep since adolescence, but now it was carefully cadenced, so that every word seemed weighty and important. This could be Borlin's contribution.

"And to you," Hael answered, carefully neutral. "I like what I've seen of the new lands so far. Do you think there will be any trouble in settling here?"

"Most probably," Gasam answered. He gestured with his spear. "Down there to the south is a dense stand of jungle where terror-cats live. There are also wild men—outlaws and exiles from the farming and herding tribes, who live there and come out to raid. Over there"—his spear swept to the west—"are villages of the Asasa, and they will not be able to restrain themselves from raiding our herds for long. No, times will not be peaceful here until we have established ourselves and made it known that we are not to be trifled with."

"That might not be a bad thing," Hael said. "We junior warriors need battle experience, and the seniors grow slack and drink too much ghul."

"That is true," Gasam said, nodding solemnly. "I hope that this place restores our warrior spirit. Well, I must go and see where the Night-Cats are to be encamped. Good day to you, Hael."

Hael watched the broad back perplexedly as Gasam strode toward the gathering. In no way had Gasam's words or manner been hostile or even condescending. Another man might have been disarmed, but Hael could not forget the look of evil triumph he had seen on Gasam's face when he had been downed by the longneck. Only Gasam's manner and bearing had been altered, Hael believed, and he was as dangerous as ever. Perhaps far more dangerous.

The next days were hectic as the villages were built. Parties had to be sent to the nearby hills for wood to build houses and lodges. As much of this work as possible was performed by hired men from neighboring villages of settled people, for the Shasinn warriors greatly disliked heavy, manual labor, which they considered degrading. During the march they had taken turns at carrying the heavy spirit-poles, but only Shasinn could perform that task and there was nothing demeaning about it, backbreaking labor though it was.

The housing was made of upright poles planted in circles with flexible twigs and withies woven between them basket fashion and plastered with mud. The conical roofs were covered with thatch. The meeting lodges and larger storage sheds required larger timbers and had plank floors. The greatest demand for timber, though, was for the palisades that surrounded the villages. Not until these necessary structures were finished would the junior warriors be allowed to erect their much simpler camps.

Hael went on one such timber-cutting party into the low hills to the west. He and a few other warriors were supposed to be supervising the workmen, but their real purpose was to protect the party from the wild animals of the forest. The village men knew their work and the warriors would have had no idea how to supervise them.

The trek to the hills took half a day, and Hael took the opportunity to acquaint himself with the villagers, who were for the most part farmers, raising small herds of quil, kagga and nusks. They were short men, dark of skin with long, black or brown hair, occasionally with a startling reddish tinge. Their eyes were mostly brown but sometimes blue. They were cheerful and unselfconscious, happy to spend a few days away from farm drudgery and earn some fine kagga.

The other warriors held themselves aloof, but the villagers, who called themselves Cana, did not seem offended. In fact, had he not known such a thing was absurd, Hael would have suspected that the Cana considered the Shasinn warriors' prideful arrogance somewhat humorous. They were stocky, heavily muscled people, with thick wrists and forearms corded from years of straining at their plows. Strong as they were, they had none of the lithe swiftness of the Shasinn. Their movements were bluntly forceful but lacking in grace.

As always, Hael was curious about these peoples' spirits and magic. He found that their practices were extensive but unimaginative, and not at all exotic. They had spells to prepare the land for plowing, and songs to be sung while plowing, and ceremonies to be performed after plowing, and during planting, and so forth, until the harvest was in. All seemed to involve one of two things: fertility and rain. He asked if they had any gods and they acknowledged that there was an overall spirit who controlled most of nature, both wild and agricultural, but this being was remote, and they concentrated their attentions on the smaller, more approachable spirits. Hael found this interesting, but not very enlightening. He was still curious about gods, but perhaps they dwelled only on the mainland.

The first evening, as the group sat around campfires in the forest, Hael asked the Cana about their styles of fighting. This the other warriors took an interest in despite themselves. While they knew that the Shasinn were the greatest warriors in the world, each worth ten of any other people, still it did no harm to know how lesser folk made war.

"We do not have your great spears," said a shock-headed young man who had parallel rows of scars carved down both cheeks, "But our own suit us well." He gestured with his weapon, a stout, three-foot shaft tipped with a six-inch bronze point as broad as a man's palm. "We use them only to thrust. Our shields are tall but narrow, to make a thrust easy to deliver. We stand in lines close together, so there is just enough room between shields for the spears."

"With such short spears," said a Shasinn warrior, "you are helpless at more than arm's length."

An older man grinned wickedly, nodding. "Yes, we like to get close."

"That is not much metal to fight with," said Gota, who still walked with a very slight limp from his longneck-broken thigh.

"Look at it," said the shock-headed young man, his smile twisted by his ritual scars. "A hand long and a palm broad. How thick is a man's body? This is like thrusting a gardening spade through an enemy. No man survives having one of these thrust through his belly. Ask the Asasa and the wild men."

"Do you use javelins or other missiles?" Hael asked.

"We throw stones," said a man with one milky eye. "And there are some who are skillful with the sling and javelin."

"And the bow?" Hael said.

"Only a few have the time to learn skill with the bow. We have some hunters among us who kill vermin and hunt in the hills for the pelts and feathers we must have for our ceremonies." The milky-eyed man scratched abstractedly. "And, although many will not admit it, we like to eat wild game now and then. It is supposed to be forbidden, but who cares when the spirit-speakers are not around to see, eh?"

The other Cana chuckled and a young one asked, "Is it true that you Shasinn live on milk and blood?"

"That's right," said Sounn. "The blood we bite from the necks of our enemies. The milk we get from their kagga, if there are not enough nursing women among them."

The boy gaped, almost believing it, until the older man slapped his shoulders and hooted at his credulity.

"That's their oldest tale for gullible youngsters," said the milky-eyed man. "They pulled that one on me, when I was younger than you are now. I believed it for months, ran every time I saw a Shasinn."

Hael steered the talk toward practical matters. "We have heard that the Asasa dwell near here. Do they trouble you here much?"

"Every month or two," said the scar-faced

man. "Usually a small kagga raid. We don't have much else they value."

"We've never seen them," said Sounn. "We were children when the tribe last stayed here. What are they like?"

"They are tall, like you," said a man whose hair was heavily streaked with gray. "But their skins are much paler, and most have black hair. They paint themselves all over, and they fight with spears much like yours, but many also have long swords that are good both for cutting and thrusting. Their shields are round, made of nusk hide with the hair still on. They take their enemies' scalps and wear them as ornaments. They fight singing."

"They'll sing sadly if they come for our kagga," said Gota.

The next two days Hael watched as, with axes of stone and bronze, the Cana cut timber with amazing skill. He wandered in the forest, absorbing the sights and sounds of its animal life. From time to time, he saw hunters watching them resentfully from hiding. Once, he called out to them.

"We mean no harm," he said. "We just need wood."

"Go away," called one. "You disturb the forest. You make the spirits of the beasts uneasy."

He wanted them to come closer, so he could speak with them, but the hunters were a notoriously shy folk. There were other things of interest in the forest. He saw man-of-the-trees, tiny creatures somewhat like men but without speech, scampering about the branches, their large, bushy tails held high. They screwed up their diminutive faces into expressions of indignation and scolded the men who cut at their trees. The other men thought this comical, but Hael felt that they had first claim to the forest, which was their home.

He always took one of the night watches. After the others had gone to sleep around the fire, he would sit with his back against the trunk of one of the great trees, the glow of the coals dim on his face, and listen to the forest. It was even quieter than the plains, often with little more than the whisper of the wind among the leaves to break the silence. It was at these times, when he was without distractions, that he could feel the forest.

It was far different from the plains, where herds of large beasts made their stately progress along the landscape, with small creatures scurrying to avoid their feet. Here, most of the life was small, and it lived in a strange, vertical world, with much of the life swarming in the rich leaf mold of the floor, and many larger animals, although still small by plains standards, living on the ground, browsing among the lower plant growth. In the branches of the trees were innumerable creatures, each adapted for life in a particular level, and above them all the birds that dominated the skies by day, the bats by night. There were even a few of the rare flying lizards that aspired to flight in the fashion of bats, with wings of bone and tight-stretched skin, their jeweled hides flashing in the piercing shafts of sunlight like the ornaments of chieftains flung through the air.

Among all these, Hael could feel the workings of the spirits. This forest lived on a level invisible to men, although even the dullest could feel some of its vibrancy. They were not his spirits, and he knew that while the hunters were undoubtedly in close communion with them, he could at least sense their presence. They did not welcome him or his kind, yet he felt that they did not greatly resent them either. Men and their depredations were but brief, fleeting things, while the spirits and their forest lasted forever, and they would be here when the flesh and bones of all the men who ever lived were nothing but elements in the soil, to be turned into the fabric of plants and animals and back into soil again.

Hael could understand, after a night of such contemplation, how the hunters, although they lived by killing, could be such peaceful, gentle people. It was not for him, however. For good or ill, he was born to be a warrior, and he was eager to be about his business.

When they returned from the expedition, Hael felt that he knew a little of their new home. He had formed a favorable opinion of the Cana, although they could never be a people as fine as the Shasinn. Still, they had their good points, among which was a certain warriorlike toughness it would be unwise to underestimate.

When Hael approached the temporary warrior camp outside the village, Luo waved his spear in the air, grinning and all but dancing in his exultation.

"Look who comes!" Luo shouted. "It's Hael, great warrior and would-be spirit-speaker." He ran down to Hael and waved his spear beneath the other's nose. "What do you call that, Hael? Surely you see what stains my spear?"

Hael took the weapon by the shaft just above Luo's hand to steady it and studied the long blade carefully. There were spots and streaks of ugly brown.

"Is this rust? You really should be more careful, Luo, this is a fine weapon, and once it served a genuine warrior. It calls for more respect than this. The bronze is not so perishable, but the steel must be guarded."

"Pendu, Raba!" Luo shouted. "Come here and tell this fool who has been out herding two-legged kagga what we real men have been doing while he was away." He turned back to Hael. "What have you harvested, Hael? Wood, that's what! And what have I harvested?"

"Rust?" Hael hazarded.

"Blood! The blood of our enemies!" The two warriors summoned by his cry had arrived, grinning and chuckling.

"I see," Hael said. "A great force of Asasa, armed and painted, came against you. And you repelled them, single-handed. My admiration is boundless, Luo. It even excuses that rust on your spear."

Luo turned to the other two, fuming. "Look at him. A mere untried youth, without the blood of a single enemy on his spear, and he speaks ridicule to a genuine hero of a kagga raid. Shall I endure this?"

"Come on, Hael," said Raba. "We've got some ghul from those Cana villagers you've been working with. Let's sit down and drink and we'll tell you all about it. It wasn't quite the great battle this fool likes to make out, but it was a pretty good fight. Maybe it's a portent of better things to come."

They went into the camp and Hael heard of the excitement he had missed. The very night of the day he had left, a small party of the wild men had been seen lurking around the herds. The next night, they had made a serious try, and it had been for a herd guarded by the Night-Cats. Luo, Pendu and Raba had been among the guards that night. Danats had been on the wrong side of the herd.

They had been hungry, desperate men, armed with crude spears, their features those of a number of peoples. Luo had been first to see one; a thin, wiry fellow with a shaven head who had tried to cut out some kagga, then turned snarling upon the warrior who rushed shouting toward him. Luo had taken a spearpoint in his shield, and he displayed the gouge proudly. He had given the man a bad cut on the side and at that time the other warriors arrived and encountered the rest of the kagga thieves and a brief, general fight ensued. As far as anyone could tell, nobody had been killed on either side, but wounds had been numerous and there was some blood on the ground the next morning. The men who had been on night watch now felt like seasoned veterans, much to the amusement of the senior warriors.

Hael would not admit it, but he envied those who had been there for the fight. Still, he felt that there would soon be plenty of opportunity for each warrior to distinguish himself. Or die. That was nothing to worry about, because the Shasinn were not greatly preoccupied by death. Everyone died. There were a great many ways to die, and nearly all of them were far worse than a quick demise in battle.

Over the next few days, while the Cana assisted in erecting the village, the young warriors built their own huts in the encampments. The saplings for hut frames were available in the swampy area nearby, and the sewn-bark coverings had been brought from the old camp, carried on the backs of nusks. With a final, brief ceremony, they erected their spirit-pole.

Because of the hostile activity, patroling went on without pause, day and night. Most of this was the duty of the young warriors, who trotted along their assigned sectors tirelessly, eyes searching the skyline for enemies, the ground for tracks or other signs of intruders. Occasionally they found footprints in the soft soil, prints of feet broader than any Shasinn's; there were the marks of spear-butts of a shape different from their own. The young men lived in a state of perpetual tension, anxious for something to happen. The senior warriors, some of whom remembered previous brushes with the Asasa, were grim and watchful. They did not boast as much, and during the nights they could be seen standing outside the palisade, leaning on their shields and conversing in low voices.

When the battle came, it was without warning. Hael and his companions entered the camp three hours after sunset and another patrol trotted out to resume the vigil. The returning men put their shields in the shed and walked to the central night fire to talk with the other wakeful warriors and see if there was anything to eat.

A strong, cool wind was blowing, pushed ahead of a towering bank of clouds to the northwest. Lightning flashed luridly, although there was as yet no rain and the clouds were too far away to hear the thunder. The fitful illumination overpowered the low fire, causing the warriors' faces to show almost white every few seconds. With fighting imminent, most wore paint and ornaments, wanting to look their best for the occasion.

Hael automatically registered the faces of those present. His usual companions Raba, Luo and Pendu were there. Gasam had gone out with the last patrol; Danats, Sounn and Gota had been with him. Kampo was the oldest warrior present. About twenty others were in the camp, and most were awake, although he could hear snoring from some of the huts. He picked up a bowl of blood-laced milk and was drinking when he heard shouting in the distance, followed by the bawling of alarmed kagga.

In an instant, they were scrambling to their feet, fumbling in the shed for their shields in the dim, unsteady light, shouting for the sleepers to turn out, all their heads turning in the direction of the sounds. They could now hear more voices shouting a single word: "Shields! Shields!" It was the ancient call to battle.

"Assemble at the spirit pole!" Kampo shouted above the confusion.

Hael thrust three throwing-sticks into his belt and snatched up a javelin. His heart was thumping madly and he suddenly felt, somehow, that he was lighter, that he could move more swiftly, that he could see in the dark. In no more than fifty heartbeats they were all together at the spirit-pole, all fully armed.

"There they are!" someone shouted, pointing toward a spot on the far side of the main herd, where torches waved. A few of the young men began to run that way.

"Halt!" Kampo shouted. "We defend our own herd unless the drum sounds to assemble at the village spirit-pole! That must be a feint, anyway.

What kind of idiot takes torches on a night raid? They intend to strike somewhere else. Is everyone here?" There was a quick head count. "Let's go." Kampo set off at a steady trot and the others filed behind him at three-pace intervals. He began a warrior chant and they took it up, thumping their shields with weapons. Lightning reflected from polished bronze and paler steel. The sounds and the strange, flashing light transformed them from a group of lighthearted young men into a frightening spectacle.

Hael was second in line, directly behind Kampo. Like all the others, he strained to see what they were running into. In the lightning flashes that came every few seconds, it seemed he could see for miles, but so brief was the illumination that they eye had no time to register more than a colorless vista of waving grasses before the darkness was complete once more.

Somewhere ahead of them, they heard shouting and war cries. The patrol that had left the encampment just a few minutes before was under attack. Kampo raised a shrill war cry of his own and they all broke into a fast run, spreading out so as to meet the enemy in something like a battleline.

A hundred paces ahead of him, Hael could see the pale patternings of Shasinn shields, revealed by lightning and in violent movement. But where were the raiders? The land around them seemed bare of anything but grass. Thus they came among the Asasa before they actually saw them. Then it seemed that the raiders were everywhere.

Dark against a greater darkness, a man suddenly loomed before Hael, and he knew why they had not seen the enemy; the raiders were painted black from head to foot! The round, hair-covered shield of the man facing him was also dark, and only the flashing teeth and eyes in his grimacing face assured him that this was not some night spirit in human shape.

Reflexively, Hael jerked his shield across his body to block the thrust of the man's spear. He thrust the javelin as hard as he could against the dark shield, but it lacked the mass and sharpness to penetrate. Jumping backward to gain room he dropped the javelin and took his spear from his left hand, which also gripped his shield.

As he defended himself from another spear thrust, he cursed himself for a fool. How could he have forgotten that javelins and throwing-sticks were all but useless in a night battle? Just seeing at arm's length was a considerable feat. All around him men were shouting war cries, calling out names of friends, and sometimes grunting in pain, and the Asasa sang their war-chants. There was a great rattle of weapons against shields, an occasional clashing of weapon against weapon.

The man facing him tried to thrust around the left side of Hael's shield, but Hael jumped to the right and had an opportunity for a shield hook; he got the left edge of his shield behind the other man's shield and jerked hard to the left, spinning the man around and exposing his side. Hael thrust with his spear and felt it sink into the man's flank. The man grunted and fell.

For a moment Hael stood as if stunned, staring down at the form that writhed all but invisible in the grass. Then he leaped into the air, shaking shield and spear, howling a victory cry.

He came down and remembered that he was still

in the middle of a fight, and there would be plenty of time to celebrate later. He went in search of more enemies to fight. There were plenty.

Almost immediately, a man came for him, swinging a club, and Hael exchanged blows with him for several seconds; then they were separated when a knot of brawling warriors blundered into them. Hael drew aside, where he could get a better idea of what was going on. As near as he could see, the other patrol were fighting raiders who were trying to drive off the herd, while his group had run into a force left to engage reinforcements. It was not so hard to see them, now that he knew what to look for.

He saw another man who stood to one side like him, shouting words Hael could not understand above the nearing thunder. Hael made for him, and the man turned to face him. This one was covered with vertical black stripes, his hair in a great knot on top of his head. Snarling, he came to meet Hael, swinging a weapon. To his amazement, Hael saw that it was a long sword, a weapon he had never before encountered. As it slashed down at him, Hael blocked with his shield and thrust, his heavy spear penetrating the other's shield and lodging there. The Asasa tried to slash and jerk his shield free at the same time, causing the two men to whirl around one another. With a hard twist, Hael managed to free his point, but before he could thrust, the other charged him and they met shield to shield. Hael was not balanced or braced, and he went over on his back, holding his shield above him and frantically blocking the descending slashes as he tried to regain his feet.

In a lightning flash he saw that the Asasa was

so anxious to kill him that the man forgot to cover himself with his shield. By the light of the next flash, Hael thrust beneath the shield, driving his spear upward beneath the ribs to the heart. The other man froze as still as a spirit-pole, then toppled stiffly.

Hael scrambled to his feet, gave another victory cry, and listened. The sounds of combat were fading. The enemy were in the process of withdrawing and there was no fighting nearby. Above the fading shouts and the approaching storm, he heard the voice of an elder: "Warriors, stay with the herd! We will count bodies by daylight! Bring the wounded to the village!"

Relaxing and trembling with reaction, Hael jammed his spear into the ground and leaned his shield against it, then he stooped to strip his slain enemy of trophies. He took the sword, having to twist the grip from the still-tight fingers. Its sheath was suspended from the man's shoulder by a long belt, and these he transferred to himself, sheathing the sword for examination later. The dead man wore numerous ornaments, apparently all of silver. These and the sword indicated that this had been a man of importance, perhaps a minor chief. He thought of going to find his first enemy, who was surely dead, but he knew that his duty was to go to the herd and in this gloom it would be almost impossible to find a body in the high grass. There would be plenty of time to search in the morning.

As he walked toward the animals, he called for wounded Shasinn, but no one answered. Before he reached the outskirts of the herd a hard rain descended, making it impossible to converse with the other men he found there. For the rest of the night he walked among the beasts, and the rain seemed to quiet them. In this enforced solitude, he reflected on the events just past. He was a warrior in truth now, with two dead enemies to his credit. He would have to see Tata Mal as soon as possible, to seek protection from vengeful spirits. It was unlikely that they would plague him, since the men had not learned his name before they died. Still, it would do no harm to be sure.

With dawn's light he examined his new weapon, and was astonished by its richness. The steel edges were broad, with only a central strip of bronze holding them. When he held it at arm's length and turned his wrist back, the point reached three inches past his chin. Its short guard curled down toward the blade, and the pommel was weighty, in the shape of a fantastic beast's head. The grip was just large enough to accommodate his hand, and was wrapped with purple cord. All of the bronze was finely worked in strange designs. The sheath and belt were nearly as splendid, all of red leather tooled in the same designs as the sword, and studded with bronze and silver bosses.

The ornaments he had taken from the dead man were mostly of heavy silver, but there was also a chain of gold links and a bracelet covered with jade, topaz and coral. He knew that the sword and jewelry had to come from the mainland.

A party of warriors and elders came up from the southern end of the herd, tallying the dead. He was relieved to see Danats and Luo among them. Danats' eyes went wide when he saw Hael.

"Here is one who had a profitable night!" The others admired his trophies and he took them to see the body. Already the scavengers were nosing about, but they had not yet worked up the nerve to attack the body. An elder nodded and made a notch on a tally-stick.

"That makes eight so far," he reported.

"I'll show you another," Hael said. He looked around, trying to orient himself. "Let's see, I think he's over that way. I see somebody standing over there."

As they walked toward the standing figure, Hael asked after the night's casualties.

"Two killed," the elder said, "and three, maybe four more who aren't likely to survive. It is looking as though we inflicted more losses on them. They won't be back soon."

Hael felt a stab of apprehension when he saw the black shield propped against a pair of spears. Gasam stood watching them, his impassive face somehow radiating triumph.

"Is this another of yours, Gasam?" said the elder. Hael was about to correct the impression when Gasam spoke.

"It is. I ran up here when I heard Kampos' band encounter this force. We had finished with the others by that time."

Hael felt a coldness in his belly. He had a great desire to hurl his spear through Gasam, but something held his hand and his tongue. There Gasam stood over the corpse, in possession of the dead man's weapons and ornaments. If Hael called him a liar, which of them would be believed?

"This makes two," said a senior warrior. "I saw you spear that raider down by the southern end of the herd. I don't think anyone else killed two." Gasam said nothing.

Hael turned and strode toward the village, unable

to trust his powers of self-restraint further. Moments later, Danats and Luo caught up with him.

"What was that all about?" Danats demanded. "What happened back there?"

"Nothing," Hael said.

"Did Gasam claim your kill?" Luo pressed. "It would not surprise me. He wants to be the only one with two kills in our first real fight."

"I will say no more about it," Hael insisted. "I am content with my accomplishment." He patted the splendid sword that hung at his side. "Were any of our brothers killed?"

"No," Danats said, clearly unsatisfied with Hael's answers. "Bundu of the Fur Snakes and a senior warrior, I'm not sure which one. But Rendil is one of the badly wounded who may not pull through." Rendil was one of the Night-Cats, although Hael did not know him well.

The mood in the village was one of elation, as the warriors who were not out looking for scattered stock boasted of their deeds. The Shasinn did not mourn extravagantly, and when a man died bravely in battle the death songs were joyous. Among the wounded they found Raba having a severe cut on his side treated with hot pitch. He forced himself to grin through his pain and admire Hael's sword and other trophies.

"Just my luck that you should encounter a rich weakling! The striper who gave me this got away, but I'll wager he does not reach his village alive. He was bleeding from worse wounds than this when he staggered off."

As his indignation toward Gasam cooled, Hael found himself amused at the battle stories of the others. Of those who had fought, every one who did not have an unquestionably dead enemy to display claimed to have mortally wounded one or more.

"If all these stories are true," Hael commented to his friends, "we must have annihilated every able-bodied man in their village."

The Night-Cats and the Fur Snakes had done most of the fighting, along with a roving patrol of mixed fraternities and seniors who had arrived in time for the last stage of the fight. Those who had missed out on the battle were downcast, vowing that, next time, they would make their weapons felt.

When the livestock were counted, it was found that no more than twenty head had been lost. The Asasa had made a poor exchange in their raid. Minda called a council of chiefs and a feast was decreed for all the warriors, even the ones who had not fought.

All the next day there was music, dancing and eating, although the warriors were not allowed to overindulge in ghul, in case the Asasa felt an urge to retrieve their honor while their enemies celebrated. As one who had killed an important enemy, Hael was lavishly complimented. Gasam received even more adulation, having killed two, by his own claim. Hael now saw the little group who fawned on Gasam, and he saw that several of them had painted their shields black in imitation of his. Oddest of all was that Gasam behaved normally toward him.

A strange thought came to Hael. Could it be that Gasam actually believed that he had killed both Asasa? He did not claim Hael's kill out of cowardice, because he had slain the other before witnesses. Just how mad was Gasam?

FIVE

Settling in the new land went smoothly after the first few months, during which the Shasinn, as newcomers, had to prove themselves capable of defending their pastures, their livestock and their people. The Asasa troubled them no more after their unsuccessful night raid, but there were others to convince. Among these were the wild men who dwelled in the southern jungle. After a number of small raids and thefts, during which several Shasinn were killed by ambushers, it was determined that the best course would be to clean out the nest of outlaws.

An expedition was mounted, in which half the warriors from each of several villages were chosen to march south. The rest had to stay and guard their homes. Hael was overjoyed to be among those to go on the short campaign. The warriors assembled at the southernmost village; several hundred excited young men itching for action. The painted, chanting mass marched south for two days, and on the third morning stood within sight of the forest edge.

It was a daunting spectacle; tall trees growing so close together that little light shone between them. The noises that came from it were disturbing, the squawks and occasional roars of beasts they did not recognize. They were not used to the jungle and did not like it, but there was no choice save to enter. Hael did not feel the affinity for this place that he had felt for the mountain forest where he had been with the wood-cutting party. The life here was too abundant, and there was the sensation that it was brief as well; that things were spawned and died with unnatural swiftness in such a place.

The jungle was extensive, but it was no great trouble for them to find the tracks and droppings of kagga, and to follow these to where the beasts had been driven into the woods. Wherever such an entry place was found, a strong band of skirmishers was sent in under the direction of an experienced warrior. When these contacted the wild men, they fought while the rest of the force threw a wide crescent around the area. When its horns closed in, the wild men were trapped within a tightening circle of spears, and those who could not escape died.

Three days of this bush-beating all but annihilated the outlaws. The Shasinn were amazed at the variety of their catch. There were men from most of the peoples of the island, and men from other islands, even a few mainlanders, all of them fled—so the Shasinn understood—to this savage place for deathly offenses in their homelands. The haul of plunder was not great, but that had not been the intention of the campaign. Its purpose was to eliminate a threat, and this had been done.

Once they started up a terror-cat, and were amazed that none of them were killed. It was at least twenty feet long from whiskers to tail-tip, its yellow pelt striped black on the foreparts and spotted brown on the hindparts, with a fine white mane from the back of its neck to its shoulders. It was like a piece of the jungle come to life. It gave a strangely shrill snarl, baring long fangs, then bounded away, leaving the skirmishers who had disturbed it shocked and shaking.

They also acquired a group of over a hundred women, all of whom claimed to be held captive by the wild men. It was decided to take these women with them. Those who were not repatriated to their homes could become servants of the Shasinn.

They marched back happy, driving a small herd of liberated kagga with them. The campaign had been a great success, with elements both of sport and of war about it. Casualties had been light, for the wild men were no match for organized warriors, but the jungle was an unhealthy place and a few men came down with illnesses severe enough that they had to be carried, and any who had suffered wounds found that these quickly festered. These were comparatively minor difficulties, though, and almost everyone was satisfied with how it had turned out. All who had taken part had a good store of tales to tell around the fires in the months ahead.

The expedition also solidly established their reputation as a people not to be attacked lightly. It had been years since they had lived in this area, and local people had short memories. Now a reminder had been delivered. The villages round about were content with the new state of affairs, because they liked to see the Asasa humbled, and the wild men had been a plague to everybody. Kagga raids dropped off to nearly nothing, and every day envoys from the neighboring villages dropped by to express good will and to compliment the warriors on their accomplishments.

This suited the Shasinn warriors well, because they liked to be praised for their bravery, beauty and many manly qualities. If these compliments were delivered with equal parts flattery, groveling and trembling, they liked it that much better. When they were held in awe, fear and admiration by everybody else, all was right with the world.

Life, for Hael, seemed good. He was an accepted warrior, with more credit than any other of his age in the village. He had been blooded in the kagga raid and had done quite well in the expedition against the wild men. All he needed now to complete his warrior education was a stand-up daytime battle against another people. These were rare among the island people, though, and he might have to wait years before an opportunity came along. But he should be able to look forward to a few such battles during his warrior years, before having to pass his spear on to some untried youth.

All was not as he might have wished, however. There was the problem of Gasam. He grew more arrogant and overbearing daily, always pushing and ambitious, always trying to assume credit for things done by others, always insinuating himself with the people of influence. His circle of followers was expanding, and it seemed to Hael that black shields were to be seen everywhere he looked these days.

Not surprisingly, few of these were from his own fraternity. The Night-Cats knew him too well. Even so, Hael had noticed that his brothers no longer made as much fun of Gasam's pretensions. They, too, were beginning to fear him. As a defiance of Gasam's assumed austerity, Hael had taken to wearing all the ornaments he had taken from the slain Asasa chief. He even wore the sword everywhere, although he had not yet mastered its use.

The problem was that there was no one among the Shasinn he could practice with. Their weapons were the spear and short sword, the javelin and throwing-stick and the occasional axe. The long sword was not used by them and only rarely seen among enemies. In recent years, these weapons had come from the mainland, traded by merchants who dealt in arms and metals. Many thought an expensive sword lent the bearer an aristocratic appearance but little else; Hael believed it could be devastating if used properly.

Trying it against targets, he found it difficult to control the point in a thrust, whereas his spear found the spot he aimed for as if it had eyes, since the butt-spike exactly counterbalanced the head. When he practiced cuts, some bit deep and others barely gouged the target. It was a perplexing weapon, but seeking its mastery relieved him of worrying about other problems.

One of these was Larissa. Despite Tata Mal's good advice, he could not give up his aspirations for her, and she occupied his thoughts during the long night watches, which were the only hours he spent truly alone. Even then, he questioned his own feelings about her. They had been children together, but they were children no longer. He saw her little since being sent to the warrior camp. He suspected that he did not really know Larissa the woman at all, that the woman who inhabited his thoughts was his own creation, that what obsessed him was her face and her body. To these he devoted more than passing thought.

On the rare occasions when they met, she always wanted to talk about Gasam. He was not experienced in the ways of women, and could not tell whether she was truly infatuated with Gasam, or merely looking for a jealous response from Hael. Whichever the case was, the latter was what she always received. Worse, there was no one to whom he could speak of this. His brothers would mock him unmercifully, and Tata Mal would simply tell him to forget her. His young man's pride would not let him seek out one of the older women for advice, which would have been the most sensible thing to do. So he suffered. Young men set great store by suffering where women are concerned.

In the meantime, he had distractions, especially during the day. There were kagga to be tended, there was training to accomplish, there were occasional feasts and festivals. There were trading expeditions, too. More calves than expected had survived the long march, and many of these were traded to the other peoples of the southern plain for goods or labor services. Two days' journey to the east was a port called Turwa, and twice Hael went on kagga escort to this place. It was almost identical to the other port he had seen, and he had inquired there about the *Wave-Eater*. Neither time had it been in port, but the villagers said that the ship made regular calls there during the season. They expected it to be back sometime during the next few weeks. Hael still hoped that he would encounter the vessel again someday, so that he might continue his conversation with Malk.

It was toward the end of this time of settling in, when it looked as if things were going to get dull, that something extraordinary happened.

It was evening when he came in from herd guard, talking with the others who were coming off duty. They were no longer quite as laughing and carefree as before. They were an older group now, and the long months of conflict and watchfulness had made them a little more serious, although still far from solemn. They passed near the village on their way to the encampment, and as they did Hael saw someone standing by the spirit-pole, as if waiting for them.

From the bright-patterned wrap, he knew even at a distance that it was a woman. As they drew nearer, she waved and called to him. With some stumbling words of excuse, he separated himself from his companions amid much unseemly advice. It was, as he had suspected, Larissa. She had a smile for him as he came within speaking distance. The sun was lowering, and the shadow of the spirit-pole was long on the ground.

"Good evening, Hael. I haven't seen you in too long."

"That would not have been, had I had a choice," he answered, wondering what this might portend. She seemed nervous and unsure of herself, unlike her normal manner. With the vanity of youth he hoped that it was his presence that so flustered her.

"In ten days is the Third Moon festival. I have been given the task of gathering herbs for the ceremony. Some of them grow down near the swamp, and I must have an escort. Would you go down there with me tomorrow morning? You warriors have made the land safe from outlaws and Asasa, but the beasts of that place are numerous."

"Just the two of us?" Hael said, mystified. Usually, a number of warriors escorted a group of women for this task.

"We already have most of what we need. Once there, it should take me no more than an hour to gather what is necessary. Of course we won't need to rush."

Had he been older or less besotted with her, he might have been more suspicious. As it was, he willed her story to be no more than she told him. She had found an excuse for them to have some time and privacy for themselves. She wanted to go into the low country with him, and tarry there.

"Of course," he said, his tongue suddenly thick. "I will go with you. Danats can take my day watch." He would have to repay the favor soon, but that was a small price for such a chance.

"Then I will see you when the sun clears the horizon." She turned to go into the village, and he was too confused and anxious to call after her.

That night, he arranged with Danats to take his watch. Danats complained, but then he always complained. Hael told nobody exactly where he was going or with whom, because he didn't want to endure their inevitable raillery. He found it difficult to sleep with the images that filled his mind. He woke red-eyed but eager.

She met him at the spirit-pole, wearing a wrap

of red-and-green checks, her ashen hair waving softly in the morning breeze. She held a basket of wicker on one arm. In it were a waterskin and a small, sickle-shaped bronze knife for cutting herbs. She smiled and bade him good morning, somewhat solemnly, it seemed to him, and they set off toward the east.

The ground descended gently as they walked, passing the herds and the warrior encampments. He tried to speak of inconsequential things as they walked, but she was moody and made only short replies, or none at all. He found this most perplexing, for he had allowed himself to hope that she had intended this as an opportunity for some dalliance. She was so preoccupied with her own thoughts that he felt he might as well not be there.

Two hours of walking brought them within sight of the swamp. It looked something like the jungle where the wild men had lurked, but the growth was both lower and thicker, and it had none of the jungle's dark majesty. As they neared it the odor that came to them was one of rotting vegetation, stagnant water and worse things. Even so, it was not without a certain beauty. The foliage was many intense shades of green, and it was riotous with huge, colorful flowers. The voices of the birds were unmelodious, but their plumage was brilliant. There was a constant buzzing and clicking of insects, and an occasional cry as some unfortunate creature became a meal for a luckier one.

"Let me see," Larissa said. "I think that spot over there—yes, that's it, by the tree with purple flowers and a great broken branch. There is a patch of blueweed near that spot."

"Have you been here before?" Hael asked.

"What?" She looked at him, startled. "No, it was described to me. Come on." She began to stride toward the spot, and Hael began to wonder whether she was well. She had begun the day moody and withdrawn, then she had been confused, and now he was sure, by the rigidness of her back and the quick, short strides she took, that she was afraid. But afraid of what?

As they neared the tree with the broken limb, he noticed that the ground nearby was torn and trampled as if by many animals, and recently. But there were no large beasts that he could see.

"I think this is a bad spot, Larissa," he said, fingers flexing on his spear-grip. "I don't like the look of these marks. Let's try somewhere else."

"No, this is the spot," she insisted, a little breathlessly. She stepped slowly to the margin of the swamp, where the water began, and splashed her feet in it. Hael was no expert in the lore of herbs, but he knew what blueweed looked like, and he saw none nearby.

"Larissa, I see no—" He was silenced by a thunderous roar from a clump of brush just inside the swamp line. The brush split, leaves and branches, roots and mud flying to both sides as if hurled by the explosion of a volcano. The nightmare shape that exploded through the brush towered over both of them, half-sunk though it was in watery mire. Hand to mouth, Larissa screamed and backed away, stumbling as she did.

"Longneck!" Hael shouted. He wanted to run away, but could not. Instead, he flew toward the beast, knowing only that he had to place himself between it and Larissa.

Splashing wildly, the monster got its front feet

on solid ground and scrambled with its rear feet
to get free of the swamp. Still screaming, Larissa
darted aside, but the beast paid her no attention.
Its eyes were fixed on Hael. Hael knew that animals were not human and could not feel human
emotions, but the eyes of this creature held hate
as pure as any he had ever seen.

Almost in a daze, as if things were happening very
slowly instead of with hectic swiftness, he saw it
emerge dripping from the swamp, hissing and roaring. He saw the gaunt decrepitude of its huge body,
the many healed and half-healed wounds and the
running sores. He recognized the wounds, some of
which he had inflicted himself: it was the longneck
they had fought on one night during the Calving Festival, which now seemed so long ago.

It lurched for him, and he avoided its strike only
because one of its forelegs was crippled. Things
still seemed to be happening slowly, although he
escaped death by inches several times in those
first moments. It was almost as if he and the great
creature were engaged in a stately dance. He
darted his spear at its neck but it could not penetrate the massive muscles more than a few
inches. A sideways jerk of its head sent him stumbling back, almost dropping the spear.

As he fought for his life and Larissa's, he could
not help but marvel. This was an animal of powerful magic, and it remembered. The thing had
lurked in the swamp near the old village as its
wounds mended. Then, when the Shasinn had gone
on their long migration, it had followed, coming
southward in the nights from swamp to swamp,
pursuing its vengeance. How it must have suffered and hated. Then, abruptly, Hael understood.

This was why Gasam had run off to the swamps to commune with his "spirit." He was keeping track of the longneck, making sure that it did not lose them. All so that he would know where it laired near their new home. All so that he could trick Hael, a gullible fool who had angered it, into—*Larissa!* She had betrayed him for Gasam.

Then he had no more time for thought. The beast was working close, darting its long, flexible neck around the probing spear, seeking his life. It would rear its head back, jaws gaping, and shoot it forward with thunderbolt power. But each time it was a little slower, for the thing had never fully recovered from its wounds. Unfortunately, Hael was tiring even faster. Never in his life had he done anything as strenuous as fighting this monster. He knew that he had seconds to live, that it was too late to run. He darted back and stood still, spear-arm drawn back, facing the longneck squarely.

The animal hesitated as if expecting a trick, waiting for him to move to one side or the other, trying to anticipate his direction. When he did not move, its head reared back for one last, fatal strike. Its jaws gaped as it paused for a split second— and Hael's hand flew forward with all his remaining strength. The long blade flew straight between the rows of teeth and struck the palate, piercing through it and into the wild, feral brain, stopping against the back of the skull.

The longneck stood trembling for a moment, then the eyes darkened, its knees buckled, and it toppled sideways. The huge body rolled over onto its flank and the head came down violently, snapping the spearshaft as it struck the ground. The sides heaved reflexively for a minute or two and the feet twitched with the creature's unwillingness to die; then it was still.

Hael could not move for several minutes. He waited for the thing to rise and continue the fight. With some surprise, he noted that he had drawn the long sword, as if such a puny weapon would be of any use against so terrible a creature. But then, he had killed it, hadn't he. It took some time for that to sink in. He looked around for Larissa, but she was gone. Undoubtedly thought him dead, too. According to plan.

Well, however things turned out, a Shasinn warrior had to have his spear, and he set about retrieving it. This was no small task, as it was wedged at an awkward angle. By probing and gouging with his swordpoint, Hael was able to free it after about half an hour. He cleaned it on some dry grass, wrapped the blade and the butt-spike in his gut sheath, and slung the package across his back. Then he stood for a while and looked at his late adversary, happy now that the battle was past, that its sufferings were at an end.

"This is most serious," said a deep, resonant, ringing voice behind him. Slowly he turned. It was Gasam, of course. With him were at least ten warriors, some of them his black-shielded lackeys. There were also about fifteen women, come to gather herbs for the Third Moon rites.

"Where is Larissa?" Hael asked.

"Larissa? What has she to do with this?"

"Nothing, I suppose, any more than any other tool."

"You speak foolishness," Gasam said. "You have killed a tabu animal, a longneck! You must pay, or the whole people will fall under spirit-curse!"

Hael drew his sword. "Not before I kill you. The spirits will love me for that. It will balance out." He began to run up the slope but his deadly fatigue slowed him. A black shield batted aside the sword and arms seized him. He had no strength left to struggle.

"Kill this fool," Gasam said.

"That is not for you!" said one of the women. He saw that it was Badira, Minda's senior wife. "This is a spirit matter."

"Yes," said one of the warriors. "We'll hold him, but we dare not harm him." Hael looked around. He saw no brothers among the warriors, but they watched with awe. And why not? he thought. He had slain a longneck single-handed, something never done before in Shasinn history. Only legendary heroes with magical weapons ever did such things.

Disarmed, with several warriors behind him, Hael was marched back to the village. He understood how brilliant a plan Gasam had conceived. Undoubtedly he had expected the longneck to kill Hael, but even if it did not, Hael would violate a serious tabu. Even if he had merely wounded it and escaped, it would have been a grave offense.

Once on the trek he tried to speak, but Gasam struck him across the face with a spear-butt, almost breaking some teeth. The women scolded him for this action, but he merely snorted haughtily. After that, Hael kept his silence.

A swift runner was sent ahead of them and when they reached the village there was a great assembly, as if for a festival. He saw his brothers of the fraternity, looking stricken. He saw Tata Mal, looking even worse. He did not see Larissa at all. The only face that showed joy was Gasam's, though he fought to remain impassive.

The hearing was brief. It was not as if there were a matter for trial, where guilt or innocence would be debated. Minda stood before Hael and asked, in a loud voice: "Hael, junior warrior of the Night-Cat fraternity, did you slay a tabu beast, a longneck?"

"I did," Hael said. He did not bother to protest the defense of his own life, or of Larissa's, nor did he say anything of Gasam's plot that had brought this about. There were no extenuating circumstances in a violation of tabu. The offense was absolute. The spirits had no interest in human intent.

"This is a serious violation, Minda said. "Spiritspeaker, what does the law require of us?"

Tata Mal came forward. Old as he was, he looked a score of years older. "Of the human evils that have brought Hael to this I am empowered to say nothing." He shot a venomous look toward Gasam to make his meaning clear. "But of the facts, there can be no doubt. Hael has slain a tabu beast, at a time when it was not lawful." The old man took a deep breath and let it out in a sigh. "He must be exiled from among us, never to live with Shasinn again."

"No!" shouted Gasam, his newly acquired orator's voice going shrill. "He must be killed! He tracked the longneck to its lair to kill it!"

Tata Mal turned on the youth, sneering. "When did junior warriors become our interpreters of ritual law?"

"Silence, Gasam," Minda cried. The elder turned to face the people. "It shall be done as the spirit-speaker says. Hael shall spend this night isolated, under guard. At the rising of the Sun tomorrow, he will be taken to the edge of our grazing lands and he will be gone from us by the Sun's zenith. If he is ever seen again, any man may kill him and suffer no guilt. Until then, let no one molest him or his possessions. He is ritually unclean."

The crowd began to disperse, many of them looking their last at Hael with mixed horror and awe. He had done something truly unique and unprecedented, both in its heroism and its sacrilege. He was taken to a small house and told to go inside and not emerge until daybreak. Two warriors with black shields stood guard.

Hael stooped in through the low doorway. The place was bare of furnishings, and he remembered that the elder who had slept here had been bitten by a serpent one night and had been found dead the next morning. No one would live in a house where someone had died, so it was abandoned, although still new and sound. Since he was now cast outside ritual law, Hael decided that he would not be defiled by staying here one night.

Indeed, he was so stunned by events, so stricken by fatigue, that he scarcely cared about anything. To be cast out from his people was little less than a death sentence. He sat on the floor, his arms on his knees and his hands dangling between them, feeling more dead than alive.

Sometime during the night, when moonlight slanted through the hut's little window, a face appeared there.

"Hello, Larissa," he said. "Have you come to gloat?"

"I should. You are suffering the fate of a fool

and deserve it. But I didn't know about the long-neck. Gasam told me to lure you to that spot, but I truly didn't know what was to happen."

"Yet you did Gasam's bidding," Hael said, bitterly. "What was the price of your treachery?"

"Treachery?" she said. "What did I owe you that you accuse me of that? You are just a foolish boy like any other. You would moon and sigh over me, and proclaim your love, but when the time came some foul old man would make me his wife and you would do nothing, like the obedient junior warrior you are!"

He had to admit that there was some justice in this. "And you expect Gasam to be different?"

"Yes! Gasam is no ordinary warrior. He will be a king! And when that happens, I will sit beside him as his senior wife. I will not be the fifth wife of some old fool with a great herd of kagga."

"So this is what he has promised you? Gasam will be a king? He who steals other men's glory, who uses women to lure his enemy to be killed by an animal?"

Shockingly, she laughed. "Do you think I hold him less worthy because he is clever rather than brave? Any fool can be brave, what of it?"

"The longneck might have killed you," Hael said.

"No. Gasam knew that I can run fast and that the crippled longneck couldn't. And he knew that you are a fool who would place himself between the beast and me."

"I am such a fool, truly. It is a mistake I shall not make again, be assured. But the day will come when you will regret what you did this day. You will wish a thousand times that the longneck had eaten you, rather than that you had lived to become Gasam's queen, or wife, or toy. He is evil, and all who have anything to do with him will suffer."

"That isn't true!" she hissed. "He will be great, and so will I! You will be dead, or at best a pitiful outlaw, like those ragged brutes you and the others hunted recently. Anything that is not Shasinn is nothing, and you are not Shasinn now."

"Then why do you bother to speak to me? Why do you want to justify your actions? Is it just to reassure yourself that you have made the right choice, in casting your lot with Gasam? Or is it guilt, knowing that you used my love for you to bring me to destruction?"

She was silent for a moment. "The love of one like you is worth nothing!" And she was gone.

When morning came he was called outside. There were fifty warriors to escort him from Shasinn land. None were his brothers, who undoubtedly nursed their shame in their camp. Then he saw a single Night-Cat. Without surprise, he recognized Gasam.

"Let's go," said a senior warrior. They walked from the village. Tata Mal sat beside the spirit-pole, and he waved sad-eyed as Hael passed. Another man waved with his spear from a low hill nearby. Hael waved back. It was Danats, defying scorn to give his disgraced *Chabas-Fastan* this farewell. Then they set out toward the east. Before the sun was more than two spans above the horizon, they were out of sight of village and herds.

"This is far enough," said the senior warrior in charge. At his signal, Hael's sword and the package containing the broken halves of his spear were returned to him. The warrior pointed eastward with his spear. "Go."

Hael ignored him, adjusting his burdens until they were comfortable. "Gasam," he said when he was satisfied, "some day I will return and kill you. If my spear were not broken I would do it right now."

"You hear!" Gasam shouted. "This disgraced outsider threatens me! Kill him!"

Reluctantly, a few of the warriors raised their spears. Hael rounded on them and glared. They flinched, lowering their weapons. "You expect *these* to kill me?" He turned back to Gasam. "You may become what you like, a king or a gibbering madman. You may have the tribe, and all its women if that's what you want. But one thing you will never have: as long as there are Shasinn, it will be remembered that it was Hael who slew a longneck single-handed. You will always be one who gained his ends through other men's deeds." He walked away and did not look back.

It was a strange sensation, being an outcast. He had no protection, no determined future. Just the day before, there had been no question of how his life would progress, any more than for any other Shasinn male. He would be a junior warrior for a number of years, then a senior warrior, then an elder, if he lived that long. Somewhere in the second half of his life would come marriage, children, perhaps prosperity in the form of a private kagga herd.

Now all of that was gone. His future was a vacuum, a great void. On the other hand, he had no duties. There was no one to tell him to assume herd guard, or to carry water, or any other task suitable to his place in life. The feeling, though unfamiliar, was not wholly unpleasant.

He had not thought out where he would go, but his feet seemed to know. It was past noon when he realized that he was walking toward Turwa, the little port town. It seemed to be as good a destination as any. He did not want to encounter Shasinn any more, and the only way to ensure that was to leave the island. There were, after all, other islands. There was even the mainland, although that was too far ahead to think about just yet.

As he walked along that day, and the day after, people in the villages, or out grazing their small herds, looked at him with awe and surprise. The awe was because he was Shasinn, and now everyone hereabout feared the Shasinn. The surprise was because they were not used to seeing Shasinn walking alone, especially junior warriors.

It amused him, wryly, that they should think him a Shasinn, because he no longer felt like one at all. Yet he knew that his outward appearance was unchanged. What had made him Shasinn was not simply blood, but adherence to a set of customs and beliefs that directed every facet of the people's lives. Now that he was outside those customs, he might as well have been born to a different race entirely.

By late afternoon of the first day, he grew hungry. He brought down a springer—small cousin of the branch-horn—with a throwing-stick. At the next farm he encountered, he traded half the meat in exchange for the farmer to clean the animal and give him a gourd of smouldering coals. He could have eaten there, but he did not want company just yet. He made camp near a clump of trees and cooked his dinner. He knew that his days of kagga milk and blood were over, and that he would have to learn to eat other people's food, even that which he had always considered to be tabu. All tabus were over for him.

The next morning he finished the springer meat and continued his journey. Before noon, he reached the port village. He had thought it would be farther away, but before he had always been driving kagga. He was regarded with much wonder by the villagers: a Shasinn junior warrior alone, so far from the nearest Shasinn settlement. He did not bother to enlighten them, but he asked whether the *Wave-Eater* had called recently. It had not, but it was expected once more before the change of winds ended the season, which would not be long.

The element of time meant little to him, since his future had no aim. But he would need to eat, and he knew little about money. Some questioning led him to a money-changer near the dock. This was an elderly man, who wore a knee-length kilt of good trade cloth, and a short jacket with sleeves, and a length of cloth wrapped many times around his head. What astonished Hael was none of this, but rather a pair of little circles of glass hung before the man's eyes, held in place by a framework of thin gold wire.

From his pouch Hael took one of his ornaments—a bracelet of silver, heavy but ornamented only with raised designs. He handed it to the money-changer. "I need money," he said.

The old man took the bracelet and held it close, peering at it through the pieces of glass. This was astonishing. Hael had seen glass before, bottles from the mainland, and a few places in the coastal villages had small panes of colored glass set in their roofs to make a colored light, but this was mystifying.

"How much do you want for it?"

"I don't know," Hael said. "I have never used money before."

"Hmm. You would be easy to cheat, but men who value their lives don't cheat Shasinn. I'll show you something." The man sat at a table like the ones in the taverns Hael had seen, and he placed upon it a curious device, consisting of a t-bar upright in a solid base, with two small trays suspended by fine chains from the two arms. He put the bracelet in one tray, which sank; Hael saw that the crosspiece was hinged. On the other the money-changer placed small weights, all of the same design, but each of a different size. With a last, tiny weight, the two trays balanced.

"This is a balance. These graduated weights on one tray tell me exactly what the object on the other tray weighs. In this case, six ounces."

"That seems simple enough," Hael said.

"Indeed. Now this"—he held out a tablet inscribed with tiny figures—"is a price scale for metals. In one column"—with a spidery finger, he showed how one line of figures went up and down the tablet—"is a list of weights. I go down to six ounces." His finger went down to stop at a figure, then it traced slowly across. "And each of these other columns gives the value of that weight in gold, in silver, and in copper. Those are the three metals used for money."

"What about steel?" Hael wanted to know.

"Steel is too valuable for making tools and

weapons. Likewise tin, which is needed to make bronze."

"And these weights of metal are money?"

"You are quick," the old man allowed, "but that is not quite the case. Here are the coins most used in trade." He opened a small chest and took out three coins. They were flat, one of them of yellow metal, square with rounded corners, the other two thick disks. All three had edges milled with close-set grooves. "This one"—he indicated the smallest coin, the square, yellow one—"is an auric. It is of gold and is worth twenty of these"—he touched the silver coin—"which are called argentines. Each argentine is worth fifty cuprics." He touched the largest coin, which was of a ruddy metal darker than the bronze of his spear. "The words are very ancient ones, meaning 'made of gold,' 'made of silver,' and 'made of copper.' These coins are minted in Neva, where the government guarantees the purity and weight of each coin. Now, as to your bracelet: I can give you five argentines for it, with twenty cuprics. That is slightly less than the actual value in silver. The difference is my profit on the transaction."

Hael shrugged. "That sounds fair. I suppose I will get used to it. It is not like kagga, though. Kagga are living animals."

"Coin is much easier to store than kagga. And metal does not get sick."

"Kagga make calves, though," Hael said.

"Money can be made to multiply, too, if one has the knowledge."

"Is this magic?"

"No, but it is not easy to describe briefly. You will quickly learn how to use money. You will have to try to be careful not to let anyone charge you excessive prices until you learn the values of things."

"I thank you for your advice. Now, if it is permissible to ask, what are those things in front of your eyes?"

"My spectacles?" The old man took them off and looked at them, his eyes suddenly bleary. "They are made in the south, in The Zone. My eyes are not as good as they were when I was young. These lenses correct the defect to an extent."

"That does sound like magic." Hael took the spectacles from the old man's hands and examined them.

"No, it is just a property of shaped glass to distort things. If your vision is already distorted, a correct shaping of the lenses will redistort things so that defective eyes see them as they are. It isn't magic, nor even especially costly. They are quite common on the mainland."

Hael looked through them, but the picture he saw made him dizzy. "They don't make me see more clearly."

"That is because there is nothing wrong with your eyes to begin with."

After thanking the money-changer, not knowing whether he had gotten a fair price for the bracelet and not greatly caring, Hael went to the shop of a woodworker. There, for three of his cuprics, he had a new haft of flamewood crafted for his spear. With the weapon repaired, he felt much restored. He spent the day idling about the little port, which had a crude tavern like the one he had visited before.

He found that his money would last a long time if he bought only food with it. He saw no sense in paying for lodging when he could easily build himself a hut somewhere outside the village. Curious about the foods here, and no longer bound by tabu, he tried a wide variety, even sampling fish. He found that he did not like the taste, and it was difficult to overcome the revulsion, even knowing that it was no longer forbidden. The shellfish were out of the question. At least the fish was a recognizable animal; it had eyes, mouth, even limbs of a sort. He could not imagine himself to eat anything as repulsive as shellfish. For several days, he suffered cramps and other digestive disorders as his body adjusted to the abrupt change in diet.

One morning he saw a man come to the tavern with a fresh-killed springer. The owner paid him for the animal, and Hael asked about this arrangement. He found that this tavern, and the other two establishments in the village that sold prepared food, would buy fresh game, which was especially in demand when sailors were in harbor. Hael asked if he would like something more substantial than a springer, and the man answered that he would pay generously for whatever Hael could bring him. Any meat that was not consumed fresh he could salt and sell to the shipmasters as as sea rations. He was much surprised, because it was known that the Shasinn did not hunt game animals.

Hael found two dockside idlers who eked out a living helping to unload the ships, and made them a proposal. The next morning the three men trekked into the hills past the coastal farms. There they found plentiful game. Moving low through the grass, Hael selected a good-sized branch-horn and stalked it. When he was within range he charged it. These animals, when startled, always broke right or left, because a charging cat would have to make a sharp turn and thus lose speed. Seeing by the twist of its horns which way the beast was going to dart, Hael hurled his spear and pierced it behind the shoulder.

As his two helpers trussed up the animal for carrying, Hael muttered a chant to put its spirit at rest. He was unsure if this would work, since he was no longer Shasinn. Walking behind his bearers, spear slanted over his shoulder, Hael felt as if he now had some control of his life. He was determined not to allow Gasam's plottings to destroy him. He would go away, and he would learn about the world, and, when the time was right, he would return and destroy Gasam. It was a simple plan, and he found it very pleasing.

The tavern-keeper was pleased with the fine, large animal, and said that he would like to have more. Hael paid his bearers the agreed-upon share, which he knew to be more than generous, and told them that they would be going out again the next morning. At sunrise he found that his helpers were fond of drinking up their earnings in the tavern, and they discovered that he had not the slightest sympathy for their suffering. He hauled them to their feet and drove them into the hills with kicks and blows of his spear-butt. For the first half of the day they complained bitterly of their aching heads, their shaky stomachs.

By the time he marched them back that afternoon, with a fat toonoo slung from a pole on their shoulders, they were far more content, knowing that there would be another night of carousing. In this they were disappointed, because Hael had determined that they should not be paid every day, but only when he did not intend to spend the next day or two hunting. They did not like his new arrangement, but they were in no position to alter his decision.

Thus Hael sustained himself, and in time the townsmen grew familiar with the strange, solitary Shasinn who hunted. Ships came to the harbor and departed, but Hael took little interest in them. Somehow, he had conceived a fixation on the *Wave-Eater* and would wait for whatever span of time was necessary until she returned.

Toward the very end of the season, when it looked as if he might have to spend several months in the village before the ships should return again, he came down from the hills with his bearers, a fat three-horn slung between them, when he saw a ship tied up at the dock, its sides streaked yellow and black.

On the pier he looked down into the ship and a familiar face looked up at him. "Shasinn! I had heard that your tribe had come down to these parts."

"And I came to find you," Hael said. "There were some things we had not time to speak of when last we conversed. I would like to continue."

"And so we shall, at the tavern. But I fear it will be only for this evening. I sail on the morning tide. I've waited out the season foolishly, and I'll be lucky to reach the main before the killer storms strike."

"We'll have plenty of time," Hael assured him.

SIX

Life at sea proved to be a very strange experience. It was a constant wonder, the more so because Hael had no preconceived notions of what it would be like. The Shasinn knew nothing at all about such matters, and Hael had been impressed even by the boats of the fishing people. The lives of those fishermen, and the lives of the farmers and the hunters, had differed considerably from the life of the Shasinn, but Hael had never imagined a life so different from the one he had known.

In place of the slow, rather easy-going routine of a herdsman's life, the life of a sailor was an intense one, with a hundred duties to be seen to every day, a hundred dangers to be overcome to ensure the safety of the ship, and many maritime perils occurred with brutal suddenness. The discipline required of a seaman was almost unprecedented in his experience; ordinary vigilance at sea was not unlike waiting for an Asasa raid. Hael had been astonished at the change that came over his friend Malk from the moment the *Wave-Eater* cast off from its mooring. The easy-going, talkative, ever-inquiring companion of the night became a demanding tyrant, who required and got quick, unquestioning obedience whenever he spoke an order. Hael found it surprising and galling, but he quickly learned, both from conversation with his new shipmates and from observation, that this was the proper way to run a ship. Once they were out of sight of land, he began to understand that a ship is a fragile sustainer of life in the midst of an utterly hostile and unforgiving environment. Every man's life depended on the actions of every other man, and all of them on the competence and seamanship of the master.

After a few hours of voyaging, the motion of the ship made Hael very sick, and he found that this was a source of great amusement for the others. Eventually they told him that every man new to the sea suffered thus, and there was a great tradition of seasoned sailors having sport at the wretched landsmen's expense. Hael's rugged constitution quickly asserted itself, however, and by the third day was able to perform his limited duties with full strength.

At first, lacking any skills, those duties requiring strength were all he could do. He hauled on windlass ropes, he manned the capstan bars, and helped muscle the great tiller for the helmsman. He scrubbed and pulled and pushed and did whatever else he was told. Most of all, he learned. There were many periods of frantic action in a sailor's life, but there were also some long idle times, when the ship ran before a following wind and all could rest, save for the helmsman who steered and the master, whose task it was to worry constantly.

At these times Hael talked with each man in the crew about the mysteries of his craft; of sail-making and sea carpentry, of steering and navigating. He spent hours with the leadsmen, learning the arts of sounding and, most of all, he spoke with Malk, who was as approachable as ever when not preoccupied with the urgent necessities of running the ship. At those times, his tongue was as sharp toward Hael as to any of the others.

Malk showed him the compass: a disk of thin white substance, similar to the ivory of a toonoo's tusk, floating in a bath of spiritous liquid and enclosed in a bronze vessel, the disk visible through a glass window. Inset in the ivory was a needle of iron, charged in some mysterious manner so that it always pointed north. Malk explained a little of the properties of magnetism, and showed Hael how, by use of the marks engraved around the periphery of the disk, he could navigate and figure his position.

Together they studied the stars, and Malk showed him the fixed star that was always to the north—Hael had known that one since childhood—and the "wanderers," the stars that had irregular but predictable motions, and the "moonlings," the ones whose motions seemed to be independent of the other stars, but rose and set with great frequency and regularity, although they were just points of light, like the stars.

"Now these," Malk said, with his usual enthusiasm for other peoples' legends, "are supposed by many to be children of the Moon, since their motions are moonlike. There are some people, though, who hold that these are creations of men. Those legends say that they are little worlds, or self-contained vessels, made by means of the same magic that created the fiery spears that were hurled at the Moon. How this all came about the legends don't explain."

There were also charts—pictures drawn on sheets of thin, scraped parchment made from the underskin of sleens. This substance was extremely costly, but was nearly immune to the effects of water and salt. Gradually, as Malk's finger traced for him the contours of the islands and the mainland, Hael began to comprehend how these marks translated into genuine, three-dimensional features of land and sea. It was his first inkling of the principle behind writing, another mystery he was now determined to master.

Another skill was made available to him at this time. Among the crew was a man named Kristofo, who had been a soldier in the armies of several nations. He was a master of the long sword, and owned a weapon much like the one Hael had taken from the Asasa chief he had slain. Kristofo examined Hael's sword, and proclaimed it to be of superb quality, if somewhat overdecorated for his own taste. On days when the ship did not lurch about too much, he gave Hael lessons in the use of this weapon, which was devastating in the hands of one who knew its capabilities.

"Don't lunge like it was one of your spears," Kristofo explained one day as they stood before the mast, the other sailors sitting with their backs against the gunwales, watching this activity with interest. "The point won't go where you want it to, that way. You have to step in and use the point in short jabs, upwardlike. No great follow-throughs, mind you. Try that in battle and the man standing next to the one you're fighting will take your arm off. That's something to remember in battle with professional armies; each soldier watches out for his mates. You attack one, the men standing to either side of him will get you, soon as they have a moment to spare from the men right in front of them. So, you make your jab, and you get that arm back behind your shield as quick as you can, see?''

Hael saw. Kristofo also explained the cutting qualities of the long sword, which were what made it the frightening weapon it was. After all, the spear and short sword were superior for thrusting, the axe was the best weapon for chopping, but there was no weapon for cutting to match the long sword. This was new to Hael because, like most people, he was unaware that chopping and cutting employed entirely different principles. Kristofo showed him the difference. With an axe, against a straw-stuffed target, he showed how the massive axe head, at the end of a swinging arc, forced itself into the object. It was a wedge on the end of a pole. Then he demonstrated how a long sword could be swung and its edge drawn along the point of impact, to produce a devastating wound. The advantage of the sword was its lightness, so that a blow could be delivered much more swiftly than with an ax.

Kristofo took him through the motions of the swordstroke a hundred times, perhaps a thousand. The sword was drawn back behind the shoulder, then slashed forward, vertically or horizontally or in other attitudes, the last snap of the wrist added for the extra speed it gave to the edge. They practiced with the small, round shields used at sea, which handled quite differently from the long shields of the Shasinn.

In the course of their voyage to the mainland, they stopped at a number of islands, loading and unloading cargo at each. Usually, as one island was lost astern the next would become visible on the horizon. Even so, Hael was astonished at the distances the *Wave-Eater* covered. More amazing yet was Malk's assertion that this patch of islands was but the tiniest part of the world, which was of a vastness Hael could not envision. The other sailors averred that this was true, so Hael could not doubt it.

The people of the port villages varied little from island to island, and in some places he saw Shasinn, who seemed much like his own people, although their speech was strangely accented. He had no desire to fraternize with them, even though they had no knowledge of his outcast status.

They also encountered other craft, some of these being of designs differing from the *Wave-Eater*'s. From the south there were long, double-hulled vessels and once in the early evening and from a distance, they spied a huge warship. From a watertight chest, Malk removed a long wooden tube bound at both ends with bronze and put it to his eye.

"Let's see what nation she sails for," he said. He lowered the tube, looking puzzled. "She's Chiwan, and far north for this time of year."

"What is this thing?" Hael asked. Malk let him examine the instrument, which was made of two tubes, one sliding inside the other. At each end was a glass lens, like the ones on the spectacles Hael had seen. Malk showed him how to adjust the focus and through it he saw, in an odd, flattened perspective, the Chiwan war vessel. It was far larger than the *Wave-Eater*, and had two masts. There were large devices on her decks, but he could not guess their function.

"In battle she'll maneuver with oars," Malk told him. "Those are missile-casting engines you see on the deck. I suppose it could be on a diplomatic mission, ferrying some prince or ambassador or such between Chiwa and Orekah."

Hael wondered what this meant, and Malk had to explain to him something of how kings exchanged diplomats, who then represented their sovereigns in foreign courts. He also explained the large part played by intimidation in diplomatic affairs, and that it was not uncommon for such missions to be transported in a nation's latest, most powerful war vessel.

"There is a very ancient saying among sovereigns," Malk expounded, "in many languages and with slightly different phrasings, but all to the effect that, when dealing with other nations, it is always well to speak in a soft voice, but to keep a formidable weapon where everyone can see it."

Hael asked whether sea power was the only means by which these rival nations contended, and Malk explained that they also maintained extensive land forces. Hael found it difficult to visualize when Malk spoke of the numbers of these forces, for he spoke not merely of thousands, but of tens and even hundreds of thousands. These were numbers Hael could not relate to men, but only to animals.

"There was a peak," Hael said, "above our northernmost pasture, where as boys we would climb to look out over the entire upland plain. There we could see for many days' walk in all directions, and from that vantage point we could see many thousand head of kagga, and many times that number of wild game. I suppose that in those times I saw as many as a hundred thousand living creatures at once. But I confess I find it hard to picture that many human beings in one place, nor can I conceive how such a multitude might eat without devastating the countryside, nor yet how anyone could control them."

By this time it was dark, and the ship was almost silent, running before a following breeze, with nothing but flashes of distant lightning to interrupt the serenity of the night.

"It is a sight not soon to be forgotten," Malk told him. "Nor is the smell, after they've been on the march for many days, or too long in camp. As for devastating the countryside, well, they do exactly that. For which reason kings usually assemble such hosts only when a major campaign is imminent, and disperse them as soon as possible. Control is effected by what is known as a chain of command. The king or his marshal is in uttermost command, and beneath him may be generals, each in command of an army or a large part of one. Under each of these will be subcommanders, each in charge of perhaps a thousand, a hundred, and so on down to the squad leaders who have charge of eight or ten men. Orders may be relayed down this chain of command with surprising swiftness, if the conditions are right."

This was most amazing to Hael and he turned to Kristofo. "Can this be true?"

The older man nodded. "It is in theory, and much of the time it does work that way, on the march and in maneuver, at sieges and the like. But once battle is joined there is neither time nor quiet for such niceties. Then, certain basic orders are relayed by trumpet, or pipes, or drums, or cymbals. Battlefield generalship consists largely in moving men by great masses. It is impossible to give each man detailed instructions."

"And kingdoms are conquered in this way?" Hael asked.

"Sometimes," Malk said. "I think most kings go forth to war with the ambition of conquering their enemy. Usually, they are happy in the end merely to preserve their own holdings. They may simply fight for an advantage, control of a piece of territory or a trade route; and then other factors can enter the equation and upset everything. Disease and famine have often brought wars to a halt."

"Do they use magic upon each other?" Hael wanted to know.

Malk thought long about this. "Some claim to. It is a rare king who sallies out to war without holding great solemnities to gain the favor of his god, or gods, or goddesses, or whatever. If he is successful, he may later claim that his god took a personal hand in the victory. Few blame their gods for defeat, save to say that a god witheld favor because of some slight or sin, or a ceremony or sacrifice that was overlooked. Usually, someone is found to be blamed for this and punished.

"But it sometimes happens that sorcerers are brought in to wreak harm upon an enemy, cursing him or laying some baleful spell upon him. I cannot say whether this works or is merely superstition."

"I have seen things," Kristofo maintained, "that were the result of sorcery. Once, when I was a foot soldier in the Nevan army, we went down to campaign in The Zone. That is a very strange place. There are animals in The Zone you won't find anywhere else, and some of the people are just as strange. There are villages in the desert that are like little nations to themselves, and the folk there say they have strange powers. I saw this for myself that time."

"What happened?" Malk asked.

"Well, we were marching down into the country along the River Kol, at the southern end of the lake, where there are some big ruins, things built by giants in the old days. We met the Zoner army there, drawn up in battle line. They were a much smaller force, so we expected an easy victory. Our general rode out front on his cabo with its gilded horns, and he called out for the Zoners to surrender and for their king to come forth and pay tribute. Their king came forth, all right, but it wasn't to pay any tribute. He was mounted on a humper, the kind that can live in the desert without water, and he was all wrapped up in robes and veils and a crown on his head, and he yelled something.

"Next thing you know, out runs a ragged-looking little wretch rattling with bones and charms, and he sets up a wailing and dancing and gesturing fit to make your hair stand up. What was strangest about him—he was blue! And some of my mates said it wasn't paint, but there's people up the river and to the west, in the Canyon, that have blue skin, and they have powerful magic. Well, this one was blue, and he had magic, all right. At the end of his dance he starts spitting and waving and throwing things and howling down some kind of curse, then he points a finger straight at our general."

"And what did your general do?" Malk asked, an eyebrow slightly raised.

"Why, he fell stone dead right out of his saddle, that's what! I mean to tell you, it took the spirit out of us, and there was no fighting that day. We stayed around a while and there was some parlaying among the leaders of both armies, but in the end we turned around and marched back to Neva. Now, if that's not sorcery, I don't know what is!"

Malk rubbed his chin through his black beard. "Could be. I've always heard that the most powerful magicians are in The Zone, and they say those Canyon people have most of it, but there could be other explanations. I've seen plenty of *false* magic and conjuring. They could have had a blowgunner hidden in the rocks, with a poison dart. Easy enough to have it look like magic, once the sorcerer had everyone primed for it, with his dancing and howling."

"Well, maybe," said Kristofo, frowning, "but it looked to me like—"

"Storm coming!" the lookout's voice cut across their conversation and Malk rushed to the stern rail.

"I knew this luck wouldn't last," Malk said. "We're in for a blow." Quickly he barked out orders and the great slanting yard was lowered and the sail bound tightly to it. Everything loose was lashed down and extra men detailed to bail or help with the rudder. By the time all preparations had been made, the storm was upon them.

It was Hael's first experience of a big storm at sea, and he found it terrifying. The vessel pitched about as if it were no more than a twig, and the winds were deafening. Lightning sizzled everywhere, and it seemed impossible that it would not strike the ship. The rains were blinding, and he was almost swept off the ship twice before a seaman passed him a line to secure himself with. He tied one end around his waist and the other to a lifeline that ran the length of the vessel. That done, he could help bail or heave on the tiller, as he was directed.

Several times, it seemed to his horrified gaze that the whole ship, not just the bow, plunged beneath the water, but each time it erupted back through to the surface again. Surely, he thought, the fragile structure of the ship could not hold up under much of this. But the spirit of the ship, housed in the thick part of the keel where the mast was stepped, was stronger than he would have thought, for the vessel came through the storm with little damage, as did Hael himself.

The next morning they were sailing beneath clear skies and little to show for the storm save a slightly roughened surface to the water and some leaky seams which his shipmates were caulking with pitch and tow. Hael felt that they had survived a terrible experience, but the others laughed at the thought, and said that this had been no great storm, but a mere gale such as one endured several times in an ordinary season.

"When you have a hard blow from seaward, and rocks alee, inshore, that's when you know it is time to consult with your gods," said one.

"Aye," said another. "A wind five times stronger than that one can blow for two or three whole days together, and raise waves that look like mountains."

Hael did not know whether they spoke the truth or were indulging in the sport of frightening the inexperienced landsman. But Malk affirmed that it had been but a trifling storm, and nothing like the truly fearsome tempests that came from time to time, usually late in the year.

"At such times," he said, "you had better be in a snug harbor, one well protected from the winds, or well out to sea. If you are too near shore, you are surely doomed, and a windy harbor is almost as bad. I have known great storms to lift a ship the size of *Wave-Eater* and set it down atop houses a hundred paces inland."

This seemed like an extravagant claim, but Hael knew better than to question Malk's word. What was certain was that the storms that gave this part of the world its name were of unimaginable power, and that power was compounded when one was at sea. It gave him pause. The night before, he had been sure that, once he was ashore, he would never leave dry land, not even to return to Gale to accomplish his vengeance upon Gasam.

Now, thinking back on it, the night's storm did not seem all that terrifying. In retrospect, it took on the dimensions of adventure, which in truth is little more than hardship and danger remembered in circumstances of comfort and safety. Perhaps he would stay with the ship a while longer, and see more of the world in this fashion, before taking up life ashore.

On the next day they sighted the mainland. Hael

was anxious to see this fabled land, and was disappointed at first that it looked no different from a large island. As they sailed southward, though, the land stayed to their left, although with occasional capes and indentations, and he began to get a sense of how vast it was. He asked Malk how far it stretched inland.

"No man can truly say. If you sail far enough to the south, you will round Cape Rika, and there the main turns northward. From there it takes many weeks of sailing to reach as far north as we are now. So the mainland is in truth a great body of land, and much of the interior is unknown. There are great deserts, and parts called Poisoned Lands, where nothing lives and where any life that dwells too near may take on strange forms, and there are jungles too thick to penetrate. The coastal kings sometimes send expeditions to explore into the interior, to find new resources and new peoples to trade with."

This sounded intriguing to Hael, who thought it would be a fine thing to explore unknown lands. "For what do they search?"

"Metals are always scarce. Not gold and silver, which don't perish, but any expedition that finds a good store of iron makes a profit. The ancients used to bury beams of iron within great masses of stone, and that is about the only way it is ever found in a quantity and a state of preservation that is useful. There are other things; spices, various kinds of horn and ivory and feathers, rare sorts of earth used in trades like glass-making and ceramics, dyes. The list is long, and a new territory almost always produces something that is valuable, if you but have an eye for such things."

"Why did ancient people bury their iron, do you

think?" Hael asked, knowing this was just the sort of knowledge Malk loved to collect.

"Some think it was to preserve it, but that seems unlikely, since a prodigious effort is needed to break it free of the stone matrix. Lucky for us they did, or there would be no iron at all. No one has ever found deposits of iron, although gold is sometimes found in nature."

They put in at a port called Floria. It was situated where a small river descended from mountainous country and made its way to the sea. The fine, deep bay was encircled by steep hills, and the city was built upon the slopes. The buildings were of a permanence Hael had never before seen, some of wood but more of stone or brick, and much of it whitewashed. Many of the roofs were of baked clay tile, so that the overwhelming impression of the city was a vision of red and white.

Besides innumerable dwellings, there were much larger structures, some of great magnificence. "Are those temples?" Hael asked, pointing to a group of such buildings set on a hillside a short way above the port.

"Some," Malk said. "But that lower one on the right is a law court, and the one next to it, with a shingled roof, is a covered market."

"I want to see the temples," Hael said, eagerly. He was still fascinated by the idea of gods.

"You shall," Malk promised.

Another intriguing thing about the city was that it was, in truth, a city. Hael had never seen anything larger than one of the coastal villages of Gale, and this was easily a hundred times larger. He was somewhat prepared for this, because his shipmates had talked casually of cities with tens or hundreds of thousands of people. Most of all, they spoke of Kasin, the royal city of the kingdom of Neva. It was rumored to have as many as a million inhabitants, a number so immense that Hael had no conception of its meaning. The other sailors had themselves no really clear idea of what it meant, save that it was a tremendous amount.

"I can write the sum," Malk said, proceeding to do so on a plank, "but I can no more picture it in my mind than can you. In truth, nobody can. Let nobody mock you as a barbarian because these numbers puzzle you. The best-educated sage who ever lived could never picture in his mind more than a score of individual objects. These things are—abstractions. Do you understand that word?"

"I think so," Hael said. "But if a man can hold no more than a double handful of things visualized in his mind, how is it that I can scan one of our herds, with perhaps three or four hundred head of kagga, and know within seconds when a single one is gone?"

"That is not picturing all those animals in your mind at once," Malk said, with his usual relish for this sort of brain-cracking dispute, "but rather the working of a trained memory. Once you have learned all the animals of a particular herd, you know when one is missing. That is because your mind acts as a filter, such as is used in making beer. It does not take note of that which is meaningless, but calls your attention immediately to what is important. Your eye, which is far quicker than your mind, can scan the whole herd, register that each one is there, and then tell you that one shape of horn or pattern of markings is missing, without you actually thinking about it, do you understand? Now"—

he slapped the back of one hand into the palm of the other, which meant he was approaching his point—"if you were suddenly to be put in charge of another herd, one unfamiliar to you, after one day, would you know on the next if one was missing? Or even ten? If too few were missing to definitely reduce the visible size of the herd?"

"I confess," Hael said, laughing, "I would not. I concede your point. But what is beer?"

"Enough!" Malk said, throwing up his hands. "You are like a ten-year-old child, that knows nothing of the world and can never have enough answers to his questions! Leave me to dock my ship. We will go ashore later, and perhaps teach you about beer."

That contented Hael, who was looking forward to this. He looked quite different from the Shasinn junior warrior who had boarded the *Wave-Eater*. His paint was gone, and his bronze-colored hair hung free on his shoulders. He no longer wore it in hundreds of tiny plaits because he was no longer a junior warrior of the Shasinn, and, in any case, it was prohibitively difficult for a man alone to maintain such a hair style. At home, the young men would spend hours plaiting each other's hair, or arranging their face paint, or any other task that was deeply involved with their warrior pride.

That was something that puzzled Hael about this business of "civilization." While these city-centered peoples had armies and fought wars, it seemed that those who fought for them were not true warriors, but rather something called "soldiers" who lacked the sense of personal style that warriors considered essential.

He wondered somewhat at this, because in those

times when he had bothered to think about it, he had always assumed that when the time came when he would have to earn a livelihood among the civilized folk, he would simply follow the warrior's trade. Now that did not seem so simple. There were specialized skills expected of a soldier, and soldiers had no style nor personal loyalties. Ability to fight was only a small part of their requirements. This would bear thinking about, especially the part of which Kristofo had told him: Soldiers were not of high status, especially those who merely did the fighting. The higher the rank and status, the less fighting a soldier did.

This matter of exploring, though, that sounded promising. A man who was an accomplished warrior, and who was at home in many terrains and climes, and who had an affinity for all sorts of animals, surely would have no difficulty in finding a place on such an expedition. When he felt it was time to give up the sea he might try for such a position. He had not decided on leaving the *Wave-Eater* yet.

When the vessel was secured to the pier and a watch set, it was time for the rest of the crew to go ashore. It was too late to begin unloading cargo and, in any case, that was the task of the dockmen, not the sailors. Washed up, dressed in their best and in some cases perfumed, the seamen swaggered ashore.

Most headed for the nearest tavern or brothel, but Hael was determined to seek out one of the great temples. He attracted no little notice from the townspeople, especially the women. While he had discarded a few of the attributes of his nation, the local people were still not used to seeing such a towering youth, dressed scantily in the skin of a night-cat, wearing a long sword and bearing an elaborate spear. Especially rare were young men so handsome, who seemed to be both aware and unaware of the fact at once.

Many invitations were called to him, which he declined as politely as he could. He was climbing uphill, toward the temples. The rough-cut paving stones felt strange beneath his bare feet. The buildings hemming him in on either side were strange as well, but after the break from his former life followed by his time at sea, any further change of environment seemed minor in comparison.

After a few minutes Malk caught up with him. "You waste no time, lad. I take it you're headed for the temple district?"

"I am. Why are there so many people in the streets? Is it always like this?"

"The markets are just closing, people are going to their homes. Do you feel crowded in, among such a throng?"

Hael shrugged. "It's no worse than kagga." Indeed, it was rather like walking in the midst of a herd, for while the people were numerous, he was a head taller than all but a few. They wore colorful clothes, and many of the women wore wide hats of woven straw to protect their pale complexions. The garments were far more elaborate than he was used to, with much fitting and tailoring, unlike the simple wraps worn by his own people. He corrected himself; his *former* people.

A group of guards walked past them, and they eyed Hael suspiciously, noting his prominent spear and sword. These men wore short tunics that left their legs bare above heavy sandals, and their bodies were protected by armor of laced horn or bone, arranged in overlapping scales or rows of splints. They wore close-fitting caps of hardened leather, except for an officer who wore a larger helmet covered with what appeared to be plates sawn from the iron-hard tusks of the toonoo. Their weapons were spears and short swords.

"Those are soldiers?" Hael asked when they were past.

"Yes," Malk answered. "Probably the gate guard going out for the evening watch."

"They aren't very impressive," Hael said.

"Five aren't impressive, ambling along a city street. Ten thousand in formation in the field make a very impressive sight indeed."

"Where should we start?" Hael asked.

"I have to make a call at the temple of Aq, the sea god. It's expected of shipmasters to offer to Aq, in thanks for a safe voyage. Since this isn't my home port, the offering needn't be great. When I return to Kasin, I'll be expected to make a substantial donation to the great temple, in thanks for a prosperous voyage and safe return."

"Is Aq an important god?"

"In maritime nations, yes. Especially in the port cities. Here is the temple." They had come to a tiny plaza, and on the far side was the front of the edifice, a columned portico beneath a pitched roof. The steps leading up to it were of sea-green marble, and the columns were decorated with tile of the same color. The wall of the shaded portico was painted with a stylized wave motif, amid which played painted sea life. On this portico, men with clean-shaven faces accepted offerings from those who entered.

The interior carried on the sea-green motif, even the light coming through panes of green and blue glass set in the high-pitched roof. At the far end of the single great chamber the god sat enthroned. Malk had explained that these sculptures were rather like spirit-poles, containing some of the essence of the god. The figure was beautifully carved, but Hael couldn't tell of what material, for it was painted. Garments, flesh and hair were of differing shades of the dominant color and the god was draped with seaweed. Unused to such art, Hael had to study the sculpture for some time before he saw that the throne upon which the god sat was an enormous seashell. The god himself was depicted as a handsome, middle-aged man with a square-cut beard. In one hand he held a fisherman's spear, the other resting on a ship's wheel.

Hael was much taken with the beauty of the place, but he could feel no presence of the spirits. Perhaps it was because he was not of this place, and was not familiar with its spirits. Malk had explained to him that the gods dwelled far away, in some vague, splendid homeland of their own, from which they sometimes took a passing interest in the affairs of men. That might be why he felt so little spiritual presence here, because the god was far away. It was perplexing, because he could not imagine how the artisan made such a beautiful image without spiritual aid.

Malk went through a consultation with the priests—for this was what he told Hael the shaven men were—and something passed between them. Then the shipmaster tossed a handful of incense on a brazier that smoked before the statue of Aq. He jerked his head toward the entrance and the two left. As they descended the steps, Hael confided his doubts concerning the god inside.

"You are not the only one to be sceptical," Malk told him. "The worship of gods can become mere form, and sometimes priests are greedy. Still, the people hold these gods dear, and it is best to show them no disrespect.

"I would not!" Hael protested.

Malk laughed and clapped him on the shoulder. They walked through a few streets and came to a temple of the fire god. The dominant color here was red, and the god was not greatly revered by the townsmen. There was a fire that was kept burning perpetually, and here the householders repaired when they needed to restart the home fires.

Hael inquired about this god's less than ardent devotees and the shipmaster said, "Here the sea god is preeminent, because the people live by his bounty. But should you ever travel to the cities near the Smoking Mountains, you will see the fire god worshipped with rare devotion. In any district menaced by volcanoes, people worry incessantly about fiery lava and other evidence of the fire god's displeasure."

"Is that always the way?" Hael asked. "Do people pay their devotion only to gods who have an immediate hand in their welfare?"

They stopped in front of a food and wine stall and Malk ordered them some refreshment. "Not exactly, although that has a part in it. People usually revere all the gods, but with special emphasis on those who are likely to do them the most good or harm. In the desert areas, the gods of wind and sun hold sway, and everywhere that farmers live the gods of earth, and your spirits, and the bringers of rain, have their devotions."

Hael accepted a skewer of smoked meats from the vendor. "But are they *real*?"

Malk bit into another skewer and washed the mouthful down with a draught from a clay cup of sour wine. "You ask one of the great questions posed by scholars. For my part, I think that gods have the reality accorded to them by their believers. That is not to say that they are less than real, but that the—oh, the form they take may be determined by the number and fervor of their worshippers. Does that make any sense to you?"

"It does," Hael said. "Our spirits had little form, save what the spirit-speakers chose to give them. I think these gods may be like that, on a larger scale."

"I must remind you not to get into dispute with the learned doctors here," Malk said. "You would probably win, and they wouldn't like it, then the authorities would be after you and who knows where it might end?"

They visited a number of other temples before it grew too dark, and while each was interesting, there was a certain sameness to Hael's taste. Each was housed in an impressive edifice, each contained a splendid depiction of its tutelary god and a decorative motif suggestive of that god's attributes; agricultural, warlike, meterological and so forth. The temple erected to the goddess of love and fertility was rather startling to Hael's unsophisticated eye, but the worshippers there behaved as solemnly as in the other temples.

"And then," Malk said as they finished their tour, "there are some gods people simply like, even if they have no great power and can't do their worshippers much good or ill." He led Hael into a tiny temple whose façade was covered with a riot of flowers made of ceramic and glass. Some were so realistic that Hael touched them to make sure they weren't real. Inside, the air was heavy with natural perfume, and heaps of flowers lay all around the figure of a smiling goddess who sat enthroned in a giant blossom.

"Fleura," Malk said, "goddess of flowers and patroness of the spring festival. Would that all gods were so benevolent."

"Are some evil?" Hael asked as they left the little temple and made their way back to the harbor.

"There are some . . ." Malk began, hesitantly, "some whose worship is forbidden in the civilized kingdoms of the mainland. They are spoken of little, but there are said to be temples of their cults in the hinterlands. Their worship is very dark and bloody, and their priests are sorcerers, or so they claim. Have nothing to do with them, Hael. If someone offers to take you to such a temple, restrain your curiosity and flee.

"Now, come. That's enough of religion for the evening. Let's find ourselves some real food and entertainment."

SEVEN

Two days later they continued their journey south. At first Hael's stomach was queasy and his head ached from the rich food and wine, although his indulgences had been moderate by sailor standards. The others had made some sport of his abstemious habits, but this had ceased after one of them had challenged him to a wrestling match, a sport at which the Shasinn were famed. Almost without effort, Hael had thrown each of them in succession, with painful results. After that, they let him eat and drink as he chose, without critical comment.

This was the last leg of their journey, a two-week run south to the great port of Kasin, the huge double city which was both port and capital of the kingdom of Neva. This legendary metropolis lay in the lush lowlands of the central southern coast, an area rich in agriculture, in population and in wildlife.

Each day, as the *Wave-Eater* clove the swells southward, seldom straying from sight of land, the shoreline grew more densely green. Some evenings, when they put in at small, village-sized harbors, the sounds from the nearby jungles were riotous; squawks and roars, buzzings and clickings without end. Hael longed to go into those strange woodlands and examine their mysteries, but he knew that he had plenty of time before him, and that he would have ample opportunity to seek out the world's secrets.

Finally, racing ahead of a pursuing storm, they rounded Point Shipwreck and sailed into the estuary of the Shonga River. They passed the gigantic Lighthouse of Perwin, reputedly the tallest structure in the world, which Hael could scarcely credit to be a work of human hands. Its sheer walls were of white stone, with stairs slanting up around its sides to the enormous fire basket at the apex. Gangs of slaves toiled up these steps all night to carry wood-knots and fistnuts to burn brightly during the hours of darkness. During the days, the ashes were left to send up a pillar of smoke.

Near the lighthouse, they waited for the tide to carry them upriver. When the tide began to run, they ran out the oars and made a quick progress past the naval harbor, a huge, circular pool surrounded by roofed docks where the warships were kept out of the weather when they were not cruising.

The storm broke as they entered the vast harbor. The rains came heavy but the winds were gentle in the protected anchorage. Hael was glad to be in sheltered waters when the storm came, but disappointed that he could see nothing of the fabled city. They dropped anchor and lowered the yard, drawing the sail to one side. Then, carefully and laboriously, they lifted the mast from its step and lowered it to rest upon a pair of brackets erected at bow and stern. With the mast secured in place they stretched the sail across it to make a ship-tent and huddled beneath it. The cook had a smoky fire going in a box of earth, and they passed around a wineskin as he prepared a meal. They were exhausted but elated, knowing that the season's work was done and they were safe in harbor, with their pay to be distributed soon. In no time the dice were out and rearrangements of that pay commenced.

Hael was impatient to see the famous city, and disappointed that the weather deprived him of a view. "How long until the next sailing season?" he asked Malk.

"For four months no one will sail. After that, some of the bolder captains will set sail, risking the late storms for the chance of being first to do trading at the far ports. One who survives the trip gets the best prices there, and likewise when he returns. By the end of the fifth month, everybody sails."

"And you?" Hael asked.

"That will be decided later. I have to consult with the owners. Some of them are great omen-takers and never sail unless the signs are right."

"You don't own the *Wave-Eater*?" Hael said, surprised.

"I am only part owner, one of a company. If you put all your savings in one ship, you lose everything if that ship goes down. Our company owns a number of ships and everyone gets a part of all the profits. Likewise, a loss is spread out among many."

"Like tribal property, held in common?"

"Something like that. What do you plan to do? You are welcome to a berth here when we sail again. You are learning the sailor's trade quickly."

"I want to see the city, but I want to travel inland as well, now that I have heard something of the interior. If one of those expeditions you spoke of is being planned, I might be able to join it. Surely they must need warriors."

"That may be. But be careful and let no one talk you into joining an army. They will make it sound glorious and adventurous, with war and booty, but new soldiers usually get sent to lonely outposts in the desert or the jungle where battles are few but boredom and disease kill off thousands. If you must take service, go into the navy. The conditions are better and you spend much of your time in ports like this one, where there is at least something to do between cruises. I don't think you would like any kind of military service, though. You are always taking orders from fools who enforce discipline with a whip."

Hael's head buzzed with possibilities and that night he went to sleep with the rain thundering against the sail-tent overhead.

The next morning dawned bright and cloudless, and Hael crawled out from under the tent and dashed water from a bucket over his face, then blinked at his surroundings. Then he blinked again, unable to credit his eyes. He had known that Kasin was a city, and a large one. But never in his wildest imaginings had he thought that he could stand in one place and see nothing *but* city in any direction.

Kasin surrounded the bay in rolling hills that retreated to the limits of vision, all of them clothed in manmade structures. There were stands of greenery to be seen, but they appeared to be orchards or gardens rather than wildland. Some of the hills were crowned with great temples and for a while Hael was puzzled by a number of tall objects of strange shape before he saw that they were colossal statues. Smoke rose from chimneys and altars to mingle with the morning mist.

The bay itself was crowded with ships now that the sailing season was over, some at anchorage, others hauled up onto shore and stored in long sheds. A great deal of unloading was going on at long stone piers. From some of them loomed wooden cargo cranes where men toiled inside giant windlasses, endlessly climbing horizontal spokes to power the great side wheels. Seabirds swarmed overhead, their cries blending with the creak and clatter of the cranes and the calling of men as the morning's work picked up tempo.

At Malk's orders, the tent was taken down and the anchor hauled up. The long oars were run out and Malk steered as the ship was rowed to a place at a long pier. Lines were cast ashore and the vessel was made fast to bollards as the sailors began a rhythmic chant signifying that the voyage was now officially over, except for the sacrifice to the sea god. The inevitable dockside idlers cheered the seamen and offered their services as stevedores. Within minutes, the bales in the hold were moving onto the pier, where port officials hurried down to record the cargo and levy port fees and taxes.

"I will be very busy for the next two or three days, Hael," Malk said. "But now you've seen a little bit of civilization and I hope you'll stay out of trouble while you seek a livelihood to sustain you during the winter months. If not, and should you end up in the city dungeon, contact me through the Brotherhood of Shipmasters. Our hall is across from the sea god's temple. I'll come and fetch you, if possible."

"I promise to be careful," Hael said. He collected his few belongings and climbed up the stone steps to the pier.

Each of the sailors had been given a small advance against his pay, which would be tendered on the third day after docking. The first day was dedicated to unloading, the second to auctioning the cargo and calculating each man's share, the third to payday.

None of this was Hael's concern, save collecting his own pay. At present, his concept of money was still too nebulous for that to be a matter of anxiety. With his spear, his sword, his scraps of nightcat fur, his pouch and waterskin, he was ready to challenge the world. His ornaments and the money he had collected back on Gale would sustain him for a while, and in the meantime he would find something suited to him by way of employment.

From the docks, Hael began making his way into the city, always tending uphill. He came to markets where a stunning variety of goods were offered for sale, and he lingered to examine all of them. He, in turn, was examined, but not with great interest. Kasin was the greatest port in the known world, and outlanders were a common sight. Hael was of an island people who were well known but seldom seen, and as such attracted a certain notice. Still, there was no true shortage of great, handsome barbarians.

He had decided that the best place to seek his fortune would be the city's hub, an area called the Common. In the days when Kasin had been no more than a port village, the Common had been a civic pasture, where anyone, citizen or visitor, could leave his livestock to graze. As the city grew it became a market, then a meeting place, and now it was a complex of shops, temples and public buildings, completely paved and without a blade of grass to be seen. The streets of the city were chaotic, winding among the low hills surrounding the bay, following the terrain rather than any city plan. The Common, however, was dominated by a colossal statue of the war god, easily visible from most parts of the city. As long as Hael kept the statue in sight, he knew that he was headed in the right direction.

The buildings were mostly low structures of wood or brick, with a few imposing residences of stone. Much of the building material was re-used, for fire and earthquake devastated the city from time to time. Occasionally, Hael saw walls that seemed disconcertingly to have parts of human bodies built into them, but these proved to be pieces of shattered statues scavenged as building material.

After an hour of trudging through winding streets, meeting dead ends and retracing his path, asking questions of citizens who could barely understand his dialect, he found a wide boulevard leading to the Common. Flanking the boulevard were strips of earth planted with flowers and shade trees, and this made the place seem a little less alien to Hael. Never could he walk for long without encountering a fountain, usually surrounded by women with water jars. In the narrow streets these were usually just streams pouring from a clay pipe into a basin, but here on the boulevard were elaborate constructions of stone and ceramic sculpture, with multitudes of high-arching sprays fracturing the morning sunshine into rainbows and filling the air with a cooling mist.

At the end of the boulevard, Hael found himself standing in the shadow of the war god's statue, which was merely the largest among many such monuments, some of them aged and weathered, others little more than fragments left by long-ago earthquakes. The place was thronged with people wearing the costumes of many nations.

He saw tall, thin, hawk-faced men from the deserts, tiny bells plaited into their black beards, leading the grotesque animals called humpers. There were stocky men from the southern jungles, their hair decorated with extravagant feathers. There were a few slaves, who wore little more than loincloths and thick copper collars.

Most of the women in evidence were local, the wealthier ones stitched into elaborate, complicated gowns and bodices. This manner of dress was ostentatiously impractical, demonstrating that the wearer was not expected to work. These fashionable ladies wore veils to protect their complexions, and they were attended by slaves with fans and parasols. When they encountered one another, they exchanged elaborate, formal courtesies that were meaningless to Hael.

He passed a stall where a man sat, dressed in a rusty red tunic of thick cloth and belted with a short sword. His leather leggings were studded with copper and beside him rested a cuirass of laced bone splints, lacquered bright scarlet. On a table before him was a helmet of hardened leather plumed with a long, white kagga tail. He eyed Hael's height and build, his spear and long sword.

"You seem a likely lad," he said, smiling broadly and falsely. "A warrior from the islands, am I right? There's not much call for your trade here in Kasin, my friend, but I know where there is. The royal army is always looking for fine, strapping young men with a taste for adventure; exotic travel, the blood of enemies on your blade and their loot in your warbag and their women wherever you choose to keep them. Sounds good, eh?"

The man's whole attitude and manner reminded Hael too much of Gasam. "Do you get many recruits this early in the day," he asked, "when most men are still sober?"

The recruiter scowled. "No, but duty hours are duty hours. You've just arrived, haven't you? Come back in a few days, when you're hungry and have found that there's little work for a primitive in a civilized town. The army will look better then."

Hael walked to the base of the war god's statue and stood leaning on his spear, unconsciously adopting the stork stance, causing small children to giggle and point. He ignored them, assuming that city people didn't bother to teach their children good manners. Standing thus, moving only his head, he let the sensations of the place wash over him. The sounds were cacophonous, a melange of different languages, animal sounds, the cries of vendors, even distant music. The smells were as varied; spices and cooking smells, perfumes, rank animal odors and less identifiable stenches, all overlaid by the aroma of incense drifting from the temples.

Clouds began to tower on the western horizon, promising a storm before the day was over. Sometimes Hael felt the stirrings of spirit life, very faintly, but it seemed that the overwhelming human presence here kept all such things suppressed. He suspected that cities, being human creations, had little place for doings other than those of men and manmade gods.

A new set of sounds made him turn his head. A procession came toward the Common, traveling along the broad boulevard Hael had found. The sounds he had heard were musical, although of a type he had never encountered. At the head of the procession, fat, smooth-faced men blew into pipes and great conch shells, while behind them women in filmy gowns beat cymbal-jangling tambours, their hair flying wildly as they danced and whirled. Farther back yet, tall men in feather headdresses beat long, deep-voiced drums. In the center of the procession, powerfully built men bore a litter on their shoulders, and as this litter passed even the richly dressed women bowed low before it.

The crowd parted as the procession entered the Common, and its path took it near the pedestal where Hael stood. He wondered whether he should bow like the others, but he had never been trained in the gesture, which was foreign to his people. As the litter passed him, he inclined his head as a compromise. To his amazement, a young woman sat on the litter amid a pile of cushions, beneath a canopy of emerald-colored cloth. Her eyes widened when she saw him, her head continuing to turn as the litter went by.

Hael hoped that he had not offered offense. This was obviously someone of importance, accustomed to deference. She might feel that his failure to bow was intended as an insult. He had not had time to gain more than a fleeting impression of the woman, but she had not resembled the highborn women he had seen here, either in dress or in physical appearance. She seemed to be of a different race.

Luckily, everybody else had been too busy bowing to notice Hael's lack of conformity. Behind the litter trailed a line of attendants leading a number of beautiful animals draped in flower garlands, among them a magnificent white kagga male. Its horns were gilded and across its back had been flung a network blanket of colored cords, fringed with tassels and bells. It cared nothing for its finery. Its eyes rolled and it pranced nervously as attendants fought to keep it under control. It pained Hael to see a kagga handled so incompetently.

When the procession had passed, wending its way toward one of larger temples, Hael went to the stall of a perfume merchant.

"This is my first day in the city," he said. "Would you tell me who that woman was, and what sort of procession that was?"

The merchant looked him over. He wore the same dress and had the same general look as the money-changer back in Turwa, save that this one wore no lenses. "That was Shazad, the high priestess of the storm god. Now that the season of storms is upon us, she performs this sacrifice each month."

"Are all priestesses due such reverence?" Hael asked.

"She is also the daughter of the great nobleman Pashir, who is head of the Royal Council and general of the armies. Since the king's own daughters may never be seen in public, she is the most powerful woman the citizens ever see."

This was interesting. The woman had instantly fascinated him, for reasons he could not have named. There had been something in the way she had stared at him. He began to walk toward the temple of the storm god, where he could still hear the wild music of pipe and drum, of conch and cymbal. A crowd had gathered on the esplanade before the temple, clapping and chanting in time to the music.

The bearers halted just as Hael reached the leading edge of the crowd, and they were beginning to lower the litter from their shoulders when the frightened kagga broke loose from its handlers and ran in panic, plowing into the bearers on the left side of the litter, knocking four of them sprawling. The litter tilted and overturned, sending the lady Shazad tumbling in a mass of flying cushions.

The crowd gasped, either from concern for the priestess's safety or fear of a terrible omen. The kagga leapt amid the struggling bodies, butting and goring, its forehoofs inflicting wounds as it bawled in rage. The woman struggled to get up but she was knocked down once again by the kagga's shoulder as it struggled to get one of its horns free from the litter's canopy.

Since there seemed to be no one present who knew how to handle a panicked kagga, Hael strode forward. The animal had worked itself loose from the canopy and spun around, seeking an escape but seeing only humans in every direction. Since there was no escape, it could only attack, and the nearest target was the tall young man walking toward it. The kagga put its head down and charged.

Hael studied the animal. From the angle of its neck he could see that it habitually gored with its left rear horn, so he quickly sidestepped to its right, bringing his spear-butt down sharply between its horns. The crack of the blow echoed across the esplanade and for a moment the kagga stood half-stunned. In that instant Hael grabbed its right ear and twisted it forward as he kicked it behind the foreleg. The beast collapsed to its knees, then struggled to get up, but the constant, painful pressure against its ear held it still.

"Rope it," Hael said to the attendants who stood by gaping. They scrambled among the wreckage of the litter to find enough cord to secure the kagga. When at last they had it trussed up, Hael released its ear and stood back.

"Who are you?"

Hael looked down to see who was speaking to him and saw to his great surprise that it was the priestess, Shazad. She was barely tall enough to reach his chest, although her body was anything but childlike. She wore green trousers and a gold-colored bodice sewn with scallop shells of thin gold. It was quite unlike the clothing of the local women.

"My name is Hael. My people are—were—the Shasinn."

"You come from the northwestern islands, don't you? And what do you do besides fight kagga?" She rubbed her sore backside, apparently feeling that she had lost no dignity before the crowd, which she ignored. Her hair was black, and her dark eyes tilted in her broad, beautiful face.

Hael smiled, leaning on his spear. "You don't fight kagga. You handle kagga. You fight cats, and fur snakes, and longnecks. And you fight enemies, of course."

"So you are a warrior as well as a herdsman?"

"The two are one and the same where I come from. I've even learned a little of being a sailor, although I don't think that life would suit me forever."

"I can see that you know your trade. Far better than these worthless slaves." As she spoke he realized that this was a girl no older than himself, although her eyes and bearing were those of a far older woman. Her voice was low and husky.

Two fat, oddly costumed men came hurrying down the temple steps, their sandals slapping the stairs, their breath coming in puffs. "Are you unhurt, my lady?" said one in a piping voice.

"Quite," she murmured.

The other stared at Hael, scandalized. "Bow down, you oaf! The Lady Shazad should not have to look up to the likes of you!"

Hael studied him coolly. "Where were you when that kagga tried to trample and gore this woman? I don't remember seeing any fat man running this way then."

The man began to turn purple, but Shazad quieted him with a raised hand. "Don't be tiresome, Priest Phulug. This man saved me from injury if not death. He is an outlander and we can't very well expect him to know our customs. The ceremony will have to be cancelled, of course."

"B-But," the other priest spluttered in his high, fluting voice, "this is the appointed day!"

"Look at that kagga," she said, pointing at the gouge between the animal's eyes where Hael's spear-butt had plowed a bloody furrow. "A sacrificial animal must be without stain or blemish. We can't offer the god a beast with a great, bleeding cut on its brow. Another will have to be selected from the sacred herd. Besides, some of my attendants are wounded, and it's forbidden to drip blood on the temple floor. You'll have to select another day. Surely there's a procedure."

The priest named Phulug sighed loudly. "Oh, there is. When the gods show that it's a bad day, by lightning or earthquake or something of that sort, we consult the divination books to find an alternate day."

"Excellent. Do so." She dismissed them by turning away and surveying the wreckage of her litter. "Soulis," she called, "is there enough slavepower left to carry me back to the palace?"

A man in a long white tunic bowed deeply. "Assuredly there is, mistress."

"Good." She turned to Hael. "Come with me." She walked to the litter and seated herself on the restored cushions. Having nothing better to do, and still fascinated by the strange woman, Hael followed. She watched the two fat priests as they toiled up the stairs. "Eunuchs are always so testy when you interfere with their schedules and routines."

"What are eunuchs?" Hael asked as she was lifted.

"Men who've had their—you really are from the hinterlands, aren't you? What do you do to male kagga when you don't want them to breed?"

"We castrate them," he said.

"That's what is done to eunuchs."

"It seems drastic," Hael said, "but I can see why you wouldn't want those two to breed."

She laughed, covering her mouth with both hands. "That's not why—oh, you'll have plenty of time to learn."

"Where are we going?" Hael asked.

"To the palace. Actually, it's my father's palace. There are others, but ours is the finest, except for the king's." By now Hael knew that a palace was a very large dwelling place, where important and wealthy people housed their families, their belongings and their great retinues of servants. Instead of a man's wealth being judged by the number of huts in his enclosure, as in his homeland, it was judged by the size of this single building.

It was a strange experience, walking alongside the litter, with people bowing on all sides. The musicians did not bother to play their instruments. In fact, the cancellation of the ceremony seemed to leave everyone at a loss, so they just trudged in no particular order. The litter lurched a little, because some of the slaves were limping. Hael felt no great sympathy. In what had seemed to him a very minor emergency they had all proven to be spectacularly useless, and some of them might have been dead but for his actions. He had been impressed by the seafarers, who grappled daily with a hostile environment and had mastered demanding skills, but these city dwellers seemed to him detached from some of the sterner aspects of reality.

The woman was something else. She was strange, but she didn't frighten easily. Her manner with people was arrogant but somehow not rude or discourteous, as if in tacit recognition of a natural relationship between her aristocratic self and the rest of the world, her natural inferiors. Her beauty was of a sort totally alien to him, and for that fact all the more compelling. He had always thought of feminine beauty in terms of the tall, long-limbed, fair-haired women of his people, with their coppery skins and blue eyes. This woman's tiny but lush figure, her abundant black hair and strange, dark, slanting eyes, her pale gold complexion, these were all features he would never have associated with beauty. Yet he found himself to be transfixed with admiration. It did his young male vanity no harm to know that the most famed woman of this immense city took so much interest in him as well. If the other men he had seen here were any indication, it was hardly surprising.

"Why are you taking me with you?" he asked.

"Partly from gratitude," she said. "You did me some service, and now I would be of some aid to you. If you just wander about the city, you will either end up in the army or become a drunk like all the other barbarians. I think I may have some employment for you that will make better use of your qualities."

This sounded interesting. "What might that be?"

"I must speak with some people. I can make no promises now." And she would say no more.

The palace sprawled over an entire hilltop in the southeast quarter of the city. Its grounds were surrounded by a high wall which they entered through a ponderous wooden gate guarded by low-browed men who carried knotty-headed wooden clubs. From the gate paved path ascended through an artificial forest, across a bridge spanning a stream and past ponds in which huge, strange fish swam solemnly, as obese as the eunuch priests.

The palace itself was a formless building, its wings scattering from a rectangular central structure, with low towers protruding here and there and some wings seemingly abandoned and fallen into ruin. They arrived at the main structure in time to take refuge from the long-impending storm, which finally broke in gusty winds and flashes of lightning seconds before the deluge began. In the trees that grew every ten paces along the approach to the palace, Hael could hear the screams of man-of-the-trees, their voices subtly different from those of his island.

Shazad descended from her litter and dashed up the steps to the covered portico as the first drops began to fall. Seconds later, the rain was coming down full force as slaves and attendants scattered for shelter. Hael watched with bemusement as two near-naked slave girls rushed forward with towels to blot up the few drops that had splattered Shazad. She paid them no heed, as if they were a part of the air she breathed. A tiny, spotted cat padded from the entrance and rubbed against her legs, and Shazad stooped to pick it up and stroke it, making absurd baby-talk to the purring creature. It seemed odd to Hael that she could ignore two beautiful young girls, yet fuss over an animal of doubtful utility. It increased his sense of being in an alien world.

He followed the woman into an atrium floored with polished marble, its walls ablaze with colored mosaics. One wall depicted an underwater scene. On another, figures that were part human, part animal enacted the scenes of a complicated myth. Above a small central pool, a rectangular opening in the roof admitted the rain. On a pedestal in the pool stood a serene statue of a nude woman, possibly a goddess, realistic to the smallest detail but unearthly in its beauty.

They passed on into another room, this one illuminated by panes of clear glass set into its roof, presently mottled by rain. "Wait here," Shazad said as she disappeared further into the palace's interior, still carrying her cat and trailed by her slave girls.

Nonplussed at this dismissal, Hael studied the room. Its walls were decorated with battle scenes and atop small wooden chests stood man-shaped frames bearing armor and helmets. A stand of swords was next to a circular rack of spears. Shields hung from one wall like decorative medallions. The armor was made in a variety of styles, mostly of laced splints, finely lacquered, but one cuirass was of beaten bronze. A few were covered with thin leather dyed and stencilled in elegant designs. All of it was beautiful, much finer than the soldiers' armor he had seen, but none of it looked any more comfortable.

All the battle scenes emphasized champions dueling in the foreground. The armies were mere, vague shapes in the background. Below some of the figures ran lines of what Hael could recognize as letters, which he assumed identified the combatants. Most interesting to him were the scenes depicting men fighting from the backs of animals. He was curious how this might be done. As a child, he had ridden on the backs of quil and kagga like the other children, but the idea of grown men not only riding animals but actually fighting from so precarious a position seemed wonderful to him.

The swords were mostly elaborate, expensive weapons like his own, but the spears were simple weapons, just long wooden shafts with points containing no more metal than a dagger. From this he deduced that the swords were carried by warrior aristocrats, while the spears were probably for arming common soldiers, perhaps the guards or serving men of this palace.

The drumming of rain on the skylights ceased and a sudden burst of sunlight washed across the tessellated floor. From its angle he knew that he had been in the palace for more than an hour. He wondered whether he should leave. Surely he had stayed as long as courtesy would dictate. Probably the woman had forgotten him. He wanted to know her better, she was quite unlike anything he had ever encountered before. But he had no taste for being ignored, as he had seen her ignore her slaves. He was about to leave when a voice from the interior doorway stopped him.

"I see you have a taste for warrior accoutrements." Hael turned and saw the speaker was a man as tall as himself, powerfully built, but at least thirty years older. He wore an ankle-length robe of a shiny material Hael had never seen before. Thrust into his sash was a sheathed dagger with a handle of carved coral.

"I am a warrior," Hael acknowledged. He rapped a cuirass with his knuckles. "But I've always fought in my own skin, not a turtle's."

The man smiled, the expression slightly twisted by a scar that ran from one corner of his mouth down into his graying beard. "You'd soon learn the virtue of it if you ever fought in a battle of armies. Fighting in close formation robs you of individual mobility, as does mounted fighting. And when arrows come in storms, you can't keep an eye on them all." He crossed to the elaborate bronze cuirass and stroked its surface, ran his fingers through the bronze helmet's scarlet-dyed plumes. "This armor has saved my life in many a fray. A commander has even less attention to spare for flying missiles than a foot soldier." It came as no surprise to Hael that this was a man of importance.

"And yet these pictures"—Hael waved toward the wall decorations—"show warriors fighting man to man, just as they do on my home island."

"Those are scenes from old stories," the tall man said, gazing fondly at them. "They are my ancestors. To hear the old poems, all the battles were decided by duelling champions. That is no longer true, if indeed it ever was. Fights like that sometimes happen in the confusion of battle, but the battles themselves are decided by the armies. Victory goes to the larger army, or to the better led."

"I am not sure such fighting would suit me," Hael said. "How could a man distinguish himself?"

"Wars are not fought for the benefit of soldiers, although a man of bravery, talent, and skill will make himself known. But it is probably true that you would be wasted carrying a spear in the army." The man stepped closer and his narrow eyes widened very slightly. "Why, you are no more than a boy!"

Hael bristled and he gestured with his spear. "I am not considered so in my homeland."

The man held out a hand. "Peace, my friend. I know you are a warrior, but things are judged differently here. When my daughter spoke of your deed this morning, I expected an older man, and indeed your bearing makes you seem such, yet you cannot be more than seventeen."

"I am glad she thinks I was of service to her," Hael said, "but I would never have thought quieting a fractious kagga to be the act of a hero."

The older man laughed. "Nonetheless, the danger was there and your act kept it comical when it might have turned serious. My daughter is small, young and unused to half-tamed livestock. A kagga's horn can kill, and its hoofs can shatter bone. I am grateful."

Hael was impressed by the man's graceful manner. It struck him that this must be the Councilor Pashir, a man of great stature, perhaps second only to the king himself. Yet he stood here and spoke familiarly with a barbarian youth of surpassing unimportance in this great city. He reminded himself not to take this affability at face value, remembering that Gasam had also cultivated an ingratiating manner.

"I confess," Hael said, "that I don't understand why your daughter brought me here. What I did was little enough, and I wasn't looking for reward. Perhaps I should go."

"No, stay. You seem to be a promising young warrior, and you are at loose ends in this city. It may be that I have employment for you. It will involve travel and no little danger, and a possibility of great profit, just the thing, I believe, for one of your mettle."

This sounded intriguing. Before he could ask what the nature of this employment might be, Pashir held out a hand and his fingers snapped loudly. At the signal, a man dressed in a brief kilt of yellow cloth padded into the room on bare feet. He said nothing but stood waiting as if that were all he was designed to do.

"We will speak further of this at dinner. I must attend at the royal residence now. This one will show you to a room I have put at your disposal. If you will consent to be my guest for a few days, I think you will not regret it."

This was precipitate, but Hael knew better than to pass up such an opportunity, now that it was so clearly stated. "I accept, with gratitude."

"The gratitude is mine. Until this evening, then." The man swept from the room, and only then did Hael realize that the Councilor had not asked his name, nor spoken his own. The ways of the mighty were indeed strange.

"If you will come this way," the slave murmured. Hael followed him from the room into a long, featureless corridor.

"What is your name?" he asked the slave.

The man looked back at him with mild surprise.

"Name? I'm number three of the seventh squad, main house, day shift."

"But don't you have a *name*?"

The man shrugged. "Nothing that would interest a freeman."

They came to a small, square courtyard. Rooms opened off its perimeter and they entered one. It was small compared to the great chambers Hael had just seen, but was still larger than any village hut. There were chairs and a table, and what, after a moment, he recognized as a bed, of carved wood covered by plush cushion. The walls were decorated in abstract patterns.

The slave pointed to a door in the wall opposite the courtyard. "There is a privy down this hallway to the left, and a guest bath to the right. You have freedom of the palace, save those places where door guards will not admit you. Do you wish to eat?"

Suddenly Hael realized that he was famished. Much had happened since leaving the ship that morning, but eating had not been among the happenings. "I do." Before the man could dash off, Hael asked something that had been bothering him. "Tell me; why are you a slave?"

The slave looked at him as if he were insane. "Why? Because I had no choice, of course." Then he was gone.

The answer made little sense to Hael. A man could always choose death instead. Or perhaps all the ones he had seen here were born to be slaves?

He stood before the one open wall of his room, where, in the courtyard, played one of the inevitable fountains. There were thick drapes to close the room off at will. Around the fountain were planted an abundance of flowers, now all abuzz with bees. The recent rain steamed on the flagstones.

Sounds of music drew his attention and he crossed the courtyard. Through the drawn-aside curtain of a room like this, he saw a woman seated on a floor cushion, playing a harp. Around her waist she wore a string of large pearls, and rich bands of gold and strings of gems adorned her neck, arms and ankles, but she wore nothing else, and the heavy copper collar proclaimed her a slave. The whiteness of her skin astonished him, in stark contrast to the rich blackness of her hair, and he wondered what strange part of the world had been her home. He heard a sound of low voices from within the room but could not see who spoke. He backed away, not wishing to intrude. The woman watched him with cool gray eyes, but her fingers plucked the strings automatically, as if controlled by a will other than her own.

He retreated to his room and explored the facilities the slave had indicated. The bath was a small, beautifully tiled room with a sunken basin in its floor. Scented water swirled lazily to an unseen current. This he had to try. Removing his swordbelt and his skimpy garments, he descended the few steps into the tub. His astonishment was great, as he had never bathed in hot water before. He found the sensation inexpressibly sensual, made the more so by a thin film of scented oil that dotted the surface. The current was supplied by hidden jets in the sides of the tub. He had a feeling that he could grow accustomed to living like this.

He returned to his room to find the table set with platters of bread, fruit and cold roast poultry, and a beaker of chilled wine. Despite his hunger he ate slowly and carefully from long habit. He wondered how the people here would react to a bowl of mingled milk and blood. With disgust, probably, although that still seemed strange to him. The subtle seasonings of the food were another new experience. The poultry was honeyglazed. The bread was fragrant with tiny seeds and saffron, a seasoning Malk had shown him, one highly valued in Neva.

His meal finished, Hael found himself with several hours free before the evening meal and, possibly, knowledge of his future course. The slave had said he had freedom of the palace, so he decided to do some exploring, since he would not be wandering about the city for a while.

He quickly wearied of the lavish furnishings and decor of the palace, and wondered what else there might be to see. Slaves went about their business silently, while the free staff strode importantly about and paid him no heed. A wall painting of a procession of mounted men reminded him of his curiosity about these strange animals, and he asked a guard if there were any on the estate. The man gave him directions to something called the stables and Hael left the building. He emerged onto a back terrace from which he could see that the estate almost abutted the city wall on this side. From the terrace a stair descended a slope planted with fruit trees, and at the foot of the stair began a meadow that extended almost to the city wall. To one side stood a series of low buildings and pens from which came the unmistakable sounds and smells of a livestock enclosure.

It felt good to feel living earth beneath his bare

feet again, and Hael savored the sensation as he
sauntered to the nearest fence. Within a small enclosure, near a post, stood a little group of men.
They wore short, leather trousers and little else,
but none had a slave ring on his neck. They were
dusty and short-haired, and looked very business-
like. An odd arrangement of leather straps and
pads lay on the ground by them. Someone called
to them and an animal was led from a nearby
building into the enclosure.

Hael looked to see what drew their attention
and he gasped at the sight. Two men led a pranc-
ing beast by a pair of lines attached somehow to
its mouth. It was the most beautiful animal he had
ever seen, its beauty not in its color or patterning,
for it was plain brown, but in its splendid proportions. Its legs were long and slender, yet they
looked as powerful as those of a longneck. Instead
of claws or split hoofs, it had a single hoof to each
foot. Hael had never seen a single-hoofed animal
before. Its body tapered from a massive chest to
narrow loins, then flared into powerful haunches
decorated with a long, flowing, glossy tail.

Its high-arched neck supported a long, narrow
head with small ears and large, intelligent eyes. A
short, stiff mane crested the neck and a beard dangled beneath the chin. Its horns were short, curling backward almost into full circles. As it came
closer he saw that the controlling straps were attached to rings that passed through the animal's
pierced lower lip.

Although its beauty was extreme, that was not
the only cause of emotion that Hael felt upon be-
holding it. The animal radiated a spiritual force
so powerful that Hael was momentarily stunned.

Not even from the longneck had he felt such an aura. So total was his enthrallment that he did not hear the footsteps approaching from behind.

"You found our paddock quickly, I see." Even though the voice was Shazad's, it took an effort of will to tear his gaze from the animal and turn it upon her.

"I've never seen anything so beautiful. Is this a cabo?"

"It is. You've never seen one before? I can believe it. A woman could be made very happy if you were to look at her the way you were looking at that cabo just now." She had changed clothes and now wore short leather trousers like the men, save that hers were drawn tight at the knees above high boots of supple leather that laced up the sides of her calves. Above, she wore a shirt of the shiny material, a spotless white. Its sleeves were billowy.

"Can it be true that a beast of such pride and nobility would allow humans to ride on its back, to do their bidding?"

"Not easily," she said. "First they must be tamed. This one is no more than half tame. He is Moonfire, a purebred of one of the oldest bloodlines. These animals are used only for hunting or war, or sometimes for racing. They are too high-spirited for anything else. There are lesser breeds for everyday riding, although only the wealthy can afford to keep them."

"Why are there so few? I would think they would be bred like kagga, and everyone would have them."

"Breeding cabos is a long, expensive process. The ancestral stock was far smaller in stature, and each generation must be carefully matched to keep their size up, lest they degenerate. In centuries past, they were used to pull chariots, because they were still too small to ride. Only in the last three or four hundred years have they been practical to use as riding beasts. The young are borne singly, some must be cast off as unfit, and the training process is lengthy. It is not something for the common people." She shouted at the handlers in the pen. "Saddle him."

Hael watched enthralled as the two leaders held the animal by its mouth-straps while the other four picked up the mass of leather and wood and cloth from the ground. Acting smoothly, for they were a well-drilled team, one threw a folded blanket across the cabo's back while two others placed atop the blanket a complicated framework and buckled its straps beneath the cabo's belly. Another snapped a pair of chain-ended leather lines to the lip-rings. In no more than ten seconds, the process was done.

"Ready, mistress," said one, knuckling his forehead. "But he is fractious today. Let me ride the roughness off him before you mount."

"Do so," she said. Then, to Hael: "I've been dumped to the ground once today, and I want no more."

The handler gripped the top of the leather-covered framework and put one foot in a wooden loop that dangled on a strap down the cabo's side. Using this as a step, he swung a leg over the cabo's back and was seated atop it. He took the shorter, chain-ended lines in his hand and the longer lines were freed. At his signal, the others backed way.

The cabo had been squirming and fidgeting, but now it burst into violent action, bucking and rearing, its hindquarters twisting as its forelegs came down stiffly and repeatedly. After a few moments of this, the handler lost his seat and went flying over the beast's neck. He landed loosely and expertly and was up immediately.

"This is not a good day to ride Moonfire, my lady," he said. "Perhaps tomorrow he will be in a better mood."

"How disappointing." She pouted, making her face appear ten years younger.

"I want to try it!" Hael said, impulsively. Indeed, he had never wanted anything so much in his life.

The handlers laughed. "There are some old, gentle geldings in the barn, lad," called one. "Perhaps her ladyship will let you ride one of those."

She turned and truly looked at him, all over, for the first time. For a long, tense moment she said nothing, then. "All right."

The man who had ridden strode up to her. "My lady, you must be joking. Anyone can see this one has never ridden."

Something strange and perverse entered her look and she smiled. "I want it."

The handler looked decidedly uncomfortable. "My lady, Moonfire is a half-tamed and dangerous animal. It might be good sport to see this naked savage thrown, but if Moonfire kills even one man, he could be ruined for life."

She lost her smile and the corners of her mouth began to quiver strangely. "Do not argue with me," she said in a near monotone. "Just because you are a freeman doesn't mean I can't have the hide flogged off your back."

He bowed and touched his forehead with the knuckles of one hard-callused hand. "As you wish, my lady." He turned to Hael. "Come with me, boy."

Hael was too excited to take offense. He stuck his spear in the ground and hung his sword from a post before vaulting over the fence. The other handlers had the animal under control again, holding it still by tension on the lip-rings. Still, it quivered and its eyes rolled.

"Never ridden before, eh?"

"This is the first cabo I've ever seen," Hael admitted.

"Well, there are worse ways to die. Under the lash, for instance. If you'd prefer to live, try not to tense up when he throws you. It hurts far worse if you do. Fall loose and if you can't get up right away, try to roll toward the fence. We'll try to keep him from trampling you to death." By this time they were standing by the cabo and the handler pointed at the wooden loop. "This is a stirrup. You put your foot into it and haul yourself onto this," he slapped the leather-covered frame, "the saddle."

"Just a moment," Hael said. "We must get to know one another first." He reached up and touched the animal's brow, slowly drawing his hand down to its muzzle. The sense of its spirit was so thick around him it was like a scent in his nostrils or a taste in his mouth.

"Careful," said one of the holders, "they bite." But the animal began to quiet down, and its trembling slowed, then ceased; the shimmering of its spirit changed as well. Repeatedly, Hael stroked its head, and soon the cabo tried to nuzzle his palm with its nose.

"I will mount now," Hael said. A handler held the stirrup and he stepped into it and reached up. The rider showed him how to put both hands at the front of the saddle and with a long flexion of his leg he swung up and across and then he was seated, his other foot in the stirrup on the far side. The leather controlling straps were put in his left hand. He had never felt such a sensation, elevated above other men with a powerful beast beneath him. He could feel its lungs working between his knees.

"You sit well, for a beginner," said the head handler. "Get your heels down. That's better. Those straps in your hand are reins. When you want him to turn, you pull in that direction, and you press with your knee on the opposite side. If he were trained, rein pressure on the neck and knee pressure would be enough. As it is—" He shrugged. "As it is, you won't be up there long enough to worry about it. If you want him to go forward, touch his sides with your heels. It's worth a try."

"I'm ready," Hael said, his heart racing.

The lead straps were unsnapped from the lip-rings and the handlers stood back. Their broad grins turned to looks of consternation when Moonfire failed to burst into violent action. Instead, he pranced excitedly, as if eager to run, but he showed no resentment of being ridden.

Cautiously, Hael touched the animal's ribs with his heels. The cabo trotted forward. He bounced uncomfortably on the saddle but he remembered to rein the animal to the right to keep it from running into the fence.

"Loosen your back and knees," the head trainer called out to him. Hael did so and soon adjusted himself to the animal's motion. All through him he could feel the animal's spirit, and he knew that it wanted to run.

"Open the gate!" he shouted. The handlers milled about looking puzzled.

"Do it!" Shazad ordered. Bars were drawn aside and the heavy gate swung open.

Without thinking, knowing instinctively what to do, Hael let the reins relax and he leaned forward slightly. Moonfire was out through the gate with a bound and running across the meadow at a full gallop. Hael was amazed at the way the animal's movement smoothed out at this gait, and the two of them were moving as one. He could feel its exultation as it did what it was made for. The sensation was as new as going to sea had been, but it was far more enthralling. It was partnership, power and mastery all in one. The cabo responded to his slightest wish almost without his needing to use rein or knee pressure.

He felt the great muscles working between his legs and he realized that this animal was so high-spirited that it would run until its heart broke, had he wished it. Gradually, he straightened up and the animal slowed by increments until it was trotting again. He leaned back, giving the reins a faint tug, and the cabo stopped. He pressed with a knee and the animal spun in place, making a complete circle. He tried the other knee and it reversed direction. He wondered why these people made such a mystery out of something so simple.

Of course, he thought, they might be so spirit-dead from living in cities that they could establish only physical dominance over their cabos.

He nudged Moonfire into a trot and returned to the enclosure, where the handlers stood with mouths agape. The head handler scowled at him. "Why did you say you had never ridden?"

"Because it was true," Hael said. He kicked a leg free and slid to the ground. He winced at a slight soreness in his thighs and backside. Apparently riding, like seafaring, was not without its initial discomforts. He patted Moonfire a last time as the handlers were reattaching the straps to his lip-rings. He began to snort and twist once more.

Shazad's eyes danced as he climbed the fence. "You are a man full of surprises."

"You surprise me as well," he said, resuming his sword and spear. "But then, I had no idea what to expect of you. This is my first day in a great city, and I've never met any sort of noblewoman or priestess. Things were different in my homeland."

"You seem to adjust quickly."

"I have to. I am an exile, and I can't convert the rest of the world to the life I grew up with."

"That is very wise. You'd be amazed at how many people try to do exactly that." She looked back into the pen, where another cabo was being led out, this one far calmer and more docile. "Well, I still must get in my riding for today. I will see you at this evening's dinner, and perhaps after that we may find time to talk." She turned away with her usual abrupt dismissal. Hael vowed inwardly that the day would come when she would not dare act thus with him.

As he returned to his room, though, there was little place in his mind for Shazad's arrogance. He was still excited over this new experience of riding a cabo. Never had he dreamed that anything could be so enthralling. Most of all, he thought of ways that these marvelous animals might be employed. What had Shazad said? That they were used only for fighting, hunting and racing? It was plain to him that the aristocrats here merely wanted to keep the animals to themselves. And he wondered about the ones culled out as "unfit." Unfit for what?

Apparently the aristocrats did no work themselves, and it never occurred to them to use their cabos for anything except their own pastimes of war and sport. But Hael thought of what such an animal could mean to herdsmen. Mounted, a very few men could control immense herds. He remembered the long, arduous trek his tribe had made from one pasture to another, going only as fast as the slowest member of the tribe. What a difference it would make if the people were mounted, using pack animals for all their belongings. Their mobility would be infinite, their mastery of the grasslands total. This would bear much thought.

He found his way back to his quarters and washed the dust from his body. When he returned from the bath, he found new clothes laid out for him; a tunic of the shiny cloth, a jewelled belt, sandals of finely worked leather. He began to put them on, then stopped. Were these people showing him courtesy, or merely trying to make him one of them? Not even one of them, but a poor imitation of them? He tossed the clothes back onto his bed and retained his hard-won pelt of night-cat fur. He did not wish to insult them, but he had no intention of discarding his pride either.

The sun was low when a slave came to summon him. This one was a woman with very dark skin, like the hunters of his island, but her coarse hair was reddish. He picked up his sword and spear.

"That will not be necessary, master," the woman said, eyes downcast.

"It is to a warrior," he said, following her from the room.

The dining room was illumined by oil wicks burning in globes of blown glass. The guests turned and their eyes widened at sight of Hael's barbaric attire. Pashir was already seated at the head of the long table, and he gestured toward a vacant place. A slave stood behind each seat, and Hael handed his weapons to the attendant as he sat. Shazad was seated across from him, her eyes glittering with amusement. There was also something malicious in her expression, which he did not fail to notice.

Pashir introduced him to the others. There was a merchant named Shong, a hard-bitten man with a weathered face. Next to Shazad sat Marakh, the ambassador from Omia, a nation to the northeast. Next to Hael sat Marakh's wife, Meletta. She was a woman of great beauty but her face was dissolute. Above her complicated bodice her breasts bulged so that dark half-circles of her nipples showed. She was already well into the wine.

The introductions over, Pashir said, "My daughter tells me a very strange tale of happenings at the paddock this afternoon, young man. So strange that I would not credit if from another source."

"Oh, I must hear of this," Meletta said, smiling

at Hael, giving him a look of such evaluation that he wondered that her husband didn't take offense. That gentleman, however, merely looked bored.

"It was *most* enthralling," Shazad said. Breathily, and with many embellishments, she described Hael's easy mastery of the half-tamed Moonfire, despite his inexperience.

"It took me many long, painful lessons to learn to ride," said Pashir at the end of the recitation. "Can it be true that you never saw a cabo before today?"

"It is true, but my people are herdsmen, and I have handled animals all my life. Perhaps the cabo could sense that." Even though he was cast out from his people, Hael still did not like to talk of spirit matters to strangers.

"Amazing," Pashir said. As the first course was brought in he steered the conversation to an expedition being mounted by Shong. It seemed that the man was a sort of merchant-adventurer, who opened new territory for Nevan commercial exploitation. While his immediate motive was profit, such ventures were expensive, and were partially underwritten by the king, since any intelligence thus gathered was of value, even should the expedition prove commercially fruitless.

"What course do you plan to take?" Pashir asked him.

"Northeast, through Omia and across the mountains, then up into the high plains country of the Dakos. That is unexplored territory; only trappers and hunters have seen it. It could be rich."

"Or it could be wasteland," Shazad pointed out.

"Whichever," her father said, "it would be good to know. His Majesty King Oland of Omia has graciously granted permission for our expedition to cross his nation and to return the same way."

Marakh smiled professionally. "And most happy he was to grant such permission, as peaceful and prosperous relations between our two nations are ever uppermost in his mind."

Hael suspected that far more than good will lay behind much of this hearty cooperation. His people were not so primitive that he had no knowledge of false smiles and insincere words, although it seemed to him that these people assumed he was too innocent to see through them. If so, that was an advantage he could well need in this strange place.

"Hael," Pashir said, "I spoke earlier of a place for you in a project suited to a man of your adventurous spirit. How does this sound to you? Would you like a place on Merchant Shong's expedition? An experienced warrior is always an asset on such, and one who has your way with animals might be doubly valuable. And you may be of special use to me."

"It sounds interesting indeed," Hael said. "How might I be of special use to you?"

"You would render me a full report upon your return. Different men see different things. Our esteemed Shong, for instance, is a merchant of rare vision. By your return, he will know everything about trade goods, both what the local people have to trade with us, and what they desire from us in return. He will know all about the local merchants, and the rules and tariffs, should you encounter organized states, and the factors or officials we must deal with in the future. There will be a royal map-maker on the expedition, and there may be an herbalist as well, to find medicinal herbs or rare plants of other value, and possibly a master miner who may locate minerals of which the local people know nothing. You, I think, may learn valuable things about the wildlife of the lands you pass through, and perhaps of the customs of local peoples, a thing we tend to neglect to our later regret."

This sounded eminently reasonable to Hael. "How are these expeditions conducted?" Hael asked.

"Starting from here," Shong said, "we load nusks with the sort of trade goods we usually find a demand for inland. On the way, we may encounter desert, in which case we will have to trade the nusks for humpers. If the terrain is such that animals cannot be used, as in the jungles down near the Cape, we may have to hire local bearers. Always we look for rivers flowing in the right direction. Traveling by river is easier and can save much time. I do not anticipate much of that this trip, unless it be returning. By all reports, you must go far, far inland before you encounter rivers that flow eastward."

"Does everyone travel on foot?" Hael wanted to know.

"The drovers do, and most of the guards," Shong said. "The leaders may ride, if they have animals."

Hael looked at Pashir. "As your special emissary, would I have a cabo to ride?"

Pashir smiled widely and, it seemed, honestly. "Somehow I knew you would ask that. Yes, I think something can be arranged. I will see to your outfitting. Believe me, you will need more than a

spear and a sword. Not such a high-blooded creature as Moonfire, but we have some geldings in
the stables that are past their hunting and fighting
days. No one uses a blooded war-cabo as mere
transportation."

Hael's heart leapt. He longed to ride Moonfire
again, but that would be far too much to expect.
But to have *any* cabo for his own sounded glorious. "How can I refuse so generous an offer? Of
course, I accept. When do we leave?"

"In eight or nine days' time," Shong said. "The
mountain passes will be blocked with snow when
we get there, and we will winter at the foot of the
mountains, to be through the passes as soon as
they become clear and, it is to be hoped, back
through them before the snows fall again."

"Then," Hael said to Pashir, "with your permission, Councilor, I would like to attend your stables in the meantime, to learn the care of these
animals."

Meletta smiled into her wine glass. "Spoken like
a true herdsman."

"I would hope so," Hael said. "In my homeland,
there is no nobler calling." The woman reddened,
but everybody else seemed pleased by his answer, even her husband.

"Of course," said Pashir. "My men shall give you
every assistance. Every man of merit should know
the care of cabos." As the next courses were
served, the conversation fell to small talk about
the eccentricities of those nobles whose love for
cabos was carried to extremes, including a prince
of royal blood who insisted on cleaning his own
stables. Another, who had inherited enormous es-

tates, took his greatest pride in the invention of a superior currycomb.

As the dinner broke up, Pashir saw his guests off with gifts and fine, effusive words, then he took Hael to one side.

"A moment before you retire, my friend," the Councilor said. "Hael, you are a most remarkable young man. I do not say this as flattery."

"I believe you," Hael said. "Such a man as you has little need to flatter an outland nobody like me."

"It is good that you appreciate that. Your deed this morning when you came to my daughter's rescue was fine, but I expected a competent countryman to whom I could give a small but honorable reward. When I met you, I realized that you were different. Your very strange behavior at the stables this afternoon reinforced that judgment. Tonight you conducted yourself well in company that would have awed many a man far higher in station than you, and I mean no offense by that."

"I take none," Hael assured him.

"Especially your handling of that slut Meletta. Well, that's another story." They walked out onto a terrace where guards stood by smoking braziers and popped to attention as the master arrived. "And don't think that I missed your gesture of wearing your tribal clothing to a formal dinner. The others may have attributed it to ignorance, but not I."

"I meant no—"

"I realize that," Pashir cut him off, "but there is more I wish to say. You have great gifts, my boy, but do not think that these will sustain you forever in the higher circles. I had a reason for wishing to place you with Shong's expedition. It was to get you out of Kasin as soon as possible. Does that astonish you?"

Hael felt himself out of his depth. "Well, I—" He cursed his hesitancy, but Pashir seemed to expect it.

"Quite so. You are rising swiftly here. Your fall would be as precipitate. Intelligence is not enough, nor is courage, nor ability. Experience is what counts in these matters, and you lack it. This place eats up young men of talent. Go out with Shong's expedition, and gain experience with a wide range of peoples. Gain some years and some maturity, and then come back. If you live, I think that it will then be time to consider you for real advancement."

Hael was unsure what to say. This man seemed to be sincere, but how was he to know? The man was certainly correct about Hael's lack of experience among the great and near-great of the cities. Taking a somewhat confused leave of his host, Hael began to make his way back to his quarters. It had been a long and extremely eventful day, but it was not yet over.

Waiting by the entrance to his room was another slave, this one a woman of the same black-haired, white-skinned race as the one he had seen harping earlier. "The lady Shazad wishes to see you, master," she said. Like the others, she kept her eyes downcast while speaking. When she raised them, they were gray.

"Then lead me," he replied. His weariness vanished with the resilience of youth and the excitement roused by the prospect of seeing Shazad privately. He reminded himself not to relax his vigilance, remembering the last time a woman had lured him to a private meeting.

The halls and courtyards were illuminated by candles and oil lamps. There were slaves whose sole task seemed to be keeping the wicks trimmed and the oil basins filled. Incense burned in braziers to perfume the air and ward off night-flying insects.

The slave woman left him in a room glimmering with dozens of candle flames. It was at least ten times the size of the room he had been given, its walls hung with richly worked fabrics and its floor nearly invisible beneath a scattering of pillows and low tables.

A complicated sculpture drew his attention. It was perhaps one-fourth life size, and he studied the tangle of entwined limbs for some time before he realised that it represented a man and woman locked in carnal embrace, their faces contorted by what might have been ecstasy or rage.

"The god Palumwa and the goddess Rheone creating the universe," Shazad said. Hael turned to see her standing in a doorway. She had changed clothing yet again and now wore a gown so sheer that the candlelight behind her turned it to little more than mist. "The act of procreation is performed among gods as among humans, you see."

He glanced at the statue. "Except that gods seem to be more flexible than humans."

"Ah, but they are not!" she said, smiling. "That is a position practiced by the sect of Palumwa and Rheone, although it takes much practice and usually more than two people to accomplish."

"I thought you were a priestess of the storm god."

"That is because of my father's position." She came into the room. No longer backlighted, her thin garment became semi-transparent, briefly revealing darkness at the tips of her breasts and the base of her belly as it brushed those areas. It was tantalizing, and obviously intended to be so. "As the most socially prominent lady allowed to appear in public, I am priestess of a number of the civic cults."

"Including this one," he gestured to the statue.

"Oh, no. That sect is forbidden in most places." Her tone was one of regret. "Couplings like this are among the mildest of their rites."

"I had heard," Hael said uneasily, "that there were gods whose rites were forbidden in the great cities."

"Many," she agreed. "Probably just as well. Most ordinary people lack the strength to cope with occult things. Besides, there is a special thrill in doing that which is forbidden." Her eyes glowed strangely.

"I did that which was forbidden, once," Hael said. "I was lucky to be merely exiled instead of being slain."

"Tell me about it," she said, barely whispering. She stood so close he could feel the heat from her body.

"It would mean nothing to you," he said, having to force the words past a sudden constriction in his throat. He felt there had been enough talk. He put his hands to her waist, just above the swell of her hips, and pulled her to him. She was so tiny that the tips of his fingers almost met in the crease of her back, his thumbs over the indentation of her navel. Her arms slid over his shoulders and she pulled his mouth down to hers.

Their tongues entwined and he felt a great surge of power flooding his loins, a feeling as consuming as his mastery of the cabo had been.

She broke away for a moment, her breath coming in hard pants. With trembling fingers, she fumbled at shoulder-clasps and the thin gown drifted to the floor. He had only seconds to admire the miniature perfection of her body before she tugged urgently at the thong supporting his pelt of night-cat skin. Impatiently, she made little whining sounds as she tugged it downward, freeing his arousal. He pulled her to him and kissed her hardened nipples as she slid her hand along his erection, from tip to base and back again.

Her arms went around his neck again. "Lift me," she whispered, her voice shuddering. Slowly, his hands beneath her arms, he raised her, marveling at the softness of her skin as she slid up his hairless belly and chest. Her legs wrapped around his hips and she released his neck with one hand, reaching beneath herself, taking his manhood once again and positioning him at the juncture of her thighs, then let her weight fall, impaling herself with a cry she might have made in dying.

His hands cupped her buttocks as they churned powerfully. She breathed into his mouth and an intoxicating scent rose from the juncture of their bodies. Her motions never slowed as he walked to a pile of cushions and dropped to his knees. The motion drove him violently deeper into her, and her head snapped back, her eyes squeezed tightly shut and mouth agape, its corners drawn almost grotesquely downward as she screamed in pleasure-pain.

Hael fell forward onto her, needing to subdue her, almost mindless in his urgent drive for completion. She called out words in a language he did not understand, clawing at his back and buttocks, urging him ever more frantically as their bodies drove together again and again with wet, slapping sounds.

Finally, just when Hael was sure that he could stand no more, that he must die within seconds, she screamed something that sounded like the name of a god and she reached behind them where their bodies came together, ran her fingers along the base of him till she gripped and squeezed his balls. At this extra touch, the intense, shuddering ecstasy overwhelmed him, making him helpless for long seconds while all of his strength gathered, pooled at the base of his spine, then pumped into her with a force so powerful that he felt neither of them could survive it.

When he awoke, only a single, low-burning candle lit the room. She was gone, and it was as if she had never been there, save that her scent, animal-sharp, rose from his body. Weakly, drained, he fumbled for his clothing and weapons, then made his unsteady way back toward his quarters. He felt as if he had been consumed from within by a spirit that fed on youth and strength, leaving him a shell. And he longed to experience it again.

EIGHT

Hael vigorously brushed the cabo, careful to keep the direction of the strokes the same as the lie of the animal's hair. The cabo's coat was growing longer and coarser, preparing for the winter to come. He found the work to be pleasant, more so than tending kagga. Kagga were herd animals, and it was difficult to feel anything for a single kagga. Each cabo, he had discovered, had a distinct personality.

These gentle riding beasts lacked the ferocious heart of a young purebred like Moonfire, but they were still creatures of deep spirit, and in many ways he found them more familiar and congenial than the people of this city. Only a few of the cabo handlers felt anything like his rapport with the cabos, and those were all outlanders like himself, from primitive tribal peoples.

He was glad that they were soon to be leaving, but he was torn by it as well. The lure of far lands was strong, and so was his desire to get away, for the city and the palace now seemed a perilous place, full of hidden danger and smiling enemies. Every day, strangers found excuses to speak with him, always friendly, always steering the conversation toward his host and his host's daughter. Sometimes there were subtle hints that high rewards might be his should he find any interesting information about the pair and pass it along to his new friends. Inexperienced as he was, Hael had better sense than that. Always, he put them off with polite words. At a dockside tavern, he had spoken of this to Malk.

"By every god that is, boy, get away from that place!" the shipmaster had cried, his eyes wide with alarm.

"But who are these people?" Hael asked.

Malk held a hand before his face, fingers spread. As he made each point, he bent a finger down. "First, there are enemies of Lord Pashir, looking for any evidence of treason with which to denounce him. An intimate dinner with the Omian ambassador might have been a good opportunity for that. Second"—another finger went down—"agents of the king, keeping tabs on the Councilor on general principles. Third"—another finger—"Pashir's own servants, checking to see if you are a spy planted on him by his enemies, or, possibly, the king. It may have occurred to Pashir that it was an amazing coincidence that an expert kagga-handler was there just when her ladyship needed one; a temple servant sticks a thorn in its rump and the handsome young stranger leaps forth to save the day. It would have made *me* suspicious. You can bet that the temple servants who had charge of the sacrificial animals that day have been rigorously questioned."

"So many deceitful people to watch for?"

"Those are only the most obvious possibilities," Malk warned him. "These are only the people who have roused *your* suspicions, remember. Others will have been far more subtle. The slaves who clean your room, the stable hands, the guards who stand silent by the doors, never moving, all these could be spies, in any man's or woman's employ. Get away from there, Hael."

"As quickly as I can," Hael promised him, raising a cup of the heady sailor's beer.

He had decided to tell his friend nothing of Shazad. She was the only reason why he was not even more anxious to leave. Since arriving, he had spent every night with her, and the very thought of those nights set his knees trembling. She was no older than he, yet she had taught him things only an experienced courtesan far older should have known. Not only with her sex but with fingers, lips and tongue, and teaching him to use the same members, she had transformed their bodies into a single instrument of pleasure so exquisite that it could almost make suffering seem preferable.

Yet as great as was the pleasure she gave him, he felt almost as much fear. No matter how intense the bliss she could coax from their bodies, yet it was less an act of love than of ritual. In the moments when she seemed to go out of herself in sensual transport, she babbled in a strange tongue, its rhythm and cadence like that of a spell or prayer. Whether it was magic or some unholy religion, it was almost enough to unman Hael at the ultimate moment of their coupling. Almost, but not quite. The thought of giving up those incredible moments distressed him almost as much as the prospect of remaining in the city and in the palace.

He was grateful when a call distracted him from his upsetting thoughts.

"Hael! Come here!" It was Shong, the adventurer-merchant. He stood by the stable fence, impatience on his face as always. Hael patted his beast's shoulder and tossed his currycomb into a box of grooming instruments by the door. Walking out into the sunlight, he saluted his soon-to-be leader and, without conscious thought, picked up his spear from its place at the right of the doorway.

The corner of Shong's mouth quirked upward very slightly. "Wouldn't recognize you without that sticker." Hael already wore his sword belted, awkward as that sometimes was in the stables. Animals were important, but it was disgraceful for a warrior to be without his weapons.

"There are worse things to be known for," Hael said, thumbing the keen steel edge of the weapon lovingly.

He had confidence in Shong. The merchant had been doubtful of Hael at first, since it was no novelty to him to have a courtier, a remittance man or a ne'er-do-well son inflicted on his expeditions. Hael had taken pains to assure Shong that he was not only competent but outstanding when it came to fighting or handling animals, and the merchant had taken the extra effort of contacting Malk and grilling the shipmaster about the strange youth, making sure that he had not been planted on the expedition as a spy or an excuse to get rid of an embarrassing idiot in the family. Now the two were conditionally satisfied with each other. Actual performance on the expedition would cement or rupture their relationship.

"We leave at first light," Shong said. "Be at the Moon Gate with all your gear before the third opening gong sounds tomorrow. If you are not there, we leave and you may catch up or vanish as you see fit."

"I'll be there," Hael assured him.

"Good. If you will go back to your quarters, I am told that Lord Pashir has outfitted you rather handsomely."

Puzzled, Hael took his leave and went back up the hill to his quarters. In the courtyard before his room he found goods to stop his breath. There was a saddle of beautifully worked leather stretched over splendid wood. There were garments for all weathers and boots of surpassing workmanship and blankets of woven quil hair. There was a tent of heavy fabric, complete with cleverly jointed collapsing poles.

"Not many start out so well equipped," Shong said from behind him, having followed at a slower pace.

Hael wasn't sure how he felt. He had never had any feeling for posessions beyond his weapons. "How do I carry all this?"

"You'll have a nusk for your personal gear."

At Shong's suggestion, Hael arranged for servants to take his new goods to the expedition's assembly-camp near the gate. After taking his leave, Hael would spend the night there with the others. He sought Pashir, but the Councilor was at the royal residence, and likely to stay there for days.

When he had done all else he could do, Hael went to Shazad's apartments. He found her seated before a glass mirror, having her hair dressed by three of her women. The intricate coiffure required the services of all three. An elaborate gown stood on a mannequin near the women, complete with jewelery and odd ritual accoutrements.

"Good afternoon, Hael," she said absently, not taking her eyes from the mirror. "I'm rather preoccupied just now. I have to perform the first of the harvest rites this evening. The goddess is quite demanding in matters of dress and hair style. Could you come back tomorrow?"

"I won't be here tomorrow. The expedition leaves in the morning."

"Really? So soon? Well, you'll be back."

Hael was not naive enough to expect transports of grief from her, but he expected more than this. "How do you know that? I could die on the journey."

"That could happen, of course. But if you live, you'll come back to me." With a tiny brush, she applied cosmetics beneath her eyes.

"Are you so irresistible?" he demanded.

At last she looked at him, smiling. "Yes, I am. Besides, I have ensorcelled you. You are a person of destiny, and so am I. Our destinies are entwined, and there is nothing you can do about it. You will come back to me."

Her assurance was maddening. He could not tell whether she was serious or merely having sport with an unsophisticated, superstitious barbarian. And he always disliked it when she spoke thus in front of other people. Of course, to Shazad, they were not people at all, only slaves. With this thought he studied the three woman and saw that they looked at Shazad with undeniable fear.

Around them the city was silent. There was bustle in the camp, though, as handlers began to load the pack animals and kick dirt over the faint-glowing coals of the night's fires. The air was decidedly cool, a reminder that the hot days of summer were past, a foretaste of what they would soon encounter. It would never grow truly cold in this port, but the higher elevations where they were headed were different. There they would encounter true winter.

The first gong rang out when the guard atop the gate tower spied a band of paleness at the eastern horizon. The last of the packs were lashed down tight. A few minutes later the second gong sounded and there was a final tightening of cinches and straps, and those who were to ride mounted their cabos. The third gong rang when the captain of the gate could see the first milestone, looking like a white needle in the distance. Shong rode to the head of the column as the massive gates began to swing open, pushed by chanting slaves. Eagerly, Hael mounted and slid his spear into the long leather socket attached to his saddle behind his right leg. He was impatient to go, but no one would move until Shong gave the signal. The master rode a complete circuit around the column, seeing that all was in order. Satisfied, he rode to the head of the column once more. When the gates were fully open, he lifted his right arm and swung it forward. The handlers raised a loud chant for good luck and prodded their animals into motion.

Hael trotted his cabo toward the front, but did not try to pass Shong. He rode beneath the massive stone lintel of the gate and onto the plain outside. Waiting without were several trains like their own, arrived too late the night before to get in. There were many countrymen bringing produce and livestock to the city markets. Somewhere he could hear the music of a lone flute.

His feelings upon leaving the city were somewhat mixed, but the first breath he took outside the city walls carried the very taste of freedom. The whole wide mainland beckoned, and he was eager to see it all.

The cabo he rode was named Surefoot. It seemed to fit the animal, but Hael knew that cabos had no use for names and would never recognize those that men had given them. Surefoot was a steady and reliable creature, just what was needed for the long journey ahead.

The nusks that bore their burdens were larger than the island breed, with shaggy white manes covering their shoulders and necks. The handlers were a strange breed as well, dark-skinned men who wore white cloths wrapped from waist to knee, their ears laced with copper wire and their front teeth knocked out as part of a singularly brutal manhood ritual. He had been told that they were Kereels, and that their home was the land bordering the southeastern desert. He was also warned that they were a rough and villainous lot, and he could believe that. Their headman was a tall, wiry man named Agah. He was missing two fingers and part of one ear, and bore a great many scars.

The stone paving extended only to the first milestone, then they were on a road of hard-packed earth, which the daily rains of this season kept from becoming dusty. To each side of the road stretched wide grazing lands and close-planted farmlands. Stalks of grain nodded beneath the weight of nearly ripe ears awaiting harvest within a few days. Near every field Hael saw tiny shrines from which smoke rose. Looking for someone he might ask about this, he spied Choula, the royal map-maker.

"Those are shrines to the gods of air and rain, and to the storm god," the man answered. "What the planters will need desperately is a brief return of summer weather, about six days without rain so that they can get the harvest in and stored while it is dry. In some years much of the crop is lost to damp. Some have been ruined entirely. Of late, wet harvest times have been more numerous than in centuries past."

"Why should that be?" Hael asked. "If these things are controlled by the gods, shouldn't all these rituals and sacrifices be enough to ensure good weather?"

"So one would think, but gods may change their minds or their needs. It may be that, at some times, one god gains ascendency over another. Or"—he looked around to see who might be listening—"or it might be that the gods have little to do with this."

Hael scratched behind his cabo's ears and the animal snorted contentedly. "How is that?"

"Well." Choula looked around again. "You don't

see that fool Gilipas around, do you? He's in the college of priests and hates to hear doubting talk." Satisfied that Gilipas, who was to join the Nevan embassy to Omia, was nowhere within earshot, Choula continued. "Well, there are many of us who believe that much of the world is of little, if any, interest to the gods. They function by laws of their own that no amount of prayer or sacrifice will alter. See this." The map-maker took a piece of twig from his cabo's beard, held it up, then dropped it. "See?"

"It fell," Hael said, waiting for the point.

"Exactly. It fell. Things always fall if there's nothing to support them. The lightest bit of fluff, without a breeze to impel it, falls. It takes no god's will to make it so. This is a law of nature. Do you think that there is a god someplace who spends all his time sitting around and willing that things should fall? Nonsense!"

This was something that had never occurred to Hael. These things simply *were*. "So you think that the weather behaves according to laws as unalterable?"

"The weather and many other things. Most things, in fact, that are not directly controlled or altered by human action. One must be careful, of course, where one expresses such ideas. In a cosmopolitan city like Kasin, where many philosophers dwell, one may express oneself freely, within reason, although the priests complain. In the hinterlands, though, the people are so fearful of their gods that they kill disbelievers. Most dangerous are primitive towns where the power of the authorities rests on the supposed favor of the gods. In these places, you may be put to death with many imaginative embellishments for voicing doubts such as these."

"I will remember," Hael said. This business of the gods grew more complicated all the time. He asked about the cultivated land they were passing through, which was so different from the patchwork of tiny farms he had known on his island. He had found that Choula was a fount of such information. He was, indeed, as difficult to stop as a spring-fed fountain once he warmed to a subject.

"These are not your peasant-worked family farms," the map-maker expounded, "but plantations. A great landowner may hold an estate whose borders you could not ride around in two days. Some such plantations are worked by tenant farmers, others by gangs of slaves."

"Where do the slaves come from?" Hael wanted to know.

"Some are born slaves. Many others are captured in war. A great war means an abundance of cheap slaves thrown onto the market. At such times a man of enterprise may buy up the land of impoverished farmers and staff it with a great multitude of slaves. It is immensely profitable and productive."

"If you win the war," Hael amended.

Choula waved a hand dismissively. "No matter who wins, *somebody* will profit."

The countryside changed little during the first day. Just before sunset they made camp by a stream near a small village. Out of habit from his herding days, Hael rode to a low rise of ground and watched the camp being set up. Some of the others made sport of him for taking on sentry duty while they were still many days from the Nevan border, but he saw no reason not to establish a watchful routine early.

Besides, he felt a need to be alone, as he had been in the days when he had kept watch over his tribe's kagga. New knowledge was pouring into him at a tremendous rate, and he needed this time to sort through it, to understand it all and make firm his knowledge of the world. He felt that he had some strange destiny to achieve, and he would need all this wisdom in the future.

He was also grateful that the first part of the journey was being taken in easy stages to give men and animals a chance to become accustomed to travel and to caravan conditions. It was not that the routine was so strenuous. But the end of his first full day's travel in the saddle left Hael as sore as he had been after his circumcision rite, although in different areas. The more experienced riders derived great amusement from his discomfort, much as the sailors had at his seasickness. It seemed to be the way of the world, he mused, that those accustomed to any arduous activity took pleasure in the agony of a newcomer. He bore up under the pain stoically, reflecting that it was not the pain so much as the indignity of it that rankled. He picketed his cabo and rubbed it down, then tried not to let his stride wobble as he made his way to the first night's campfires.

By the fourth day of travel his discomfort was gone and they were near to the border of Neva. The land had risen slowly but steadily and the farms, once virtually continuous, were now widely scattered. It was hilly grassland, and besides large herds of kagga and other domestic animals they began to see increasing wildlife, animals rare near the larger cities.

At this time, Shong also enforced night watch and sentry discipline. This far from the capital, enforcement of royal law was spotty at best, and outlaw bands were not unusual. When they crossed the border, the danger would be far greater. Omia was not as centrally organized a nation as Neva, with many local lords and few army patrols. In that land, Hael fully expected to earn his keep with his warrior skills.

He had wondered how they were to eat on this trek, for the coarse meal and dried fruit they carried seemed like poor fare for men on an arduous journey. He need not have worried. At each encampment, local farmers and villagers came out to barter for their produce, so that there was an abundance of flesh and milk, of cheese and fresh fruit and greens. There was even fish from nearby streams and lakes. If there was a tavern nearby, sooner or later someone would arrive in a nusk-drawn cart with casks of wine and ale. They scarcely had to dip into their travel rations at all.

"This is not at all as bad as I had thought it would be," Hael said to Shong between bites at a juicy kagga rib.

The merchant smiled grimly. "Not now. This is fat, settled land, and this is the time of year when produce is the most abundant. Wait until we reach the mountains where men leave bloody footprints in the snow, and you have to melt snow just to have water. And if there is desert on the other side of the mountains, it will be worse. Then you will be glad to have a handful of coarse meal and a few dried berries between you and death."

"That sounds demanding of a man's perseverance," Hael agreed. "When I was a child, there was a year when no rain fell. The year after, a bloody flux struck the kagga. The kagga were already weakened by the drought. They died in great numbers, and so did we."

"Good," Shong grunted. "I do not mean good that your people died, I mean it is good that you know the meaning of hunger. Some of these city-bred men have no knowledge of the real world beyond the walls. They will eat their rations foolishly and complain incessantly. I have had more trouble out of such men than out of bandits."

"Can you not simply expel them?" Hael asked.

"Would that I could!" Shong raised eyes and hands to the heavens in heartfelt appeal to the gods. "If it is one of the handlers, then something may be done, expulsion or the whip or, in extreme cases, the sword. But all too often the whiners are those with influence in Kasin." He glared toward a fire around which sat a tipsy group of merchants' factors and government officers. Choula the map-maker was there, and Gilipas the priest and ambassador, along with a physician named Tuvas.

"Do you expect trouble from Choula?" Hael asked. He hoped not, for he had taken a liking to the man.

"Not him." Shong brushed at crumbs on his long robe. "I have traveled with him before. The only trouble he causes is when he becomes so wrapped up in his work that he forgets to eat or lets his toes freeze while he draws a map. No, the natural troublemakers are the ones like Gilipas, pampered all their lives and fools to boot. Some of the others as well, those whose experience of commerce has been in the counting-houses, not out where men must find new goods and new markets."

In these early days, though, problems were few and the experience was enthralling. Hael grew so used to mounted travel that he was unsure whether he would ever willingly take to his feet again. The land was wild and beautiful as they left the cultivated territories behind, and they began to see mountains. These looked high to Hael, some with snow on their peaks, but his fellow travelers assured him that the range many weeks' travel to the east would dwarf these and make them seem to be little more than hills.

Out here on the high plains he could feel the spirit-force of living things, a great relief after the dead sensations of the city. It was not as intense to him here as on his home island; but here life was somewhat more spread out, and he was not bred to this place. Now, everywhere he looked there were herds of curlhorns and branch-horns, toonoo and other grazing and browsing animals for which he had not yet learned the names. Along with these came the predators and scavengers that fed off the herds of herbivores.

In this land they encountered people whose herds were migratory and so, perforce, were the herders. Their animals were a sort of half-wild kagga, smaller than the type raised by his tribe, as well as being noisier, more rambunctious and evil-smelling.

The border with Omia was marked only by a small fort, its upper works made of timber and mud atop a far older structure of finely-cut stone.

Its banner flapped listlessly and on its battlements soldiers leaned on spears and stared at the caravan with stupefied boredom. Hael shuddered at the thought that he might have been tempted to enter such a life, instead of having a cabo between his knees and the whole wide world before him.

He sought to converse with the nusk handlers, but they were a surly, clannish lot who seemed to have scant regard for anyone save their own kind. Agah, their headman, never spoke words of insult to Hael, but his look was always sly and condescending. They were notorious thieves and brawlers, adept with the short, curved knife tucked into each man's belt. Yet Hael could see why they were tolerated, for their skill at handling the balky, ill-tempered nusks was little short of magical.

The nusks glared at the world through a mop of foolish-looking hair that hung from their polls to cover their tiny, red eyes. They seemed conscious of their own ugliness, and determined to make the rest of the world pay for the indignity. Yet the Kereels coaxed these intractable animals to near docility. They could get them to stand still for packing with chants and crooning songs, and they could urge them to greater speed with flexible wood whips, without being kicked or bitten. Hael had already had several close calls with the creatures and wanted to learn their ways, but the Kereels would never let him near their beasts.

As they traveled, they roughly paralleled the course of a river called the Shell. Its headwaters were far to the northeast, beyond the boundaries of Omia, in which land it was greatly enlarged by the runoff from the mountains. The river looked inviting, but Shong explained that it was too swift and shallow for convenient navigation in their intended direction, although it was marginally navigable when traveling downstream, either on rafts or in boats of very shallow draft. Hael saw a few flatboats being poled upstream with great toil, and decided that travel by cabo suited him well.

The grasslands appealed to him. First, he liked them because he was a herdsman, and grass is always of paramount importance to herdsmen. Second, he enjoyed their limitless expanses. He had been told that this great band of prairie stretched from the desert of the south far into the unknown expanses of the north, separating the coastal plain from the mountains with an unbroken steppe that was sometimes hilly and other times rolling or nearly flat, cut only by frequent small rivers, most of them easily fordable.

It astounded Hael that so much of this plain went unused and unoccupied. To the coastal people, this was wasteland, no better than the sand and rock desert of the south. The water sources were too far apart, they said, and the outlaws were numerous. Worst of all, only nomads could live there, migrating with their animals from one pasture or water source to another, and nomads were contemptible primitives.

Only the city-bred, Hael thought, could hold such a view. The distances were formidable only to those who thought in terms of fenced pastures and people traveling only on their own feet. A tribe mounted on cabos would own this plain, all of it. As for outlaws, a warrior people who went armed from birth had nothing to fear from such.

Hael had spoken much with Pashir's cabo herders, and had learned something of the breeding of cabos. The mares had one or at most two young per year. Of these young, many were rejected as unfit for the pursuits of the aristocracy. Hael had seen pictured on the palace walls how they were used in warfare. The nobles wielded long lances with which they rode against one another. Much emphasis was put on excellence of armor and having the larger, more powerful cabo. This struck Hael as a foolish way to conduct warfare, as a game where status was more important than prowess.

He needed two things: a great number of cabos of sufficient size and hardiness to bear men over great expanses of ground, and a weapon that could be wielded from cabo back. And the men, of course, but that was one breed that seemed to be plentiful everywhere. He spoke of none of this to his companions of the journey. He knew that they would be scornful of a homeless youth who dreamed of being a great conqueror. But to Hael it seemed natural. The fact was simply that he was not as other men, and there was no reason why he should feel constrained by the petty dreams of such men.

He had been an outsider even when he belonged to a tribe, and there was no place for him elsewhere save by adopting a role created by others: sailor, soldier, explorer, even slave if he were not careful. Very well, he would create his own role. If there were no tribe or nation to support such a role, he would create that nation.

One day, as they rode within the borders of Omia, Hael was riding far ahead of the train, musing upon these things, when he saw something extraordinary.

His cabo shied at a sudden motion to his left front. Hael smiled when he saw that it was a duster. This was a flightless bird native to these lands, a cousin of the killer birds but without that creature's predatory habits. The duster was mostly legs and long neck, with a bulbous body covered with black feathers except for an upstanding ruff of bushy green feathers across its back.

To Hael's amazement, the duster was running from a man. This startling individual looked rather like a bird himself with a short, spare body and incredibly long, thin arms and legs. He ran with a steady high-kneed stride, twirling something in his right hand, holding something coiled in his left. As he ran, his head was thrust forward on a long neck, emphasizing a pointed beard the length of Hael's forearm. The man was very dark, almost black, rather like the hunters of Hael's home island, although otherwise he looked nothing like them.

Hael was astonished to see the man gaining on the bird. Then the right hand flashed forward, underhanded, and a noose sailed out. Now Hael could see that the man held a long, thin rope coiled in his left hand. The noose settled over the bird's small, silly head and slid down its neck to settle just above the stumpy, useless wings. The man stopped and jerked back on the rope and the duster tumbled over into the grass. In an instant, the man was almost upon it. Hael expected to see him kill the bird, but instead he immobilized it. Its powerful legs kicked violently, and with a flick of his wrist he cast a loop of his rope over them, drawing it tight, then swiftly tying a slip-knot. He then sat on its body, and the bird quieted to await its fate. Methodically, the hunter began plucking its spectacular backfeathers.

Hael rode over to the man, intending to learn what this extraordinary spectacle was all about. With great efficiency, he had all the green feathers stripped and in a pile at his feet and was beginning to take some fluffy white feathers from the undersides of the wings. He looked up and smiled as Hael approached, his teeth flashing white in his dark face.

"Aren't you going to kill that bird?" Hael asked.

"What for?" the man said, still smiling. "Can't eat. Tough like leather. Let it go, grow more feathers, catch again."

"That makes sense."

"You want to buy some feathers?" The man wore no clothes whatever, just some strings of beads and broad leather straps on both wrists, along with a pouch slung from one shoulder. From this pouch he took some thin strings and began to bundle his feathers.

Hael dismounted and drove his wooden picket-pin into the earth, securing his reins to the pin. The cabo began to crop grass contentedly as Hael went to look at the feathers. In truth, he was far more interested in the rope. As he drew near the man stood and dextrously flicked his noose up the bird's neck and over its head.

"Stand back," he warned. "Kick very hard. Gut you quick." He jerked on his slipknot and the bird's legs were free. It took a moment for this to register, then it lurched to its feet. Squawking at the indignity, it ran off, denuded of its bright feathers, but with a whole skin. Both men laughed as it dwindled in the distance.

"How much?" Hael asked, pointing at the green feathers. The hunter shrugged.

"What you got?"

Hael decided that he might as well begin his merchant career. He went to his saddlebags and dug out some metal ornaments. This man did not look like the type who would have much use for coined money. With a few words and gestures, they quickly came to an agreement. For a bracelet of silver ornamented with a little gold, Hael got all of the green feathers. For two thin armlets of copper, he got the white ones. Hael was not sure of the values, but the hunter seemed quite pleased. Now Hael expressed his true interest.

"How much for the rope?"

"Rope?" The hunter frowned in puzzlement.

"Yes. I have never seen one like this, or used the way you used it. May I see it?"

"Sure. You like, I show how to use."

That was just what Hael wanted. He ran the surprisingly light cord through his fingers. It was made of a plant fiber, that much was plain. It had been oiled and handled to great suppleness and seemed to be quite strong.

One end had been cunningly braided into an eyelet and the rest of the rope passed through it to form an adjustable noose. "How do you cast it?"

The hunter took the coil of rope from Hael and once again held the noose in his right hand, the greater coil in his left with a large bight of slack between. Something glittered in his ear and Hael saw that a line of tiny gold dots outlined the outer curve of each ear. Bands of raised scar tissue decorated his chest. He shook his hand and the noose enlarged, then he swung it in slow circles. With a sidearm sweep, he tossed the noose, releasing a part of the coil in his left hand as it flew. The noose opened into a circle and settled over the upright stalk of a long-dead plant fifteen paces away. With a snap of his wrist, he sent a bight snaking along the length of the rope and the noose leapt off the stalk and he recoiled it.

"Let me try," Hael said. He tried to imitate the hunter's action and the coil sailed ten paces and the noose shrunk into a tiny circle as it flopped ignominiously to the ground. The hunter grinned and showed him how to release the left-hand coils more efficiently and he tried again. This was better, but the noose flew wide of the target. The hunter corrected his stance and release and the results were better yet. By the tenth throw, the noose settled over the stalk. Hael was very pleased, but he needed six more tries to do it again. By the last few casts, the hunter assured him that he was doing everything right, even though his accuracy was deplorable.

He knew that the man was not mocking him. It was as he had suspected: Casting the noose was rather like throwing the javelin. The technique was minimal and could be taught in a matter of minutes. After that, it was up to the user to practice hour after hour for as long as it took to acquire the coordination of body, eye and hand necessary for expert use.

A few minutes sufficed to strike a new bargain. Three small finger-rings of thin silver and a pair of silver ear-studs set with garnets and turquoise made Hael the owner of the rope. As the transaction was concluded, the hunter raised his head and stared over Hael's shoulder, his eyes narrowing, his nostrils flaring. Hael turned to see what he was looking at and saw the caravan in the far distance to the southwest.

"Those are just my friends. Don't—" But he turned to see the hunter sprinting away, faster even than he had been when chasing the duster. In an incredibly short time, the speedy black man was out of sight.

A while later the caravan reached him and Hael rode over to Shong. He held up his bundles and saw the merchant's eyes widen.

"Where did you get these?" Shong asked. Hael described his experience of the past two hours and Song shook his head. "The man you met was a Nightrunner. They are a shy, elusive people, the most primitive I ever heard of. They show up at outland markets from time to time, with rare goods to trade. Their needs are few, so they feel little need for contact with other people. Why this fellow was so casual about meeting with you I cannot guess, unless it was because you were alone, and young, and perhaps a kindred primitive."

"Did I make a good trade?" Hael asked, holding the bundles of feathers across his saddle. "Or was I robbed?"

"About the rope I can tell you little," Shong said, stroking his short, pointed beard. "I never had any use for one like that. The feathers are a different matter. Dusters are notoriously difficult to catch. Usually they are killed in the process, which increases their rarity. These, the green ones"—he touched the glittering bundle—"are worth well more than their weight in gold in Kasin. They are much used for priestly ornaments, fans for rich ladies, and such. Down south, they are worth even more since every village chief needs a few for his headdress. The feathers have some religious significance for them. The white ones"—he touched the other bundle—"are much esteemed by soldiers, to serve as plumes in their helmets. You will get a small silver piece for each one. In short, young Hael, you have done rather well, taking an afternoon off from your sentry duties; this little cargo packs down well, weighs little and is worth about fifty times what you paid for it. It is the ideal trade good; low bulk, light weight, cheap at the buying end and expensive at the selling end. This is the very essence of commerce, you understand."

Hael was pleased to learn this, but he was far more pleased with his rope. In succeeding days, he took every opportunity to dismount and practice tossing the noose at targets. When he felt that he had achieved sufficient competence with the rope dismounted, he began to try it from his saddle. At first he made the cabo stand while he whirled and tossed the noose. This was not immediately easy, because the cabo shied away from the rope whistling past its nose. But once it grew accustomed to this strange new habit of its rider, he tried it at a walk, then a trot. Finally he threw the noose at a canter, and on his first success, roping the broken stump of a large tree, he was jerked from the saddle and dashed senseless onto the stony ground.

He took several days of very slow riding to recover from his injuries, and this bestowed ample time to reflect upon his folly, and to devise remedies. For a man to rope an immovable object from a moving platform was, upon reflection, a foolish thing to essay. By extension, a rather large and reluctant animal could have a similar effect. It might not be as drastically immovable as a tree, but a tree could not bite and kick a fallen man to death, as a fractious nusk or cabo could.

By the time Hael had recovered, he had thought of an answer. At least it was an experiment worth trying. As soon as he found a settlement with skilled saddlers, he planned to have a saddle built with a stout post on its front. With this, he could tie or snub the running part of his rope to this post and let the saddle, its girth and his cabo take the greater part of the shock. While he mused thus, many of the others laughed at his enthusiasm and some said within his hearing that it would have served him right to break his neck. Foremost among these was Agah, who had taken an unreasonable dislike to Hael.

Another thing that occupied Hael's thoughts while he recovered was what to do about Agah. The man now lost no opportunity to insult him, growing more unbearable with each passing day. While Hael was disabled, he scarcely bothered to disguise his hostility and contempt, once going so far as to slap Hael across the face when Hael reached for a skewer of meat ahead of him. Had Hael not been so weakened by his injuries, he would have killed the man without hesitation, but the moment had passed, and now Agah acted as if Hael were a natural inferior.

One evening, Choula came to sit with Hael where the younger man was eating, still nursing a tendon-torn arm. The map-maker proposed a sensible but eminently citified solution to the problem.

"Hael, my friend, there is no reason for one such as you to put up with this insolence. Agah's second is the man Karvas. He would very much like to have Agah's job. Simply hire Karvas to kill Agah while he sleeps. It will not cost much and you will feel immeasurably better."

"No," Hael said, "among my people a man is expected to kill his own enemies." The memory of Gasam and Larissa and the longneck still burned within him. "I'll have to do it myself, when I am recovered. I thank you for your concern, though."

Some days later, when his wounds had diminished to a faint soreness and he felt that he had full command of all his limbs, Hael approached Shong. "Master, I hate to bother you, and I hesitate because I fear I may deprive you of a valued subordinate, but would you mind it terribly if I were to kill Agah?"

"Agah?" Shong said. "I marvel that he is not dead already. By all means, kill the rogue. That other rogue, Karvas, will do his task as well. Are you sure you feel up to it? Agah has killed a number of men in brawls. It is expected of a Kereel headman. How do you intend to fight him?"

Hael had not decided this. "How is it done? In my homeland, we could challenge an enemy, and it was fought in an area confined by a single kagga-hide cut into a continuous strip and pegged out in a circle. The weapons might be spears or short swords."

"On a caravan there will be nothing that formal," Shong said. "Call him out and you will fight then and there. I recommend that you do not fight with daggers. The Kereels are masters of that weapon, and you know nothing of it."

That evening, after the man had eaten, Hael took his weapons and went to the fire where the Kereels sat drinking wine and talking loudly among themselves. Several wore dirty bandages, for there had been a number of fights among them. Even a stern caravan master like Shong could not completely suppress the belligerent urges of his men. Agah looked up at Hael's approach and a cruel smile creased his features.

"Look who comes! It is the bronze-haired boy from the islands! He has heard that we are short of women, and has come to do the woman's service for us! As your headman, I demand the right to go first. Drop that scrap of cat-fur, boy, and come over here." The others roared with laughter and watched to see what Hael would do.

"Agah, I don't know what I've done to earn your dislike, nor do I care greatly. I'm a free warrior and I don't tolerate such insult."

"And what would you do about that, child?" Agah's eyes slid right and left, taking in his men's reactions. They were eager for a fight. Karvas looked back and forth between the two, a calculating gleam in his eye.

"I intend to kill you. You have earned it and there is no sense in merely beating you and then leaving you alive behind my back. I'm not sure why this has come about, but I will end it here and now. Get up and fight."

Agah's smile was gone. Slowly, he stood. "Will you fight with knives? Real men do not need long spears or great swords." His tone of sarcasm told Hael how much the man feared those weapons. It was tempting simply to draw a sword and cut him down, or skewer him with his spear. But to do such a thing would cause the others to think he feared to fight, and some day down the road he might have to deal with another challenge. Better to demonstrate his mastery in terms they could never dispute.

"Use what you like. My people only fight armed duels with our equals." He jammed the butt-spike of his spear into the ground and lifted the sword-strap from his shoulder. Bare-handed, he faced Agah.

The man looked nonplussed, then he grinned, his thin lips spreading back over his teeth in an animal expression that conveyed no humor. "Die any way you wish, boy. Perhaps I shall make use of you before I cut your throat." He drew his dagger and unfastened his knee-length kilt. It dropped to the ground, leaving him dressed only in a brief white loincloth. His dark skin glistened in the firelight. The Kereels anointed their bodies with animal fat, raising a high gloss and a great stink. The unsheathed bronze blade, ten inches long, curved and double-edged, flashed luridly.

Hael had already oiled himself with fragrant fistnut oil in which flower petals had steeped. If he lost, he thought, he could die with the satisfaction of knowing he made a better-smelling corpse.

Word of the impending fight spread quickly and men hurried over from other fires. There were people from the village nearby as well, congratulating themselves on their luck in being present at such a fine entertainment. The lives of villagers were surpassingly dull for the most part.

Walking on his toes like a dancer, never taking his eyes off Hael, Agah took small, mincing steps as he walked around the fire to meet his enemy.

Hael stepped out and back, so that when Agah reached him, the Kereel would not have the flames behind him.

"Do you back away from me, boy?" Agah crooned, seizing the opportunity for another psychological attack.

"Do you intend to talk me to death? You bore me, Kereel."

"Then," Agah hissed, "let me provide you with some amusement!" He slid forward, the knife lancing toward Hael's side. Hael slapped the attack aside, swatting with his palm against Agah's forearm, not foolish enough to make a try for the knife hand. He did not try for an offensive move, content for the moment to observe and analyze Agah's fighting style.

Agah continued to move like a dancer, continually shifting his feet in intricate patterns, moving his hands in patterns as intricate, apparently trying to bewilder Hael with the complexity of his maneuverings. Some of the spectators murmured appreciatively at this, taking it for mastery of a formidable fighting technique.

Hael paid little attention. He knew that in mortal combat every move a man made should have one of two purposes: to defend himself or to threaten his enemy. Hael stood crouched, his arms slightly forward, hands open at chest level, watchful and alert. He would take note when the dagger actually came toward his body and ignore the meaningless gestures in the meantime.

With a loud cry, Agah slashed at Hael's face, then, with a sudden change of direction, drew his arm back and thrust for the belly. Hael sucked in his belly as he sidestepped and the knife lanced past. Agah tried a back-handed slash but by that time Hael had stepped in behind him, kicking behind his right knee, gripping his left shoulder and hauling backward to send the Kereel sprawling on the ground.

Hael was almost able to finish it then; to crush the man's larynx with his heel or fall on his belly with full weight behind an elbow, rupturing internal organs and paralyzing the man with shock. But in pulling back his hand had slipped from the greasy shoulder and Agah did not land as hard as Hael had intended. Still slashing to keep the younger man away, Agah whirled over, got his free hand beneath him and scrambled to his feet.

In moments their circling, shuffling dance resumed, but now there was fear in Agah's eyes, fear that he sought to mask with a great deal of hissing and waving of his knife, as if he were already skinning Hael alive.

Hael had the man's measure now, and he was ready to commence attacking. He knew nothing of knife dueling, but wrestling was his people's favorite sport. While he had no weapon, he had use of both hands, which, with his expertise, evened things considerably. He could see that counterattack was his best tactic. It would be necessary to know which way the knife was moving when he made his own move. He was in no rush, perfectly willing to wait as long as necessary for Agah to commit himself.

With a snarling curse, Agah lunged forward with his whole body, his knife dipping low then flashing upward, its sicklelike upper edge ready to pierce Hael's groin and rip upward to his breastbone, spilling entrails and blood like wine from a slit skin.

Instead of dodging back or sideways, Hael

stepped straight in, his forearms crossed before him to block the knife arm. He felt the very tip of the knife touch his skin just below his navel as he slammed his forehead into Agah's nose, sending the man staggering backward with blood gushing from his nostrils. Hael pressed close, turning his palms inward and grasping the wrist of Agah's knife hand, then digging in his heels and yanking back with his full strength and weight. Agah screamed as his shoulder dislocated and Hael whirled to send him flying across one hip and land face-down in the fire.

Sparks flew upward along with a stench of burning hair and the men standing nearby drew back to avoid being scorched by the flying coals. Hael stepped forward and knotted his fingers in Agah's hair, drawing him back out of the fire, burned and injured, all but senseless with pain and shock, his arms hanging limply at his sides.

Hauling the man half upright by the hair, Hael kept his eyes on the watching Kereels as his right hand flashed across, the edge of his palm snapping the neck vertebrae with terrible force. He released the greasy hair and the lifeless body dropped by the fire, still smoking faintly.

"This situation was not of my making," Hael said, scanning the Kereels, his gaze stopping at Karvas. "Is it over, or shall we contest this further?"

There was a great silence among the watchers, then Karvas stepped forward. "Agah was our headman, not our lover. He has no kin here to seek vengeance. Now I am headman and I say it is over." He looked at the other Kereels and slowly, reluctantly, one by one, they nodded assent. Karvas looked back to Hael. "There. It is over."

Shong stepped forward and nudged Agah's body with his booted toe. "Get this carrion out of the camp before it draws scavengers. Perform whatever rites you must to keep his spirit at rest, but be ready to break camp at the usual time in the morning. You"—he pointed to a boy who tended harness. "Fetch the dead man's dagger and sheath. They are Hael's now."

Hael resumed his sword and picked up his spear. The boy handed him the knife and he tucked the sheath under the thong supporting his loincloth.

"You are acquiring quite an arsenal," Shong observed as they walked back toward the leader's fire.

"I killed a man for the sword, too. It was the better bargain. There was certainly more honor in it."

"You cannot always be motivated by honor. Sometimes a man has to take drastic action to preserve his standing or his life. Better to die than to let scum like that lord it over you. You did the right thing, and now no one will treat you other than with respect."

"I still do not know why he wanted to provoke me to fight. Do you think he might have been put up to it?"

"The thought had occurred to me. He was a bullying loudmouth and probably many times a murderer, but he was not the type to fight with no prospect for profit. Of course, perhaps he just wanted your fine sword and spear. They would have been his had he won."

Hael did not think so. The man might have been

greedy, but he would not have risked his life thus just for the weapons. If he had been hired, and it was not just some mad hatred, who had hired him? Was it someone here on the expedition? Or was it someone back in Kasin? This would bear thinking about.

That evening as he sat by the fire, most of the others avoided him. Somehow a man with fresh blood on his hands seemed to be something to keep at a distance. To his surprise, though, Choula came to sit with him, bearing a skin of wine and a pair of cups. He handed Hael one, then poured for both of them.

"Congratulations on your victory," he said.

"Victory!" Hael said, smiling wryly. "It is not much of a victory to kill a worthless rogue in a dirty little scuffle."

"Congratulations on being alive then. That's always something worth celebrating. Here, drink up. You might have lost, then who would I have to talk geography with?" Hael had been pumping the map-maker for information about the neighboring lands for the entire journey.

"Not Agah, surely," Hael agreed. He confided to the map-maker some of his thoughts concerning Agah's motivation.

"It is not at all unlikely. It is never difficult to gain enemies at the best of times and in the best of places. In Kasin it is easier than in most places, and easiest of all in the home of a powerful man. You were seen to rise quickly in his estimation. That could be galling to an ambitious man who has spent years toadying to the mighty."

Hael did not suggest to Choula that it might be Pashir himself who had paid for his death. Might he have found out about Hael and Shazad? Even worse, could it have been Shazad? He might now be an embarrassment to her, a mere lowborn outlander who had shared her bed. There were many old tales of women who, like the legendary spider, had their lovers killed. He could see that, should he pursue this line of thought much longer, few would escape his suspicions. It was time to change the subject.

"It will be a long time that we winter at the foot of the mountains, will it not?"

"Two or perhaps three months," Choula confirmed. "It will be a long, boring time in a town with few amusements."

"I want to learn from you in that time," Hael said.

Choula smiled. "You shall learn all I know of the lands. I shall teach you to draw maps."

"I want you to do more than that," Hael said with all seriousness. "I want you to teach me to read."

NINE

Hael paused on a hilltop near the foot of the mountain. He felt something unfamiliar, but the impression was so fleeting that it passed before he could grasp it. He had been coming out to exercise his mount every day at this time, when weather permitted. The altitude and season were such that most of the expedition preferred to stay indoors, for the cold was bitter at times, with an almost constant drizzle and occasional snow.

Now for a change the sky was clear and the sun shone dazzlingly on the snow-covered flanks of the mountain that dominated the horizon. The mountain, and others like it, ran to the north and south as far as vision would allow, forming an insurmountable barrier to eastward travel during the winter months. Nearly every day, Shong's waiting caravan would hear a distant rumble like thunder. It was the avalanche of unthinkable quantities of snow, sliding from hillsides into the valleys. Sometimes, riding as high up the slopes as he could go, Hael thought he saw manlike shapes, impossibly tall and so white they were difficult to see against the snow, seemingly on mysterious missions of their own as they crossed the snow-fields as silent as ghosts. When he asked the townspeople about these, they shrugged and turned away, with looks of superstitious fear.

Hael was reluctant to turn back and face the boredom of another evening in the drab little town whose sole reason for existence was its location at the western end of one of the very few passes through these mountains. Its huddle of buildings within the earthwork wall consisted of little more than a few score single-roomed huts, half buried as protection from the winter weather, coils of smoke rising from their turf roofs.

Hael had himself been forced to make no few concessions to the elements. He now wore a jacket and leggings of finely tanned skins lined with blanket-woven quil hair. His feet and lower legs were encased in soft boots of similar construction, and he wore a cloak of woven quil hair. He had never gone heavily clothed before, but then he had never been anywhere this cold before.

The sensation came again, and this time he seized it. It was a shift in the wind, and it was slightly warmer than the ambient air had been. It was from the south. Spring was returning. With a whoop, Hael spurred his cabo downslope toward the town. They would not be stuck here forever, something he was beginning to fear. The snows would melt, the passes would open, and they would be on their way, across the mountains and into the unknown.

It was not to be over as quickly as Hael had anticipated. For the next four weeks, the thunder of avalanches was almost continuous as entire mountainsides divested themselves of their snowy coats. Mountain streams became savage torrents as the snows melted. In this time the animals were tended to and gear was readied and repaired. The Kereels had long since been paid off and made their way home, having no liking for the highland winter, and had taken their nusks with them. Local handlers were hired and new pack animals purchased. These were a shaggy, hornless breed of nusk, more tractable than their lowland cousins, with smaller hoofs for negotiating narrow mountain ledges.

At last the day came when Shong gave the order for departure. Flowers had already appeared in the mountain meadows and beasts were returning to the high pastures after a winter in the lowlands. For the first days Hael felt impatient as the caravan trudged along behind their guides, local men who traveled on foot. At least they were moving. And haste would have been foolish, for the paths were narrow and often treacherous, the precipices sheer. As they ascended, the cold returned and there was sometimes ice to contend with. After some men and animals were lost in falls, Hael no longer chafed at the slow pace.

Every time they dismounted for rest or to make camp for the night, Hael took a pointed stick from his sash and practiced forming letters in the soft earth. This, he sensed, was a power as great as that of weapons and armies. He was only beginning to learn how knowledge could not only be transmitted but stored in this fashion, but he sensed the power. The letters he found fairly easy to understand, because each meant a sound and the sounds formed words. Numerals were more difficult. There were only ten to remember, but combining them to form ever-larger numbers did not come easy, and arithmetic promised to be challenging. Still, he knew he would master them.

Their guides took their pay and went home once they reached the mountain crest, leaving the party feeling a little vulnerable. The air was thin at the high altitudes. It made men sluggish and unalert; there were times when it caused them to see things that were not there. One day after they had passed over the crest of the range and were descending the eastern slope, Hael saw something, and for a while he thought it was but yet another of the delusions bred in his mind by the thin air and the fatigue of the long, arduous mountain crossing.

What he thought he saw was a woman, alone, dressed in strange clothing, trudging up the mountain path toward him as if dazed. It was impossible, of course. There was no possibility that a woman would be wandering this desolate mountain path alone. He blinked and shook his head, expecting her to disappear when he looked back. She did not go away. He looked behind him to find out if any of the others could see this apparition, only to find that he had once again gone out far in front of the caravan. He looked downslope again. There she was, but now she was staggering. After a few minutes, she fell sideways, tried weakly to rise, then lay still.

Hael nudged his cabo and let it walk forward slowly. He was curious to know how close he would get before the hallucination disappeared or changed into something sensible. As he drew closer, though, the vision remained. More, it grew plainer, more solid, the nearer he approached. When he was ten paces away there could be no doubt that this was no vision. He dismounted and hurried to the fallen woman. She lay on her side, a cloak drawn over her face, her knees drawn up like an infant's.

He put a hand on her shoulder, turning her gently so that she lay on her back, her head cradled in the crook of his arm. He drew the cloak aside and, to his great astonishment, gazed upon a face of great beauty. It was long and fine-boned, drawn with fatigue and hardship, but the beauty was unmistakable. Her skin was bone-white, her full lips bluish from the thin air. Abundant, tan-colored hair spilled across his supporting arm.

Her clothes were like none he had ever seen before, brightly colored like the cloth traded in the islands, but the fabric was heavy and coarse, woven in patterns of complex intersecting lines. The garments had once been a heavy jacket and close-fitting trousers, but now comprised little more than rags. Her footgear were buskins of soft leather, but they were shredded as well, the remains of the soles blood-stained.

Her eyelashes fluttered for a moment and opened wide. Her eyes were green, the irises so large that little white showed when they opened their widest. He could not read her expression. Probably, he thought, she felt nothing at all. This beautiful creature was near death from fatigue and exposure; and the cold ground would leach what little warmth remained to her. He lifted her in his arms, amazed at how little she weighed, and carried her to his cabo. Its head was down as it nudged at the turf with disappointed snorts. The grass had not yet grown long enough to crop at this altitude. Awkwardly, trying not to upset the animal, he placed her across the front of his saddle and mounted. The cabo seemed undisturbed by the extra burden.

Slowly he walked the animal back uphill. The woman had closed her eyes again. Apparently the warmth from his body was enough to make hers surrender its losing battle against the elements and passively accept his shelter. Who could she be? What was she doing high on this mountainside, where she surely had to perish, and still *climbing* when he first saw her? The answers to these questions would have to wait.

When he met the caravan a short way uphill, Shong's eyes flickered over the bundle Hael held on the front of his saddle. "I believe you were to scout out pasture and camping grounds below," he said. "Instead, I find you have collected a woman. Explain this."

Hael did so, and Shong nodded. "And it occurred to me," Hael concluded, "that she might be running from something. We might do well to find out what is ahead of us before we go much farther, if she is strong enough to speak."

"That makes sense. Perhaps she will speak when she has recovered a little."

They continued downhill. The eastern slope of the range proved to be far less rugged than the western slope, and already they could see an inviting plain stretched before them, with no dangerous precipices or narrow, crumbling paths between. They could be on level ground before sundown, if there were no delays.

"And if there is somebody pursuing her?" Hael asked.

"Then we give her back to them. We are not an army, after all."

"No," Hael said, unconsciously tightening his grasp on the unconscious woman.

"Ah, I see. You are learning to be a merchant. Very well, we will *sell* her back to them."

"I am keeping her," Hael said.

Shong put on a look of great exasperation. "My young friend, this is not a fish you have caught, to keep because it is large enough. This is a woman. She may have an owner, or even a husband. Women frequently run away from both. I shall not endanger this expedition because you have conceived a fancy for a starved and half-frozen runaway." He was silent for a while, then, "Let me see her."

Hael uncovered her face and displayed her like a mother showing off a sleeping infant.

"Hmm. She is comely, I must admit. Her clothes were once of good quality, not what a slave would wear." He sighed. "I suppose you feel you must play the hero. If there are those who would take her back, and they are strong and willing to attack us, I will not try to keep her. If you feel you have to do something foolish, make sure you do not involve the rest of us."

"Fair enough," Hael said.

The sun was beyond the mountain behind them when they came off the main slope and entered an area of rolling foothills above a great plain. The temperature rose dramatically, so that as soon as they stopped and dismounted for the evening, heavy cloaks, jackets and leggings were stripped off, rolled and stowed away, in all probability not to be resumed until the next winter. The spring was well advanced in this area, the meadows and hills riotous with bee-buzzing flowers. Cabos and nusks were picketed, and the animals commenced to munch blissfully on the fresh green grasses. All the beasts were lean from the long mountain trek, and Shong had to leave strict orders to the handlers not to allow the animals to eat and drink until they were foundered.

Soon there were roaring fires going, and several riders went out in search of game. Most were content to sit by the fires and luxuriate in the warmth. Hael saw to the woman's comfort, then went to the nearby stream, found a fairly deep pool several minutes' walk upstream of where the livestock were drinking, and stripped off his musty garments. The water was gooseflesh-raising, scrotum-tightening cold, but he clenched his teeth and waded in. Confined in heavy clothing since autumn, he had felt like a man imprisoned. He scrubbed himself with sand from the streambed, ducked beneath the water and wrung out his hair repeatedly.

When he felt clean enough and could stand the numbing cold no more, he climbed up the low bank and let the last rays of the sun dry him. His hair still darkly damp, lying heavily on his shoulders and upper back, he put his night-cat fur loincloth back on for the first time in months. With his sword, spear and dagger, he felt like his true self again.

Shong looked up from his seat by a fire as Hael approached. "It is still somewhat cool for such attire," he said.

"I was suffocating wearing the hide and hair of so many other animals. I'll wear my own for a while, and this scrap of my totem animal. How is my find? Any signs of life?"

Shong looked toward the huddled bundle near the fire. "Aside from regular breathing and an occasional groan, none. She is fortunate to be able to do that much. It must have taken her days of climbing to reach the spot where you found her, though it took us less than a day to cover the same path going downhill."

"Do you think we should try to wake her? Feed her?"

Shong shrugged. "Leave her for the moment. I doubt she has the strength to chew our preserved rations."

Before it was dark, the hunters returned. The riders had had no luck, for the mountain springers were wary and ran away with great bounds at first sight of the mounted men. The handlers, on foot and wielding slings, had better fortune. They brought down a number of small animals and some birds, and soon a savory smell of roasting meat filled the air. Shong ordered some meat broth prepared, in case the woman should revive.

As Hael ate, he watched her, absorbed in her enigmatic presence. It was something that went beyond her beauty, beyond the extraordinary place where he had found her. There was a sense of something destined. How had she come to that spot exactly when he had? If she had collapsed so much as an hour before she did, he would have found her dead. She groaned and rolled weakly, tossing off her cloak. Her jacket had ridden up and he could count each rib along her flanks. Even through the thick cloth of her trousers, the jut of her hipbones showed plainly. If she was so beautiful in this condition, what must she look like when she was full-fleshed and healthy?

At some time during the evening, after everyone had finished eating, he realized that she was looking at him. There could be no doubt of it. Not only were her eyes open, they were focussed on him. She did not seem to be alarmed, but neither was she apathetic. There was a wariness in her expression.

Casually, Hael rose and found a bowl. This he filled from the pot of broth and carried to where the woman lay. He placed an arm behind her shoulders and raised her to a half-sitting posture. She made no protest when he raised the bowl to her lips. She sipped at it warily at first, then with greater urgency, lifting trembling fingers to steady it. The touch of her fingertips on his hand was cool. When the bowl was half emptied she drew back, shaking her head. He lowered the bowl and held her while she trembled violently.

"She's been too long without food." Hael looked up to see Shong. "Give her no more for a while." Hael nodded assent. He lowered the woman back to her pallet, and within seconds she was asleep again. That night Hael slept next to her. When she awoke during the night, he gave her more broth. He heard her mutter in her sleep, but he could not make out any words he understood.

Since the area was fair, the grass lush and the water sweet, with game available, Shong decreed two days for men and animals to rest and recuperate. Hael soon found that Shong's idea of rest did not involve much leisure. Among the animals, every hoof, hide, mouth and eye had to be inspected and, if need be, treated. Every strap, buckle, and length of rope was overhauled, every bundle of goods inspected for damage to its contents or its watertight wrappings.

At every opportunity, Hael checked on the woman. The others made sport of his solicitousness, but they were careful that he should not take offense, for everyone remembered Agah. Late in the afternoon of the first day, he found her sitting up on her folded cloak, a bowl of broth by one knee, a cup of watered wine by the other. Bits of meat floated in the broth.

"She seems stronger," Shong explained, "so I ordered some more substantial nourishment brought."

"Has she spoken yet?" Hael asked.

"Not a word. But I don't think she is mute, or simple-minded. I think she just wants to know what her position is before she says anything."

"She spoke in her sleep last night, so I know she can speak," Hael affirmed. He went to the woman and sat before her. She looked at him, but said nothing.

"What is your name?" Hael asked. She said nothing. He pointed to himself. "Hael." He pointed to her and raised his eyebrows, hoping she would recognise the gesture.

Slowly, as if it were very weighty, she raised a hand and placed it, fingers spread, against her chest, just beneath the u-shaped depression where her prominent collarbones joined.

"Deena," she said, her voice little more than a whisper.

This was progress. Hael thrust an arm out, indicating the mountains behind them and the path they had descended. "Stormlands. We," he indicated the others, "all of us, came here from the Stormlands. You?" Once again, he made broad gestures of enquiry.

She frowned, as if she had not quite heard him. Yet it was not a look of utter bafflement as he had half expected. Then, "Storm-lands?" Her pronunciation was very strange, but he could understand her.

Choula came to join them. "Stick with simple words and speak very slowly," he advised. "Most people speak a dialect of Northern or Southern, and even those two languages may have had a common origin. From the way she forms her vowel sounds, I think she speaks a type of Northern."

Trust Choula to be pedantic, but was undoubtedly right. Hael tore up a handful of grass. "Grass," he said.

This time she nodded. "Grass." He could tell that she was not just repeating the word he had used, but was speaking her own word for it. It sounded strange but was perfectly recognizable.

"Northern," Choula said, triumphantly.

Hael settled down for a lengthy language lesson. A few dozen words sufficed to demonstrate that her language shared much of the same vocabulary as the dialects of Northern spoken to the west of the mountains. The only word she had no cognate for was "nusk". Apparently the animals were unknown here. Happily, Hael found that she was quite familiar with the cabo, although she pronounced the work "cabiyo."

At intervals that day and the next, he established communication with Deena, always careful not to tire her out. Tuvas, the physician, examined her and pronounced her undamaged but very frail from long deprivation. His primary interest was medicinal plants and he was always impatient when asked to treat a mere human, especially so when the human was a foreign woman of uncertain standing, possibly a slave. Hael's stony glare and short words convinced him to make a thorough diagnosis.

On the morning of the third day, as they prepared to break camp and resume their trek, Hael arranged a makeshift saddle for Deena on one of the nusks. The handler was a man he had come to know in the village where they had wintered, and Hael trusted him. Nobody said anything to him about it. Perhaps nobody dared.

That day, Hael found occasion to ride by her from time to time. He felt that they had established sufficient mutual understanding for some meaningful exchange of information.

"How came you to be so high on the mountain?" he asked.

She looked at him for a long time, apparently gauging his trustworthiness, before speaking. "I—escape from the Amsi. I knew they never go on the mountain. I thought I could get to the other side. Did not know the mountain was so high."

"You were lucky. It isn't just one mountain, but

a whole range you must pass through to reach the other side. Many days' travel."

She shrugged. "I would have tried anyway, to get away from them."

He scanned the terrain, seeing only occasional wild beasts. "And are we likely to encounter them?" If she was so desperate to get away from them, they might prove to be a problem.

"You surely will." She looked grim, but not alarmed. "But you are a large band, well armed. They will not attack. They will want to trade."

"Good," Hael said. "That is why we are here. Why were you their—prisoner?" He hesitated to say "slave." She might take offense.

She raised a trembling arm and pointed to the northeast. "My people live there, the Matwa, the People of the Long Bow. We are enemies of the Amsi for many generations." She had to repeat the last word several times before he understood it. Despite such occasional lapses, they were quickly establishing conversational fluency. This mainly involved getting used to each other's pronunciation and slight differences in grammar.

By the third day of their trek, she had recovered enough to show a little animation in her speech, and she agreed to guide them to some of the nearby settlements. In return, they would not let the Amsi recapture her, and would return her to her own people when they had secured the services of another guide. Shong had been reluctant at first.

"If she is our guide," Hael urged, "then she is entitled to our protection, is she not?"

"That depends entirely on how much these Amsi want her back," Shong said.

"If they say she is a runaway slave, we will buy her back," Hael insisted. "Surely they cannot want much for her."

Shong eyed the woman, still emaciated from her ordeal. "Not if they charge by weight, certainly. I will put it to you thus: We are merchant-explorers in a strange land where we cannot afford to make enemies. We will negotiate with these people if they insist, but I will pay no more than a fair price for one skinny woman. Any extra you must make up with your own profits from the expedition, since it is clear that you are concerned only because you are smitten with her. I think that, were she old or ugly or, worse, male, you would not be so anxious for her safety and freedom."

Hael knew better than to dispute with that. He would be quite happy to part with all his gains to have her safe. Everything about her intrigued him. Not just her beauty, as Shong had intimated, but the great inner strength that had carried her so far, the determination to be free that had sent her up a mountain she must surely have realized that she could not climb, alone and weakened as she was.

"Why did you not try to escape back to your own people?" he asked her. Her answer stirred him to excitement.

"I could not outrun them. They ride these," she pointed to his cabo, "not so big, but very fast. But the mountain is forbidden to them, so I went there."

"Do your people ride?" Hael wanted to know. She shook her head. "We live in the forest hills, the Amsi on the grassland. Oh, some of the tribes on the edge of the forest keep cabos, they try to hunt from them, but most Matwa want nothing to do with them."

This was interesting, but Hael had ceased to be surprised by the things people believed, their customs and tabus. By now he knew that each people had such beliefs, and thought them to be the laws of nature, and that everyone else was wrong or at least strange for holding otherwise. When he thought of his life on the island, which seemed so long ago now, he marveled at the odd things he had believed without giving them the slightest thought.

Had he still been Shasinn, he would have thought Deena and her people were contemptible, because they used bows and hunted animals in the hill forests. Now they sounded interesting. He was also anxious to meet these Amsi, even if they were a danger to him and the others. These were a people who rode cabos, and they could be very important to what he now believed to be his destiny. He had known that Deena was a part of that destiny the moment he had seen her on the mountain.

He felt a surprising eagerness for this land on the far side of the mountains, as if he had come to some place where he was meant to be. On foot, the grasslands looked dreary and limited. From the saddle of a cabo, they were limitless vision of freedom stretching to the horizon in every direction. There were possibilities here that he could only faintly sense, but unclear as they were, the feeling was powerful.

On the fourth day, as they neared a village Deena had identified as Hard Wind, they encountered the Amsi. Hael saw them first. He was riding

point, as usual, but only a few hundred paces
ahead of the main body. Shong had instructed
that, since visibility was so great anyway here on
the plains, there was no cause for the point, flank
and rear guards to go beyond sight. In the distance, riding toward them, Hael descried at least
a score of riders. Since he knew that they saw him
as well, he was casual about wheeling his cabo
and trotting leisurely back to the caravan. At his
report, Shong ordered a halt and signaled the
other guards to come in.

"Be friendly," Shong ordered, "no show of bel-
ligerence. Keep your weapons handy, but make no
threatening moves. A simple misunderstanding
can turn into a feud over nothing. I've seen it happen." He turned to Hael.

"Hael, you have had the most conversation with
the woman, so you will probably be handiest with
their dialect. Choula, you stay by me as well. Converse, answer questions, be friendly. But when I
speak, be silent, and translate for me at need. Is
that understood?" Hael nodded. As always, he admired the merchant-adventurer's swift competence in these matters.

In minutes, the riders were near them. They did
not ride swiftly, whooping and waving weapons,
but rather they trotted along casually. Hael took
this for a good sign. Their appearance was wild
enough even without any demonstrations of feroc-
ity. He could count at least thirty now. They were
dressed mostly in skins, finely tanned but decorated vividly with paint and embroidery. Most of
them wore hoods made from the head and neck
skins of animals, often with the beast's mask atop
the head like a cap. Some of these headdresses

included horns or antlers, while others included manes, tails, a few feathers and what might have been human scalps. Their saddles were clever, light constructions of wood and hide, also well decorated. He saw little metal save for silver and gold ornaments. There were a few knives, and each man had a long lance tipped with a bronze point.

The Amsi halted, forming a line twenty paces from Shong and his two representatives. Then a man ambled his cabo forward from the center of the line. The others were men of middling size, but this one was very tall, his legs dangling within a foot of the ground as he sat easily in his saddle. He wore a greater profusion of ornaments than any of the others, and his richly embroidered hide shirt was almost white. Atop his head he wore the red-furred mask of a predatory animal, its pointed ears raised as if listening for prey.

"I am Impaba, sub-chieftain of the Northwestern Amsi. Who are you, strange men, and what is your business on our land?"

Shong nodded for Hael to speak. "We are a trading mission sent by the king of Neva. Our intentions are peaceful. As you can see, we are few in number, and we do not have many weapons. This is our leader, Shong of the Honorable Guild of Merchants. I am Hael of the Islands. I speak because I have learned a little of your dialect. This is Choula, a scholar." They had decided not to mention that Choula was a map-maker, lest the people of this land think their mission was a cover for espionage.

Impaba seemed interested. "Did you come over the mountains? We rode along the foot of the great mountain just a few days ago, yet saw no sign of newcomers."

"We did," Hael said. "We crossed from the far west as soon as spring cleared the passes of snow."

Impaba shook his head, apparently a gesture of wonderment. "Few, few people have ever crossed, people like those"—he gestured to the nusk handlers—"who live in the mountains, on the far slope. Is this a great land you come from?"

Hael was about to answer when Shong broke in, apparently now confident that he could express himself clearly. "Great, and populous, and powerful." It never hurt to let men understand that one's sovereign was well able to avenge any injury done to his representative. "My king has decided that it is time to establish contact with the people east of the mountains. We have now discovered that the way through is not too arduous to travel, and my king would like to establish trade with the people here. Trade is the basis for friendship between peoples."

Impaba gave every indication of listening closely, as if he needed to concentrate in order to understand what to him must have been thickly accented speech. He seemed to comprehend well enough. "That is good. What do you bring to trade?"

"We have brought a mixed cargo of goods; cloth, lenses of glass, dyes and pigments, medicines. You understand, this is a preliminary expedition. We must find what the people here want that we can supply, and what they have to trade for our goods. Future caravans will arrive loaded with the goods most in demand."

"Iron?" Impaba asked.

"We bring no metal, save for some spools of copper wire. In fact, we would gladly pay well for iron, had you any to trade."

Impaba nodded. "We will speak further. You are welcome here. There is a village nearby, Hard Wind. Come with us there and we will see your goods. You may rest and we will speak—" He broke off and squinted past Hael's shoulder. Hael turned to look and saw Deena seated atop her nusk, her eyes wide but her face impassive. He was sure she was terrified.

Impaba pointed at the woman. "Where did you find her? She is our captive."

"She may have been," Hael said, "but she is with us now. She has been our guide since we found her on the mountain, and she is under our protection."

Impaba turned hostile in an instant. "She is mine! I want her back!" He began to urge his cabo toward her, but Hael interposed his own and gripped his spear. The Amsi behind Impaba milled for a moment, readying their weapons.

"Wait." Shong's impassive voice and raised hand stilled them more effectively than a shout. "This is nothing to disagree over. If she is your property, perhaps we will buy her from you. Let us discuss it at the village, as friends."

Impaba shook himself and calmed down. "Yes, that would be best. She is just a woman. And a Matwa at that." He pronounced the word as if clearing a foul taste from his mouth. "Come with us." With that he wheeled and rode off, and the other Amsi rode behind him.

"That was a near thing," Choula commented. "Brave but foolish of you."

"Not necessarily," Shong surprised them by saying. "It would have been foolish to fight, but it is often a good idea to establish at first meeting that one is not to be intimidated, if for no other reason than they may get the idea that they can bully you into lowering your prices." He turned and signaled the handler to bring Deena to them.

"Thank you," she said, with a slight tremor in her voice.

"We will not let them have you back if we can protect you without endangering ourselves," Shong said. "But you must know that we cannot endanger ourselves or our mission for you."

She nodded. "I understand."

"Who is he?" Shong asked her. "Is he important, or just the leader of a war band?"

She took a deep breath, let it out with a sigh. "Impaba is an important man among the Northwestern Amsi. They have no home, but move their tents from place to place as suits them. There are six major bands of the Northwestern Amsi, and he is the war leader of one of them, newly come to the position." She looked at Shong inquiringly, uncertain that he could follow her speech as well as Hael could.

"Go on, girl, I understand you. Just do not speak too fast."

"Many weeks ago, he and his band raided my village in the hills. Some of my kinsmen were killed. I was captured, along with some other women and children."

"Did your people not fight back?" Hael wanted to know.

"Oh, yes!" she said proudly. "The Amsi fear our bows. But riding on their cabos, they can sometimes strike swiftly, before we can get ready. Our warriors drove them off, but they had time to catch some of us who were out gathering wood."

"They capture women and children for slaves?" Shong asked, as he would about any other form of commerce.

"Yes," she said, nodding.

"And what do they do with these slaves?" Shong asked.

"Some they keep to work for them, others they sell in the south."

Now Shong showed more than passing interest. "And what lies to the south?"

She shrugged. "I have only heard stories. Rich cities, strange places where there is much magic, poisoned lands where anyone who sets foot dies. I only know for sure that they buy slaves. They trade metal, bronze and silver and gold, and sometimes iron. I heard Impaba say that I would be worth three pounds of iron if traded to the southerners."

"He had better not ask such a price for you now," Shong said.

She laughed mirthlessly and held up her arms, which were still as thin as a child's. "That was when I was still fresh-caught, plump and fighting and trying to kill myself. You may not believe it, but I was considered well-favored once, by men." Hael was about to say something, but decided that the moment was too serious for gallantries.

They came to the village within two hours. It was surrounded with a mud wall built up man-height and topped with a palisade of peeled logs sharpened to points. Hael wondered at the labor involved in dragging the logs across the treeless plain, but then he thought that perhaps they might have been floated from the hills to the north by river. A wide ditch surrounded the earth wall, its bottom covered with a few inches of muddy water.

The huts within the wall were circular, built of squares of turf and cleverly roofed with the same material. Outside the walls there were fields laid out for cultivation, at this time of year little more than earth scratched up by wooden plows. Apparently the occupants lived primarily by farming, although they also had small herds of quil and a species of plump though dwarf curlhorn. Among the huts ran scores of flightless birds.

The villagers themselves were a stocky, dark people, plainly not of the same race as the Amsi. Men and women alike wore kilts of skins or cloth and all were barefoot. Children watched wide-eyed as the procession wended through a notch in the encircling wall. The gap was closed by a crude gate pivoted to an overhead beam and swung upward and outward to admit traffic.

"Who are these?" Shong asked Deena in a quiet voice.

"Byalla. A village people and harmless. They would rather pay tribute to the Amsi than fight." Her contempt for such people was clear.

"What form does their tribute take?" Shong asked.

"Food that they grow, the sort that can be carried, some of their children for slaves. The Amsi care little for the looks of their women, so they are safe enough." She sounded bitter about that.

"Such is the fate of the spiritless in this world," Shong observed philosophically. They passed a kiln still radiating heat. Around it stood many crude clay pots, ugly and irregular in shape. "A good market for fine ceramics, if those are any indication," Shong noted. "Assuming they have anything to trade for them."

There was an open area in the center of the village, its earth hard-tamped. Here the Amsi were already dismounted, and the others quickly followed suit. Impaba spoke curtly to a gray-haired man who was apparently a village headman, and he came to speak with Shong. His accent was too thick for Hael to understand, so Deena translated. He welcomed them and put several large huts at their disposal. Despite their status of near servitude, the man spoke with considerable dignity, which surprised Hael. How people could crawl before other men and keep a sense of self-worth was still beyond his understanding.

Shong gave the order for the nusks to be unloaded. Impaba approached them with the awkward, rolling gait of one who is unused to walking. Hael braced himself for conflict, but the chieftain ignored him and Deena alike.

"We must go hunt now," he said to Shong. "We will come back in two, three days. You rest here. These slaves will see to all your needs. When I come back, we talk." Without waiting for an answer, he turned and shouted to his followers. They remounted and within minutes they were all out through the crude gate, which dropped behind them.

"Gone to tell the others, I'll warrant," Shong

said. "Well, there is nothing we can do about it, and we came here to establish relations, after all."

The huts assigned to them proved to be spacious if dark. Each had a single, low doorway and a circular smoke hole in the roof. By way of furnishings there were hanging pegs for gear and pallets stuffed with grass upon which they could spread their bedding. The villagers supplied them plentifully with food, although they seemed to have no strong drink.

That night, the whole village took part in a complicated ritual, which Deena explained was not in their honor but rather was one of many they performed throughout the year. They wore fanciful dress and their bodies were painted in incredibly complicated designs, and to the music of flute and drum they danced in complex patterns while costumed dancers acted out some sort of myth involving humans and animals and, apparently, spirits and gods as well. There were specialists who mimicked the actions of animals and birds with astonishing fidelity, and at one point a group of young girls acted the part of what seemed to be a rainstorm. The dancers looked utterly rapt, almost transcendent. It was quite incomprehensible, and Deena was unable to enlighten them.

"They are farmers," Shong said, "so it probably has something to do with rain and fertility. Most farmers' religion is centered around the weather and the soil. It might be bad manners to enquire, though."

Hael watched with interest after the others had retired. He had never seen people so totally involved in a collective ritual. These people lived a mean, sordid existence of poverty and subjugation, yet they had a spirit-life of great richness, color and variety. He decided that this must be the source of their dignity. The everyday world was not real to them, or at least it was not important. On the spirit plane, they were at one with the forces of nature. Here, these people who were little more than slaves were in control of the universe. They had reached an accommodation with life and the world, and as far as Hael could see it was no worse than many others. He could not live this way. There was too much of the warrior in him. But he understood the attraction of spiritual exaltation. These people spent much of their lives in that state, it seemed.

He retired to bed with the sounds of flute and drum still throbbing on the night air.

TEN

The Amsi had been gone for five days and there was still no sign of them. This was no surprise to anyone, as primitive peoples were never strict in matters of time. Shong was prepared to wait a week, if need be, then he planned to push on to the next town to the south-east. Undoubtedly they would reencounter the Amsi somewhere along the way.

Hael had a try at speaking with the Byalla, but their language was difficult, more than a mere dialect of Northern, with only a few words that Hael could understand. Choula believed that they spoke an extremely adulterated version of Southern. They were quite taken with the trade goods the caravan carried, but they had little to trade for them. Shong traded for hand-ground meal and dried legumes and some bundles of medicinal herbs that Tuvas identified as valuable, paying mainly bright cloth and copper wire in exchange.

Choula, lacking anything else to do, unpacked his sketchbooks from their waterproof envelopes of sleen hide and made faithful drawings of the people, the village and their products, each item carefully labeled. It did not add up to much, although the Byalla made oddly beautiful baskets, of dyed grasses and withies woven into complex designs.

Hael admired these drawings and asked Choula if they were a part of his mission.

"Very much so, although I fear His Majesty's intelligence advisers will be disappointed with these particular works of art. This portfolio will go into the royal archives when we return, for the information of future expeditions to this area, commercial or military. These"—he waved airily at the drawings of the circular huts, the poor pottery and the excellent baskets—"are trifling, but all knowledge has value."

"Interesting," Hael mused, "that merchants and map-makers can be so important in the plans of kings."

Choula dipped a brush in an ink-and-water wash and shaded a drawing of one of the domesticated dwarf curlhorns. "Oh, it is very true. The mightiest army is weak if it marches forth blind. Intelligence of what lies ahead is absolutely necessary if catastrophe is to be averted. Every army lives always on the edge of catastrophe. A work such as we shall compile on this expedition,"—he lifted his portfolio—"may be worth ten thousand soldiers to a general some day. To know where water is, what foods are available for man and beast, the nature of the natives, whether they are rich or poor, warlike or peaceful, even the matters of their religion, ceremonies and such, these can prove to be surpassingly valuable."

Hael filed this knowledge away, for it made excellent sense. Some day, when he was in command of an army—for he fully intended to be so in the future—he would make this sort of reconnaissance his highest priority. Not just scouting, but this careful preparation, thought out far in advance, groundwork carefully laid, perhaps many years in advance. This caused another thought to come to him.

"When Shong speaks of the need for friendship and trade, is this simply a cover for spying, to seek out the best paths for conquest and the weaknesses of the people in the king's path?"

Choula considered this for a while. "It is all tied together. Truthfully, there is need for commerce, and friendship is no bad thing. As for conquest, surely His Majesty does not contemplate such in the near future. After all, the whole kingdom of Omia lies between Neva and those mountains we just crossed."

"A kingdom we crossed from one side to the other," Hael noted, "taking what was probably the best invasion route. You made notes back there, as I recall."

"Well, yes," Choula said, hesitantly, "but it is inevitable that trade and war follow the same paths. Relations between Neva and Omia are rather good at the moment. But sovereigns must take the long view. Never can they assume that, just because a certain relationship exists, it will always exist thus. There is always the future, and one must watch out for the interests of one's heirs. The country must be protected should your sons prove to be weak or foolish. Though the king of Neva and the king of Omia be as brothers now, you will notice that neither of them demolishes his border forts or dismisses his troops."

Hael thought about this. The Byalla were poor conversationalists, so he spent much time speaking with Deena and with Shong. The merchant confirmed much of what Choula had said, although he was much preoccupied with the delay they were experiencing. He had the merchant's eternal impatience to be on with it, to finish trading in one spot and go on to the next, always knowing that the season wore on inexorably and soon would come the time when all trading had to stop for winter, or the stormy season, or whatever condition signaled the end of trading season locally.

"Oh, yes," Shong said, closely inspecting the legs of a nusk. "Any time there's a war in anyplace, or even one just contemplated, we traveling merchants are consulted. The king or local governor or whatever the nearby authority is, will suddenly be overcome with affection for the honorable guild of merchants and will invite all members to a grand banquet where, somehow, the conversation will always be about the country that he is planning to attack, or which he thinks is attacking him: How many soldiers we saw when we were last there, were the forts in good repair, are they wealthy, things like that." He pried the nusk's mouth open and checked its big, flat, yellow teeth.

"What we are doing now is a little different, you understand. This is a semi-official expedition of exploration, and presented openly as such. Nothing deceitful or underhanded about it." He paused. "Well, we did decide not to present Choula as a map-maker, but that's different. You would be surprised at how some people regard maps. Think they're magic, and evil magic at that. Primitive peoples sometimes credit their defeat by civilized armies to the fact that the civilized generals have maps. They are right, but for the wrong reasons. They think that the map is somehow a spell cast upon their whole land."

"And what we've found thus far?" Hael asked. "Do you think that the Royal Councilors will find this of interest?"

"Very little," Shong answered. "But then, we are still early in our expedition, which may go on for another two or even three years. After a brief time among the villages of this desolate plain I intend to turn south. From what little we've heard, that is where the rich cities are to be found. Of course, even here we have found valuable intelligence of a negative sort."

"How is that?" Hael asked, puzzled.

Shong waved an arm in a gesture that managed to be all-encompassing and contemptuous at the same time. "This great steppe is all but empty. There are nothing but primitive peoples of little importance; ragged hunters, and wild, cabo-riding raiders, and grubby farmers in palisaded villages. Although His Majesty the king of Neva and His Majesty the king of Omia are as brothers, which we all know to be irrefutable fact, still"—he made a rocking gesture of the hand eloquent of the changeability of man's condition—"still, the time could come when the gods decree otherwise. Should our king decide that conflict is inevitable and should he subsequently prove victorious, adding Omia to his already broad domains, it would be a comfort to him to know that he need fear no interference from the northeast, across the mountains. When I return, I can truthfully report that nothing will come westward through those mountain passes except a trickle of trade for many, many years to come."

Hael read the situation somewhat differently, but he said noting of this to Shong. The merchant would have laughed at his boyish ambitions, or considered him insane. To Shong, interested primarily in trade routes, markets and natural resources, it was a wasteland. To Choula, a city man, interested mainly in geographical information, it was of no further interest once it had been mapped and certain notes and sketches made concerning its peoples and products.

But to Hael? Hael saw a limitless expanse of grass, and every herdsman knew that grass was life for livestock and, by extension, for men. As a tribesman, he had thought in terms of kagga. Now he thought of cabos. Here he had seen a people who were mobile, a nation that rode. And such people could travel wherever there was enough grass to feed their cabos. This he knew was a part of his destiny.

He wanted to visit Deena's people, the Matwa. He felt sure that they, too, held a part of that destiny. The problem here was that the people were divided into many tribes riddled with suspicion, hostility and contempt for one another. He had seen civilization, and he had understood the power that unity confers. The kings and their kingdoms were likewise divided and hostile, and that seemed wrong too, but that was a problem he would take on when the time for it came.

Just now, he needed an instrument of great and unexpected power to fulfill his destiny, and he felt sure that the people of this wild land could be forged into that instrument. Even the degraded Byalla would have their place.

And always he asked questions. He asked Shong about the details of commerce among nations. From Choula he wanted to know everything about royal politics and the handling of agriculture and land holding on the scale practiced in civilization. Like most men, these two loved to discuss the details of their trades with someone who took a flattering interest in them, but even they had eventually to beg for mercy from Hael's incessant questioning.

He did not neglect Deena. She was quickly recovering, and willing to cooperate, but it was plain that her experiences with the Amsi had left her with a distrust of all men. Hael patiently set about winning her trust. She seemed genuinely grateful that he had saved her life and had not sought to take advantage of her. Many times he assured her that he would not allow the Amsi to take her back, but she was not going to believe that until she was returned safely to her people.

"Do you live in villages like this?" Hael asked her, seeking as always to understand the people he would move among.

She shook her head. "We have villages, but we do not huddle behind walls of log and mud. The valor of our bowmen is our defense."

"Not always a sufficient defense," Hael pointed out. "They did not save you from the Amsi."

"There is no certainty in life," she said, wooden-faced. "Even the bravest, the most alert, can be taken by surprise. The Amsi are very swift. It was a small raiding party, the hoofs of their animals muffled. They struck at first light, when we had gone out to get water. That is a time when people are still half asleep, and the pulse of life beats slowly. They chose their time and place well, swooped in like birds of prey, threw those of us who were not swift enough across their saddles and sped away. Even so, it was a poor bargain for them. Two were killed by our arrows, and three more wounded. That made them very angry and they were hard with us in their anger." She lowered her eyes and would not raise them. "I am so defiled I do not think my people will want me back."

"That is nothing," he said with great serious-ness. "That is the past, and you are unchanged by it. Do not worry about your people. I will make them give you the respect that is your due."

Now she raised her eyes and looked at him as one would at a madman. "And who are you to im-pose your will upon a proud and free people?"

With this one woman, he felt that he could speak what was in his mind. "I am Hael of the Islands, and I will be a king. I cannot inherit a kingdom as most kings do, so I shall build by own. I shall build it here." He gestured widely, to take in the broad plain.

He had not thought that she would mock him, and she did not. "These are ambitious dreams for a former herdsman who is now a guard riding in a merchant's train." There was disbelief but no scorn in her voice.

"I have never been as others are. Even among my own people I was different. I should have been a spirit-speaker, but the circumstances of my birth did not allow it. I was cheated even of warrior and tribesman status by my foster brother, who made me truly an outcast." He looked back toward the mountains, now a low, irregular blue line in the west, as if seeing through them to his past.

"The spirits are strong in me," he went on. "All through my youth they spoke to me, but in words I did not understand. I could only feel them, and for a long time I did not know that others could not feel them as I did. Only our old spirit-speaker had some understanding of this, but there was little he could do.

"When I came to civilization, I thought that the gods of civilized men might hold answers for me, but I found that their gods are just natural forces made into human image. They have become so far separated from the spirits they once were that they are all but dead now, and their rituals are little more than public shows."

She was confused. "But now, without these gods, you think that you way is clear to you?"

"My path is not completely clear," Hael admitted, "but its destination is."

For the first time, he saw her smile. It was not a wide smile, and it clearly required an effort, as if the muscles of her face had not formed the expression for so long that they were reluctant to try. Nevertheless, it was a smile, and to him it doubled her beauty.

"Well, then," she said, in a voice of half-amused wonderment, "how can I do other than put my faith in the man who will one day be a great king?"

He smiled back. "Good. Already your spirits rise. By my side, you shall grow great, as I shall."

Now she actually laughed, but it was an honest sound, expressive of delight. "I think you are quite mad, but that is no evil thing. Mad people are highly thought of among the Matwa. Be my protector and I will be your first and firmest follower." Her face sobered. "There is still the question of Impaba and his Amsi."

"Leave Impaba to me. I will deal with him. Now that I know where my destiny leads me, I will let no man stand in my way, least of all one who has treated you brutally."

"If you can do that," she said levelly, "be assured that I will be yours forever."

On the sixth day, the Amsi returned. This time there were not thirty of them. Hael, standing on the walk that ran below the top of the palisade, estimated that there were at least a thousand. They covered a very large segment of the plain outside the village, and a number of the villagers were straining themselves dangerously to get the gate open as quickly as possible. It was a ludicrous sight to Hael, for it seemed to him that such a fortification would be a good defense against mounted men, but he had learned that the stockade was actually a defense against the many large and ferocious predators in which the plains abounded.

Shong, standing beside Hael, swore bitterly. "That serpent! That longneck! He resented my as-

sertion of our king's power, and now he is going
to show me his!"

"It is not good to underestimate people!" Hael
said. He was enthralled by the sight, even though
it might portend danger. To see so many mounted
warriors was a splendid vision, and a hint of what
he might accomplish with such material.

"Ah, well," Shong said resignedly, "perhaps it's
all show, after all. I shall show that I am suitably
impressed. That will take no acting on my part."

Choula had joined them. As Shong scrambled
down the ladder to the ground Hael pointed at the
mounted men, now drawing very near. "Choula,
how would the mounted men of the civilized armies fare against these?"

Choula looked them over. "These look fierce, but
they would have little chance against the disci-
plined cavalry of a great nation. These men bear
only light lances, and they wear skins and carry
hide shields. The civilized cavalry form an elite
force of well-born men. They fight in battlelines.
They wear strong armor and bear heavy shields.
They carry long, heavy lances, often tipped with
iron, and they wear swords. The wild charge of
these savages would be like chaff thrown against
the waves of the sea."

Hael nodded, reserving judgment. He descended the ladder and went to join Shong in the
village center, where their wares had been unpacked and displayed. In minutes, the Amsi began
to arrive. They had expected Impaba to be leading
the warriors, but they were mistaken.

The first to ride in were a group of men past
middle years, their hair graying or pure white.

They were mounted on small but beautiful cabos, their harness richly decorated.

"Chiefs, I'll wager," Shong muttered.

Hael remembered Tata Mal's words when the spirit-speaker had explained how their whole tribal system had the aim of concentrating power, property and women in the hands of a few old men. He suspected that the same held true here; he thought it might well be true everywhere.

Beside him, Shong relaxed a little. "If the chiefs are here, they probably don't intend to fight."

Surely, Hael thought, they could not all intend to ride into the village at once! To his relief, the influx stopped when about forty cabo-mounted men occupied the village circle. All of them showed signs of wealth and importance by their age, the fineness of their mounts, their clothes and cabo trappings. They used little cloth, but the skins they wore were beautifully dyed, embroidered and otherwise decorated. Jewelry of silver and gold and colorful stones was plentiful.

Three of the Amsi, white-haired men of especially distinguished appearance, now rode a little ahead of the others. With them was Impaba. Arrogant as ever, Impaba spoke.

"These are the high chiefs Rastap, Migay and Unas." As each chief was named, he made a gesture of his hand, circling horizontally, palm down, at chest level. All three had stern faces deeply lined. "These chiefs wish to meet with the new men who have come into our land from the west, across the mountains. I have told them of your words, but they wish to hear them from your own mouths."

"Welcome to you, great chiefs," Shong said,

with broad, welcoming gestures. "I bring you offerings of friendship from His Majesty, the king of Neva." Since these people seemed to set much store by solemnity and ceremony, he launched into an especially fulsome version of his official speech, this time emphasizing the wealth rather than the might of his nation, the generosity rather than the power of its king.

While the merchant did this, Hael took the opportunity to study the rest of the Amsi party, all of whom still sat their cabos a little behind the four advance men. So far, nobody had made a move to dismount. They spoke quietly among themselves, most of them looking with some eagerness at the trade items laid out for display.

One man was different from the others, and he attracted Hael's attention at once. Unlike the rest, he bore no lance, nor any other edged weapon that Hael could see. His garb was elaborate but not rich, made up of many small skins with the fur left on. He wore many amulets and strings of small, skin bags. In lieu of a spear, he bore a carved staff in his right hand, its length decorated with feathers, pelts and what appeared to be human scalps. His face was painted or tattooed in intricate whorls and his headdress was the headskin of a huge reptile, apparently some kind of serpent. Most strangely, he ignored Shong, the chiefs and the trade goods. He was staring directly at Hael.

Hael, who came from a people no less primitive than these, had no difficulty in recognizing a spirit-speaker when he saw one. More than that, he could feel the spiritual force of the man. This was not a posturing fraud, like the civilized priests he had seen, but a man who was daily in contact with the spirits of this land.

As Shong's presentation ended with an invitation for the chiefs to dismount and examine his goods, the spirit-speaker rode forward and halted to the left of the line of chiefs. Slowly he raised his curious staff and pointed it directly at Hael.

"Who is this man?" he demanded loudly. The other chiefs looked startled. Clearly this was something unexpected. Hael was shocked, but not so unsettled that he failed to notice Impaba's reaction. The war band leader turned a look of undisguised hatred toward the spirit-speaker.

"Why," Shong began, surprised, "this is Hael, a man from the islands of the great ocean. He is one of my guards. Why do you ask?"

The spirit-speaker said something to the others, too swiftly and in too low a voice for Hael to make it out. They looked at him, astonished, except for Impaba. He was protesting something vehemently. At last one of the chiefs silenced him with a raised hand and turned to Shong. It was the one named Rastap.

"This is Naraya, our Speaker-to-Spirits. He has told us a strange thing. He says that this youth is a changeling, a spirit in human form." A murmuring began among the mounted Amsi behind him.

"I assure you, Chief Rastap," Shong said, "he is just an ordinary young man who has, like the rest of us, only the most benevolent intentions toward all your people. He is a fine warrior and scout, but no more."

The spirit-speaker rode to within a few paces of Hael and leaned forward in his saddle, searching Hael's face for several long minutes.

"Hair like knife bronze, skin like copper, eyes the blue of sky," the man said, his speech in the cadence of a chant. "You are a spirit. Why do you come among us? Are you one of the prophesied great spirits come to guide us, or a demon, come to deceive?"

"I am Hael, once a warrior of the Shasinn, now outcast and sent to wander the earth. I was born of a mortal woman."

"Many spirits are," Naraya asserted. "The question is: are you good or evil?"

Shong, seeing his trading mission about to collapse in confusion, began to protest. "Great chiefs, this is—"

"This is nonsense!" barked Impaba, drowning out other voices. "That"—he pointed a finger at Hael—"is just an insolent boy who stole my woman! She is my captive and slave, taken in honorable raid, and I want her back!"

Shong, seeing a way out, spoke again. "I am sure that can be arranged. What is one woman slave between—"

"No," Hael said, calmly but forcefully. "She is a free woman and belongs to no one."

"Quiet!" shouted Rastap. He turned to Impaba, frowning. "Impaba, you captured this woman, but you let her get away. Are these strangers at fault for finding her when you could not? Do you hand over slaves that you have found wandering on the plain without demanding payment?" The chief's glare said more. Impaba had displayed weakness and division before strangers, just when the Amsi were intent upon a show of strength.

Impaba flushed crimson but he calmed his voice. "Your pardon, chief. Of course I would not. I but let my warrior's anger overrule my head." Rastap nodded as if satisfied with this lame apology. By now Hael knew the type well: If Gasam were Amsi instead of Shasinn, he would be Impaba.

Rastap turned to Naraya. "These spirit matters can wait. You speak to this one, test him and tell us what you find. We will speak with this trader."

"Trader and representative of His Majesty the king of Neva," Shong reminded him modestly.

"Yes, this—ambassador." He spoke the word with an odd inflection, as if he knew it from a foreign dialect. Shong smiled, having gotten his point across. He addressed Hael.

"By all means, Hael, go aside and speak with this learned holy man. Set his mind at ease about you. I am sure he will rest easy when he knows that you are a mortal man."

One of the other chiefs called something and the rest all dismounted. Villagers hurried in to hold the cabos while the riders began to examine the trade goods.

Hael looked at up Naraya. "Where would you like to speak?"

The spirit-speaker jerked his head toward the village entrance. "Out there, on the plain where the spirits can hear us. You have a mount?"

Hael whistled and his cabo came trotting from behind the hut he now shared with Deena and some of the others. The beast wore no saddle, but its reins were looped over its back. Hael caught them and swung onto the cabo's bare back in a single motion, spear in hand. Now that the head chief had made a point of denying Impaba's claim, Hael did not worry for Deena's safety as long as he was here.

As they walked their mounts through the village Naraya spoke. "Your people on this island, are they riders?"

Hael shook his head. "A year ago, I had never seen a cabo, nor ridden any animal save a kagga for sport when I was a child."

Naraya nodded as if this confirmed something. "You whistle and your cabo comes. Few men can train a cabo thus, and then only if they have it from birth to train. You ride as if raised in the saddle, like an Amsi."

"I am not like other men," Hael averred. "And the spirits have always had an—an affinity for me. But that is not the same as being one myself."

Naraya grunted. "We shall see."

Outside the palisade, they rode through the great mob of Amsi warriors. The men were now dismounted. Some had started small fires and were cooking over them, others were intent on games played on boards scratched in the dirt with stone counters. They looked up with cautious interest to see the spirit-speaker riding with the bronze-haired stranger, but no one spoke to them. Hael guessed that the spirit-speaker was held in awe by these men, and he was not someone with whom they struck up idle conversation.

They rode through the camp and beyond, to the small river that looped around the village, then across it. They rode until they came to a low place on the plain, where a spring surfaced and formed a pool, surrounded by small trees. These were slender, with drooping branches and leaf-lined twigs that were like tough grass: they grew thickly but were small and narrow. Everything about the little trees was designed for survival in a land where the winds were often terrible.

"This is a holy place," Naraya intoned. "All water is holy, but the standing waters of this plain are sacred to us. The rivers have their beginning in a place we know not, and they flow from here into the lands of strangers, but the springs are for us alone. Their spirits are our spirits. The animals of the plain drink here, and their spirits are ours. The spirits of the grass sustain us, and they are ours."

"My people are herdsmen," Hael said. "I understand water, and beasts and grass. I do not understand spirits that well, but I know of them."

"No man understands spirits truly," Naraya said, "unless he is one of them."

They walked their cabos down to the spring and let them drink. The water was so clear that they could see small fish swimming in it. "You speak of spirits in human form," Hael said. "My people never spoke of this. We thought spirits sometimes appeared to us as animals, but usually in dreams."

"Spirits can enter a human at birth or before, sometimes the spirit of one who is dead but very strong. Did your father or mother speak to you of strange circumstances surrounding your birth?"

"My father died before I was old enough to know him," Hael said, bitterly. "And my mother died bearing a second child. That is the only thing unusual about my birth. Orphans are not highly thought of among us. My foster parents did not think I was anything special. Far from it. When I was old enough to go live as a warrior, they were glad to be rid of me."

"You say more than you know with these words.

For the mother to die before she can perform all the necessary protective rites, that can leave the child vulnerable to many spirits. Had you been born among us, I would have watched you closely."

"That is strange," Hael said. "The only elder who took any interest in me was our spirit-speaker, Tata Mal. He wanted to take me on as apprentice, but that, too, was forbidden to an orphan."

"Then he saw as I have. You are a spirit-man, but not like those of us who talk with the spirits, who seek their favor, and try to interpret their will. You are in a way one with them."

"You think that I am controlled by spirits?" Hael asked.

"Not controlled, but in a way sharing in their power. You are tied to them, but whether you are their instrument, or they yours, that is unknown to me."

"You mentioned evil spirits. Among us spirits were neither good nor evil, they were just *there*. They could be helpful or harmful, but they did things for their own reasons. Tata Mal said that only humans are good or evil. Beasts and spirits act according to their natures and not in the way of men. He said that they have little interest in human affairs, but I am not so certain of that. When I was in Neva, among civilized people, I learned that there are good and evil gods, but I do not believe in them."

Naraya dismounted and sat cross-legged on the grass bordering the spring. Hael did likewise. Above the surface of the water dragonflies darted busily, like tiny spears. A plopping splash followed a frog's dive.

"In the southern towns they talk of their gods," the spirit-speaker said. "I have seen the carvings they make of them, great lifeless things of stone and wood. Even the wretched Byalla would not degrade themselves further by worshipping such things. They are a slave people, the Byalla, but they are strong in spirit-craft."

"I saw that," Hael said. "It seems strange that they cannot use that craft to better their condition."

"They think they do," Naraya said, surprising him. "Their ideas about this are different from ours, and suited to slaves. They live among the spirits during their rituals, and they believe that, after they die, they will be united with the spirits forever. They think that in their rites they keep the world on course, that without them it would end, and in the afterlife they are rewarded for this good work."

Hael smiled. "Even slaves can think themselves masters of the universe. I suppose it is just as well. They have little enough in this life."

Naraya managed the slightest of smiles. "You are a spirit-man. But now I do not think you are an evil one."

"The chief—Rastap, was it? He said you had some sort of test for me."

Naraya reached into one of his skin bags and took out a small bone. He tossed it into the spring, where it made a minute splash. "What does he know about it? Does he think that spirit-men come among us so often that we have a regular test for them, such as the warriors give the boys prior to circumcision? He just wanted the two of us out of the village while he does his chief's business, which is mainly talk."

Hael found himself liking this spirit-speaker, who reminded him of Tata Mal in more ways than just the similarity of their professions. But now the older man turned serious again.

"No, I do not think you are an evil spirit. But that does not mean that no evil will come from you. We know of the prophesied ones, the leaders who appear from nowhere with the spirits strong upon them. They bring greatness with them, and much turmoil, and I now believe that you are one such." After a moment he glanced sidelong at Hael from beneath his reptilian headgear. "It does not surprise you?"

Hael shook his head. "I have always known I was different, and since becoming an outcast, I have come to feel further that I was destined for something. When I came on this party of exploration, I knew that it was to be something great. I felt it most strongly when I found the Matwa woman, Deena."

"Ah. And what have the spirits revealed to you?"

"Only hints, thus far." It was strange talking to the man like this, but he felt that this spirit-speaker could be of much help to him. "I have seen how the world is split up into tribal lands and kingdoms. Each people oppresses the weaker, and I feel this is wrong. In here, I feel it is wrong." He tapped his broad, bare chest with the tips of his fingers.

"Is it wrong for the strong to oppress the weak?" Naraya asked. "That is how it has always been. It keeps the weak from becoming too nu-

merous and making us all degenerate. Would you
like to see a whole world full of Byalla?" His eyes
glistened with amusement.

"No, but I have seen that the strength of the
kingdoms is mostly show. They think of themselves as conquerors, but they fight only foolish,
indecisive wars amongst themselves and then
build great monuments to their victories. They
speak of their slaves as captives, but I found that
most of them were born in slavery, or bought from
their parents in places where there was famine.
Their armies huddle in forts most of the time, and
the soldiers are little better than slaves themselves. They have a small mounted force called
cavalry. These ride mainly to show the excellence
of their birth." He waved a hand contemptuously.
"And they think they are strong! Had we Shasinn
not been so few in number, we could have conquered them all."

"This warrior pride is very fine," Naraya said.
"But the southern kingdoms are much as you describe, and we find their strutting armies laugh-
able, yet we do not conquer them. Their discipline
sometimes serves them well. More important, they
are very numerous. An army defeated can be replaced, and replaced again. Our warriors sometimes serve as scouts and mounted auxiliaries in
these armies and we have seen for ourselves. They
are poor in warrior virtue, but sheer accumulated
wealth and greatness of population make them
strong. Otherwise, we would have conquered them
long before now, and reduced them to the level of
the Byalla."

Hael smiled. "And that is why I have come

among you; I, Hael the spirit-man, the prophesied leader."

The spirit-speaker stared at him and let his eyes go wide. He smiled as well, and the smile grew into a deep laugh. "Oho! So that is how it is. There is still the little matter of Impaba, however, a strong and ruthless man, who bears you a grudge."

"Yes," Hael said, "let's talk about Impaba."

When the two returned to the village, serious trading was going on. Shong sat amid a circle of chiefs, with piles of goods all around them and Byalla bringing food and drink. From time to time a chief would call out and a warrior would come forward with a bundle of finely dressed pelts or colorful feathers. Shong would hold up his bolts of cloth or spools of copper wire or other goods until a deal was struck.

Shong looked up as Hael returned. "Worked it all out, Hael? Good. Come here and see what progress we have made. Splendid furs these people have. The hills and mountains nearby are full of fur-bearers and they trap them in the fall. The feathers are excellent as well. Some odd items, too. There is a powder—would you show us again, Chief Unas?"

The chief signaled to a warrior, and the man brought him a wooden tube a foot long and as thick as a man's thumb. The chief took a stopper from its end and shook a tiny pile of grayish powder into his palm. He handed the tube back to the warrior and cast the powder onto the fire before him. With a hiss and a flash, startlingly bright, the powder vanished. It produced a great quantity of white smoke that stung the nostrils.

"Strange, isn't it?" Shong said. "They say it comes from far in the east, near what they call the Great River, and they swear that the people there use it to power some kind of weapon, although they cannot describe it very well. I want to take a tube of the stuff back to Neva. I have a feeling that it could be worth the whole expedition. Or would be if we could find out how it's made and how it's used."

Hael found the powder intriguing but he had other things on his mind. The chiefs looked at him with curiosity, wondering what had passed between him and the spirit-speaker outside the village. He looked around for Impaba, but did not see him. If Impaba was like Gasam, and Hael was certain that he was, he would be out with his closest cronies, talking them into backing him in his next maneuver, which would be a fateful one for Hael and Deena.

Since they had made a promising beginning, Shong decreed a feast be held that evening, inviting all the chiefs. He purchased some fat curl-horns from the Byalla, to be slaughtered for the feast. Even in this his mercantile instincts were foremost: he ordered his cook to make profuse use of western spices, in hopes of creating a demand for them.

"They tell me there are large salt deposits to the south of here," the merchant told Hael. "We will not be exporting salt to this area. Just as well. Salt is too bulky."

Tuvas, the physician, came striding up with his hands full of bundled herbs. Normally a sour and taciturn man, he now beamed. "Look at these! Quilherd's Foot, Black Lady, Wargod's Vengeance, Trembling Moss! Valuable medicines, all of them, and plentiful as garden weeds here!" He addressed Hael as he saw the young man's mouth open to ask the inevitable question. "Two of these are the most powerful of purgatives. Wealthy people live on an over-rich diet, with consequent ill effects on the bowels. One dissipates drunkenness. When one considers the trouble and expense required to get drunk in the first place, it would seem rather useless, but it is much in demand. The fourth is esteemed as a remedy for hangover, and therefore much demanded of apothecaries who open for business in the mornings."

"There is much profit to be made from the degeneracies of a wealthy people," Shong agreed.

That evening, the savory smells of roasting flesh filled the village. Hael was too nervous to anticipate the feast with any pleasure. He knew that tonight would bring his confrontation with Impaba.

"I am happy," Shong said, eyeing the gathering chiefs and warriors, "that these people know nothing of strong drink. Otherwise they might easily forget that they have decided to be our friends." Hael agreed that that would, indeed, be lamentable.

Soon the party settled down to serious eating, and the Amsi brought out flutes, stringed instruments and drums, and commenced a high-leaping dance. While it had none of the solemn dignity of the Byalla ceremonial dances, it had plenty of vigor. Hael watched with admiration. He had yet to see an Amsi woman, and he wondered what they might be like.

His stomach tightened when he saw Impaba coming forward, trailed by a knot of brutal-faced warriors. The fierceness of their looks had been increased by the use of paint, blackening their eye sockets and slashing their cheeks with long, blood-colored streaks. Unlike the ranking chiefs who still sat, gnawing the last vestiges of flesh from curlhorn bones, these men were armed with daggers and with a type of club favored by the riders: a fist-sized stone ball mated to a slender wooden handle. Ball and handle were covered with a sheath of rawhide which was stitched on when wet and allowed to dry and harden. The whipping flexibility of the handle gave the rather lightweight mace terrible force.

One of the seated chiefs spoke up angrily, demanding the meaning of this interruption. Why did the warriors come among peacefully celebrating people thus accoutred for combat? He was not answered.

Impaba strode to the largest fire and the music faltered. The dancers ceased their leaping and gyrations and stood looking about, puzzled. Gradually, all conversation ceased as the feasters noticed that something untoward was in progress. All attention centered on Impaba and his little group of bravos.

"I have come for my woman!" Impaba shouted. His eyes shone like coals in their blackened pits.

Rastap stood and pointed at Impaba. "This has been settled! Leave us and do not return until you have disarmed and taken off your paint!"

"It had not been settled! It was only delayed.

Well, the trading has been concluded and you former warriors"—he pronounced the words with scorn—"have arranged the peaceful matters of trade and safe conduct. Now I want *that* man"—he raised an arm and pointed at Hael—"to give me back my woman!"

Chief Unas stood. "Have a care, Impaba. You are a war leader, and you earned your rank through deeds, but we have many brave warriors. Your unseemly behavior could cost you your chieftainship."

Impaba laughed loudly. "Your words are empty! I gained my rank through strength and they follow me because I am the strongest, the bravest and the most cunning among them all. They will not leave such a leader for the words of old men."

A loud, ululating howl put an end to all talk and every head in the village snapped around as one. The shaman Naraya leapt into the firelight, shaking his staff and rattling his innumerable amulets. He began to cry out in a high, shaky voice.

"Do not touch Hael! He is beloved of the spirits! He is a prophesied one! He will lead us to greatness! Disaster awaits any who interfere with the beloved of the spirits!" He said all this in a singsong chant, then continued in a loud but conversational tone: "Desist, Impaba. You trifle with things beyond your feeble powers."

"What do you mean, old fool?" Impaba demanded. He looked at his men, but saw looks of superstitious dread. "How is this thieving boy to make us great? We are already great!"

"It is prophesied!" Naraya cried out. "You all know the prophesies of Asula, mother of all the Amsi!" Like all curators of ancient knowledge,

Naraya first told his listeners that they knew what he spoke of and, assuming that they had actually forgotten, proceeded to refresh their memories. "She prophesied that six great leaders would come among us from unknown lands. Each would guide us into greatness, each touched by the spirits. First was Wan Cabo-Tamer from the south. He found us in the hill forests, living like the wretched Matwa. He gave us the gift of the riding cabo, which before he had hunted only for their meat. He taught us to breed them, so that with each generation they grew larger, stronger, swifter.

"Next came Black Martin from the east. He led us onto the plains, the limitless world of grass, and made us one with the spirits of this land. He gave us dominion over the Byalla, the Onco, the Okla who dwell at the edge of the Poisoned Lands, and all the other sedentary peoples of the plain.

"Now among us comes Hael, from the islands of the sea far to the west. He bears the prophesied marks: the hair like copper, the skin like bronze, the eyes like the sky. That cabo was unknown to him a year ago, yet he rides like an Amsi, and his beast obeys him without the pull of rein. He is a spirit-man, a prophesied one. He is the third of those prophesied by Asula, and he will lead us to new greatness!"

At this a great shouting broke out, but Naraya waved his arms for silence. "Impaba, the woman Deena is Hael's. Will you relinquish your claim on her and acknowledge Hael as your leader, as the leader of us all?"

"Never!" Impaba almost screamed. "The woman is mine, and this outland boy is no prophesied leader. Let him come forth, if he has the courage, and I will prove it! I will kill him, and that will put an end to your ravings!" He called out a wordless challenge, waving his stone-headed club, brandishing his knife in his other hand.

Hael stood, and all eyes were on him as he walked toward the fire. Spear, sword and dagger he had left where he had been sitting.

"See!" Impaba shouted. "He comes without weapons. He dares not approach me bearing arms. What say you, boy? Give me the woman and leave this land, and I will let you live."

Hael spoke calmly, but loudly enough for all to hear. "I am the prophesied one, the spirit-man. I have come to fight you, Impaba. I have heard that the Amsi are great wrestlers. My people are the greatest wrestlers in the world. I will fight you unarmed. You may use your weapons or not, as you wish."

Impaba stood with his mouth half opened, stunned like a sacrificial beast just struck by the priest's axe. A furious but low-voiced argument began among the highest chiefs and Hael could easily guess its content. They would be happy to see Impaba defeated, but they saw Hael threatening their position, and they did not like the idea of a stranger, a man of another race, becoming their overlord by winning a single combat. Hael now essayed his first exercise in statecraft.

"I am a stranger among you, and though I tell you I am the prophesied one, I do not expect you to accept that on no more than my word and the word of the spirit-speaker. Let my future deeds among you determine my place. For now, I will fight for the woman Deena, not because she is mine, for she is not. She belongs to no man and I will restore her to her own people, as I have promised."

"Your only future deed will be your dying," Impaba spat, "and I need no weapons to best you!" He threw down his club and his dagger, and stripped off his leather shirt. There was much excited chatter from the onlookers, for whatever the spiritual and political changes this portended, it promised at least to be a good fight.

The two men did not look well matched, for while Hael was the taller by an inch or two, Impaba was far more heavily built, with massive arms and shoulders and a chest like two bucklers fastened together, his back seeming as wide as a man's arm is long. Standing before him, crouched with legs spread, arms wide in a wrestler's guard position, Hael seemed frail by comparison.

To some observers, though, the inequality of the match was not so clear. While Hael's build was slender, his neck was unquestionably that of an experienced wrestler. And while his long, smooth-muscled arms and narrow waist were more calculated to please a Nevan sculptor than an Amsi warrior recruiter, the more experienced men recognized that strength dwells as much in the proportions as in the bulk. Most telling of all, Hael had long, powerful legs with swelling thigh muscles and heart-shaped calves above high-arched, runner's feet. Impaba's legs, while knotted with muscle, were thin and bowed from a lifetime in the saddle. With his massive upper body and spindly legs, he looked like a beetle standing on its rearmost set of legs. Every man knowledgeable about wrestling, and every Amsi male considered himself to be an expert, knew that legs were as important as arms in wrestling. Legs powered the rushes, provided the stability, did the tripping when men were on their feet. On the ground, legs could lock a limb or, if the wrestler were strong and expert, they could squeeze a man unconscious.

The combatants circled patiently, each waiting for a good opening. Each sought to get the firelight in the other's eyes before attacking. Since both were using the same maneuver, nothing came of the stratagem.

Impaba feinted as if trying for a neck-grapple. Hael did not respond. Seconds later, Impaba made the same move, but this time he carried it through. Hael had been expecting it, and when Impaba's body lurched forward, Hael swept the other's right foot from beneath him with a sidewise sweep of his own foot. Impaba went down, but he took advantage of his predicament by turning his forward lunge into a dive, catching Hael in the midsection with his shoulder and wrapping both arms around his waist.

Hael was dancing backward as Impaba caught him, otherwise the shoulder blow might have struck him with paralyzing force. As it was, the shock was brutal and almost took the wind from him. The move had been from desperation, however, leaving Hael's arms free. He could easily have brought his fists down on Impaba's neck, bringing swift unconsciousness or even death, but this was forbidden by the Shasinn rules of wrestling and he assumed that the same held for the Amsi.

Instead, Hael dug in his heels to stop Impaba's

forward momentum and leaned forward, grappling the man about the waist. With a wrench and a backward heave, he hoisted Impaba upward so that his legs were in the air and, twisting, threw him past his hip. The massive leverage forced Impaba to relinquish his hold and he went flying, to land solidly on his back. Had this been true battle, Hael would have instantly jumped on the fallen man, to crush his larynx with a heel or snap ribs with his descending knees. As it was, though, he waited for the man to get up.

Impaba was up with commendable speed, chagrin all over his face. Now his teeth showed like a hunting cat's. The paint was smeared over his face and he looked more than ever like an animal. He moved now as swiftly as a striking serpent, and the two men were struggling for an upper body grip, each trying to get an arm around the other's neck while simultaneously preventing the other from doing the same. For a few seconds, Impaba had both arms around Hael's neck, a position from which he might have broken the neck with proper leverage, but Hael used his legs to lift Impaba clear of the ground, depriving him of the necessary leverage. In an instant, the hold was broken and the two men broke apart.

Now Hael knew that Impaba was stronger than himself in the upper body. This was a formidable advantage but far from decisive. The man had no idea how to use his legs, which made him only half a wrestler by Shasinn standards. He was quick as a striking adder above the waist, though, and his hands were as strong as a vise.

At the moment, Hael's best advantage lay in Impaba's ungovernable temper. The man was letting his anger and frustration overrule his guile. A wrestler in such a frame of mind forgot all craft and sought to win through sheer brute strength.

This time, as Impaba charged straight in, Hael stepped lightly across to his left front, and bucked a hip into Impaba's midsection, reaching behind Impaba's back with one arm and grasping his other shoulder with his free hand, twisting and letting Impaba's forward momentum carry him off his feet and over Hael's hip to land once more on his back.

Now he was fractionally slower in getting up. Hael took advantage of the moment to sweep his opponent's feet from under him, felling him a third time. Impaba grabbed Hael's ankle as he fell and brought him to the ground. With a furious scramble, the men rolled on the ground, each seeking an unbreakable hold. Impaba wrenched himself onto Hael's back and tried to force his arms beneath Hael's, to obtain a double-handed grip on the back of his neck, which he could then quickly break.

Desperately Hael tried to keep his elbows tight to his sides, at the same time using his hands to dislodge the legs wrapped about his waist. Within seconds, he knew that this would not work. He had only the muscles of his shoulders and chest to keep his arms against his flanks, while Impaba had his whole, powerful upper body to work against them. In a move that seemed suicidal to the onlookers, Hael opened his arms. Instantly, Impaba's arms snaked beneath them, around the front of his shoulders and back again to lock just behind the base of his skull, finger interlaced.

As the terrible, neck-breaking pressure commenced, Hael let his long, flexible neck bend forward so that his lower jaw rested against his chest. This would preserve his neck for a few seconds longer. With a backward heave, he coiled his legs beneath him. When his feet were solidly on the ground, Hael reached far behind him and twisted his fingers into Impaba's tangled hair. As all watched gaping, he heaved himself to his feet, Impaba still attached to his back like some grotesque barnacle.

Squatting low, Hael leapt upward and forward with all his strength, curling into a full somersault, landing on his back with Impaba beneath him. He heard Impaba's breath explode from his lungs. The hands behind his neck unlaced and the arms flung wide. Hael rolled free and scrambled to his feet, trying to hold his neck rigid lest he be incapacitated by the cramps that threatened to put knots in his neck muscles.

Impaba came jerkily to his feet this time, roaring with outrage. But there was more than anger in him now, there was fear as well. He lurched to the spot where he had stood before the match commenced and stooped. When he straightened and whirled round, the terrible, stone-headed club was in his right hand. He ignored the shouts of indignation that arose from all sides.

This was what Hael had been waiting for. He had had several opportunities to defeat Impaba, and had taken advantage of none of them. His defeat of Impaba had to be total, dramatic and unquestionable. He had had enough experience of life and human beings by this time to discern easily the weakling and coward who always dwelled inside swaggering braggarts like Impaba. He had known that, as soon as he saw he could not win fairly, Impaba would go for his weapons.

The leather-cased stone head came whistling toward Hael's head, but the body behind it was staggering. Hael caught the wrist as it began to descend and held it immobile. He held it long enough for everyone to see that this was no trick, that he now was stronger than Impaba. With a sidewise wrench, he brought the arm down. A simultaneous kick behind Impaba's knee brought him down as well.

Hael knelt on the calf of Impaba's leg, bent over him and slipped one arm beneath his and around behind his neck. Slowly, he began to apply pressure. With one hand he still grasped Impaba's right wrist, the arm held at full extent. With an inexorable twist, he forced Impaba to open his fingers and drop the weapon. This simple action brought a solemn murmur from the onlookers, as if it had taken more strength than the superhuman effort with which Hael had sent the two of them tumbling through empty air. In the great silence which followed, Hael's words were clear to everyone.

"Yield, Impaba." The two men formed a composition of sculptural stillness.

"Never!" Impaba said, his voice twisted into a strangled yelp by the unnatural angle of his neck. Hael could feel the empty bluster in the word, and he knew that this would merely take time, which he now had in plenty, as long as Impaba's friends did not interfere. He applied more pressure.

"It is not a good way to die, Impaba," Hael said, calmly. He fought his own bellowing lungs to keep the tremor from his voice at this crucial moment. "A warrior should not die before a crowd of on-lookers, many of them Byalla. I would have you in my following, Impaba, to fight my battles. Yield."

"I will not yield to spare myself ridicule!" Under the circumstances it was a lengthy sentence, and Hael was impressed. It also told him that Impaba, like all essentially weak men, was merely looking for an excuse.

"There is no shame in yielding to a spirit-man, Impaba," Hael said. "It is an honor. You will be known as the man who challenged the prophesied one, and was defeated, and became thereby first among his captains." As he had hoped, there were sounds of agreement from the onlookers, most loudly from Naraya. After a long pause, Impaba spoke again.

"It is true. I yield."

Immediately Hael released Impaba and stood back with folded arms. Naraya cried out something in the very ancient tongue used by spirit-speakers and the surrounding warriors cheered. The chiefs showed less enthusiasm, but even they knew that they had witnessed something extraordinary. Impaba lurched to his feet. He stood swaying, battered and bruised, his paint smeared and blood streaming from his nose. Before him Hael stood serenely, elegant as a dancer at the end of a performance. It took a mighty effort of will to keep up this front, but Hael was determined to wring the highest impression from these moments.

Impaba stared at him with awe and fear. Slowly, reluctantly, as if his hand weighed more than his body, Impaba brought it up from his side and touched his knuckles to his forehead in salute. Without further words, Hael turned and strode from the firelight.

He found Deena standing in the shadow of the hut they shared. Her eyes glowed as she took his hand and led him back inside to the darkness. They sat together in the stillness and she wrapped a blanket around them both.

"Are you their prophesied one?" she asked.

"I believe that I am, though I am a mortal man and not half spirit as they think."

"You are my spirit-man," she said, "whatever anyone else may think." She kissed him then, and he responded. But when she made it plain that she would gladly lie with him, he told her, gently, to desist.

"That may not be between us yet. You are not recovered, and I would reinstate you with your people before I make you mine."

She nodded, and they both recognized her weariness. She was soon asleep, and he simply held her through the night. He would not take advantage of her weakness, her relief or her gratitude. In this, too, Hael was unlike other men.

ELEVEN

Hael finished the last lashing of the complicated hitch the handlers had taught him.
The two bundles of his goods now rested
evenly on each side of the nusk's spine. This was
a far better system than the Shasinn had used.
They only made use of nusks every few years when
they migrated, and had infrequent experience with
the mysteries of packing. A poorly packed animal
would soon suffer from open sores and nusks were
ill-tempered even when they were comfortable.

Shong had allowed him one pack animal, since
the train now had less to carry. Hael had his own
cabo, and Chief Unas had made him a gift of another, to bear Deena to her homeland. Like the
other chiefs, Unas was not sure that Hael was
what he and Naraya claimed, but he was willing
to hedge against the future. Hael had learned that
the Amsi were so rich in cabos that even the
smallest children rode. They calculated their

wealth in cabos as the Shasinn did with kagga, and owned many times more of the animals than they could ever use for riding. This was exactly what Hael wanted.

Shong looked over the lashing with approval. "We will leave at first light tomorrow," the merchant said. "The Amsi guarantee our safe conduct all the way to the southern boundary of their territory. After that, we should be in civilized territory. Not that civilized men cannot be far more treacherous than barbarians, of course, but they usually perceive the advantages of peaceful trade with minimal persuasion. I had intended to swing farther east, but anything called the Poisoned Lands can wait for a later, better-prepared expedition."

"I am sorry not to be going with you," Hael said. "I would like to see those cities of the south, but that must wait."

"You can still come with us," Shong said. "Give up this lunatic plan to become an Amsi overlord."

Hael shook his head. "I must follow my destiny. That lies north just now, among the Matwa. I believe they shall supply the last element necessary to that destiny."

"You are quite mad, you know," Shong said. "But then most sane people are boring. I suspect it will be a quieter expedition without you. You have been a fine traveling companion, although sometimes a disquieting one, and none can deny that you have provided us entertainment to match our highest expectations. I wish you well, although I do not expect to see you alive again."

Hael took the proffered hand. "And good fortune to you. Tell my patron Pashir that I remain his friend, and will keep in communication with him, now that I can write. It may have been he that set Agah to kill me, but I will not believe that without proof."

The two men parted company and Hael led his animals to the village gate. He had made his good-byes to the others already. Most had come to regard him with superstitious dread and were not unhappy to see him leave. Choula was the exception. He gave Hael an abundance of writing materials, and made him promise to send intelligence of the northlands as soon as regular caravans began to ply back and forth over the mountain passes.

Deena sat smiling by the gate, waiting for him. The Byalla had repaired and refurbished her clothing, so that she now looked like what she was; a well-born young woman of the Matwa people. She was regaining flesh rapidly, although she was still thin, and Hael feared that the haunted look would never leave her face.

He helped her mount and at first the fractious cabo alarmed her, for she had never ridden one alone before, but Hael laid a hand on its cheek and instantly the animal quieted. He remounted and the other cabo followed his as tamely as a pet. The Amsi warriors who lounged nodded and spoke among themselves in low voices at this further proof of the stranger's spirit-power.

The two rode through the Amsi camp until they came to the gathering place of the chiefs. Rastap, Migay, Unas and all the lesser chiefs awaited him. He saw Impaba, who loudly proclaimed allegiance, but would always bear watching. They exchanged salutes, then Hael pointed to the fingernail crescent of moon that touched the western horizon.

"Meet me here on the third moon from this," he said. "Bring as many of the other Amsi chiefs as you can persuade. At that time, I will make my intentions known to you. It is prophesied, it is destiny, and it will mean your very survival as a people."

"We will not fail to do so, spirit-man," Rastap promised. They still had their doubts, but they were strong believers in the spirits, and every passing day would strengthen their memories of the things this extraordinary young man had done. Naraya had already left, to make a pilgrimage among the spirit-speakers of the plains and villages, and to bring them to the gathering.

The assembled warriors cheered and waved their weapons as Hael and Deena rode away. Few of them had actually seen the fight with Impaba, but word had spread swiftly and what might have passed as an ordinary fight between two enemies over possession of a woman had already grown to heroic proportions.

They rode north slowly at first, for Hael remembered well how sore his first days of riding had made him. It might have been easier to let her ride a nusk, but Hael wanted her people to see her return to them riding a cabo. She was in no wise to look like an abject captive.

These first few days the land was gently rolling, but as they rode farther north the true hills began, the low early ones covered with grass, the higher ones coated with brush. The first trees began to cast their shadows, and then the hills were small mountains, densely covered with forest.

Soon, Deena told him, they would begin to encounter the Matwa. They would be seen long before her people made themselves known, for it was her people's custom to examine strangers closely before contacting them or taking them to a village. Bitter experience had taught the People of the Bow that most outsiders were enemies, and even an innocent-looking couple—one of whom looked like their own—traveling openly could prove to be spies for a raiding party nearby.

During these days and nights Hael and Deena came to know one another, speaking of their people and their earlier lives. There was little similarity in their upbringing, he a virtual outcast and she the pampered daughter of a chief. Her people were hill-dwelling villagers who hunted and farmed, his were plains-dwelling pastoralists. Her people lived in large dwellings that housed extended families, his separated the boys into warrior fraternities and dwelled in small huts.

He told her of his days on the great sea, a thing she could not even imagine, having never seen a body of water larger than a mountain lake.

"You speak with great affection of this man Malk," she said once. "You seem almost as fond of Shong. Why is that?"

Hael considered this question for a while. "They taught me that it is not only warriors who are fearless, nor is it only spirit-speakers who are wise." He told her of his passionate but disturbing relationship with Shazad. She assured him that the woman was unquestionably a witch who had cast a spell on him, and that it was probably Shazad who had hired Agah to kill him.

Deena, in turn, told him of her captivity. It was

a long, painful recitation of indignity and abuse, and she suffered in the telling. He assured her that this was over, that she was to put it behind her. From now on, she would be a great lady, second to none. He knew, though, that she could not forget, and that the memory would remain fresh as long as Impaba was alive. He knew that he had stored up grief for them both in sparing Impaba's life, but he believed it had been a necessary choice.

They had been in the high hills for two days when they encountered their first Matwa. They rode through a small valley with a relatively level floor, paralleling a small stream. The valley was full of huge trees, larger than any Hael had seen on his island. The trees were spaced widely, with little underbrush, but flowering plants raised their colorful heads wherever the great trees allowed sunlight to filter through.

The stream flowed swiftly over a rock bed, raising a foamy spray and making a thousand musical notes and thereby, Hael later reflected, making it impossible to hear the Matwa. He had to admire their skill in choosing this perfect place to make themselves known. The breeze was in their faces, so they had not even the momentary warning of the cabos shying at an unfamiliar scent.

One moment the two of them were riding alone through the pleasant valley, the next a score of Matwa warriors stepped from behind concealing treetrunks. They held man-high bows in their hands, undrawn but with arrows nocked. They were tall men for the most part, strong but slender of build. He saw no black hair among them, most having brown or dark blond hair. One had a startling red thatch. They appeared to be mostly blue-eyed. All wore smoke-darkened skins or drab cloth. Hunting clothes, Hael guessed, for he knew from Deena that the Matwa were fond of bright clothing.

One man came forward. He wore nothing Hael could see to distinguish him from the others. Like them he was tall and of erect posture, with dark brown hair and gray eyes. "Stay where you are," he said quietly. "Who are you, and why do you come to our land?"

Hael was impressed with the man's quiet dignity and straightforward manner. They were not like the hunters of his island, who were a shy, furtive people who crouched behind bushes most of the time and never looked a stranger in the eyes.

"I am Hael of the Islands, and this is Deena, a noblewoman of the Matwa, whom I have returned to her homeland." Smiling, he looked at the surrounding archers. "Are we so dangerous?"

"You could be," the man said. "It is never amiss to be cautious. An innocent-looking rock may conceal a serpent. I am Honn, and we are from the Bluewood Village." He addressed Deena. "Who are your people, young cousin?" Hael knew this last to be a formal address for a Matwa stranger of uncertain status.

"My father is Afram, chief speaker of Broadleaf Village."

Honn nodded. "We heard about the raid. Few come back from the lowlands, once they have been taken." Now he turned again to Hael. "Why do you bring her back? We do not buy back captives."

"I know that," Hael said. "I do this from love for her, and from good will toward the Matwa people. I have matters of great importance to discuss with your chiefs, and there is little time. You can see that we mean no harm. None follows us, although I do not expect you to take my word for it."

"We have watched you since you came into the hills. We know that no one follows. You would be dead now if there were Amsi behind you."

"You are redoubtable warriors. Will you give us a guide, so that Deena may return to her village?"

"Come with us," Honn said. "We will discuss it at our village. First you must be blindfolded. This is not a sign of distrust, it is our custom. You will have to dismount and lead your cabos. We have never handled them."

"We will ride blindfolded," Hael said. "My cabo will follow you, hers will follow mine."

The Matwa looked greatly surprised at this. Hael and Deena dismounted long enough for the men to bandage their eyes, then they remounted. As they wandered through the hills, Hael found himself enjoying the sensation of traveling with his eyes covered. It was not unlike standing night watch in his herding days, or on the caravan. He could feel the spirits of the land without distraction. Between this and his superb sense of direction and orientation, he knew that he could easily retrace the route they now took. The Matwa might have been astonished to learn that blindfolding did nothing to confuse Hael in matters of direction and location. Once, after they had been winding through the hills for more than an hour, he had a startlingly clear sense of a large number of animals, uphill to his right. He turned his blindfolded face toward them.

"Curlhorn up there, fifty or more," he announced.

"Stop and dismount," Honn ordered. Hael did so, then felt the man's hands checking his blindfold.

"The bindings are tight," Honn said. "How did you know about that herd? You could not have seen them even without the blindfold. They are too far away to hear or smell. The curlhorns have been coming up from the plains for weeks, heading for their northern pastures. That herd has been in the high meadow for three or four days. How did you know?"

"He is not an ordinary man," Deena said. "He sees things others cannot. The spirits speak to him."

Hael remounted and he could hear the men whispering to each other as they wended their way through the woods. He enjoyed the many floral smells and birdsongs. High in the trees, he could hear the chitterings of daybats as they hung upside-down from the top branches, grooming their leathery wings.

An hour past midday, Honn told them they could remove their blindfolds. They were on a low ridge looking down into a small valley. At first Hael did not see the village, but his eye followed the thin columns of smoke down to their sources and saw a cluster of long, low houses that seemed to grow out of the ground. There was no palisade, and he could see no bare, open area for gatherings or ceremonies, such as characterized all the other villages Hael had known. Like all villages, though, it was situated near water, and a number of small forest paths converged upon it. It struck Hael that men could search long without chancing upon this place; they could pass near without detecting it.

As they entered the village, Hael saw that the roofs of the long houses were covered with sod on which grew moss and grass and multitudes of flowers. The walls were no more than half man-height, the rest of each building being dug into the earth. Around them children played under the supervision of women who worked at various tasks; women and children alike were clad in bright-colored cloth. In the woods, he saw boys practicing at targets with scaled-down versions of the bows used by the men. Hael was most interested in these weapons and had vowed to make their study his first priority, after seeing to Deena's safe return.

A woman took charge of Deena and led her into a long house while Hael took their cabos to the woods, followed by a group of curious children, some of whom had never seen such animals. Hael stripped off their saddles and turned them loose.

"Aren't you going to tie or hobble them?" Honn asked.

"They will come when I want them," Hael assured him. He was gratified to note that the Matwa made no objection to Hael's resuming his weapons. His spear and sword were much admired for their workmanship and abundance of metal, although these men seemed to think that the bow and knife were the only weapons suitable in their forests.

The Matwa did some small farming, but they lived primarily by hunting and trapping. Like the Shasinn, they changed village sites from time to time as the areas where they lived became depopulated of game, but this was not necessary often, for so many herd animals moved through their hills on annual migrations that they seldom had to rely on the local game. Just now, for instance, the Matwa were eating well from the herds of curlhorn, such as the one Hael had so mysteriously detected. Half the women in the village seemed to be cooking or smoking curlhorn flesh, while the other half were dressing curlhorn hides.

Despite their primitive lives, Hael saw that the Matwa were an uncommonly clean and fastidious people, and he saw none wearing paint. The women dressing hides kept leather basins nearby to wash their hands as they worked, and even the children seemed to carry no more than the dirt they could pick up in a single day. It was a far cry from the Byalla and Amsi he had seen and smelled.

Honn took him to a long house and for several minutes Hael was all but blind as his eyes adjusted to the smoky dimness of the interior. It was pleasantly cool inside, despite the fire burning on a hearth at one end of the structure. The earth walls below the logs sides were covered by woven mats, and similar mats covered the floor. The only outside light was admitted by small windows just below the roofline.

Honn gestured for him to sit at a long, bench-lined table, and Hael did so. They were joined in a few minutes by Deena, and another woman brought in a platter heaped with roasted flesh, flat cakes, and fruits.

"Eat first, then we will talk," Honn said. "The headman will be back from hunting at sundown." Both Hael and Deena ate hungrily, for they had been subsisting for the most part on preserved rations since leaving the Byalla village. Hael had not been willing to leave Deena alone to hunt, and no game animals had wandered conveniently close as they traveled north. The woman poured them cups of a sour drink made from pressed fruits, slightly fermented.

When they finished, Honn left them to rest from their travels while the village men assembled after a day spent in the woods. According to Deena, there were few men in any Matwa village during the day, and often large numbers of them were away for many days at a time on hunting and trapping trips. Most of the village tasks were done by women and there were very few elders of either sex, for life could be hard in these hills. She told him that he was seeing Matwa life at its best in this village at this time of year, when there was abundant game in the forests and fish in the streams, when wild fruits were coming in and the weather was benign.

The winters were always hard in the hills, and many froze to death or became lost in blizzards. A really severe winter meant starvation. A dry summer meant little game, no crops and terrible fires that swept in with horrifying speed and could leave hundreds of miles of forest nothing more than charred cinders.

Between these natural threats and raiding by the Amsi and other enemy peoples, prospects of reaching old age were severely limited. Even so, these people seemed to be as happy as any Hael had encountered. Like the Shasinn, they were proud and independent, holding their freedom more precious than ease or security.

"Are your people like these?" Hael asked when they had finished eating.

"In everything," she answered. "There is much intermarriage between villages, and there are gatherings and celebrations every year. We do not isolate ourselves from each other so we all have the same customs and dress."

"Where do you meet?" Hael asked. "Where do you hold assemblies and ceremonies?"

"There are meadows where several villages at a time may assemble. We hold our religious rites in forest groves, and there are caves where the men go to make hunting magic."

"With those bows and the way these men move through the woods, I am surprised that they need any magic."

"Hunting is never easy, and the spirits must be propitiated. Men can meet with accident in the woods, and all these things must be looked to."

Hael wondered about the cloth he saw and asked her about it. "Some is loomed in the villages, using plant fibers and dyes we make from the forest products. The thinner, brighter cloth we get from traders who come up from the south. They trade mostly for furs and toonoo teeth. Sometimes we find nuggets of gold in the streams. Once a very strange expedition came here from the south and hired a whole village to spend the summer capturing animals and birds alive. They said their king had a great collection of animals and wanted to own examples of everything that lives. The village earned great wealth that year, but they ended up spending most of it to buy food, since they had spent the best hunting months gathering animals for this mad king."

Hael found to his surprise that these woods, rich in game, had few predatory cats. Here the feared predators were mostly relatives of the fur snake and the longneck. Fortunately, the giant longneck native to his island home was unknown here, but there were varieties twice the bulk of a man and sufficiently dangerous and numerous to take a regular yearly toll on the human population. There was even a small, aquatic longneck that lived mainly on fish. No wonder, he thought, that he could feel this spirit-force in these woods so strongly, with this many longnecks about.

As the light dimmed in the tiny windows, men came in and hung their bows from pegs along with their quivers of arrows and their hunting bags. Many took off their drab hunting leathers and donned colorful shirts and leggings. Some looked curiously at the strangers, but they did not stare. Hael was amazed at how quietly they spoke. He had yet to hear a Matwa voice raised. Soon the long house was crowded with men, women, and children, but to them it was a matter of course. The Matwa spent their days scattered widely in woods and fields, but the nights were spent packed virtually on top of one another. Of all their customs, only this one made Hael truly uncomfortable.

Last to come in was a man of middle years who, unlike the other men, wore a full beard. Perhaps this was to compensate for his scalp, which was devoid of hair except for a crescent above the ears. He nodded to Hael and Deena as he entered, and then everyone sat down to eat. The headman and some senior hunters sat at the long table, the rest sitting cross-legged on the floor, with children scrambling over everybody as platters of food were passed from hand to hand. There was little conversation while the people ate. The headman insisted that Hael and Deena sit at the table, although they could no more than nibble at the abundant food.

When all had eaten, the headman rapped on the table with his knuckles and all the platters, pitchers and drinking vessels were passed out the door, where a clean-up detail awaited them. He turned to Hael.

"I welcome you among us. I am Venaman, village headman of Bluewood. You two must have a very strange story to tell. I make no demand, but we would all like very much to hear it."

"I will speak first," Deena said. In a few, spare words, she told of her capture and subsequent captivity. She did not detail how she had suffered, but she left no doubt of the severity of her ordeal. She ended with an account of her escape from Impaba and her flight into the forbidden mountains. When she had finished, the villagers looked at her oddly, as if uncertain how to regard a woman returned from slavery.

Hael gave them a much abbreviated version of his adventures, promising a detailed recitation at some future date. The listeners wanted to hear more about his days as a warrior on his island. They had heard of oceans before, from traders who spoke of the great southern sea, and they were fascinated by the idea of whole peoples living out their lives on a mountain surrounded by water. To them, it was as wondrous as a village built on a cloud, and Hael knew that his best efforts of description would not convey to them what such a place was like.

Before the fires were banked for the night, Venaman promised them a guide to Deena's village. "You will be expected," he said. "I sent a runner to Broadleaf when I learned of your arrival."

The next morning they set out to the east. Travel through these hills was not as arduous as in the mountains, but there were many small streams to cross and it was impossible to see very far in any direction. Their guide kept them supplied with small game. With blunt-headed arrows he could knock birds off branches without damaging the flesh and he plucked them as he walked along the narrow path.

They spent two nights camped by small fires beneath the overarching trees, ruddy light reflecting from the undersides of the leaves. Venaman had told them that three days of travel would bring them to Broadleaf, but they did not need to travel that long to make contact. On the morning of the third day, a small party of villagers met them on the path. In the forefront were a man and a woman no longer young and wearing clothes of better quality than the others. Hael heard Deena gasp at the sight of them. He had little doubt who they might be. He looked at Deena's face and saw that it had gone white, her lower lips trembling.

Then the woman rushed forward, reached up and swept Deena from her saddle amid such laughing and sobbing, and it was difficult to know which was doing which. In all probability, both women were doing both at the same time. The man was less demonstrative, but he was also choked with emotion. He blinked back tears as he took Hael's hand.

"You have brought back our daughter when we

thought she was lost to us forever," he said, simply. "All I have is yours. Anything I can do for you, that shall be done."

The other men looked on wonderingly. Most were young men, and their expressions combined joy with dismay. Former suitors, Hael guessed, glad to see her back, but resentful of Hael. Possible future trouble, but the least of his worries for the moment.

Hael thanked their guide, and he returned to his village as the rest set out for Broadleaf. This time Hael and Deena walked so that they could converse with her parents. The cabos followed tamely and were the occasion of much comment. After a brief and tearful reunion with his daughter, Afram and Hael drew a little ahead of the others, where they could converse privately. The rest maintained a respectful distance.

"We will arrive at Broadleaf late this evening," Afram said. He turned and said something to one of the young men and the youth set off at a fast run. "He's one of our best runners. He'll tell the village that my daughter is truly returned and to get the feast started. It will be the biggest feast you ever saw. I have casks of wine I was saving for her wedding. We'll open them now. And ale! A great tun of ale." The man chuckled and sniffled slightly. His eyes still swam in tears.

"I am very happy that you rejoice so in her return. She was terribly afraid that she would meet with rejection."

Afram snorted. "Women always think things like that. As if what those animals did to her could make her less precious to us." He leaned close and said in a half whisper, "They, ah, did not get her with child, did they?"

"They did not," Hael said, solemnly.

"Good, good. No harm done, then. I'll kill with my own hands any man who dares to say she is less than when she was taken from us. Her mother will handle the women. Always does."

"Those men who came with you," Hael said, "are they her suitors? I would not wish to have bad blood between me and any of your people."

Afram looked over his shoulder at the men in question. "Them? Yes, they all courted her. I did not see a single one of them pursue the Amsi raiders and bring her back, though. It was you who brought her back. I would waste no worry on them, were I you."

"As you say." Relieved on that score, he went on to the next topic of importance. "I wish to learn about your bows." He indicated the one that hung cased across Afram's back, along with its quiver.

"You shall have the best bow in these hills. I shall teach you to use it myself. The bow must be learned in childhood to have its true mastery, but I shall make you proficient."

"Thank you. I also need an assembly of all the Matwa chiefs. Could you arrange that?"

Afram stopped in his tracks and stared at Hael. Everyone stopped behind them. "Just like that? An assembly of all the chiefs?"

"Yes," Hael agreed. "I have some things to tell you all, and there is little time. It involves your survival as a people. I have demonstrated that I can do extraordinary things."

"So can a cave bat," Afram retorted, resuming his pace. "They can fly at night and that is extraordinary. You must tell me more. My personal gratitude might not extend to my peers."

For the next two hours, Hael told him of his journeyings and adventures, of his sense of destiny, and of what he had learned in Neva and on the caravan and among the Amsi.

"You see, my patron, Lord Pashir, was right: I am able to see things that most civilized people miss, but more than that." He paused to choose his words carefully. "I see the shape that things are taking. I see the consequences of the things men do, and how all these things involve the spirits. This is why I must address all your chiefs."

Afram strode along for a while, deep in thought. "Well," he said at last, "I could never get all the headmen together, but a good many would come as a personal favor to me, perhaps one-third. But those would be the heads of all the most important villages."

"That may be sufficient," Hael said, using his long spear like a walking staff. "And I wish to marry your daughter."

"Hmm," Afram said, still deep in thought, "that could present some problems. You're from outside the tribe. Could be remedied, though. Adoption, that sort of thing."

"I've been adopted before. I was an orphan," Hael said.

"Yes, well, good, that can be managed. Also, you're perfectly insane. Not necessarily a problem. We hold the mad in some esteem."

"Yes, Deena told me."

Afram remained bemused for the rest of the journey to the village, where preparations for the feast were in full swing. It was already dark, but

Afram would hear nothing of putting off the celebration until the next day. The village was similar
to Bluewood, but it was transformed by the festival. Torches and lanterns lined each path and
decorated the long houses. The air was full of the
music of flutes and stringed instruments and tiny,
thumping drums.

Deena's mother, whose name was Reveca, immediately took charge. There would be no crowd-
ing into a long house this night. All the tables were
dragged out into the open areas between the
dwellings and the casks of wine taken out and
broached. Long fires had been preparing since the
runner had arrived, and now carcasses rotated on
spits over beds of coals so that the smells of roasting meat were interwoven with the tunes of the
musicians on the night air.

Afram, Reveca, and the rest of their party, who
had spent the last twenty hours on their feet, first
going out to meet Hael and Deena, then returning,
immediately sat down—but to spend the night in
revelry, not even thinking of pausing for rest.

Hael found the dancing customs of the Matwa
most unusual, for the men and women danced together in pairs, a practice he had never seen before. It seemed to be a part of their courting
procedure, although he noticed that married couples also indulged in the diversion.

As the hero of the hour, Hael was made much
of, and Deena's mother made it her special duty
to see that his plate was always heaped and his
cup always filled. The details of the later evening
grew fuzzy, but the next day he vaguely remembered having a try at the odd dancing, and having
found it delightful. The sun was high when he

woke and he was dismayed to find that the festival was still at full roar. His stomach lurched when Reveca tried to force yet another platter into him, and he begged off, saying he was anxious to have his first lesson in archery.

Afram immediately ordered that targets be erected; great, grass-stuffed hide bags with aiming points painted on them. Hael was amazed at the power and range of the bows. The Hunters of his home island had used small, weak bows, relying on their arrow poison to kill game. During his stay in Kasin, he had seen the military bows used in Neva's wars and these, though stout, were short and not capable of great range or penetration. The small bronze tips of the arrows would only penetrate the lightest armor. The Matwa bows were as tall as the men who bore them, thick at the grip and tapered gracefully to their tips. They were made of a light but stiff wood, with sheathings of horn and sinew artfully wedded to front and back.

The youngest of the archers could easily strike the mark at two hundred paces, more than twice the distance Hael had seen the Nevan archers attempt. After some pointers as to stance, string-grip, draw and sighting, Hale tried a near target with the bow Afram had given him. His arrow flew wide, naturally enough, but the onlookers were impressed that he, a non-archer, had been able to bring the bow to full draw at all.

By late afternoon, Hael could reliably hit the nearer targets. He knew that he would master the weapon soon. Since childhood, he had been accustomed to the automatic calculation of speed and trajectory demanded by spear-casting, and this art required only accustoming himself to the weapon and training certain muscles. His arms, shoulders and back were not unduly strained by drawing the powerful bow, but the fingers of his string hand quivered with strain on his last few shots.

By nightfall the village was subdued, the revelers finally exhausted. Hael had little chance to speak with Deena, whose mother insisted that she was an invalid, keeping her bundled in a curtained end of the long house, forcing her to eat. Reveca allowed Hael a few minutes with her patient, then shooed him away, insisting that he was exhausting Deena, that he should come back when the girl had more flesh on her, perhaps in a few months.

The next days, while Deena recovered and runners went to summon as many Matwa headmen as could be contacted, Hael practiced assiduously with the bow. He knew that he might never achieve the expertise possessed by the Matwa archers who were trained to it from childhood, but he quickly attained practical proficiency.

As soon as he became comfortable with the bow, he did something to further arouse suspicion for his sanity. He began to shoot while mounted on his cabo. At first, he shot from the saddle while the animal stood still. When he was confident with that, he tried it while the cabo walked. At a trot, the beast's gait was so bouncy that archery was all but impossible, but it was somewhat more feasible at a gallop. The length of the bow was a problem, especially when switching fire from one side to the other, necessitating lifting the bow high to clear the cabo's neck.

The Matwa watched these strange experiments with open-mouthed wonder and admiration, their earlier scepticism finally giving way to grudging approval as he galloped past man-sized targets, shooting as rapidly as he could, striking the nearer ones more often that not. Hael noted that, while the older men scoffed at the very idea of mounted archery, the younger men and youths were excited by the idea. He began to give some of them riding lessons.

Afram was among the skeptics. "It's the novelty of the thing that has these boys interested," the chieftain said one day as Hael wiped off the sweat of a long practice session. A boy now sat astride the cabo, firing arrows at a distant target as the animal placidly munched grass. "But it is not real shooting. I admit that it is spectacular because it is so unexpected. But you've yet to hit a target more than thirty or forty paces distant when the cabo is moving."

Hael grinned. "I am just establishing that it can be done. I never held a bow until a few days ago, and my experience with cabos is not great, either. But when truly experienced archers become cabo riders, what might they not do? The bows will have to be shortened, though. It could be done without reducing their power, I think. Perhaps with more use of horn and sinew and a deeper curve."

Afram snorted. "Shorten our bows? When we are known as the People of the Long Bow? You might as well ask us to shorten our—well, never mind. The men would never approve."

"The boys would," Hael said. "And enthusiastic boys grow into bold warriors."

Afram shook his head. "You don't have me convinced, and I am already kindly disposed toward you, my boy. How my fellow headmen will react to this I hate to think."

During the next weeks the chieftains in question arrived and all were treated to Hael's demonstration of the cabo-back archery. By this time, a few of the youths could shoot passably from the moving animal. Hael had not told them that this was a rather gentle beast of advanced years. What was important now was to accustom them to the *idea* of riding, a concept they associated with their despised enemy, the Amsi. None of them had his all but supernatural ability to become one with the animal, but the majority of the youths who tried immediately conceived a passion for riding, and were eager to gain their own cabos. They were not at all upset at the idea of using shorter bows for convenience while riding.

The chieftains were another thing. The whole concept seemed outlandish to most of them. They agreed that Hael's deed of returning Deena to her people was estimable, but they thought that Afram was letting himself get carried away with gratitude in giving the young man such a hearing. Sceptical as he was himself, Afram feasted the chiefs, plied them with ale and wine, and urged them to give Hael a sympathetic hearing. When the last delegation arrived, Hael addressed them en masse after yet another demonstration of mounted archery.

"Let me see if I understand this," said a gray-bearded elder from the village of Evergreen. "You are proposing that we *ally* with the Amsi, to obtain the beasts and learn the skills of handling them, and that we in turn teach them the bow?"

"Exactly," Hael said. When the subsequent uproar died down he continued. "If this enmity goes on, it will be the death of both peoples."

"Why?" asked another chief. "We have fought each other for generations, and both peoples are strong and fierce. Why should we teach them archery, which is our best defense against them? Why should they teach us to tame cabos and ride, when that is what gives them mastery of the grasslands?" Others agreed that these were valid questions.

"Because the world is changing," Hael said. "I can tell you this because I am not only a warrior but a seer. I came here with a trading caravan. It was a peaceful expedition, true, but military penetration will follow. These nations with their kings are forever contending over prestige and territory. The king of Neva plans to conquer the kingdom of Omia to his east. That will put his border at the mountains. By the time he has made his power in Omia secure, he will know all about this land to the east of the mountains; the rich grazing lands and herds of cabo on the plains, the furs and mineral wealth of these hills. And he will know that the people here are divided into tribes that fight each other incessantly.

"There is more: You have been accustomed to trading with the kingdoms of the south. Soon there will be competition in trade, then the armies will come. The west and the south may not take the field against you; more likely they will hire you and the Amsi as auxiliaries while they fight each other. The result will be the same. The peoples of this land will be ground to nothing between the millstones of these kingdoms. You must unite now, and you must have a way to fight them. They have nothing like what I propose. Out on the plains, away from their forts and strong places, they would be helpless against an army of men on cabo-back with powerful bows."

Pandemonium followed these words. The chiefs argued with him, they argued with each other. Those in whom pride was foremost refused to believe that the valor and skill of their archers might not be proof against any threat. Those of little imagination could not conceive of danger from anything so distant. But Hael saw that there was another group whose protests were no so vehement, who seemed to be considering his words.

When the evening meeting broke up and the serious drinking began, a small group of these chiefs sought Hael out. Their spokesman was one of the youngest of the headmen. He wore leather trousers and a brightly striped tunic of southern cloth. His yellow hair was braided on the right side, the braid tied up in a complicated knot. A long, soft mustache framed his mouth. He handed Hael a horn of ale as they lounged beside a large outdoor fire where the carcass of a sizable animal rotated slowly on a spit.

"I am Aron, headman of Featherbrush. My village is south of here, on the edge of the grassland. Do not be discouraged by the hostility of the old ones. Some of us"—he gestured to the other young chiefs who accompanied him—"have taken your words to heart. We think there is wisdom in them."

"I am glad to hear it," Hael said. Then he admitted, "I was growing discouraged. Sometimes things seem so clear to me that I cannot understand why others do not see them as well."

Aron sat cross-legged by Hael and the other did likewise. "You have vision. It takes an outlander like you to see things that we cannot see. These people here, the ones who dwell in the deep hills, know the Amsi only as occasional raiders. Those of us who live next to the plains see them almost daily. We fight with them, of course, but we also trade with them. Once in a while, there are intermarriages. Often their women long for a settled life in a village. Our young men sometimes want to go riding across the plains."

The young chief laughed self-consciously. "I confess, when I was a boy, many times I would see Amsi parties riding wild and free across the steppe, and I would wonder what it would be like, to enjoy such freedom, to be the terror of all who dwelled in villages. But I felt bound to our hills and woods."

"And yet," Hael said, "I learned from them that they were once just like you—a people who lived in villages and hunted the hills on the edge of the plain. They learned to tame the cabo and ride it, first hunting on the grasslands, then spending long periods there while they hunted the animals that roam there, finally cutting loose from their villages and roaming the plains as a way of life."

Another of the chiefs spoke up. "You speak of things that many of us have thought about, but you propose that we move so fast! If the Amsi became what they are from origins in the hills, it must have taken many generations. It is not so easy to do the same thing so quickly."

"And yet it must be done, if you are to keep your independence," Hael said. Then, in a reassuring tone, "But the hurry is not so great: I do not propose to merge you with the Amsi and lead you all to war as cabo-archers next year. The threat will take time to develop, for one thing. Not next year, not the next, nor even the next. But in twenty years you will be facing extinction. I do not expect everything to happen at once, but the first steps must take place now."

A man a little older than the others spoke. "I am Hosha, headman of Twineweed. I notice that you speak of yourself as organizer and leader of this great change in our lives. Is it that you are not only a seer, but a conquering hero? You have warned us about kings. It seems that you have ambitions to be one yourself." The corners of the man's mouth quirked sardonically. He had a long, intelligent face.

"It is true," Hael said, honestly. "There are times when someone of unusual gifts must appear, to take a people in his hand and turn them from their traditional path into a new one. I am one such. The world is plunging into an age of great men and the clashings of peoples. I can face men individually or in groups and change their thoughts. I can see what lies ahead. The spirits of a land speak to me. Here, in this huge land of plains and hills, they speak to me as never before, even in my homeland. They tell me that the time of the plains and hill people is at hand. I was exiled from my people for this. I was led to become a sailor for this. I gained entry to one of the greatest houses of Neva for this. It looked like chance, but it was not. For this I was assigned to the caravan of the merchant Shong. And for this Deena was sent to me. Through her, I became a man of prestige among the Amsi. Through her, I have been accepted among you. There are no accidents here. This is destiny. This is the spirits working through me. I will save you from extinction. I will make you the greatest people in the world."

The others looked at him, but they could not hold his gaze for long, and lowered their eyes. It was not that his eyes blazed, for they did not. His eyes remained mild. It was his voice, which was likewise mild, but which carried an incredible weight of conviction. It was as if his words could compel things to happen. At that moment, had Hael said that the Earth would open and swallow them all, none would have been surprised to see that event take place.

After a while, Aron looked up again. "We will back you," he said. "We will follow you to the meeting with the Amsi. It may be to our deaths, but we will try it. Some of the others, the old ones, they may come as well. We will do our best to bring some along but"—he gave Hael a level gaze—"we are your first followers among the Matwa. Whatever comes in the future, we must be your favored ones."

Hael reached out and took Aron's hands. The rest put their hands atop his. "Among the Matwa, among all people," Hael promised. "you will be my favored ones. Only proven treachery will ever cause me to break faith with one of you."

TWELVE

It was a moment to bring sweat to the palms, to dry the throat and tie the vitals in knots. Hael, with fifty headmen and other important men of the Matwa, stood atop a low rise, looking down into the Amsi encampment. This time, it was not just a war party of mounted warriors but a mobile nation. Their low tents of felt and hide stretched along the little river for miles, with herds of cabos and nusks pasturing all around them, guarded and controlled by the boys and young warriors. The unfortunate Byalla of the nearby villages were being worked mercilessly, fetching and carrying for their masters.

Hael's group had been seen and a party of mounted men galloped toward them. Hael could hear an indrawing of breath behind him as his followers saw the vast assemblage of Amsi and the party riding for them.

"I will speak for us all," Hael said. "Say nothing until I have their guarantee for your safety."

"A good idea," said Hosha, drily, "since our voices would tremble too much for clear speech."

As the mounted party neared, Hael had misgivings. He had assured his Matwa friends of the unprecedented prestige he enjoyed among the Amsi. What if they were now hostile? In that case, he decided, he would have very little opportunity for regret, so he ceased to worry about it.

Hael allowed himself to relax when he saw that among the riders were Naraya and the chiefs Unas and Rastap. The band rode around Hael's little troop, raising a shrill, yipping cry. The Matwa's faces were pale, but stern and set. They looked fearless, regardless of any internal trembling. After a few minutes, the Amsi stopped.

"I had thought that you could no longer surprise me," Rastap said, "but I was wrong. Why have you brought us these slaves from the woods?"

"They are my friends," Hael said, "every one of them a chief of a Matwa village, come here under my promise of safety to confer with you, the great men of the Amsi. Have I your assurance that they will be unmolested while here and on their return to their homes?"

The chiefs laughed long at this. "Assuredly," said Unas, still grinning. "We are not so terrified of them that we must wipe them out in fear for our safety. Bring them in, and no man will harm them."

As they made their way to the encampment, Naraya pulled up beside Hael. "All of the Northwestern Amsi are here, and most of the chieftains and important men of the other Amsi. Perhaps more important, every spirit-speaker who is not too sick or too old to attend has come to see you."

"Excellent," Hael said. "Where is Impaba?"

"Out with a hunting party. He still proclaims himself your man, loudly."

"I will believe it until he proves otherwise," Hael stated.

People were rushing from the camp to see him. The vast majority of the people here had not yet laid eyes on the storied spirit-man, and Hael could see that Naraya had been laying good groundwork. There was much cheering to go with the wide-eyed stares. For the first time, he saw Amsi women and children, the former wearing long dresses of bright trade cloth, the latter dressed only in breechclouts of hide or fabric. All looked upon him with awe.

To his amazement, people thronged around him as he rode into the camp. His knot of followers were alarmed at first, but their minds were eased when they saw that the Amsi were paying them almost no heed. The cheering turned into a deep, guttural chant. At first Hael thought that it was a wordless, meaningless double syllable they chanted, then he realized that it was his name, repeated over and over. "Hael! Hael! Hael!"

Before they reached the center of the camp, the air shook with the chant. Behind him, the Matwa took up the cry, shaking their fists in the air in time to the chant. The Amsi, liking the gesture, began to imitate it. All around, as far as Hael could see, fists shook as if threatening the sky. His task here, he thought, was going to be easier than he had anticipated.

In the following days, the council of Amsi chiefs was raucous, punctuated with shouting and threats to walk out. Like the Matwa, they were offended at the suggestion that their own skill and valor might prove inadequate in the face of the coming threat. Some refused to believe that there was a threat at all. But as loud as they shouted, as vociferously as they protested, even louder and more vehement were the plaudits of their people for their new hero, the spirit-man Hael. The Amsi chiefs were not kings to wield arbitrary power over their subjects. They were spokesmen and leaders and elder advisers, and they knew better than to defy the collective will of their tribesmen.

Gradually, reluctantly, by ones and twos, they agreed to try Hael's experiment. The spirit-speakers were almost unanimous in urging them to adopt Hael as overall leader in this great change. Hael assured them that he would not seek to usurp their power or prestige as leaders of their bands. The more southerly chiefs, without bands of tribesmen to pressure them, held out the longest, and in the end merely agreed not to defy Hael or undermine his reforms. To this Hael had to accede. He had not really expected to accomplish everything at once. He knew that, when the northwestern tribes had converted to the new way of life, the southerners would see the advantages and do the same, if not now then within a few years. Hael was patient.

In the end, when he had accomplished all he could, Hael sat outside the tent he had been given, watching the Amsi warriors who now feasted with their new friends the Matwa as if they had been allies for generations. He knew better than to expect this part to be always so easy. The enmities of centuries would not be so easily overcome, and the danger of a rift between the two peoples would never be far away for many years to come, but it was a start. His skills as a diplomat would be stretched to the fullest in maintaining the peace. They would soon have far greater enemies than each other to fight. He turned to Naraya, who sat next to him.

"I believe I am the prophesied one, Naraya. But few of these people had seen me before my return from the hills. Yet they came out calling my name, practically proclaiming me paramount chief even before I had a chance to address the chiefs. That was your doing, wasn't it?"

The fearsome reptilian headdress jerked down in a nod. "That it was. I prepared the way for you so thoroughly that they would have acclaimed a lizard had I pointed at it and told them it was Hael, the prophesied spirit-man."

"But this is only a momentary hysteria. It will not last."

"That is very true. Now you must prove your fitness by deeds, and then prove it again and again. Else it will be death for both of us."

"Yet," Hael said, "your fellow spirit-speakers believe in me."

"They were sceptical at first. But when they saw you and heard your words, felt your spirit-power, they knew you were the one, as I did. They will always be your supporters, I think, but the people will be fickle, and the chiefs will always be jealous. You must expect treachery at all times. You were lenient with Impaba, and gained great prestige thereby, but the time will come when you will have to deal with treachery ruthlessly. Let one betray you and not pay with his life, and you will be surrounded by traitors."

"I would not have it so," Hael said, sadly. "I wish to save these people, not be their tyrant."

"This is the price you pay, my friend. I think you have taken on the greatest task any man has ever attempted. You must not shrink from the sterner duties demanded by such ambition. Call your position what you like, in time you will be their king. One who would rule wisely must rule sternly. A weakling is a greater danger to his people than a tyrant."

"I know that. I will do what must be done." He surveyed the great encampment, its fires stretching as far as he could see: his people now, it came to him. He was outcast no more. "I always have."

This time, when Hael returned to Deena's village, he was greeted with joy, but also with consternation. The villagers were joyous to see him, and relieved that their men were back safe from the land of their traditional enemies, but eyes widened with wonder and disbelief at what Hael's party had brought with them: a herd of one hundred cabos. These were handled by five Amsi boys who strove to hide their uneasiness amid what to them was a sea of enemies.

"I'll arrange for the animals' pasturing," Afram told Hael, "and for quarters for these lads." He clapped Hael on the shoulder. "Now, you go to my long house. I think there is someone there who is anxious to meet you."

Hael wasted no time. Tossing his reins to one of the younger men, he raced off toward the house, its gable end decorated with curling horns and draped with flowering vines. Before it stood Deena, beaming, her arms open. Hael rushed into her embrace, then held her at arm's length. Youth and will power had won out over hardship and deprivation. She was full-fleshed and glowing with health. No sign of her ordeal remained and her eyes danced at the sight of him.

"I cannot believe it!" Hael said. "You are even more beautiful than when I left!"

"And I dreaded that I might never see you again at all, or my father or the others. How did it go?"

"Better even than I had hoped. But we'll speak of that later. Come, the day is young, do you feel up to a long walk in the woods?"

She laughed. "I have been perfectly healthy for weeks, but my mother wouldn't hear of it. I finally told her to go find somebody else to nurse. Yes, I'm dying to get out of the village and into the hills."

He took her hand and led her toward the little valley that wound up the hillside behind the village. Deena exclaimed at the sight of so many cabos being led to pasture, and Hael drank in the vision of her face transformed by joy. He had been stunned by her loveliness when he found her wasted and near death. Seeing her now, he wondered that he had ever thought Shazad beautiful. He shook his head, unwilling to let the memory of the priestess darken his mood.

They said little as they walked, hand in hand, up the narrow, winding valley. A stream tumbled musically over rocks along its bottom, and insects buzzed lazily over the little pools where the water was still. The weather was still warm in the afternoons, but the evenings were chill, and the edges of the leaves were tinged with yellow.

Deena wore a long dress of brightly checked cloth, and a green mantle of heavier cloth against the coming chill of evening. She was barefoot and where the path grew rough she sprang from rock to rock as lively and sure-footed as a young mountain curlhorn.

By midafternoon they were near the crest of the hills, in a bowl-shaped hollow where the stream had its origin: a spring that gushed from a cleft in moss-covered rocks, forming a small pool that poured over a lip of rock worn smooth and curved, to tumble into the valley below. The sheltered hollow had allowed the vegetation to grow unchecked by the stiffest of winds, and the surrounding trees dipped drooping branches into the lazily eddying waters. Only the smallest of animals came here, tree-dwellers for the most part. There were no predators to fear, and as they came to the bank of the pool, something small and timid darted into the underbrush.

Hael and Deena sat on the mossy bank and Hael took Deena in his arms. They shared a lingering kiss, then she pulled back a little to free her lips for speaking. "I have missed your touch for too long, Hael."

"We have had little opportunity," he said. "On the trail, and in the Byalla village and then on our way here, you were still not recovered. Since we reached your village, your mother has guarded you like a dragon sitting on a treasure hoard. And then I had to lead the chiefs to meet with the Amsi."

"Well"—she smiled—"none of that applies now.

I am healthy as a nusk and you are here and we are alone." They came together again, and this time their kiss was longer, deeper and far more passionate. Now it was Hael who pulled back, trembling slightly.

"I am still covered with the sweat and dust of travel. I don't know how you can endure me."

She laughed again. "By now, you surely know that I can endure a great deal. But dust and sweat are easily remedied." She waved a long-fingered hand to the pool that bubbled at their feet.

Hael had taken to wearing a shirt because of the biting insects that infested the lowlands that time of year. Now, he pulled it off, grinning. "Will you join me?"

She stood as well. "It has been years since I bathed here, but it is perfect, with a sandy bottom, and not too cold."

Hael hopped on one foot as he tugged one soft boot off, then the other. Then he stood transfixed as Deena spread her mantle on the soft bank and unlaced the front of her dress. She pulled it over her head and stood gazing at him as he fumbled with the ties of his leggings, his fingers suddenly seeming twice their normal size.

He remembered the temple of the love goddess he had seen back in Neva. The sculptured body of the goddess was awkward and ill-proportioned compared to what he saw before him now. It seemed incredible that Deena's body could be as perfect as her face, but he could not doubt his eyes. Her neck joined wide shoulders in a curve that made the joining imperceptible, and her full throat ended just above the twin swellings of breasts that were full but firm, their nipples small, prominent, surrounded by flushed aureolae. They quivered with her breath. Her waist was narrow, arching into wide, womanly hips. Below her navel, her belly swelled out slightly, then curved back in before terminating in a curly, tan delta between her long thighs. His mind near-paralyzed, he found himself admiring her knees. He had never thought that he could be so enthralled by the beauty of a woman's knees.

"You seem to need help," she said.

She came to him and brushed his hands aside. With nimble fingers she undid the thongs that bound his leggings and breechclout. As she straightened, her nipples brushed his chest, and, despite her casual attitude, they were as hard as fingertips. She gazed down at him as the night-cat pelt fell away, and he saw that her breath was coming more rapidly. With a sharp intake of breath she turned away, taking his hand and tugging him toward the pool.

At first, the water felt cold, but by the time it reached their thighs, they were used to it, not that either of them would have noticed greatly had it been icy. Hael was both relieved and disappointed when the water reached Deena's waist.

"Duck under," she said.

"What?"

"I said duck under. I intend to get you clean."

Obediently, he took a deep breath and submerged himself. Beneath the water he opened his eyes. Blurrily, he could see the sweet curvature of her thighs and the dark patch between them. He came up spluttering and swinging his hair back from his eyes. Now Deena ducked under and emerged an instant later with both hands full of sand. She began to rub the coarse stuff over his shoulders and chest, and even this touch excited him.

"Turn around," she said. He did so, and she began to give his back the same treatment.

His waist, his taut belly, her hands seemed to be everywhere. When she touched his buttocks his knees became weak. When her hand began to slip up the inside of his thigh, he grasped her wrist. He was afraid he was about to lose control. She understood and, her eyes glittering with amusement, removed her hand.

With water cupped in her palms, she repeatedly soaked his hair, scrubbed it and wrung it out, twisting it into a thick bronze rope. His body glowed almost pink by the time she was satisfied that her task was done.

"There," she said, "now you need not feel afraid to hold me." She came into his arms and pulled his head down, and this time when their lips met her tongue slid into his mouth. He pulled her to him, crushing her breasts against his chest and he felt their hearts thudding together. Their kiss broke and her chin rose as his tongue licked down her throat to her breasts, his lips taking in first one nipple, then the other, teasing them to even greater hardness. His hands slid down her back to cup her buttocks, their resiliency filling his hands as he kneaded them gently. Her hands pushing on his shoulders, he lifted her, kissing her belly and pushing his tongue into her navel.

"To the bank, my love!" she gasped. "Carry me there quickly!"

She was a more solid weight in his arms when he carried her to the mossy embankment than when he had lifted her from the frozen ground of the mountain pass, but she was no more burden than a bubble of air.

He laid her down on her spread mantle and their hands roamed over each other's bodies, his slipping between her thighs to find her secret lips half-opened, with a warm moisture that did not come from the pool, hers to grip a maleness now grown hard as his spear-shaft. They gasped, beyond words now as she urged him to her. He longed to plunge into her, but he wanted to prolong the moment as well. What he had felt for Shazad had been the blind lust of a he-kagga at mating season. This woman he loved beyond anything he could have imagined. The thought made him push himself away from her.

Her eyes went wide with surprise "What . . . ?"

He fought to control his shaking voice. "Deena, my love, I want you more than you can imagine, but not as some thoughtless boy taking a woman to himself for a night. We will marry, and we should wait."

Abruptly she collapsed in laughter. "Hael! Do you know when we will be married?"

"When?" he asked, mystified by her mirth.

"At the midwinter festival! That is when all Matwa weddings take place."

"Midwinter!" Hael exploded. "That is months away! I said we should wait, but I know I cannot wait that long!"

"No need to. Do you think all the young lovers of the village sit patiently, making eyes at each other, while they wait for the festival? No, they wed one another in private. The ceremony at midwinter makes it binding by custom. Here"—she took a thick lock of his hair and swiftly, with trembling fingers, braided it with hers. "There, we are wed. Now come into me, my love, before I die."

Joyously, he claimed her mouth with his once again as he knelt between her thighs. One hand on the back of his head, with the other she guided him to her. Slowly he began to enter her. Her head twisted back and a deep cry escaped her lips as her hips rocked powerfully into his, burying him in her warm depths. He had feared that he would erupt instantly, but from somewhere he found a deep reserve of control and their bodies began to move together in a rhythm that was so natural yet so intense that it took them out of themselves and merged them as one, and as they crested together all the spirits of the place sang to Hael, and they told him that this was right.

Later, as the moon rose, they lay together, half wrapped in Deena's mantle. Hael lay on his back, and Deena sprawled half across his chest, one of his hands gripping her waist as her hair lay spread like a cloak over his neck and shoulder. From this position he could gaze down the length of her back, admiring the cleft of her spine, how it arched from the long, convex curve of her back to the short concavity of her spine, where the abrupt flare of her hips blossomed into the full roundness of her buttocks in a volute sweep of such beauty that it brought tears to his eyes. Nowhere on her body, seen from any angle, was there an imperfection. He could see nothing that was not beautiful.

In their youth and the strength of their passion, they had made love many times that long afternoon and evening, searching out the secrets of each other's bodies with eyes and hands, lips and tongues, learning to know each other with the intimacy only lovers share.

"Everything must be fast with you," she whispered into his neck. "Warrior, seaman, explorer, now even a sort of king,—soon to be more of a king!—all in so short a time. Now you want to force a lifetime of love-making into an afternoon."

He smiled down at the part in her still-damp hair. "You have not been slow or backward, I notice."

She crossed her forearms on his chest and rested her chin on them. "I've learned that it is not good to wait. When I was captured, I thought I would die. When I was a slave, I wanted to die. And I would have died, miserably, if I had waited for rescue. Instead I ran, and I found you. I would have died content to be free, on that mountain, but instead you found me and gave me back to myself. I have learned that it does not pay to wait."

She pushed herself up and knelt beside him with her hands on her knees, her breasts swaying slightly, their nipples at last soft, subsided into the encircling dark flesh. "I know that you are not as other men, and you will be away from me much. You will not be like other husbands, to go out hunting in the days while I work in a field, to join me in the evenings. While you are with me, I intend to have all of you."

Slowly, walking by moonlight, they returned to the village. On the way, she asked him about the words he had spoken as the Moon rose, and he told her about his people's nightly apology to the Moon, and she told him of her own people's belief that in the far past, in the Time of Catastrophe, the Earth and Moon had fought a great battle, which the Earth had won by shooting fiery arrows at the Moon. Their belief was that the Moon had started the fight, and was owed no apologies.

He told her more of his victory at the meeting of Amsi and Matwa, but she did not share fully his elation, shaking her head.

"It was too easy," she said. "That the people loved you I have no doubt, and I know that Naraya believes in you, and he has probably convinced the spirit-speakers. But the chiefs are jealous of their authority. You have arranged it cleverly in leaving them their prestige, but that will not be enough."

"I have thought of it," he admitted. "Have no fear, I am not so foolish as to think that some feasting and cheering have made me the unquestioned leader of two enemy peoples."

She thought a while. "You must form a council of headmen of both nations, with you as war leader. Do not go beyond that at first. Leave the rest all other power, and defer to them in questions not relating to war. Make a show of how busy your duties keep you, and how you have no time for other ambitions. It will be close enough to the truth."

He cocked an eyebrow at her. "I can see who my chief counselor will be."

"It's good that you should know that now. And believe this: I shall be the only one you will ever be able to trust fully."

"I know," he sighed. "Already I have found that, in becoming a leader, I have lost much of the good fellowship that I once enjoyed."

"Above all," she said, "I fear Impaba. This is not because of the way he used me, save that it taught me what sort of man he is. His devotion to you is a sham, and he but looks for a safe way to kill you. You took me from him, then you defeated him in fair battle before his peers and then, most humiliatingly, you spared his life. He will bide his time, and wait for the right time, then he will try to take your life in some treacherous and under-handed way. Some way that will leave him safe."

"I do not trust him. But I don't fear him in open fight, on even terms, and who would he get to help him?"

"I do not know. What I do know is that he will try."

When they returned to the village, their long absence was pointedly ignored. The villagers, always ready for a celebration, were celebrating the return of the men who had gone into the lowlands. The next day, the representatives from the other villages would return home, and throughout the coming months men and boys would come from all the Matwa villages to learn to ride and care for cabos. It would be a long and difficult process, but it was a beginning. For the moment, unable to take his eyes or attention from Deena, he could not feel daunted by the task.

THIRTEEN

It was a long, hard autumn and winter. The cabos were unused to the hill country, and had to be coddled or else they fell to sulking and refused to eat. Learning to care for them could be hazardous, and many earned bites and kicks in mastering the task.

Saddlery proved to be a great problem. The craft of making them was exacting, and the only really fine saddles were made in towns far to the south. Until they could trade for some, and in time learn to make their own, the Matwa would have to be satisfied with stuffed leather pads tied on with woven girths. Better yet, they could learn to ride bareback, which would make their seats even more secure when they finally had good saddles.

The winters were usually hard in the hills, and there were grumblings that Hael's training program occupied the young men and boys at a time when they were vitally needed for gathering food against the lean months. Hael found himself engaging in lengthy arguments, seeking continually to justify his rigorous project.

Still, there were joyous moments. When the first cabo foals were born, people came in from all the nearby villages to gawk at the hornless, skinny-legged little creatures as they bleated and butted their heads at their mothers' bellies to nurse. Even Hael's staunchest critics beamed at the sight.

And most of his students conceived an unquenchable enthusiasm for riding, many of them reluctant to return to their own villages when a new group came in. The Amsi boys adjusted quickly, and were soon as imperious and demanding as any other teachers when they gave their lessons on the care of cabos, showing their pupils how to curry, saddle, feed, water, doctor and otherwise perform the hundred tasks necessary to keep cabos healthy, obedient and reproducing.

One day a bowyer from a far village arrived and demanded to see Hael. From his hand Hael took a strange new weapon. It was a bow, but it was short, slightly more than half the length of the usual long bow. Unstrung it curved almost in a circle. Strung, the curve was reversed, and its ends arched forward in a secondary curve.

"I saw one a little like this once, years ago," the man explained. "It was from far north, in the frozen lands. The forests up there are mostly soft evergreen. There isn't much good bow wood so they stretch their supply by using more horn and sinew and a glue boiled down stronger than what we use. Since they're short, they need this deep curve, and the extra curve at the tips seems to give the arrow extra push. When I heard what you needed, I had a try at making some. I made them stout, since they're to be used for war, and I tried a curve even deeper than the northern bow I saw. The first three I made snapped or came apart, but I think I got the proportions and the glue right with this one."

"Let's try it," Hael said, calling for a boy to bring his cabo. For the rest of the day he tried the bow at various gaits and at targets of various ranges. Stringing the bow was far more laborious than with the long bows, but in all other respects it was greatly superior for mounted archery. With its short limbs, it was easy to maneuver from the saddle, clearing the cabo's neck with a slight raising of the bow hand. Hael's eyes blazed with pleasure when he drew the bow, releasing the arrow to fly true to its target. Finally, he drew rein and hopped to the ground before the bowyer.

"This is what we have been needing! How many can you make, and how soon can you deliver them?"

"Well, it's a slow process, perhaps . . ."

Hael did not allow him to finish. "We'll have to assemble the bowyers. Can you teach others to make these?"

"I suppose I can, but I must tell you, I am more skillful than most. But these bows are still made much like our old ones, just proportioned differently. Maybe, in a few years. . . ."

"I don't have years." Hael's mind was working at a feverish pace. "We will establish a great bowyers' center here. You will be the master. We'll assemble all the materials we need and you can take on as many apprentices as you can handle. The bowyers from the other villages will come here and learn to make the new bows and then go home and start turning them out. How does that sound?"

"But, nobody has ever ... I mean ... It's just that. ..." The man's ability to protest ran down in the face of this fierce energy and determination. Finally he shrugged. "All right."

Hael clapped him on the shoulder. "Good. I like it when a man sees the right course without giving me a lot of windy argument."

Another problem was in finding privacy for himself and Deena. The packed Matwa long houses gave them no opportunity to be together. When they could snatch a few hours, they went into the forest, and when the weather grew inclement, Hael erected a small Shasinn-style hut for them. Soon, though, it grew too cold for this, too.

It seemed to them that the time of the midwinter festival would never arrive, but inevitably it did. Amid much ribald revelry, all the courting couples of the village were assembled in fine robes, the brides, many of them with swelling bellies, bedecked with ribbons and wreaths of winter berries. The ceremony took place at sunrise on midwinter day, with the village chief presiding. The Matwa had very few spirit-speakers, and these did not concern themselves with weddings, although they sometimes took part in child-namings and funerals.

The chieftain made a brief, simple address, then the married women of the village came forward to shower the couples with dried flower petals and sprinkle them with new wine. When the sun cleared the horizon a great shout went up, and the celebration began. Aside from solemnizing all the year's marriages, it was a good excuse to consume all the surplus food that could not be preserved through winter.

The following months were hard ones, with heavy snow and bitter winds. The hunters went out every day, but game was scarce. The animals taken at this time of year were valued for their winter coats rather than for food, and these pelts were dressed for trade in the spring. It was Hael's determination to trade for as many cabos as possible, and again he met with resistance, for many wished to use the pelts to acquire more traditional trade goods. Hael protested that, as they became wealthier in cabos, they would soon be far wealthier in everything else, but some were slow to see things his way.

Great labor had to be expended in finding fodder for the animals, parties ranging far and clearing large areas of snow so that dry grass could be uncovered. It was an arduous process, but by the end of winter their little herd had increased to one hundred twenty. The Amsi boys were astonished that so many foals had survived, and so few of the original stock had perished in the severe winter. They attributed this to Hael's special magic with animals, a judgment with which he agreed. Every moment he could spare, he had spent with his beloved cabos.

Whenever the weather permitted, he continued training the men in mounted archery. From his village and the three nearest, he selected a small squadron to serve as a cadre for training the forces to come. These were the fifty best archers and riders, men he also knew to be unshakably loyal to him. He determined to take them into the lowlands as soon as the spring came. He had a number of reasons for doing so.

He wanted them to have experience as an independent unit. All their lives, they had identified first with their villages. They needed to have experience in a terrain that was different from their native hills. Above all, he needed more cabos. Natural increase was too slow, trade was expensive, and the Amsi were reluctant to part with more than a minimum of their beasts. He would be stretching his fragile hold on the Amsi to demand more.

The Amsi had told him that there were herds of wild cabos roaming the plains. These were mostly domesticated animals that had reverted and mixed with the wild stock. They would be mostly degenerate, stunted animals, but he had been assured that they could be bred back up to size in a few generations and would yield excellent riding stock in just a few years. Hael proposed to take his men out on a cabo hunt.

When the last of the snows were melting on the higher elevations, Hael ordered his fifty to saddle their mounts. The animals he had chosen were sound, but not the best breeding stock. He hoped to return with many more, to make up for any losses they might suffer. Some of the men had the new, short bows. Hael had hoped to have them all equipped thus, but there had been no rushing the bowyers. Constructing the complex weapons was an exacting task, and no amount of patience would make the binding glue set faster. By the next spring, every man who rode would have a short bow, but not before.

Deena brought him some spare clothing she had

made as he was preparing to mount. "You must be back by the end of summer," she said as she stuffed the bundle into his saddlebag. Her face glowed, and her belly bulged slightly beneath her long dress of red-and-blue checks.

He embraced and kissed her and tousled her hair. "Do you think I would miss the arrival of our firstborn? I would return from the dead for that."

A shadow crossed her face. "Do not speak thus. I only want you back alive and whole."

"Then I promise to return in one piece," he said, kissing her one last time.

Hael swung onto his cabo. His short bow and his arrows were in a case by his left leg, his sword hung at his side and his spear was upright in a sheath before his right leg. The spear was not much good for mounted combat, but he could not bear to be parted from it. It was the one remnant of his former life that he had no intention of abandoning.

There were doubtful faces among the villagers who turned out to see them off, but most waved and called out good wishes. The riders, mostly young men, waved happily, eager to be off. Hael was as glad to be moving. Only the separation from Deena subdued his mood. The last weeks of winter had been galling, and only his ceaseless activities had kept him from going mad. He had found that he was not temperamentally suited to huddling with a great mass of people for days at a time when the snows were severe. This winter had in some ways been more frustrating than the one he had spent with Shong's caravan, waiting for the mountain passes to open, for all that he had much more to occupy him here. He was still too close to his origins in the warm and open environment of the islands, where his people had spent most of their lives outdoors.

Now, riding toward the open plains, he felt like a man released from a dungeon. Had Deena been able to accompany him, his happiness would have been complete. The cabos as well grew livelier as they realized that they were returning to the plains. They snorted and tossed their horned heads excitedly as they sniffed air from the lowlands.

Since men and cabos both were out of condition from their long winter's isolation, Hael decreed that the pace be slow for the first days, and that they encamp before the sun touched the western horizon.

The first day's ride brought them to the gently rolling land that separated the true hills from the grassland. As soon as they encamped, sentries were posted and the men checked their animals' hoofs and backs. Only after security and the cabos had been seen to were fires kindled and food unpacked. Small game had been bagged during the march and man set about cleaning the carcasses and preparing them for dinner.

Hael was pleased with the scene. This was a fine life for young men, and he knew that, once they were accustomed to it, few of them would want to go back to a precarious living in the hills, hunting and trapping and coaxing reluctant crops from the thin soil of the hillsides.

These men would return to their homes, and all through the winter months they would speak of their adventures of this summer. By the next spring, all the young males would be clamoring for a chance to join them. And in time . . . Hael tore his thoughts away from these speculations. He would take it one step at a time. Malk had taught him that each year's voyage began with a shakedown period, a few days during which the ship's routine was established. This was needed even by experienced mariners in a familiar ship. Hael's present preoccupation was his own shakedown period. He and his men and their animals were going to require a lengthy shakedown period, while the little troop became accustomed to each other, to their routine and their duties.

By the third day, men and cabos were over their initial soreness. Hael observed the men closely, and those who seemed to be the most natural riders, and who possessed the best sense of direction orientation on the wide plains, he gave the duty of point and flank security. These also were to shoot small or medium-sized game for the troop. Hael instructed them to take no animals that would require lengthy dressing out. Since the grasslands swarmed with migratory herds at this time of year, they never lacked for meat when time came to make camp.

Hael learned that the life of a commander was far from carefree. As the days went on, he was pleased with the progress his troop was making, but he had a thousand worries nagging at his peace of mind. He could not enjoy watching the wind waving the fresh green grasses of the plains, something he had always loved, because now he saw the grasses as the lurking place of burrowing animals. Even the humble, harmless nose-horn could bring down the mightiest cabo should its hoof plunge into a tunnel. The men got on well together, but there were inevitable rivalries and disputes, which Hael often had to settle.

It was always a nervous moment when they contacted a roving band of Amsi. The skin-clad plains warriors were unfailingly respectful toward Hael, their painted faces often alight with virtual reverence, but they looked at the Matwa with suspicion, which was reciprocated by his men. Hostility always lay just beneath the surface. Hael spread the word that he was searching for herds of wild cabo. The Amsi promised to send riders to guide him if they spotted any.

The troop did not find everything to their liking down on the plains. They were ecstatic about the incredible abundance of wild game, easily taken by a bowman on cabo-back, but they soon found that clouds of stinging, biting insects followed those mighty herds. Even more distressing was the frequent scarcity of wood, necessitating the burning of dried animal dung. They soon accustomed themselves to these things, though, and nobody grumbled very loudly or showed any eagerness to return home.

By the end of the third week, Hael felt that his men were well seasoned to the mobile life, and lacked only the experience of combat to make them competent as a cohesive military unit. He had no intention of seeking out a fight, though, being well content to build up a strong mounted force before exposing any of his warriors to the hazards of battle. His force was tiny as yet, and if they were lost in their first combat, there would never be another. Besides, for the moment they had no enemies. That, Hael knew, was a factor that would change.

One morning, Hael woke a little before sunrise, with the sounds of the sleeping camp around him. The watch fire crackled slightly as a yawning youth poked at the embers and threw on some dry twigs. The air was dew-fresh, with a tinge of smoke and cabo scent. Hael rose from his blanket and walked a little distance away from the camp, first being sure that the man assigned to the cabos was awake at his post.

Hael walked to a small rise and climbed it, at its crest turning to survey his surroundings. In the growing light, he could see far. His whole camp lay before him, and it seemed small in the limitless plain. Beyond lay herds of branch-horn and curlhorn, and the stalking forms of killer birds beginning their morning hunt. To the far west towered tremendous clouds, sign of a great storm that must have swept the western ocean the day before. He thought of Malk and all the other mariners out on that perilous sea. As the sun broke over the eastern horizon, he felt as he had sometimes in his early youth, watching over his tribe's herds, feeling the spirit-force of the land as he looked out over all its dazzling abundance of life. For a few moments, he felt that he was at the center of the world.

He came out of his reverie when he saw something moving purposefully toward the camp. It was a lone rider, undoubtedly an Amsi. Hael ran down to the camp, wanting to be there when the man arrived. The men were on their feet, stretching and yawning, some of them carving strips of meat from last night's game for a cold breakfast. Hael called for his five squad leaders.

"There is a lone rider coming," he said when

they were assembled. "Perhaps it's the news we have been awaiting."

There was subdued anticipation as the man rode in. He smiled arrogantly as he came through the camp, looking neither to the right nor the left, his eyes fixed only on Hael. He appeared to have seen more battle than most men, for his face was badly scarred, and his hairline was somewhat out of alignment: apparently a goodly portion of his scalp had been torn loose and had healed crookedly. One of his ears was missing. The skins he wore had once been fine, but now they were blackened with smoke and old blood from butchered game. He drew rein before Hael.

"I greet you, Prophesied One," he said, raising the back of his hand to his eyes. "I am Deno, of the Blue River tribe of the Southeastern Amsi. My band was out trading two days' ride to the south and we saw a good herd of wild cabo, three or four hundred. We had heard that you were here looking for such, so my chief sent me to look for you and guide you to them."

Hael felt the stirrings of excitement. "Excellent! Did they look like good stock?"

Deno grinned crookedly. "Oh, very good! Lord of the herd is a big one. It is probably some chief's prize war cabo gone wild. All his foals will be decent riders, even if the mothers are stunted. The small males"—he shrugged—"you can still geld them and break them to the saddle. They are good for teaching children to ride."

Hael smiled broadly and turned to his men. "Eat in haste, see to your mounts and put out the fires! We ride!"

Cheerfully the men hurried through their morning routine, and Hael was pleased with their efficiency. He had made a point of emphasizing the importance of putting out fires. The men felt that they knew this well enough. As foresters they were always careful about fire. But grass fire could sweep a whole plain in hours, and the Amsi had some truly imaginative punishments for anyone found to have started one through negligence.

When they were mounted, Deno rode out ahead of them, apparently having little taste for the company of Matwa. One of the squad leaders rode up beside Hael. It was Hosha, the young chief of Twineweed. "I do not like the look of this rogue, my captain," he said, frowning.

"Could you like the look of any Amsi?" Hael asked.

"No. But this one looks like he gets into many fights and loses them all. He treats you with a respect that borders on insolence. Do not trust him."

"I shall be careful. But he is a lone man and no threat to us. If he is a rogue, perhaps that is why his chief sent him out alone to find us. He would be no loss should a fur snake have him for dinner." Hosha was unhappy, but said no more.

All that day they trekked south. When they camped for the night, Deno rode off to make his own camp. Hael thought this odd, but perhaps the man felt uncomfortable sleeping in the midst of hereditary enemies, despite the presence of the prophesied spirit-man.

The next day followed the same pattern. The morning of the third, Deno rode up to Hael. "We are close now. Sometime today we will find them."

"Very good," Hael said. "I want to get as many as possible."

"Easy," Deno assured him. "Just rope the big one. The rest will follow wherever you take him."

Late in the morning, they saw a column of thirty Amsi riders. The Amsi galloped up to them, cheering and yipping, but they did not wave weapons, signifying peaceful intent. Deno scowled at the newcomers but said nothing.

A young chief dressed in beautiful white skins rode up smiling. His hair was braided with strings of beads and his ears were laced with gold wire. "Greeting, Spirit-Man!" he called. "We heard that you were looking for wild cabos. I am Twila, under-chief of the Two Rocks band, Northwestern Amsi. I saw you fight Impaba."

"I remember you," Hael said. These Amsi displayed no undue hostility, to Hael's relief. He told Twila of Deno's mission.

Twila frowned. "Odd that we haven't seen these cabos. This is far north for the Southeasterners to be at this time of year."

Deno grinned at him without good will. "We got much bronze from the south last year. We came north early to trade for the best of the winter's furs. If you didn't see the wild herd, it's because Northwesterners are more concerned with looking pretty than with knowing how to ride and hunt." He eyed the lavishly decorated skins with contempt.

Twila's face reddened. "Out of respect for the Prophesied One, I will not strike you down for that. Look me up at the midsummer trade fair. We can discuss this further on the dueling ground."

Deno laughed. "I will be at your service." He turned to Hael. "Shall we ride now? We can still have them all rounded up by nightfall."

Hael bade farewell to the young chief and they continued south, but he was uneasy in his heart. He now felt that they might be under a threat, although he was certain that the Amsi would not attack him. Who then? The answer came all too soon.

In the heat-shimmer of afternoon, Hael could see Deno riding out well ahead of the point riders. There was a rise in the ground ahead, a long ridge slanting from southeast to northwest. Beyond it, Deno had said, a river cut the plain. They would find the herd of wild cabos between ridge and river.

Within a few minutes, Hael and the main body reached the crest of the ridge and found the point riders there, halted and looking puzzled. There was no sign of Deno.

"Where did the Amsi go?" Hael demanded.

"We don't know," one of the point riders said. "He was about three bowshot lengths ahead of us when he went over this ridge. When we got here, there was no sign of him. He must have broken into a gallop as soon as he was out of our sight."

Hael scanned the scene before him uneasily. In the distance he could see the river, a narrow strip of muddy water meandering along the bottom of a shallow valley. The river's flooding had over the millennia cut up the valley floor into a maze of low hills sharply divided by gullies. Game animals were plentiful, drawn by the water and the rich grasses, and numberless water birds dotted the marshes along the river.

"Cabos!" one of the men shouted, pointing. Peering, they could see a half dozen of the animals wandering from behind one of the little hills.

"They've come down to drink," Hael said. "The rest of the herd must be behind that hill. Perhaps Deno went down there to look for them. Let's ride slowly and quietly, like another herd coming down for water. We don't want to panic them."

As they made their way down the slope, Hael readied his casting rope, making sure that the noose was supple. He wanted to rope the big leader while the others surrounded the herd. He had not yet spotted the leader. But he was still troubled by Deno's disappearance.

"Look!" Hosha shouted. All around him, Hael's men burst into furious cursing.

"String you bows!" Hael shouted. Before them, a large force of mounted men were rounding the hill, calling out shrill war cries, waving lances, clubs and axes. Now Hael could see that the cabos by the river were hobbled. They were bait, and the trap had worked perfectly.

Hosha turned on Hael, fury on his face. "So, the Amsi are our friends? We can expect a rough welcome from these!" He struggled to get his bow strung. It was difficult to do on cabo-back, and Hael had made them all practice the move repeatedly. The stress of impending battle made them clumsy.

Hael was stunned, unable for the moment to comprehend what was happening. How had the Amsi, who just last year had hailed him as their prophesied leader, turned against him? Then he saw the men in cloth tunics, and the ones who wore tattered cloaks of feathers.

"They aren't Amsi," Hael said; "not all of them."

Hosha peered at them, his bow strung and his first arrow nocked. "You are right. Look at those two." He pointed with the arrow toward two men who wore bright trousers and shirts of cloth. "Those are Matwa by their dress." He sounded as uncomprehending as Hael felt. Now other strange forms of dress became obvious. Most of the men looked ragged.

"Wild men!" Hael said. "We had their like in my homeland, outcasts and rogues of every land, turned bandit to raid for their living."

"Whatever they are," Hosha said, "they are more than twice our strength!"

"Hold fire," Hael said, "do not shoot until you can be sure of a target. Shoot the men. I want those cabos!"

Hosha and the others looked at him open-mouthed. "Are you mad? A cabo is four times the target! Kill the beasts, and the men will be helpless!"

"You heard me!" Hael roared. The men jerked in reaction, even their dread of the onrushing riders overcome by the imperative in Hael's rarely raised voice.

"As you say, Captain." Hosha nodded, his fury gone.

The raiders were almost in range and the Matwa spread out enough to give every man a clear shot. They raised their bows and slowly began to draw. Now Hael saw who led the raiders. There was no missing the hulking form astride the lead cabo.

"Impaba!" Hael said, speaking almost to himself. Despite his dread and rage, he almost had to feel a certain admiration for the man. It had been beautifully done. Knowing that his fellow Amsi would not raise a hand against Hael, he had feigned loyalty and devotion. In the meantime, he had been rounding up this pack of vicious scavengers, awaiting his opportunity. Hael had thoughtfully provided such an opportunity by riding here with a small force. If he succeeded, Hael would be dead and the other Amsi might never know that it was Impaba's treachery.

"Shoot!" Hael commanded. He aimed his own arrow at Impaba. The missiles hissed toward the raiders and at least a dozen men tumbled from their saddles.

"Now!" Hael commanded. The squads wheeled and split open, half the force riding to the right, the others to the left. It was a simple maneuver that they had practiced, and since it was unexpected, it worked. As the raiders plunged between the two forces, they poured arrows into both its flanks. When they were past, Hael rode for the river and the rest rallied behind him. At the verge of the marsh, they turned and faced the raiders, who were milling in some confusion.

"Have we lost any?" Hael demanded. Two men had been injured by stone-headed clubs hurled at short range. Another had taken a javelin through the thigh, but all three had remained in the saddle. Hael ordered the wounded men to the rear and studied his situation.

"It's not good, Captain," Hosha muttered. "River to our backs, them in front. We've hurt them, though." He smiled grimly at the litter of bodies on the ground, at the riderless cabos.

"A good thing they aren't all Amsi," Hael noted. "They'd have whirled and been on top of us before the second volley. Few of these men can ride like that."

"That one out front," Hosha said, "is that your old friend Impaba?"

"It is he," Hael affirmed. "I spared his life once, a mistake I'll rectify today."

"Just the course I would have advised," Hosha said, his sardonic manner returning. "Of course, there's the matter of the rest of this scum to attend to. Still outnumber us almost two to one, I'll warrant."

Impaba, with Deno next to him, was haranguing the bandits with many wild gestures. Apparently, he had promised that the band of awkwardly mounted hillmen would be easy victims, and they were disappointed to learn otherwise. Gradually, under his direction, they began to spread out, forming a broad crescent, then to advance at a walk. As they drew closer, Hael could see the grin decorating Impaba's ugly, scarred face. Just out of bowshot, they halted. At this distance Hael could not make out Impaba's words, but their import was plain. The raiders leaned low along the necks of their mounts. Those with shields raised them before their faces. They would not present convenient targets this time. At Impaba's barked command, the raiders began to advance.

Hael knew that his force could not maneuver swiftly on the soft, marshy ground. His men began to draw their bows. Slowly, the words came to his mouth, bitter as bile, the hardest words he had ever spoken. "Shoot the cabos!"

Abruptly, he saw a cloud of dust rising behind the raiders. Some of them were straightening, wheeling their mounts in consternation. Down the slope behind them plunged a small band of riders, in their fore a young chief in white skins.

"Belay that last command!" Hael shouted, in his excitement reverting to sailor speech. "Shoot for the men, and don't hit any of those Amsi!"

The oncoming riders, with insane bravery, collided with the far larger force of wild men, forcing them back toward the archers, who began methodically picking off every man who presented a clear target. Some of Hael's men dismounted for better long-range shooting. Within minutes, the raiders were plunging about in total confusion as the Amsi swung and thrust their weapons and the arrows hissed in, emptying saddles with terrible efficiency.

Hosha laughed loudly as he shot. "Your old friend is getting away."

Hael saw Impaba urging his cabo westward along the river. "I'll catch him. Advance the men and finish off these scum, then round up all the cabos. I'll be back soon." His men cheered and urged him on as Hael raced off after Impaba. Behind him he heard the fading sounds of battle, but his mind was intent only on one thing; to catch and kill the man who had brutalized Deena, then betrayed him. There would be no mercy for Impaba today.

The Amsi looked back over his shoulder as Hael relentlessly bore down upon him. Impaba's cabo was a good one, but the man was heavier than Hael, and the beast could not run as fast or as far carrying him. Hael drew his bow and sent an arrow sizzling past Impaba's ear. He cursed his indifferent bowmanship as he fitted another arrow to the string. A Matwa would have put the arrow through the back of the man's neck.

Impaba, alarmed by the arrow, leaned far over

his cabo's neck and slung his hide shield across his back. Now Hael had little target and too much chance of striking the animal. He had become obsessed with preserving every cabo he could. He replaced the bow in its case and jerked the thong that tied his casting rope to his saddle.

Foot by foot, Hael gained on Impaba. He shook out a wide noose and bean to whirl it above his head. Impaba was leaning too low for the noose to encircle him, so Hael had to rope the cabo. The loop snaked out and settled over the beast's head and neck and Hael reined in his own cabo. Almost instantly, the rope was jerked from his hands, but Impaba's mount was twisted sideways and fell heavily. The Amsi rolled as he struck the ground and he came up with his shield on one arm and his stone-headed hammer in the other hand.

Hael grasped his own small, circular shield and dismounted, his spear in his right hand. He did not like to give up the advantage of his mounted position, but he knew that Impaba's first move would be to smash his club between the cabo's eyes. There was no sense in shooting at Impaba, because a man on foot could easily dodge arrows, as long as they were coming one at a time.

"Come to me, little foreigner," Impaba crooned. "Carving your body will give me even more pleasure than using your woman's. Did she tell you about that?"

"You are already dead, Impaba," Hael said. "I defeated you once. You life has been mine ever since. I come now to claim it."

A look of fear crossed Impaba's twisted face. "You have no magic! I live because you were too stupid to kill me when you had the chance! Now it is I who shall kill you!"

"Did you come here to talk or fight?" Hael demanded.

Howling, Impaba charged. The hammer whirled with dazzling swiftness, and each time it struck Hael's shield the shock half numbed the arm holding it. In the middle of the furious attack, Hael began a series of short jabs with his spear, each one causing Impaba to dodge or twist or lower his shield. Hael was unable to get the point home, but twice he sliced his opponent with the keen steel edge of the blade. The wounds were not serious, but they would hurt and Impaba would bleed and weaken. The hammer came down again, and Hael raised his shield to block, catching the handle a foot behind the head. He had misjudged the whip-like flexion of the handle, and it bent enough for the stone head to smash into his shoulder with brutal force.

His head swimming with pain, Hael broke off and jumped back, his face going white. Impaba grinned and slid in, swinging high, knowing that Hael would be slow in raising his shield now. The rain of blows caused Hael to crouch low, trying to get as much of himself behind his shield as possible. Unexpectedly, Impaba threw a looping, horizontal blow that hooked the head of his war hammer behind the right edge of Hael's shield, tearing the straps loose from his left forearm and sending the shield spinning over the grass. His grin was wide as he charged in for the kill, the hammer whistling down towards Hael's head.

Hael took his spear in both hands like a staff as he swept the long, bronze butt-spike low and sideways, catching Impaba's descending ankle and sweeping it from under him with a snapping of bone. The warrior screamed in pain as he fell, twisting. He landed on his back and his eyes went wide in terror as he saw Hael looming above him, the spear raised with both hands gripping the short haft of flamewood. Then the long, lethal blade plunged down. Fear and all other expression left Impaba's eyes.

A cheer greeted Hael as he returned to the battle site, riding one cabo and leading the other. The bodies of the enemy dead were being stripped, the Amsi and Matwa wounded were being treated. The raiders' cabos were tethered by the river.

Hael dismounted by Twila and took his hand. "I will never forget this."

The young chief smiled. "You had ridden out of sight before I remembered where I had seen that lout." He pointed at the body of Deno, now devoid of weapons. "It was at a trade fair three years ago. He was having that ear torn off for cheating a fellow tribesman in a trade. I knew his people would never take him back after such an offense, so he had to be lying. The only way he could still be living was if he had turned bandit."

"Get your problems with Impaba settled?" asked Hosha, who had acquired a fine short sword.

"Satisfactorily," Hael answered. He turned back to Twila. "Are there many bands of these outlaws?"

"They are everywhere," the chief said. "About forty of these got away from us today, and they will probably join another band before the Moon turns."

"Why do you not hunt the rogues down?" Hosha asked.

"There's little honor in it," Twila said. "Warriors in search of a reputation want to fight tribal enemies, not scum no better than carrion bats. These are too weak and cowardly to confront strong bands of warriors. They raid traders sometimes, or villages. If any get bold enough to come for our camps or our herds, we chase them away."

A great inspiration spread through Hael as he saw the opportunity presented to him, the opportunity he needed. All around, he saw Amsi and Matwa cooperating in the task of stripping their enemies, their ancient animosities forgotten for the moment, the men filled with the mutual good will that comes of shared battle. Hael would not have to wait for foreign aggression to give his new force of mounted archers battle experience. He would not have to wait, perhaps for years, to make Amsi and Matwa a cohesive fighting force, wasting most of his time in keeping them from each others' throats. He now had a mission. A great good would be done in the accomplishing of it, and in the process he would gain all the cabos he needed to mount the Matwa nation.

"Twila," he asked, "what are your plans for the summer?"

Twila shrugged. "The usual. Hunt, trade a little, raid a little, court the girls in the other villages. We are on our own until our village reassembles in the fall. No married men among us, so our time is our own unless an enemy comes and the assembly call is sent out. Of course," he added hastily, "should you wish anything of us, we will gladly serve, Prophesied One."

"Splendid," Hael said, stooping to pull up a twist of grass. Carefully he began to clean off the blood that stained two feet of his spear. "Twila, how would you and your lads like to come cabo hunting with us? Not wild ones, but the good, trained riding cabos, which have been stolen. And a bit of fighting thrown in for spice? Not the sort of thing that makes a warrior's reputation, but you'll wipe the blood from your weapons knowing that you've helped to make these grasslands an even better place for people to live. How does that sound?"

Twila smiled and nodded. "That sounds very good indeed. We can use good cabos, too. But for you, Prophesied One, we will ride anywhere, against any enemy."

From the time they had ridden back into the hills, people had come running from their villages or their outlying farmsteads to stare and point. The riders, with Hael at their head, did not look like the ones who had left early in summer. These were lean, hard-bitten and decorated by many new scars. Bandages were plentiful, and many now wore Amsi-style skin clothing. Some had even taken to dressing their fair hair like Amsi. And there were no longer fifty of them. Four lay in graves on the plain, but then that many might have died in the course of a normal summer in the hills.

But it was not only the appearance of the riders that drew the attention of everyone, but also what they led: more than a thousand fine riding cabos accompanied Hael's little force of cavalry. Behind them were several hundred of the small, wild breed, to be used for training children. To help

them get the animals to their destination, thirty
Amsi rode with them, and the men of the two races
seemed comfortable together. They had tran-
scended one of the barriers that separated them,
because for the moment, they were soldiers together.

Hael, weary but proud, intended that this should
continue. As he rode, his glittering spear propped
before him, he built in his mind a vision of the
nation he would forge from these two superb warrior peoples. From now on, every summer, his
Matwa squadrons would ride into the plains with
Hael leading them. They would scour the grasslands to its uttermost limits in company with his
Amsi people, until the had rooted out every last
festering nest of the predatory outlaws. In the
process he would gain cabos for the Matwa and
good will from the villagers. A mounted force of
the two nations would be formed. The Amsi were
now eager to learn archery, having seen the efficiency of the new, short bows. Next year, his
Matwa would teach archery to the Amsi, who in
turn would teach the Matwa to use the lance for
close-in fighting. Everything was falling into place.
Hael knew that he rode the tide of destiny as
surely as any ship rode an ocean tide into port.
Where that tide would take him he was still uncertain.

He forgot about all these things when they arrived at Broadleaf, his Matwa village. He forgot
as soon as he saw the woman who stood by the
tiny bridge across the village stream, the woman
who swayed with the weight of her unborn child.
Hael jumped from the saddle, forgetting empire
and nation, army and tribe. Forgetting cabo and

bow, sword and spear, as he ran toward his wife and their firstborn-to-be.

End

The tale of Hael and his sons will continue in Book II of *The Stormlands*, THE BLACK SHIELDS, in which King Hael of the Mainland and King Gasam of the Islands contend for mastery of the Stormlands, and of how the sorcery of the Canyon Dwellers, the perfidy of the southern kings, and the fire weapons of the easterners make that struggle the greatest the world has seen since the time of Catastrophe.